Travail and Triumph

Books by the Phillips/Pella Writing Team

The Journals of Corrie Belle Hollister

My Father's World
Daughter of Grace
On the Trail of the Truth
A Place in the Sun
Sea to Shining Sea
Into the Long Dark Night

The Stonewycke Trilogy

The Heather Hills of Stonewycke
Flight from Stonewycke
Lady of Stonewycke

The Stonewycke Legacy

Stranger at Stonewycke
Shadows over Stonewycke
Treasure of Stonewycke

The Highland Collection

Jamie MacLeod: Highland Lass
Robbie Taggart: Highland Sailor

The Russians

The Crown and the Crucible
A House Divided
Travail and Triumph

Michael Phillips • Judith Pella

Travail and Triumph

BETHANY HOUSE PUBLISHERS
MINNEAPOLIS, MINNESOTA 55438

Cover by Dan Thornberg,
Bethany House Publishers staff artist.

Copyright © 1992
Michael Phillips / Judith Pella
All Rights Reserved

Published by Bethany House Publishers
A Ministry of Bethany Fellowship, Inc.
6820 Auto Club Road, Minneapolis, Minnesota 55438

Printed in the United States of America

Library of Congress Cataloging-in-Publication Data

Phillips, Michael R., 1946–
    Travail and triumph / Michael Phillips, Judith Pella.
        p.   cm. — (The Russians ; 3)

     1. Soviet Union—History—19th century—Fiction.   I. Pella, Judith.   II. Title.   III. Series: Phillips, Michael R., 1946– Russians ; bk. 3.
PS3566.H492T68   1992
813;.54—dc20   92–24496
ISBN 1–55661–174–9   CIP

To

Janet Ann Phillips Stanberry

The Authors

The PHILLIPS/PELLA writing team had its beginning in the long-standing friendship of Michael and Judy Phillips with Judith Pella. Michael Phillips, with a number of non-fiction books to his credit, had been writing for several years. During a Bible study at Pella's home he chanced upon a half-completed sheet of paper sticking out of a typewriter. His author's instincts aroused, he inspected it more closely and asked their friend, "Do you write?" A discussion followed, common interests were explored, and it was not long before the Phillips invited Pella to their home for dinner to discuss collaboration on a proposed series of novels. Thus, the best-selling "Stonewycke" books were born, which led in turn to "The Highland Collection," and the "Journals of Corrie Belle Hollister."

Judith Pella holds a nursing degree and B.A. in Social Sciences. Her background as a writer stems from her avid reading and researching in historical, adventure, and geographical venues. Pella, with her two sons, resides in Eureka, California. Michael Phillips, who holds a degree from Humboldt State University and continues his post-graduate studies in history, owns and operates Christian bookstores on the West Coast. He is the editor of the best-selling George MacDonald Classic Reprint Series and is also MacDonald's biographer. The Phillips also live in Eureka with their three sons.

CONTENTS

Prologue
Brief Interlude of Hope..................... 11

I.
Conflict and Parting........................ 17

II.
Adjustments of a New Life.................. 59

III.
A Soldier's Disgrace........................ 87

IV.
A Nation's Travail.......................... 143

V.
Aftermath of Death 191

VI.
Down the Dark Road....................... 217

VII.
Brothers in Exile 241

VIII.
Vengeance Unleashed 263

IX.
Travail and Farewell 315

X.
Triumph and New Life 363

A Cast of Characters

Anna Yevnovna Burenin
Princess Katrina Viktorovna (Fedorcenko) Remizov
Count Dmitri Gregorovich Remizov
Prince Sergei Viktorovich Fedorcenko
Lt. Mikhail Igorovich Grigorov (Misha)

In St. Petersburg

Prince Viktor Makhailovich Fedorcenko
Princess Natalia Vasilyovna Fedorcenko

Count Cyril Vlasenko—Chief of Third Section, the Secret Police
Tsar Alexander II Rominov
General Michael Loris-Melikov
Alexander Alexandrovich Rominov (Tsar Alexander III)
Pobedonostev—Alexander III's tutor

Fedorcenko and Remizov Households

Eugenia Pavlovna Remizov—Dmitri's mother
Mrs. Remington
Leo Moskalev
Nina Chomsky
Polya
Peter
Ivan

In Katyk

Yevno Pavlovich Burenin
Sophia Ilyanovna Burenin
Tanya
Vera
Ilya
Mariana Natalia Dmitrievna Remizov
Father Corygov

Revolutionaries and Friends

Paul Yevnovich Burenin (Pavlikov)
Basil Pyotrovich Anickin
Andrei Zhelyabov
Sophia Perovskaya
Stepniak
Ivan Remiga
Dr. Bobov
Evie

In the Army and in Siberia

Captain Rustaveli—Caspian Sea
General Skobelev—Caspian Sea
Lt. Plaksa—Dmitri's friend
Kaplan—Sergei's friend
Robbie Taggart—China

Prologue

BRIEF INTERLUDE OF HOPE
(April 1880)

1

Anna traced over the handwritten signature on the title page for the eighth time that day:

S-E-R-G-E-I V-I-K-T-O-R-O-V-I-C-H F-E-D-O-R-C-E-N-K-O

Her fingers carefully followed the words he had written to her only a few hours earlier. As she sat alone in her room at last, after the afternoon's succession of receptions, she stared at the words of the title, the author's name, and the inscription written underneath them. Every time she actually tried to read the prized volume, the fictional Bagraev's story paled alongside the pulsing reality of the words on the title page.

To my Anna Yevnovna, the familiar hand had written, *with the deepest of my heart's love and affection, and with great hope for our future together.*

"*My* Anna," she whispered. "*My Anna!*"

Slowly she closed the book and clasped it to her bosom, tenderly caressing the soft leather of its cover. This would be one of her treasured possessions, along with the Bible and gold cross of her father's. She would keep it with her forever. She would treasure it forty years from now, even when it was old and ragged and she had read it a dozen times! She would show it to their children, and tell them that this was the *first* and most special of all their father's many books. Although his name was famous throughout all of Russia, throughout all of Europe, *this* chosen volume, now ragged with years, was the first anyone in all of Moscow had been given. And he had given it to *her*—Anna Yevnovna, a mere servant girl!

Anna opened the volume again, and once more tried to read

the story that had sprung from her beloved Sergei's creative mind.

> *From the nobility came a youth of the Motherland, full of the optimism of his tender years. In his bosom beat a heart full of love for his country and all he thought it stood for. He came still half a boy, full of hope. When he returned, he would be a man whose hope was gone.*
>
> *His name was Bagraev. This is his saga. He left his beloved St. Petersburg in the season of . . .*

Anna could read no more.

Again she turned the pages back to the title page, gazing at the words—some printed by machine, some written by hand. She would read Sergei's book. She would read it twice . . . three times! But tonight she was tired, and she would merely bask in the glow of seeing her name on its title page.

To my Anna Yevnovna.

2

The second half of 1880 brought several months of welcome peace to the Motherland of Russia.

Foreign battlefields were, if not quiet, at least not so noisy as to echo their din all the way northward to St. Petersburg. Scattered fighting was always in progress along the distant borders of an empire so enormous, particularly in southern Asia to the southeast of the Black Sea. But with the army returned from the Balkan War, most citizens paid these scattered outbreaks little heed.

At home the terrible bombing of the Winter Palace in February had precipitated such a crisis that good seemed at last to have resulted from it in the end. The close attempt on his life had finally induced Alexander II, tsar of Russia, to heed the clamoring voices crying for moderation and change.

Summoning to the capital the governor of Kharkov, General Michael Loris-Melikov, the tsar had given the general sweeping powers, made him head of the newly formed Supreme Executive Commission, and set into motion a detailed study of the most outlandish of Melikov's proposals—granting the people of Russia a constitution, and changing the form of government to a constitutional monarchy.

Not all Alexander's advisors were happy about the turn of events. Though cautious, moderates within the court were generally optimistic, both as to Melikov's reasonable personality and with regard to his plan. Monarchists and conservatives, most notably Alexander's own son, the tsarevich, doomed Melikov to failure in their own minds immediately. It could not be disputed, in any case, that Melikov had the tsar's attention and sympathy—for now, at least. Alexander had a long history of double-mindedness, which was largely at the root of the country's present difficulties, and which all of his advisors had to weigh within their minds when assessing their own personal loyalties.

Neither could it be disputed that initially Melikov's leadership had squelched the rebellious fervor throughout the land. His immediate successes in rooting out and punishing terrorists had driven the movement sufficiently underground so as to make the streets of St. Petersburg safe again. How long such calm would last . . . one could only hope. But in this land it was unwise to make too many predictions. And it was prudent to keep one's own counsel.

Whether the tsar would continue to favor the idea of constitutional reform was anyone's guess.

In the meantime, aristocrats and noblemen, imperial ministers and advisors alike all found their own futures cloudy and uncertain. Russia was moving toward change, that much was evident.

Which direction it would take was not so clear.

Nor could anyone predict which direction the winds of personal fortune might be blowing a year from now. It was best to walk warily, watch one's words, and not say too much that could be misconstrued at some later unpredictable moment.

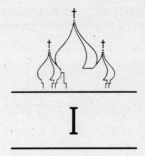

I

CONFLICT AND PARTING
(Late April 1880)

1

Cyril Vlasenko, one-time boyarin over serfs, former magistrate and chief in Akulin and Pskov, and now police chief of the mighty Third Section in St. Petersburg, was not at all happy with the recent turn of events.

His long-coveted position in the government, which he had plotted and schemed and manipulated his hated cousin Viktor to obtain for him, had suddenly become tenuous at best. Loris-Melikov's successful arrests of terrorists and rebel activists were making a fool of the police chief. It was gradually dawning on Vlasenko that Melikov fully intended to subjugate the power of the Third Section under the Ministry of Internal Affairs, usurping police powers himself, and thus bringing about the swift demise of the current chief.

But Vlasenko had bowed and scraped and groveled too long to attain his position to accept defeat without a fight!

Unfortunately, Melikov had become an imperial darling. All of St. Petersburg bowed to him. He was, for the time being, untouchable. Even if Vlasenko had some devilish stratagem up his sleeve—which in all candor he did not—it would be a dangerous game to try it now, especially against Melikov directly. The loathsome liberals had suddenly gained court favor and were making disturbing encroachments into the status quo. And at the root of it all was Melikov's increasing pressure on the Crown to approve a constitutional government. The fool would make the Motherland into another weak-kneed milksop of a nation like America or Great Britain! What was his ultimate intent—to turn Russia into a democracy? The very thought that a land of ignorant peasants could rule itself without the strong iron hand of an autocrat was worse than laughable—it was absurd!

Yet . . . this was the hour when such idiotic liberal delusions were being listened to with favor. And therefore he had to watch his step.

Nor was Cyril the only conservative in fear of his job. Dmitri Tolstoy had been removed from the Ministry of Education and replaced as Procurator of the Holy Synod. Conservatives in positions like Vlasenko's did not fear for their jobs without reason. Melikov had shown clearly enough that he intended to act, and it was also clear that the tsar would back him up.

In refilling the procuratorship, however, Melikov might well have made his first grave mistake. Cyril dared to hope it was a fatal one. In his desire to curry the favor of the tsarevich, Melikov handed the position over to the ultra-reactionary, quintessential imperialist Pobedonostev, the tsarevich's tutor. The man was violently opposed to everything Melikov himself stood for, and the appointment was perplexing, even if delicious.

If Cyril were a patient man, he had only to sit back and watch the tsar's darling destroy himself trying to play both ends against the middle. It would happen eventually.

But he was not a patient man, and he felt a sinking helplessness to do anything to speed up the process of Melikov's fall *or* to protect his own position. Before the ax fell, he would resign and return to his estate to the south. But that would be an inglorious retreat after less than two years in the capital. Remaining in St. Petersburg in essential humiliation and powerlessness was not much better. But still, it did keep him close to the action, as it were, easily in reach of . . . well, in reach of anything which might come his way for use in discrediting Melikov or his liberal cronies.

Vlasenko half-suspected his cousin's surreptitious hand in collusion with Melikov to discredit the police chief and see him ousted from power. Fedorcenko had never forgiven him for how he had used his position to gain entry into St. Petersburg's portals of power in the first place. And although he had been successful, Cyril's advancement did not put to rest his deep-seated resentment toward what he still considered the unfairly favored side of the family. Never far from Cyril's conniving mind was the ongoing obsession to gain the upper hand, once and for all, over the thorn in his side—Viktor Fedorcenko. A year ago he had come close to seeing the man's demise when Viktor's moderate stand had begun to erode his favor with the tsar. But with Alexander's vacillation, one never knew where the pendulum of fate would swing next. Now Viktor was hobnobbing with Melikov, and both had become the apple of the tsar's eye. Why, Alexander had even attended the wedding of Viktor's daughter! Cyril had been invited too—merely out of obligation, no doubt—but he had received little more than a passing nod from his snob of a relative.

But if Vlasenko could not make a frontal assault against the tsar's new dictator Melikov, he'd be just as satisfied to strike in another direction. Indeed, considering the personal fulfillment it afforded, a blow at Viktor, if it could serve something of the same purpose, might be even more satisfying.

That is why he wasted no time when the little volume entitled *A Soldier's Glory* fell into his hands.

The book was absolutely rife with sedition—couched innocuously, of course, in a tale of a youth's coming of age in battle during the Crimean War. How the drivel ever passed the censors, Vlasenko had no idea. It was probably due to more of Melikov's ineffectual liberal appointees, or, more likely, a few well-placed bribes on the part of one or both of the Princes Fedorcenko.

The tsar was afraid these days, yes. Afraid of the rebels, afraid of the public, afraid for his reputation. And in his fear he was succumbing to all the current liberal prattle. But Cyril doubted the tsar was addled enough to stand for seditious slander from the pen of the son of one of his highest governmental ministers. He was about to find out anyway.

2

Vlasenko had asked for and received an audience with the emperor. In truth, Cyril was not at all certain how the ruler of all Russia would take the chief's news. Alexander might fly off in a rage at the no-account, two-faced Prince Fedorcenko—a man he thought loyal, only to be found harboring a rebel within his own home. The tsar might dismiss him at once and exile his son—exile both, if Cyril was lucky.

On the other hand, the situation could turn against Vlasenko himself. The tsar's mind and heart was weighted with many serious dilemmas at the moment, not the least of which was his wife's terminal illness. He might be annoyed at Vlasenko's pettiness. He might even find the impetuousness of the younger Fedorcenko amusing. After all, the tsar's own father had stunned Russian society years ago by granting official blessing to the muddled rebel Gogol.

Yes, it could blow up in his stony face. But Cyril reasoned that the way things were headed, he had little to lose.

When Alexander's secretary Totiev approached him, Vlasenko was surprisingly calm, even somewhat self-assured, as well as a man might be who was holding a concealed dangerous weapon. The secretary showed Vlasenko into the tsar's presence.

The emperor was in his study, seated behind his desk, several papers scattered out in front of him. Cyril fleetingly wondered if any of those sheets were early drafts of Melikov's ridiculous constitution. But it was too early even for a driven fool like the Armenian dictator to have anything on paper yet. Cyril quickly shifted his thoughts to matters at hand.

"I have only a limited time," said the tsar. "I hope you can present me your petition succinctly."

"Most certainly, Your Majesty!" replied Vlasenko. "I am humbled that you were able to see me. And I would not presume to interfere upon your vital schedule if I felt the situation to which I have become party was a frivolous one."

He paused and cleared his throat, waiting leave to continue.

"Please go on," said Alexander, somewhat impatiently.

"This is such a delicate matter, Your Majesty," said the chief, "and I must emphasize that my brevity ought not to be taken for flippancy."

As Cyril stood before his emperor, he struck a fine pose of humility. "I have suffered much agony of mind and spirit," he went on, "before determining that I must, in all loyalty to Your Highness, bring this matter to your attention, as distasteful as I find it to do so."

He paused again, then lifted into full view the book he had been holding at his side. "I have come in regard to this book, published only this month, which recently came into my hands."

The tsar reached across his desk and Cyril laid the book in the emperor's hand. Alexander gave a quick perusal to the cover before opening the nicely bound leather boards and thumbing briefly through the pages.

"Hmm . . . Prince Fedorcenko's son, is it not?" asked the tsar, half musing to himself.

"Yes, Your Majesty," answered Cyril, although he immediately repented of his quick response. It was a bit *too* eager. He must watch himself.

"Do you have some complaint about the book?" asked the tsar.

"I have an acquaintance, Your Majesty, who is a censor. It happened across his desk, and having read it, he felt there were several . . . ah . . . a number of questionable passages."

"And why not deal with it in the usual manner? Why do you come to me?"

"There are several reasons, Your Highness. Foremost, considering the authorship, we felt you would want to be apprised of the situation."

"Yes . . . yes, that is true. What else?"

"This, Your Majesty, is the point where the matter becomes delicate," Cyril went on, his tone still more somber and humble. "As you can see, the book has already been published. I do not believe it has been released yet to the general public, however. If you will note, on the title page, it was published out of Kiev. I imagine the author, or perhaps the publisher there, must have some connection or curried the favor of some censor, thus enabling the book to pass scrutiny. I would be loathe to think that either of the Princes Fedorcenko would have used their position or prestige to influence a governmental official in such a way. However . . ."

He let his sentence trail away as if it truly pained him to even speak the words of such a possibility.

The tsar eyed him a moment, weighing the words.

"What specifically do you find objectionable in the volume?" he asked at length, his tone too veiled even for the highly observant police chief to be able to detect the motive behind it.

"If you will permit me, Your Highness, it might be enlightening and beneficial for me to quote a passage or two. Then Your Esteemed Highness can be the judge."

"Yes, by all means." The tsar handed the book back to Vlasenko.

Having already marked several of the most inflammatory sections, Cyril opened quickly to one. He removed spectacles from his coat pocket, slipped them on, and began:

" 'The young Bagraev,' " he began, " 'saw much courage and bravery that day on the front lines. If only it could have been matched in the rear, upon a grassy knoll where men in gilded equipage worked strings as of marionettes and not human lives.' "

Vlasenko paused significantly. He then turned over several pages and continued in another passage:

" 'It was now night, and the deafening bursts of artillery had faded into a ghostly silence. The respite that should have brought rest to a mind tormented by death seemed only to inspire more confusion and dismay. Bagraev could only wait in fear for when it would begin all over again, wondering if he could pick up his weapon and act as the instrument of death for yet another in an endless string of meaningless days of agony.

" 'Was he a coward, after all? Or had reality finally clouded his perception of the so-called glorious purpose that had sent him here in the first place? Had he all along been fighting for a mere illusion? His illusion of Russia had compelled him on this path to a soldier's glory. For that Russia, the beloved Motherland—Holy Russia!—he could fight and perhaps even kill and die with the zeal of a man possessed.

" 'But now the seasoned young soldier wondered if all this sacrifice was expended for a mere fiction—a country that existed only in his fantasies. Those occupying the positions of power in this Motherland he loved could not force serfs to battle for a land in which they were deprived of their own freedom. Where did justice exist in such a warped equation of rule? Nor could they place in their ill-trained hands inferior and untrustworthy weapons, with commanders and generals who knew nothing but obedience, and little of military tactic.

" 'Yet the young soldier encountered all this, and more. His idealistic eyes were thus forced upon the reality, painful as was its realization, that his beloved homeland was a nation doomed to infamy when future histories of the time were written. The subsequent disillusionment and cowardice he witnessed all about him, and even in the depths of his own soul, should thus not have surprised him.' "

When Vlasenko finished reading, a heavy silence filled the room.

The tsar interlaced his fingers together and rested them against his lips while his brow creased in thought.

Vlasenko waited. To speak now might appear too presumptuous, too eager. As difficult as it was to exercise patience, he knew his best course was to allow the emperor to draw his own conclusions. Vlasenko only prayed Alexander drew the *right* conclusions. Alexander had, in point of fact, not admired his father Nicholas's handling of the Crimean War, and technically young Fedorcenko's complaint was lodged in that direction. However, once the book was circulated throughout St. Petersburg, everyone would know that the fictional format was but a thinly disguised veil over his own bitter wartime experiences recently in Bulgaria. Cyril hoped the tsar didn't need all the implications spelled out for him.

Finally Alexander spoke. "May I have that book for a while?"

"But of course, Your Highness!" Vlasenko laid the volume back on the imperial desk. "With my compliments, to be sure."

"Thank you, Vlasenko," said the tsar. "I will deal with the matter from here."

"Of course, Your Majesty. And, as always, I am at your service."

"Yes. Thank you . . ."

Alexander paused, glanced distastefully down at the book, then returned a similar expression upward in the direction of the police chief. "You may be dismissed."

"Thank you, Your Majesty!"

Cyril bowed his way out of the august imperial presence. He wished he had gotten a more firm denouement from the tsar. But the man was clearly disturbed, that much was apparent. And it would have been most unwise to press the issue further.

3

Anna sat alone in her room. It was quiet. It had been days since she had had any meaningful work to do.

Already she missed her mistress, and she was lonely. She could not keep her mind from drifting southward to her beloved home in the country.

She took out a sheet of paper, opened her bottle of ink,

dipped in the pen, and began to write.

My dearest family,
It has been only a week since the wedding, only a week since Princess Katrina and Count Remizov left for Greece on their holiday together. The great house seems so empty and quiet. To think that one person could make such a difference in the life and vitality of a place where there are so many others may sound strange. But that is the kind of person my mistress is. Wherever she goes, gaiety and good cheer follow. I love her so much. I only hope I am able to continue serving her as I have after she returns and sets up her new home. I cannot help being somewhat anxious, however, because I do not know Count Remizov well. But he is Prince Sergei's friend, and that must say a great deal for him.

I am happy you are feeling better, Papa. The winter is over now, and surely the warmth will give strength to your body and bones. It will soon be time for planting once again. How quickly do the seasons pass! I am so glad you still have much grain left from last harvest. It makes me happy to have helped, and that you now know Prince Sergei as your own friend, too. He asks about you often and sends his kind regards.

I must tell you about Princess Katrina's wedding! How beautiful she was, and how proud of her I felt. We spoke for a long time the morning of the wedding. The princess was so kind to me and said that it was because of me she felt that she was finally ready for marriage. Can you imagine! Then she kissed me. Oh, Papa and Mama, as much as I miss you at times—and right now is one of them!—I *am* thankful that you sent me to the city when you did. God has been so good to me!

But I was trying to describe the wedding . . . the princess was covered in white from head to toe, her beautiful satin dress sparkling with diamonds and pearls. I could not keep from crying when I saw her! It was her nineteenth birthday, too. How different she looked than when I first saw her three and a half years ago. She looked so radiantly like a grown woman, mature and wise. I suppose I have changed just as much in those years, but I do not feel different on the inside. But the changes in the princess are so visible that everyone has noticed. Especially Count Remizov! She used to be but a child to him, or so the princess has told me. And now suddenly she has become his wife!

I have not seen Paul again since I saw you. It has been only a few months since my return, and I do not expect—

Anna set down her pen and glanced up. She had not intended even to mention Paul to her parents. Suddenly there was his name on the page. They only knew he was in St. Petersburg, but no more. Actually she did not know more than that either, although she had her suspicions. Those, however, she would keep to herself.

Again she inked her pen and finished the sentence.

. . . I do not expect to see him soon. The weather is very cold still, and people do not go out much yet. I am sure he is busy with the new life he is making for himself.

It was an unsatisfactory ending. But once she had written his name on the paper, she could not very well take it off. Her parents would no doubt see right through her transparent attempt to put the brightest face on their shared doubts about poor Paul.

A wave of melancholy swept over Anna, and a tear rose to her eye. She brushed it away, set her pen down, and stood up. She would not be able to write any more just now. She had to get out, to walk, to breathe the fresh air.

Anna left her room, went down the stairs, exited the huge house, and in a few minutes found herself walking alone in the Promenade Garden.

Multitudes of thoughts flowed through her mind. She was in a position that would have been the envy of any peasant girl in Russia. Her every need was provided for, and she was maid to a princess she loved. Moreover, the young prince of the house loved *her*, and wanted to marry her one day! She had every reason for joy.

Why, then, had this wave of sadness come over her? Was it thoughts of her brother? Or was it loneliness for her family or the princess?

Anna didn't know; emotions were not always easy to analyze. She brushed back two or three tears, almost laughing as she did.

"God," she said aloud, "what is the matter with me? What reason do I have to be downcast?" But no answer came.

She walked along a while in silence, remembering the time in this garden she had first seen the princess, and the times she had walked here beside the prince.

Her thoughts again turned to the wedding. It was such a happy celebration. Yet with it came new thoughts, thoughts of change. What if everything was different when Princess Katrina returned? What if the princess no longer needed her? What if their friendship . . . ?

Suddenly Anna's mind filled with questions and doubts. She had been growing more anxious every day, wondering what the future held. Telling her parents about the wedding had brought the fears on all over again. As concerned as she was about Paul, it was not her brother's future that weighed her down at this moment. It was her own.

What was to become of her?

"God, take care of me!" she blurted out. "Let the princess still want me for her maid and friend. And Prince Sergei, God . . . take care of—"

It was always difficult for Anna to pray for Sergei with words. The moment she tried, it seemed the words faded and prayers of feelings deep in her heart took over instead. But just thinking of the prince immediately lightened the burden of her anxieties.

She smiled and glanced up at the trees, still bare from the winter past, then drew in a deep breath of the frosty air and let it out in a great white puff.

She walked on to the very end of the garden, then turned and started back along another of the many paths. Thinking about Sergei made the day seem bright again. Perhaps she would be able to finish the letter home after all. She would tell them of the prince's visit to his father two days ago, and how he had contrived to see her alone.

She laughed at the memory! By the time she entered the house again, Anna was skipping along with the delight of springtime.

She returned to her room, sat down at her writing table, and once again took up her pen to write to her beloved family, this time about the young prince she loved.

You will find very humorous what happened just two days ago. Prince Sergei came to visit his father and mother. I knew he was in the house but was afraid to make an appearance for fear my face would betray my feelings. But in the middle of his interview with his father, the prince stood and . . .

Yevno roared with laughter as Vera put down the letter from Anna she had just finished reading.

"That prince is indeed worthy of our Anna!" he exclaimed. "I would so like to know his father, the elder prince. I would like to tell him what manner of son he has!"

"Anna says there is strife between the two," commented Sophia sadly. "It is not good when a man and his son do not know each other." She hardly realized what she had said until glancing up to see her husband's face. The laughter and smile had disappeared.

"Ah, Yevno, I did not mean you!" said Sophia apologetically.

"You speak the truth, wife, whether you meant it or not. It is not good, and I am to blame, just like the prince's father."

"No, Yevno. Our Pavushka went his own way and cut himself off from us. Even poor Annushka feels it. I can tell from her words."

Yevno did not reply. He did not understand what had happened to estrange his son from them. He might never understand. He merely felt the grief only a loving parent can know.

"Sometimes a child goes his way, and there is no guilt for a parent to bear. Surely you do not feel guilty, Yevno. Pavushka was always independent, always full of questions that carried rebellion."

"Yes, Sophia . . . yes, I know."

"Anna's questions came from hunger. She wanted to know things. Paul only wanted to question."

"Ah yes! And we could answer neither of them," sighed

Yevno. "How did a simple man and woman like you and me bear two who could have been so full of things we know nothing of?"

Sophia shook her head in bewilderment. "I do not know, Yevno," she replied. "But now they are out there, both in the great city, each discovering the answers to their questions and hungers in their own ways."

"God, watch over them both!" said Yevno after a brief pause.

"Amen!" whispered Sophia.

A long silence followed. There were many things to think about. The next words, when they came, were a continuation of Yevno's brief prayer.

" . . . And her prince," added Sophia.

4

Members of The People's Will were not of the sort to find themselves running scared from any man. They were, however, moving with more caution these days.

Vlasenko's successful raid of their printing operation in Grafsky Lane had portended difficult times for the movement. Not that Vlasenko himself was much to be concerned about. But he had been successful in locating the press, and its loss greatly inhibited their ability to circulate what they called "the truth." Others called it propaganda, and Vlasenko himself called it the venom of their cause.

More serious than Vlasenko's modest successes against them was the stiff hand of Loris-Melikov. He was a man to be reckoned with. They had tried to kill him, and failed, and one of Zhelyabov's key proteges was summarily hanged as a result.

Some of their number were belligerent and called for another attempt without delay. Others found cause to reconsider. Even Paul Yevnovich Burenin, as bold as his words were, took the news soberly. He himself had volunteered for the assignment, though Zhelyabov had turned him down. And whatever he said about being willing to die for the cause of freedom, he now found himself reflecting back on the horrible day he had witnessed Kazan's execution. When he was honest with himself, he did not at all relish the idea of hanging from the end of a rope—not just yet. He was still young. The blast of a bomb would be a tolerably acceptable way to go, especially if he had fabricated it himself. But not a rope.

He was not afraid, just determined to watch his step. There were no doubts in his mind about the course he had chosen, although he did find himself thinking about Anna more often at such times. To think of Katyk, and his father, was still too painful.

Yet he must try to forget Anna as well, now that she was safe and the fool Anickin behind bars for good. No matter that she was warm and comfortable, and that he was cold and hungry half the time; no matter that she would have tried to help him had he given her half a chance. He had to try to forget. He was dead to the past. His future lay with his new friends.

More and more, Andrei Zhelyabov was taking Paul under his own wing. Paul was learning the business of explosives. It felt good to be a part of the inner workings. If it could not really compare with family, it was the closest thing to it he would ever experience again.

Paul drew the thin, ragged wool coat more tightly to his shivering shoulders and hastened on. He and Zhelyabov had arranged to meet two streets down from Grafsky Lane, at a certain rendezvous point the gendarmes were not yet wise to. From there they would walk across the river to a section of the city not usually frequented by their sort. Some printing equipment was available, they had heard. It would have to be moved, and that could prove difficult. And they would have to find a place to set it up for operation well distanced from either Vlasenko's or Melikov's prying eyes—which also would not be easy.

But the equipment was to be had for a song, no questions asked. There were occasional aristocrats sympathetic to their cause, and this fellow was even willing to risk the transfer of an old outdated printing press from a newspaper warehouse. They were to meet the man today to work out the details.

If explosives were necessary for the success of the rebellion, being able to print leaflets and notices was all the more so. They had been severely hampered since Vlasenko's raid a few months ago. Perhaps they wouldn't be able to kill the tsar as easily as they might have hoped. All their efforts seemed to fail. But as long as they could continue fomenting dissatisfaction with the printed word, the time for successful revolt was sure to come eventually.

Paul turned the corner around a stone building and met a blast of cold spring wind. He winced slightly. It would do no good to try to wrap himself up any tighter. The wind knifed its way through his coat anyway. He would just have to walk faster.

He quickened his pace. Just as well, he thought. Zhelyabov was probably already waiting for him.

5

Somehow Sergei had always considered himself immune from the harsh realities of imperial disfavor.

He had known that his book contained some sections that would grate hard on official ears. But he was still naive enough to believe that truth would win out, to believe that deep down Russian officialdom really knew the sorry state of affairs in the military and would welcome such a forthright look at it, to believe that even the most tradition-minded grand duke or prince—or even tsar!—would be thankful to see an accurate portrayal of things as they really were beneath the ceremonial gloss.

He also believed somewhere in the subconscious parts of his brain, although he would have been loathe to admit it, that the family influence he spurned on the surface would protect him as it always had. As much as he thought himself unencumbered inside by the title he carried, he did not realize how strongly he still depended on his family name and prestige to shield him from the potential unpleasant consequences of what he had done.

All these illusions were suddenly dispelled with a single, swift Imperial edict, delivered to him shortly after the wedding of his sister and best friend.

In silence he read the order, each word smashing into his brain with stunning, numbing force:

Discharged . . . reassigned . . . Central Asian regiment . . . General Skobelev . . . leave St. Petersburg on . . .

The unexpected blow was demoralizing, shocking, deadening. He stumbled out of his barracks, his fingers clutching the ill-fated order, as one in a daze, his eyes unfocused and unaware of his surroundings. He walked on, came to the river, continued along its bank, and without knowing where his steps led him, came two hours later to his barracks again. His mind had gradually begun to function once more; and if the sudden news still seemed like a mockery, at least he had forced himself to take the first few steps in adjusting to it. He *must* adjust, and quickly, for it was now clear that the publication of his book was destined to change the outlook of his future—perhaps forever.

Wherever the order had originated, it was obviously intended as a direct disciplinary move against one who had dared to raise uncomfortable questions. What better punishment for a dissident who had publicly expressed his disturbance with military ineptitude than to send him off in humiliation to fight in a series of border skirmishes that were among the most representative of Russian military irresponsibility?

Nowhere he could have been assigned would have more fittingly rubbed his nose into the very dung his book had hoped to expose! It was the perfect, the most ingenious, the most debasing response possible. The book would be discredited, probably kept from ever reaching the public, and he would never receive another military promotion as long as he lived!

If any redeeming aspect could be found to being so suddenly discharged from his prestigious Guard Regiment, it was that Sergei would be under the command of the Cossack White General, whose bravery and elan he had so admired in the Balkans.

Yet, like the character in his condemned and belatedly censored book, Sergei wondered how he could possibly take up arms again. The thought of entering into battle sickened, revolted him. His stomach lurched at the very thought. He could not do it! He could never kill again ... he *would* never kill again!

Desertion ...

Once the idea began to form in his mind, it tried to obsess him beyond all reason.

It would not be too difficult to carry out!

He could take Anna with him. Tonight, perhaps! Dressed in country attire, under cover of darkness, they could take the train westward rather than south, slip out of the country, and live thereafter very happily in England. There he could write—military journals or fairy tales about princes and peasant girls!—and they could read Byron and Wordsworth together, and grow old in a small country cottage. All his dilemmas with his father, all the secrecy and uncertainty which had surrounded his relationship with his sister's maid—everything would be solved at once. They would be free!

But was it *too* easy?

Sergei Viktorovich Fedorcenko might be an aristocratic dissident, but he was a noble one. And that nobility existed not merely by virtue of the blue blood of generations that flowed through his veins.

Sergei was far too much a man of honor to run away. He would face the consequences of what he had done squarely, like a man of principle, like a man of integrity. What kind of husband could he be to Anna if their marriage was rooted in the supreme act of cowardice—running away from his own fate in the dead of night! How would he be able to look anyone in the eye again . . . how would he be able to look *himself* in the eye again!

Moreover, although it would have been difficult to admit it, Sergei still desired his father's approval too much to crush and humiliate him further. The book and the public reproach brought on by his reassignment would be belittling enough. But how could he add to the indignity by allowing his father to wake up and find his only son gone without a trace? Besides, running away would only confirm in Viktor's mind what Sergei thought the man probably already believed about him, that he was an ill-conceived blight on the distinguished family name. The last thing Sergei wanted to do was to prove his father right.

Sergei knew he had to face what awaited him—destiny, fate, God's will . . . or doom. But still he wondered if there might not be some other way, some alternative, some middle ground.

In the end, the thought of leaving Anna again, and his concern over her happiness, even more than his distaste for battle, compelled him to swallow his pride and make one final attempt at reprieve. If he was too proud to run, he was not too proud to make the effort to humble himself before the man who had, for better or worse, made him what he was.

Viktor received his son in the study.

It was appropriate that father and son met in a businesslike setting, Viktor's large desk, like a strong battlement, separating them.

"Father, I ask only that you intercede with the tsar on my behalf," said Sergei after opening formalities had been stiffly exchanged on both sides. He kept his tone steady and calm, all hint of pleading absent.

"You ask a great deal," replied Viktor. Oddly, elder prince and young soldier sounded uncannily alike as they tried to mask all emotion in their voices.

"Do I?" Sergei did not care if his bitterness showed. "I forgot, I am only your son."

Viktor winced. "I have already spoken to the tsar," he said.

"On my behalf?" Sergei's tone revealed a ray of hope. Had he misjudged his father? Had he already pleaded for his son? What was the result? Was the situation hopeless after all? Had the tsar spurned his longtime friend?

"His Majesty interrogated *me* about your activities," Viktor replied in the same stoic tone. "Imagine my surprise when I learned, from the emperor no less, of my own son's literary bent. In front of the tsar himself I had to confess my ignorance of your points of view. Here, I thought for the last year you had been off wasting your life away, when instead you were writing a book designed to humiliate the very man to whose service I have given my entire life."

"That was never my intent, Father."

"Perhaps not. But it surely has been the result. In any case, my mortification was all the greater in that I was the last to know."

"I would have told you—"

"It is obvious why you chose to keep silent about your seditious, might I even call them treasonous writings."

"Yes, Father, you have assumed correctly," Sergei replied coldly. "I wanted to avoid a confrontation with you. It did me little good."

"I am only surprised that you would have the nerve now to come and beg a favor of me."

"I *beg* for nothing!" Sergei's voice shook, his composure crumbling. He was not as experienced as his father in stoicism. "I was a fool to think I would get anything like mercy, much less forgiveness, from my own father."

"I have not yet heard you *ask* for my forgiveness."

"I suppose that is because I feel no remorse. I wrote nothing but the truth, at least as I saw it and felt it in my heart. If that is a crime in this country, then I deserve my punishment. If you read my words, I have little doubt you would agree with much of what I said. You were there—you saw the same things I did."

Viktor was silent. Sergei's words were beside the point. Both men knew he would never read the book.

"But one thing, Father," Sergei added, his voice softening.

"I should have told you what I was doing."

"Yes, you should have."

"I do regret my silence now. I am sorry."

"I doubt that my knowing about it earlier would have avoided the confrontation anyway. We cannot seem to avoid such differences."

Viktor paused. His expression revealed the barest hint of melancholy, though it would have been difficult to discern regret in his tone.

"The fact remains, Sergei," he went on, "I cannot approach the tsar again regarding this matter. It is likely more rebellious literature has escaped imperial scrutiny, but seldom anything more *personal*. You must understand how deeply His Majesty was offended in that the book came from the hand of a family whose trust and loyalty he has always counted on. It was no less than a slap in the imperial face."

"I did not intend it so."

"Perhaps not. But that is how it was taken."

"I suppose, then, it is fortunate you were not also punished."

"It is."

"I am sorry, Father, that you should have been thus affected by my views. But I cannot change how I feel."

"I did not expect that you would."

If only his father could for one moment let down the wall of his cool imperturbability. Anna had tried to assure Sergei that his father loved him, but all he could see at this moment was a solid wall of ice. Why could not his father unlock for a moment the heart of emotion deep within him? Why couldn't he at least meet him halfway in this stumbling effort at reconciliation and understanding? Was it so impossible for the man to *show* even a hint of that love Anna said he supposedly felt?

Yet ... Sergei too was hemmed in by a wall of silence. Whatever charges and questions he wanted to scream at his father, he could not.

"Then there is nothing more to say," Sergei could only manage, everything else catching in the tight knot in his chest.

"Central Asia is not the end of the world, you know," said Viktor.

Is this some inept attempt at appeasement? Sergei wondered. *Or is he merely trying to assuage his own guilt by making light of the sentence?*

"In the service of one's country, a soldier is often called upon to do what might not be to his liking," Viktor continued. "But I have no doubt as to your ability to distinguish yourself there, and thus regain your commission and regiment."

"You mean if I am a good child, the tsar may allow me back in the yard one day?"

"You need not be impudent, Sergei. It will only harm your position further."

"From where I stand, it could hardly get worse," snapped Sergei. "Though I could do better in trying to improve it by speaking to a stone wall!"

Sergei turned briskly to make his exit, but a sharp retort from the opposite side of the desk forced him to stop.

"I will not be spoken to in such a manner!" said Viktor, rising to his feet. It was the first show of emotion Sergei's father had yet revealed.

Sergei opened his mouth to shout an angry rebuttal, but no words came. He had spoken as boldly, even disrespectfully, to his father as he had ever dared, and to further ignore years of conditioning would have been impossible for him. If he said anything more, the wounds might be fatal—if they were not already.

"I'm sorry, Father," was all he said. By his tone it was impossible to tell how much he meant the words.

Sergei strode from the room in quick retreat.

6

Viktor slumped back in his chair the moment the door closed behind his son. All his carefully guarded military reserve fled from him in an instant.

It was always this way. No matter how hard he tried to communicate with Sergei, they always managed to part in anger.

He was reasonable enough to admit the fault was partially his. He could never seem to say what he wanted, or say it *how* he wanted to. And no matter how his words finally did come out, Sergei invariably took them wrong. He simply could not seem to win where Sergei was concerned.

Was it possible that now he had lost him altogether? He had finally come back after his year's wanderings. As much as Viktor had been unable to demonstrate it, he had rejoiced in Sergei's return. But this time, under the circumstances, it was entirely possible he had been driven away for good.

Viktor's hope leaped when he heard the soft knock on his study door. Perhaps Sergei had a change of heart!

But it was only Natalia. Her delicate features were taut with strain. Viktor knew this was no frivolous visit.

"I just saw Sergei," she said. "He said he asked you to speak to the tsar."

"Yes. And I told him I have already spoken to him, but to no avail."

"Viktor, I do not mean to contradict you, but when you told me of the incident, you said it was the tsar who spoke to you—that you made little argument."

"Argue with the tsar, Natalia? Is that what you both expect me to do?"

"I never took you for a coward, Viktor."

The prince's eyebrows shot up. He had never heard such impertinence from his wife. Nor had he ever known her to come so quickly to her point. He was shocked but a little awestruck as well.

"Natalia, I could not have changed his mind even had I begged on hands and knees. He was deeply hurt and annoyed by the things our son wrote about the government and, by implication, about himself. Someone he had supposed a loyal subject. We are fortunate the whole family was not shipped off to Siberia."

"Viktor, there must be *something* that can be done!"

"I fear not."

"I almost lost him in one war. I do not think I could bear the possibility of losing him again."

"Calm yourself, Natalia," interposed Viktor firmly as if rebuking a child.

"I am desperate for him, Viktor. I will go to the emperor myself if I have to."

"I believe you are making too much out of this."

"Too much! With our son's life at stake?"

"Sergei is not going to war. The troops are there mainly to keep peace. A few minor border skirmishes, nothing more."

"I don't care, Viktor." For a brief moment Natalia took on some color and almost resembled her daughter. "It should at least bother you that he has been disgraced—for doing nothing more than putting his feelings on paper. Maybe the intelligentsia is right. It is a sorry country when a man cannot even do that."

Good heavens! thought Viktor. *Has the revolutionary fervor spread to my own placid wife?*

"You don't know what you are talking about, Natalia," he said.

"Well, perhaps I don't. I only know—"

Her voice suddenly broke and tears rose in her pale eyes. "I only know I cannot stand to see my son treated in this way. Even by you. It is all so unfair!"

The tears began to flow freely, and great helpless sobs broke from her as she stood before him in all her emotional confusion and vulnerability.

As usual, Viktor had not the slightest idea what to do. He never did when his wife took on like this. At length, he rose, and in a gesture almost resembling sensitivity, left the protection of his desk and walked to his wife, laying a hand on her trembling shoulder.

"Natalia, dear . . ." he said gently. "I do not like to see this all happen to our son any more than you do. But what he did was wrong."

"Should he have to pay such a price for a small mistake?" sobbed the princess.

"I don't know . . . publishing a book hardly seems a small matter." Even as he said the words, his tone revealed the surfacing of many of Viktor's own repressed uncertainties.

"Please, Viktor! I *beg* you . . . do something to help him!"

He had never been much good at refusing his wife anything—especially when she was in tears.

"I will try," he said.

"Oh, thank you, Viktor!" She took his hand in hers and gratefully kissed it. "You will never regret this, Viktor."

"Even if I do, I suppose it must be done," sighed Viktor.

"Will you tell Sergei? It will make him so happy."

"I am sure he is gone by now."

"I asked him to wait." Natalia sniffed, then dabbed her eyes with her handkerchief. "I believe I saw him walking toward the garden."

"Why raise his hopes?" said Viktor. It was a mere excuse. He did not much relish the idea of seeing his son again so soon.

"He is terribly distraught, Viktor. He needs to know you have changed your mind."

"Why don't *you* tell him?"

"It must come from you, Viktor."

The prince shrugged in defeat. He supposed his wife was smarter than anyone gave her credit for. At least she knew how to get her way with him. Perhaps more of Katrina's high color came from beneath her mother's usually pale skin than people realized.

7

Sergei had sent a message for Anna to meet him in the garden. She already knew of the reassignment. He had hoped to tell her of his success with his father. He should have known better!

He immediately took her in his arms. Anna did not pull back. She sensed that it must have gone badly with his father, that the rift between them had widened. She knew how deeply hurt and crushed he must feel by yet another rejection. So she held him too, as tightly as she could. And as she let him talk, although she could not see his face, she could hear the tears in his voice.

"Anna, I've decided to leave the country," he said with more desperation than resolve. "I cannot serve a nation I no longer believe in."

"Sergei," she said softly, "don't talk that way."

"I mean it."

"But you are distraught now. I'm sure you will feel differently in another day or two."

"No, Anna. I am through with it all—through with fruitlessly trying to please my father and my emperor and . . . everyone but myself. Now it is our turn, Anna—*our* turn to be happy. I will not say goodbye to you again. I want you to come with me! We will leave tonight."

"Sergei . . . I don't know," Anna said hesitantly.

"I know it is sudden, but it is the only way!"

"But, Sergei . . . you could never be happy that way. It would eat away at you that you had left Russia in disgrace."

"That might have been true at one time, but no longer."

"I couldn't let you do it, Sergei. Not because I am afraid for myself. I would go with you anywhere. But I know the decision would only torment you in the end."

"I tell you, I am through with it all! I spit in the faces of all those who oppose me."

"In my face also, Sergei?"

"What are you saying?" He let go of her and turned away. "I had hoped you would want to be with me, Anna. Are you saying that *you* oppose me too, that *you* take my father's side?" His voice was cold, as it had never before been with her.

"Of course I don't oppose you, in the way of who you are and what you stand for. And I *do* want to be with you! But not like this."

She walked around to face him. "I only oppose your wanting to flee in the middle of the night. Nothing more. You would be miserable if you did such a thing. We would both be miserable. It would be no way to begin our life together."

He turned away again and covered his face with his hands. A long silence followed.

"Always the voice of reason, aren't you, Anna?" he sighed at length. He shook his head sadly. "Sometimes I hate reason altogether!"

She lifted his trembling hands from in front of his face and brought them to her lips. "I'm sure the assignment in the south is a temporary one," she said. "It is the best way, Sergei."

A long, thoughtful silence followed.

"You are right," he replied morosely at length. "I suppose I knew it all along." He embraced her once more. "But how can I bear to leave you again?"

"It will not be for long."

"Perhaps my father is right when he says I will be able to win back my favor."

"In that I *do* agree with him!" Anna smiled.

Sergei chuckled. "It is not easy to admit he is right."

"But in his words we can take hope."

"Anna, I love you so!" he said softly, kissing one of her light curls.

They had been so close to finally having each other . . . as close as talk of a midnight flight out of St. Petersburg. Now that the voice of reason had prevailed, would it ever happen? Or would they eternally find themselves pawns in a cruel game of fate, maneuvered about by voices of reason, by autocratic rulers, and by an uncaring father?

As if in answer to his unspoken questions, Sergei suddenly heard the sound of a footfall on the garden path. He and Anna parted, but it was too late. Viktor saw enough, and for what he did not see, he was well able to draw his own conclusions.

"Father!" exclaimed Sergei as Anna shrank timidly back.

"I see I was right all along," said Viktor, with such control Sergei could have exploded. "You care nothing for honor, or for a name that stands for honor."

"Think what you will, Father."

"My previous assessment of things turns out to be the correct one. Your mother's tears can do nothing to change that now."

"I don't care anymore!"

"That is obvious enough."

"What do you mean by that?" challenged the son bitterly.

"It is the lowest sort of man who would use a poor servant girl for his own ends. I had hoped I'd raised better."

"Think the worst of me if you will—you always have anyway. But I am glad you have found out the truth about Anna and me. And since you have, let me set you completely straight. This is no sordid affair, as you seem to think. Anna and I have known each other quite well for two years. Not only is she gracious enough to love me, I love her as well and plan to marry her. Thanks to you, that will have to wait, for I must go south as I have been ordered. But we will marry. Nothing you can do will stop it."

"Don't be foolish, Sergei," said Viktor in as close to a pleading tone as the old soldier could come, although it still bore the sound of command. "To throw your life away for a servant—"

"Don't even dare speak a word against Anna."

"I only meant—"

"I am through listening to you!"

"Well, at least you have enough sense left to obey your orders. I am more certain than ever that your going on this duty will be the best thing for you under the circumstances."

"No doubt you and the tsar planned it together!"

"Sergei—!" Anna tried to speak, but choking tears and her own fear in the elder prince's presence made her voice useless.

"And let me tell you this," Sergei continued to rail against his father. "My decision to obey my orders has nothing to do with you. If it were up to me alone, I would desert and leave the country, even if it meant you spending your life in shame. But for Anna's sake, and my own, I have chosen to do otherwise. Honor does mean something to me, after all, Father. Unfortunately, it is an honor different than you and your colleagues of the court will ever know."

Viktor replied only with silence. He was nearly as dumbfounded by the turn of events as his daughter's maid.

"Goodbye, Father. You are finally rid of me."

Sergei walked to where Anna stood, pale and trembling. He took her arm and together they began to walk away. But some demon of bitterness in Sergei's heart made him pause and look back for one final cruel thrust. "If you are lucky, Father," he said, "I will catch a Tartar bullet and not return!"

8

Anna went immediately to her room after leaving Sergei at the door of his father's house. The thought of running away right then with Sergei had occurred to her. But that awful face of reason—she was growing to hate it, too!—rose to prevent her.

What she *would* do she did not yet know. But just as Sergei could not run away, neither could she.

Anna sat on her bed for a long while and wept. She wanted to think, but her thoughts were in far too much disarray to be coherent.

When the knock came at her door a couple of hours later, she could not imagine who it could possibly be. Katrina had been gone almost three weeks. She had only had one visitor in all that time, her old friend Polya. Perhaps Nina or one of the other maids needed her for something. She almost hoped so. Work was just the thing she needed right now. As her papa always said, *A hand to the plow is the surest remedy for cobwebs in the brain.*

Anna dried her eyes, took in a deep, steadying breath, and opened the door.

Prince Viktor Fedorcenko stood before her. She let out a little gasp of shock and felt her knees waver.

"I believe you will agree with me, Anna Yevnovna," he said, "when I suggest that we need to talk."

Anna only nodded mutely. She prayed silently, desperately, that somehow she could find not only her voice but the courage to speak her heart to this man—her employer, her master.

"I think we may make use of Princess Katrina's sitting room," the prince went on, leading Anna, nearly having to pull her forward into the other room. "Sit . . . please."

Anna dumbly obeyed, while the prince himself stood, pacing occasionally as he spoke, and pausing now and then by the mantel.

"At this point, Anna," the prince began in a more informal tone than he had used with his own son, "I am willing to give you the benefit of the doubt. I have had, over the years, little occasion for any personal involvement with you. But that is not to say that I have not observed with interest your activities in this household. I have never had reason to find the slightest fault with you. Moreover, you have exercised a most positive influence on my daughter, for which I am grateful. Because of your influence she succeeded in her studies where no one else was able to encourage her. Fingal tells me your motivation was even greater than hers. Katrina also has confided in me how your intercession saved her from her headstrong determination to marry Anickin. In short, you have been a faithful and loyal servant, Anna Yevnovna. And thus I find myself completely baffled by this most uncharacteristic departure on your part. I must conclude, indeed I can see no other conclusion to draw, that you were overwhelmed by aristocratic force, unable to protest for fear of reprisals, and thus went along with whatever my son may have told you, despite what all reason and sensibility should have dictated on both your parts. I know how persuasive my son can be, even when he is behaving in a self-motivated and debased sense of his own—"

Suddenly Anna found her voice. She could not listen to Sergei being wrongly accused for another moment.

"If you will forgive me, Your Excellency," she interrupted, "your conclusions about Sergei are not at all correct." In the same breath she had not only found her voice but had contradicted her master!

The prince's eyebrows shot up. This insolence was not lost on him; he was accustomed to unquestioning obedience and servility from his servants. Apparently Sergei had already rubbed off more on this girl than he at first realized!

"How so, Anna Yevnovna?" he said, retaining amazing control.

"I thought you knew your children better than that, Your Excellency," Anna said, finding courage even as she spoke. "If you did, you could never accuse your son of such crass behavior."

"So . . . my son is innocent, and it was rather *you* who lured *him* into this unusual liaison?"

"Is it always a question of one luring the other?"

"I do not understand you."

"Is it not possible for a young man and a young woman, even a prince and a servant, to meet and talk and find that they have ideas and interests in common, and then discover that the friendship emerging between them one day blossoms into love? Is that so unusual . . . or so impossible, Your Excellency?"

"My son ought to have enough sense to stop such a thing before it goes that far."

"Perhaps we were wrong in that, sir. But even now I cannot truly believe what we feel toward each other is wrong. And whether you believe it or not, Prince Sergei has always behaved completely honorably toward me. You may want to think the worst of him, and of me also. But we have done nothing to be ashamed of. Whatever mistakes we have made have only been errors in judgment."

"I do not *want* to believe the worst," replied Viktor emphatically. "And I can even understand the impetuosity of youth in these matters. But the fact remains, you both made a mistake, even if only in judgment. My son may have acted honorably toward you, but he has shown beyond question his own disregard for his family and position."

He paused momentarily, then went on. "But that has nothing to do with you, Anna Yevnovna. I came here to give you a chance to speak for yourself. It seems you have chosen to use the opportunity to speak instead for my son."

He paused again, now standing by the mantel, an arm propped on the ledge, and studied Anna for a brief moment. "That, in itself, speaks as much for you as anything."

"What would you have me do, Your Excellency?"

"Sergei intends on obeying his orders. In that decision, I take hope that he is not completely lost. You both must use this timely separation to reconsider your individual positions. You are free, of course, to return to your home in the country, Anna. But you are also free to remain. In a short time my daughter will return from Greece and you will take up residence with her in Count Remizov's home—if you choose. I will not prevent you. In fact, I am sure she would be lost without you."

"And when your son returns. . . ?"

"I will hope by then you will both have come to your senses. My son may truly believe that he loves you, Anna. But I am convinced that his rebellious nature is at the root of this. He would do anything to incur my displeasure. I must rely on your good sense, Anna, of which I believe you have an abundance, to right this unfortunate situation. If you care for my son, surely you will not stand by and watch his life ruined by such a . . . hastily conceived . . . liaison."

"Your Excellency, I must be honest with you." Anna lifted her eyes until for the first time they were steadily focused on the prince. "I cannot in good conscience promise anything. I admit, there is confusion for me in all this. Yet do I simply turn my back on your son because we are from different backgrounds? If that turns out best for him, of course I will do it for his sake. But right now . . . I cannot see such things clearly. Perhaps for now it is best left in time's hands. In the meantime, I do wish to remain here, if Princess Katrina wishes to retain me after she knows—"

"Anna, this matter is best kept quiet. No one need know what has transpired today."

"As you wish, Your Excellency."

When Prince Fedorcenko left the room, Anna remained for several moments, standing silently in disbelief over the inconceivable interchange. Had anything even been resolved? She wasn't certain. The only result seemed to be that Sergei's father had, at least partially, left a resolution in *her* hands.

Slowly she turned and walked back into her own small room, closed the door, and sat down on the side of her bed. Within the short span of twenty-four hours, everything had been turned upside down.

After two or three minutes she slipped to her knees.

"Oh, God," she prayed, "I don't know how to face the choices that lie ahead for us . . . for me! Yet I know *you* are in control of my life, and Sergei's too—even though perhaps he doesn't know it—and our destiny together, whatever it is. Help me, God, to know what to do, what to think, what to say. Be with Sergei, too, wherever he goes, whatever happens. Protect him and watch over him. Whatever the final outcome of all this, Lord, strengthen us . . . strengthen *me* and make me a woman you are proud of. Help Sergei's father to see him as I see him, and to love him as I love him. Oh, God . . . I want to place the future, whatever it holds—for me, for Sergei, for our two families—in your hands. Help me to trust you in bringing about what is for our very best!"

Anna was silent a few minutes more, then rose, went to her cupboard, and took out the Bible her father had given her. She turned to one of her favorite passages, suddenly thinking of it in terms of Sergei, and read from John the familiar words: *In a little while I am going away and you will see me no more, and then after a little while you will see me again. I tell you the truth, you will weep and mourn. You will grieve, but the day will come when your grief will turn to joy.*

She drew in a deep breath, and uttered one more prayer. "Oh, God, whatever grief and mourning comes, let me trust for the day when you will turn it to joy. Keep Sergei in your hand, Lord."

9

Had Sergei been able to hear the prayers of the girl he loved, he would not have dismissed them lightly, for they were Anna's. Yet he would have had difficulty believing them to contain much present meaning for his life. As bitterness and anger sealed off his heart, the One whose voice Anna was humbly trying to hear grew more and more distant to him.

Sergei returned to his barracks and packed up his belongings. He was expected to be on the first train south in the morning. He had two more errands to attend to before then. The last would be to say goodbye to Anna one final time. But before that there was one more person he wanted to see.

He found Lieutenant Misha Grigorov off duty, in his quarters adjacent to the palace. The lieutenant invited the prince in, pulled up a simple wooden chair for him, and then seated himself on the edge of his bed.

"I heard about your unfortunate trouble with the emperor," said Grigorov. "You have my sympathy."

"Thank you, Lieutenant. But that is not why I have come."

"I didn't think so. What can I do for you?"

"I understand from Anna that you and she have become friends, that she has confided in you about us." He paused, obviously feeling the awkwardness of the situation.

"Yes . . . on both counts," replied Misha slowly.

"I honestly don't know how to speak my mind without sounding like a melancholy fool," said Sergei with a nervous laugh.

"Just speak out, Prince Fedorcenko. I will neither take you for a melancholic nor a fool. Remember, I owe my life to you. I know what kind of man you are."

"All right then, here it is plainly," said Sergei. "I received orders of transfer just yesterday. Since then I have had ominous misgivings. These are only compounded by the fact that in the last few days everything seems to have turned against me."

He paused, groping for the right words.

"My father has discovered about Anna and me, and although I do not fear that he would harm her in any way, he very well could use his influence to force her to leave his home, or St. Petersburg, perhaps even to go somewhere far away, to disappear. And even if she should remain in his home, or with my sister, he could eliminate any form of communication between us and make her life miserable if he so chose. Anything could happen, Lieutenant, and I do not want to return to find that I have lost her or that she has disappeared."

"I can hardly believe such fears are justified."

"Perhaps not. Nevertheless, I would feel much better about leaving if I knew there was someone here who understood the situation and could watch out for Anna, to see that she is not trundled off some dark night to Spain, or, heaven forbid, to Siberia."

"Do you really fear such deception from your own father?"

Slowly Sergei nodded his head. "He might do something rash, fully believing it to be for my own good," he said. "But I don't know. I have just been possessed by this dreadful sense that once I leave, I will never see Anna again. Yet . . . I must go, for reasons I hardly understand myself."

"What can I do?" said Misha sincerely.

"It would give me some peace of mind to know there is someone here for Anna, someone other than my sister, who to my knowledge knows nothing about our relationship."

"It would be an honor to serve you in this way."

"And if anything should happen to me," Sergei added, "it will be good to know . . . that she has a friend here."

"I pray, Prince Fedorcenko, that all your fears are imaginary," said Misha with conviction. "I am certain they are! But you need not worry about Anna. I will continue to be her friend, and yours through her. If the need ever arose, I would give my life to protect her—not merely for her sake but because of the debt I have owed you since the Balkans."

"Thank you, Lieutenant."

"Please . . . I am Misha to my friends."

"I am happy to be counted so," said Sergei, rising. "And you must do me the honor of using my given name also. Yours is a friendship I will value highly."

Both men embraced, sealing their friendship in ancient Russian fashion. "Godspeed, Sergei!"

"And to you also, my friend."

10

Only two more farewells were left for Sergei.

He would say goodbye to his mother in the morning, for she had insisted on driving with him to the train station. He regretted that he would not see Katrina before he left, or Dmitri.

Somehow his vague misgivings felt strongest when he thought of his sister. What would be her reaction when she learned about him and Anna, as she was bound to sooner or later? Would she hate him for it? Or worse, would she reject Anna? Or would she understand, as she had always been able to understand him? He wished he could tell her himself, but he would be far away by the time Katrina returned. He could only leave matters in God's hands, although at the moment his faith was so weak that this thought gave him little comfort.

By the time he saw Anna later in the evening, his mood had descended to its lowest ebb, perhaps of his entire life. They had arranged to meet in a little tea shop around the corner from the Marïnsky Theater. With Katrina gone, scarcely anyone paid the least attention to Anna, who found herself free to come and go almost at will. They ordered tea, but their glasses had hardly been touched thirty minutes later.

Anna tried to lift the heavy oppression weighing on them. It was a feeble attempt at best.

"I remember when I saw my first ballet at the Marïnsky," she said. "I could not believe anything under a stone roof could be so beautiful."

"And I could not believe anyone's eyes could possibly be wider," chuckled Sergei, making his own attempt at levity. "I was jealous that those eyes were not for me."

"And I thought you were concerned only for my education."

"My interest was purely selfish. The more I could talk Katrina into investing in your cultural enlightenment—with me along as advisor and chaperon—the more frequently I could see you."

"Oh, Sergei!" Anna closed her eyes against the sudden and unexpected rush of tears.

"We are always saying goodbye, aren't we?" Sergei reached across the table and took her hands in his. "But this will be the last one, Anna. When we next see each other—and it won't be long—there will be no more farewells. I swear it!"

Anna could say nothing in reply. She hoped with all her heart that they would have a future together, but her confusion over what truly was best prevented her from voicing this hope even though she knew Sergei longed to hear those words from her.

She could offer him no assurances. All she had to give was love. And she hoped that would be enough for him to take to the faraway place for which he was bound.

"Sergei," she said, "for once I do not come to one of our farewells empty-handed." She smiled. "I have a gift for you. I know it is a poor substitute, but it is at least a token of what I feel."

"Anna, I need nothing—"

She did not let him finish. "Please," she interrupted. "You always have something for me. You have given me books and other things, and now it is my turn. Please, just let me give you a little piece of myself."

He smiled and nodded in agreement.

She took from the pocket of her coat a small tan pouch made of soft deerskin. Unfastening the lace by which it was gathered together at the top, she carefully reached her fingers inside.

"My father gave me this the day I left home," she said. "He told me then that it was the only thing of material value in his possession. I have treasured it ever since, getting it out to look at when I was especially sad or just needed a reminder that my mama and papa loved me. And now it will make me happiest of all for you to have it."

She handed him a delicately handcrafted ornate Byzantine cross, made of pure gold, into which had been set thirteen exquisitely cut stones of Russian mined lapis. The deep blue on a background of solid gold was stunning.

"Anna, it's so beautiful! How can you ask me to take this—an heirloom from your own family? I could never—"

She silenced him with a finger placed lovingly over his lips.

"Will you deny me this one pleasure that will give me joy every time I think of you? Please, Sergei, for *me*. I will know that wherever you are, I am there with you. Let it be as a bond between our two hearts."

Finally realizing how important it was to her, Sergei nodded in assent and took the cross from her hand. He held it to the light and examined its every detail slowly and methodically.

The cross was not large, approximately four centimeters from top to bottom, and two and a half in width. A deep blue lapis cabochon sat in the center of the cross, with twelve smaller lapis cabochons set into diamond-cut impressions in the gold arms of the cross. The entire perimeter of the cross was edged with hand-tooled gold beads.

"What do all the stones and cuts stand for, do you know, Anna?" Sergei asked after looking it over with admiration and love.

"I asked my father that too," said Anna. "He told me that the largest cabochon stone is raised to symbolize the royalty and supremacy of Christ. The twelve smaller pieces of lapis stand for the twelve disciples of the Lord. And the gold beads around the edge represent the many ups and downs and crossroads of life."

"Besides being from your heart, it will be a special remembrance of Katyk and your father and family, and my time there," he said. "I will treasure it."

"Thank you. You have made me happy."

"But," he added, "by taking this gift, I do not make it mine. I will carry it with me as *yours*, as you yourself said, as a piece of you. I am merely agreeing to borrow it while I am apart from you . . . agreed?"

Anna smiled. "Agreed," she said.

"And because it is borrowed," Sergei went on, "I *will* return it to you, unharmed, to give it personally back into your hand."

"That will be the best part of all," replied Anna, "looking forward to that day!"

"That is my promise to you, Anna Yevnovna Burenin—a promise to place this cross of gold back into your hand."

"I accept you at your word," said Anna. "Anticipating that day will give my heart peace whatever comes between now and then. And until it comes I will keep my father's deer hide pouch, empty just like it is now, as my reminder that you carry my heart with you."

Sergei tucked the priceless icon carefully inside his uniform jacket, significantly near his heart. "We will each carry with us these reminders of our hope for a speedy reunion," he said, reaching across the table and grasping Anna's hand.

She smiled. "Our God will see to it!"

"But I don't think God will mind too much if every time I look at the blue and gold, I think of you instead of Him, and am encouraged that I will see you again soon."

"I am sure He wouldn't. Perhaps you can think of us both— of my love and the fact that *He* holds that love in *His* care."

Sergei smiled. "I will think of you *and* God when I gaze

upon my treasured piece of your heart. And I will say a prayer for you every time."

"You cannot know how happy you have made me," said Anna softly.

"You often say that God has special providences and plans for His children," said Sergei more seriously. "Do you still believe that?"

"Yes, of course," replied Anna.

"So do you think too that there is some greater purpose in everything that happens?"

"Yes, I do."

"Even this—my being sent away?"

"I don't know what the purpose is," said Anna, "but yes, Sergei, I *do* believe with all my heart that this is the way God's children must look at the events of their lives, the pleasant as well as the painful, if they are to know His peace in their deepest souls."

Sergei was silent a long while, looking earnestly and purposefully into Anna's face.

"Then, Anna," he said at length, "I am going to make one more promise to you before I go." He paused, took in a deep breath, then went on. "I am going to promise that I will do my best to see what happens in my life from now on in this way. I must admit, seeing life from what I have heard you call God's perspective has not been my natural way. But I want to, and I will try. So you must pray for me."

"Oh, Sergei, of course I will!"

"Then perhaps God can help me believe that all these events will somehow turn out for the best in the end—my leaving you, my problems with Father, whatever the future holds."

"I will pray that He will help you believe it."

"Thank you," said Sergei intensely.

"Thank *you*, Sergei! You have given me a gift far more priceless than any gold and lapis cross could possibly be."

"The time is getting late," he said. "Shall we go out and walk for a while before curfew?" He rose, and they left the tea shop.

The curfew had been recently imposed, but they had about

an hour yet to walk and talk quietly. Then Sergei hired a carriage to take Anna home. They stopped some distance from the gates of the estate. There was no sense inflaming an already delicate situation by risking being seen together again.

When the carriage came to a stop, Sergei leaned over and kissed Anna tenderly on the lips. Neither spoke. No words were spoken, only tears hidden by the darkness.

Then he climbed out and helped her down to the street.

They stood together in one final embrace. As they parted their eyes met, saying all that was necessary between them.

Anna began to walk away.

"I love you, Anna Yevnovna!" she heard Sergei's voice say behind her.

She paused, turned back for one last glance, trying to smile through the darkness even though tears streamed down her face. She opened her mouth in a vain attempt to return the words to him. But they caught hopelessly in her throat. Another moment more and she felt great sobs welling up in her chest.

She turned again and hurried toward the black iron gates of the Fedorcenko estate.

II

Adjustments of a New Life

(May 1880)

11

The newlyweds returned to St. Petersburg during the first week of May. At Warsaw Station, Katrina and Dmitri were greeted by a swarm of friends and family from both sides. Then followed several days of receptions and parties in their honor, continuing as if uninterrupted from four weeks earlier. After the relaxing days in the sunshine of the Greek coast and cruising leisurely on the Mediterranean, suddenly Katrina fell right back in the middle of an emotional whirlwind, as she had before, during, and after the wedding. Society creature that she was, she loved all the social flittering and gaiety, especially because she and Dmitri were at the center of it all. Yet gradually the months of such an intense pace began to weary her.

The frantic schedule of social engagements, however, was almost easier to take than the difficulties of adjusting to and settling into new surroundings. While on her honeymoon, Katrina had given no more than a passing thought to the prospect of no longer living at home under her parents' roof and protection. Now suddenly she was not only away from home, but, at the tender age of nineteen, a mistress of that new house in which she found herself—at least Dmitri assured her it would be so once his mother returned to Moscow.

The Remizov home in the South Side of St. Petersburg was much smaller than the Fedorcenko home, employing no more than fifteen or twenty servants. It was indicative of the declining state of the Remizov fortune, for when Count Gregory Remizov, Dmitri's father, had been alive, the family occupied an estate equal in scale to the Fedorcenko's, and, like Katrina's family, two or three estates in the country as well.

As their wealth declined after the elder count's death, his wife, Countess Eugenia Pavlovna Remizov, was forced to move into a smaller place in St. Petersburg and relinquish all but the Moscow properties. Not long after that the countess, who had been born and bred in Moscow herself and hated St. Petersburg as much as she hated St. Petersburg society, returned to the Moscow estate. Now, for the first time in years, the house was returning to permanent family use with the marriage of her only son. This was possible because Dmitri had made a good marriage—far better, in his mother's estimation, than he would have with the Nabatov girl—and it was financially feasible for them to operate the house once more.

Katrina liked the place well enough—she wasn't quite sure whether it could rightfully be called an *estate*. It was a bit cramped, with only thirty or so rooms. And it was not in the *best* section of even that exclusive St. Petersburg neighborhood. It was tastefully decorated, although there were a few changes she'd make someday. And it did feature lovely gardens with a high wall surrounding them so that you could walk about hardly aware of the location if you didn't think about it.

She could be happy there. She could be happy anywhere with Dmitri. But she decided almost the moment she set foot in the place that she would be far happier once the Countess Eugenia made her exit.

Eugenia Pavlovna was, at best, a peculiar woman. She preferred a life of solitude, not because of a particularly meditative character, but more likely because she found nearly all other human beings tedious, hypocritical, deceiving, and generally nothing but bores. In her estimation, she herself was so far superior to most specimens of humanity she had encountered thus far in her life as to make any interaction with others wearisome and dull beyond description. Thus she kept to herself, and in that company was as content as a person of her ilk could hope to be.

She was an accomplished musician and spent hours at the piano. But she did not care to share her talent, which was genuine enough, with people who could never properly appreciate her gifts. Self-generating and self-gratifying, her ability was also self-defeating and therefore spirit-killing. Even the servants, who seldom had opportunity of listening to music of high quality, found it more oppressive than pleasurable.

She had married because it was expected of her, but she found no joy in the union. As an inevitable result, neither did her husband, who eventually turned to drinking, unwise investments abroad, reckless ventures in and about St. Petersburg, and other extramarital—and some said extralegal—activities, all designed to make life bearable, if not interesting. Thus began the eroding of the century-old Remizov fortune, a tradition which Dmitri himself, as son and heir, seemed bent on continuing until very recently.

The countess would have made her son into a perfect image of herself, for no doubt that was the only way she could have accepted him. And, as his mother, she felt it was her duty to at least accept him. Dmitri, however, was not cut out to be a recluse absorbed in music and his mother—although he did manage to pick up rather advanced skills at the piano. If he must choose, he preferred his father's dissipate lifestyle, and had been proceeding along that unruly path until he had suddenly stumbled upon the sister of his best friend directly in the middle of it. Something in him now seemed to have changed, definitely if not entirely. Time would tell how deep the transformation had gone.

Katrina had expected, as had Dmitri, that the countess would return to Moscow immediately after the wedding. She had complained all throughout the festivities how horrid she found the climate in the north and how wonderful it would be to return to Moscow. Thus, the newlyweds were surprised to return and find her still in residence at their new home.

The thought occurred to Katrina that perhaps her delay was motivated by the natural tendency of a mother-in-law to desire to know her son's wife more intimately. Yet the countess made little effort toward that end, seeming almost to avoid Katrina when it was possible. Meals, if not strained, were certainly not talkative, friendly affairs, conducted rather almost as if matters of business. The few other encounters they had were not generally pleasant.

A nod, one or two words, were all that came Katrina's

way—never a smile, never a conversation. The countess seemed almost pained whenever she chanced upon her new daughter-in-law. And even when Dmitri was present, although she treated him with a distant sort of respect, the countess scarcely had a positive word to utter about anything except herself and, occasionally, Moscow.

Dmitri endured it. He had spent a lifetime learning how. Katrina eventually took to making sure she avoided the countess whenever possible. She knew her own temper well enough and did not want to take any chances.

Still Eugenia Remizov stayed, even as the unbearable St. Petersburg summer approached. There was obviously nothing to be done on either Katrina's or Dmitri's part but to make the best of it.

The mood in the household as a result was not of a sort that Katrina found invigorating for her first weeks and months as a young married wife.

One afternoon, Anna was with her in her boudoir when perhaps mirroring her own inner quandary, Katrina asked, "Anna, how are *you* finding your situation here?"

"I have to admit I miss the old surroundings," replied Anna sincerely, "and some of the people I had come to know. But I am content because I am with you, Princess, and that is what matters most."

"Thank you, Anna. But I suppose like me, you would prefer our old home, with Mama's headaches and Nina's disapproving looks, and that ornery little dog yapping and nipping at our heels. And the smell of Papa's tobacco and his deep, soothing voice."

She sighed. "Every difficulty or hardship I thought I had before is nothing alongside listening to her incessant playing on that horrid piano, and putting up with her silent stares. The other day I went into the music room, just to listen—I don't know, and maybe try again for the hundredth time to see if there wasn't something I could talk to the lady about. She stopped playing and looked down her long nose at me from where she sat at the piano as if to let me know I was not welcome in her inner sanctum. She didn't *say* a word!"

"I know, Princess," said Anna. "I have seen the way she behaves toward you. I am sorry."

"But whatever am I complaining about? I am starting to sound like the countess herself—God forbid! I am married to Dmitri, am mistress of my own home—I couldn't be happier. Well . . . *almost* its mistress. Anyway, I must be insane to be sounding so melancholic."

"I do not see how you could keep from missing your own home. As happy as I have been in St. Petersburg, I also get homesick once in a while for my parents' home and village."

"You are right," said Katrina. She took a breath of resolve, as if that were the end of it. "At least I am glad to know you are adjusting well to our new home, Anna. I've been concerned because ever since I returned from Greece, you have seemed . . . well, rather withdrawn or distracted. I feared you were unhappy, or perhaps ill."

"I am sorry, Your Highness," said Anna disconcertingly. "I am well, I'm sure . . . I did not realize—"

"Your father's health still weighs heavily upon you, doesn't it, Anna?"

"He is better this spring, but yes, I suppose so . . . more than I was aware of," Anna replied. "I'm sorry if I have neglected you in any way."

"Oh, not at all, Anna—think nothing more of it."

Anna was relieved for the excuse her mistress unwittingly provided. Yet as much as she truthfully was concerned about her father, she hated not being able to tell Katrina the whole truth. Once, long ago, Katrina had suspected her brother's attraction to Anna. But she had no idea how serious it had become. Now, Anna's fear of Katrina's opposition outweighed even the desire to confide with her everything about Sergei.

Upon their return, both Katrina and Dmitri had been dismayed to learn of Sergei's trouble over the tsar's reaction to his book. Dmitri had soothed away her fears with assurances that Sergei was no doubt having the time of his life. There was glory and adventure to be had in the outlands of the empire for members of His Majesty's army. Why not, therefore, when you are young and single, enjoy it to the full, and be where the action and dangers and excitement were?

It had almost sounded to Katrina as if her husband envied Sergei just a little. He had laughed and said being married to her was all the adventure any man could hope for. Yet still, the glint in his eye, if even for a moment, reminded her that the man she had married was not yet altogether tamed.

So the days gradually passed in the new Remizov household. Eventually, a certain routine came to be established with which both Katrina and Anna grew more and more comfortable.

12

One morning in early summer, all the capital received news that the Empress Marie Alexandrovna was dead. Because of her long illness, her death did not come unexpected; still, nothing could diminish the sadness once the end came.

The entire country mourned the loss. The Hesse-Darmstadt princess was not Russian by birth, but she had become a native in every other way possible and had been taken into the hearts of Russian people everywhere. Their grief no doubt was heightened by public annoyance at the way her husband, the tsar, mistreated her. All the court knew, even if the masses did not, that after the bombing, Alexander had brought his illegitimate family into the very Winter Palace itself to live, out of fear for their safety. The dying empress was humiliated, condemned to spend her final bedridden days within earshot of her husband's illegitimate children playing in nearby corridors. Even at the very end, she was not spared the mortification she had suffered over the years. Her husband, in his insensitivity, rubbed salt into wounds already deep and filled with acrimony.

Within two months the tsar married Catherine Dolgoruky, shocking all of St. Petersburg society and further alienating his son, the tsarevich, who promptly left not only the capital but the country altogether, moving his family to Denmark. It was the first time in centuries that a Russian emperor had married a Russian woman, breaking the long-standing tradition that an heir to the throne marry into one of the royal houses of Europe. Alexander flippantly justified his actions. "I am not the heir," he said. "I am tsar already! I shall do what pleases me."

A great fear rose within the inner circles of the court that Alexander II would go one step further and actually declare Catherine empress. As yet she was merely Alexander's wife. To become tsaritsa required the official crowning of the church. If the tsar went ahead with such an unprecedented proceeding, many feared he might even reject the present tsarevich Alexander as his heir in favor of George Alexandrovich, his eldest illegitimate son by Catherine.

Within the court, and within the St. Petersburg gossip in general, a quiet debate arose over which son, the legitimate or the illegitimate, should be the next tsar. For some, Loris-Melikov among them, the idea of George as emperor was not altogether unacceptable. For to these members of the progressive and liberal camp, the heir apparent, Alexander Alexandrovich, tsarevich in self-imposed exile in Denmark, along with his reactionary tutor and advisor Pobedonostev, represented nothing but a huge leap backward into repression for the already troubled Romanov regime.

It was early fall when stunning news of a more immediate and personal nature rocked the Remizov household. After talking to Anna about not feeling well, Katrina herself began taking regularly to her bed. After a week, both Dmitri and Anna insisted that she allow the physician to be called.

His visit turned up neither influenza nor appendicitis.

"Take good care of her, miss," was all the doctor said to Anna as he exited.

Anna went into Katrina's bedroom immediately. The princess, who had been pale for weeks, glowed with a radiant joy.

"Oh, Anna, you'll never believe it! Dmitri and I are going to have a baby!" she cried, tears already beginning to flow.

Anna ran to get Dmitri, and whether he suspected the truth

from her excited, animated face he wouldn't tell. But the moment he saw Katrina he knew all in an instant. Anna had no more than shut the door behind him when she heard several shouts and whoops in delighted exclamation.

For the rest of that day, and for several days afterward, he grinned incessantly. He stopped servants in his own house and commanders and cabbies standing with their horses and even strangers on the street to tell them the earth-shattering, delightful news that his beautiful young wife of three months was in a family way, and that *he* was the cause of it all!

"A little count, that's what he'll be . . . a chip off the old block . . . a man's man in the tsar's army! Might even train him to be a general!"

Cigars and jokes and laughter and congratulatory drinks and more boasts than could well reside on the shoulders of any infant, born or unborn, followed Dmitri about in abundant supply.

A week or ten days later, he and Katrina were taking coffee together in the parlor one evening after dinner. Suddenly in the midst of a conversation not remotely related to parenthood, a ghastly pallor flooded the count's face. He quickly set down his cup for fear of spilling it. Katrina saw the change and thought he had been flooded by a sudden wave of nausea. She jumped up and ran to him in alarm.

"What is it?" she asked.

"By heaven, Katrina!" he exclaimed softly, yet with alarm in his voice, "I am going to be a father!"

Katrina instantly relaxed.

"And *that* is what has upset you?" she asked. "I thought you wanted to be."

"Yes . . . of course," he half stammered. "But . . . but actually a *father*!"

"That is what happens when you have a baby, Dmitri," she replied with a smile, returning to the divan where she had been sitting. "You become a father and I become a mother."

"But . . . don't you realize . . . have you thought about what it all *means*?" he said in a choking voice.

"It is a little frightening, I'll admit."

"A little! What do we know, Katrina?"

"We'll manage."

"How? You're only nineteen—what do you know about being a mother? I'm only twenty-three!"

"We will make wonderful parents. You will be a tremendous father."

"How can you be so sure? How do you *know*?" Agitated, he jumped up and began to pace.

"Dmitri, it's all perfectly natural. We'll learn. Please sit down and relax."

She patted the divan next to her. But he took no notice and continued pacing.

"I've already spoken with my mother," Katrina went on. "Granted, she wasn't as much help as I would have liked. I can hardly believe she raised *two* children. But that's just it, Dmitri—if my mother can do it, anyone can!"

"That is not an altogether comforting thought! Your mother isn't exactly the picture of strength and reassurance."

"Yet look at how Sergei and I turned out. You seem to like the two of us without too many reservations." Katrina eyed him coyly, sending one of her bewitching smiles into his eyes. But her husband was not to be dissuaded from his trepidation.

"We'll have help, Dmitri, just like my mother did," Katrina went on. "Nurses, governesses—and Anna! She has lots of good sense. Anna will be our Nina and Mrs. Remington and Fingal Aonghas all rolled into one. She came from a family of five children. Why, she helped raise the younger ones herself. Nothing could be more perfect, don't you see, Dmitri? If anything at all goes wrong, we will always have Anna!"

"You place a great deal of confidence in her."

"And why not? She has proved herself worthy of it. Besides, what can possibly go wrong?"

"But I have never even touched an infant before."

"Dmitri," said Katrina in an altered and more serious tone, "if it would make you feel any better, why don't you have a talk with my father?"

"Why your father?"

"Well, your father is gone. And you couldn't find a better example to emulate than mine."

"Not according to your brother."

"Oh, pooh! Sergei is a wonderful brother and I love him. But I don't think he really knows Papa."

"He could say the same of you. *He* thinks he sees the true side of your father."

"I suppose . . . but I still think you could talk to Papa."

Dmitri shook his head. "I don't know . . ."

A long silence fell between them.

All at once Dmitri rose to his feet and started for the door.

"Where are you going?" asked Katrina. "It's too late to see my father now."

"I'm not going to see him . . . I just have to . . . I'll be back later." His eyes would not look directly at Katrina as he spoke.

"Dmitri . . . it's late."

He said nothing in reply, then turned and disappeared out the door.

13

When Dmitri arrived home much later that night, Katrina had long been in bed, though unable to sleep and dozing in fits.

She glanced up immediately when the door to their room opened. Dmitri walked in slowly, noticeably unsteady on his feet. He staggered forward, stumbled as he came close to the bed, and caught himself just in time to prevent a fall by grabbing one of the bedposts.

Katrina had left a lamp burning, and by its light he flashed her a lopsided, foolish grin as she turned over to greet him.

"Do you realize how late it is?" she asked, hardly making an attempt to hide her annoyance.

"Time...?" Dmitri slurred. "Who can tell...it's fall and gets dark so soon now, you know." He grinned again.

"Well, I was worried about you."

"Nothing whatever to be concerned about, my dear."

"If I had known you were out carousing, I might have gone to sleep. I thought something might have happened to you."

"Did I keep you awake, dear little wife? Ah, I am sorry to be such—" He could not even finish the sentence for the chuckling that accompanied his attempted remorse.

"You're drunk!"

"Am I now? Well, that *is* serious!"

"Yes, you *did* keep me awake," said Katrina angrily. "But never mind!" She pulled the blankets up and turned her back toward him.

"Well!" He drew out the word to the best effect his drunken tongue would allow. "May I not go out when I choose? Am I a prisoner in my own house?"

Katrina said nothing.

"It is a fine turn of events, I must say! We can talk about it in the morning, when you are sober," said Katrina finally, not turning around.

"No! I want to talk about it *now*! Am I or am I not master in my own home?"

"Oh, Dmitri!"

"Answer me now, *wife*!" he said sharply, grabbing at her arm where she lay and twisting her around in the bed to face him.

"Dmitri...my arm!" she cried. His grip was not so painful as that his sudden angry gesture caught her off guard. Never had she seen the slightest hint before that moment of anything but tenderness toward her. The shock on her face was clearly evident in her wide, frightened eyes—visible to Dmitri even in his drunken state.

The look in those eyes he loved jolted something inside Dmitri awake. He gasped and released her arm immediately—distressed and dismayed at what had come over him. He spun around and walked away.

Katrina slipped quickly out of bed and hurried to him.

"Dmitri, what has happened to you...to us?" Katrina asked, something almost of desperation in her voice.

He did not say anything for a few moments, breathing deeply, trying to steady his blurred and confused thoughts.

"I . . . I began to feel . . . so helpless," he said. "I'm sorry, Katrina . . . I suddenly felt closed in." His voice was soft and tentative, void of the drunken bravado.

"I'm sorry, Dmitri," said Katrina. "I was hurt that you left me so suddenly like that and went out alone. But I didn't mean to get angry at you. I just didn't . . . I felt alone and afraid . . ."

A rush of tears obliterated the remainder of her speech.

"Dear . . . Katrina . . ." He pulled her to him and wrapped his arms around her trembling frame. "I'm so sorry for leaving like that . . . I'll never do it again."

Dmitri did not exactly make good on his resolve. Throughout the fall, in fact, he was seen more and more in the company of his old army friends. Such a trend did not particularly please Katrina, but in the interest of harmony she managed to hold her tongue.

Her patience was rewarded by the unexpected and sudden announcement one day that Countess Eugenia had decided to return to Moscow. No one quite knew why she had waited so long, grumbling the whole time about the unbearable St. Petersburg weather and the oppressively foreign atmosphere of the capital.

The removal of the pall she had cast over the house injected Katrina with a refreshed sense of optimism about the future. With her departure, now they could at last really begin their lives. For a week or two Dmitri did not go out with his cronies once, convincing Katrina that his unsettledness had been entirely a result of his mother's inhibiting presence. And the stirrings of new life in her body added to Katrina's sense of hope and enthusiastic anticipation.

Soon, however, Dmitri began to slip back into what Katrina was beginning to call his "old ways"—drinking, gambling, keeping late hours with his army friends. Katrina fluctuated between hope and despair, and her temper with Dmitri was variable and volatile. One moment she could not imagine herself happier, the next she wondered how she would make it through another day. Dr. Anickin said that such emotional upheavals were quite common for young women in her condition. Katrina, however, did not tolerate them well.

When she was at her lowest, she longed for those days—they seemed like *years* ago—when she had been a normal, halfway stable young girl, in love with her brother's best friend.

But that seemed like a lifetime ago!

14

The view from the grimy tavern window was not one to inspire faith in humanity. Two boys, both smudge-faced, dressed in tatters and with wild, feral looks in the depths of their young eyes, had found a hunk of moldy bread in a garbage bin and were in the midst of a violent battle over possession of the precious morsel.

But Paul Burenin had long since ceased trying to conjure up faith in anything, be it human or spiritual.

In fact, he had almost ceased being appalled by the ugly scene in the alleyway across from the tavern. Such incidents were all too common in the sections of this city where he dwelt, a city where the contrast between wealth and poverty was as sharply defined as the stabbing hunger pains in a child's stomach. Pains ignored by the fat, content aristocratic princes and princesses, counts and countesses, whose tables were spread with luxuriant delicacies.

Still, Paul was not completely inured to what he saw. It stirred something in him that went beyond horror and outrage—something he had learned a year ago from the cold, hard words of a demented lawyer by the name of Anickin.

Travail and Triumph

"Watch! And let it burn deeply into your soul."

Neither cynicism nor moral callousness could quench the fire of rage that now burned within him. He could observe the starving boys carrying on with a detached calm, but only because his mind reminded him that soon all would be made right. Justice would be had. It might not fill the stomachs of those two with more food—not immediately, anyway. But on a larger cosmic scale of right and wrong, justice would be served.

Paul lifted his glass of kvass to his lips and drank deeply, though without relish or satisfaction. At nineteen, he was old enough to be accustomed to the foul-tasting drink, and enough of a man to pretend he enjoyed it. He was still young enough, however, to wonder why Russians everywhere drank such a brew.

When was the last time he had felt satisfied or happy? Even hate gave him no more satisfaction than the strong drink he held in his hand, not the kind of satisfaction it seemed to give some of his comrades. But he no longer expected anything so frivolous as happiness out of life. He had made his choice, and had given up all claim to happiness long ago. It was part of the ultimate sacrifice he must make for the cause. A sacrifice, not of his life—although that might come, too—but as Kazan had once told him, of his "very humanity." Such sentiments had shocked him two years ago. Now they were his life's creed.

The tavern door scraped open. Two men, both familiar to Paul, walked in and sauntered in his direction. If they had chosen this spot for a rendezvous, they could not have made a better choice. The place was busy at this hour, with the evening shift of workers from the cotton mill having just left the tedium of their day's labors. Few could afford the kopecks for the cheap vodka and kvass they were lustily consuming. But even less could they stand to face the hungry, sallow faces of their families cold and stone sober. It would not be so bad if their fourteen-hour workdays counted for anything. But once the factory owner and governmental officials deducted various taxes and expenses and fees from the meager wages, there were hardly two coppers left to jingle about in the pocket. Vodka, and the ensuing drunkenness, was nearly as vital to the survival of some of these men as a loaf of bread.

So the workers crowded nightly into whatever grimy tavern happened to be situated along the route home. Such places made a fine covering for men whose business brought them together for other reasons.

Paul glanced up casually as the two newcomers slid onto the bench at the same table across from him. He remembered when such a meeting caused his heart to pound in his temples and his stomach to quake. But they had become routine now. This was what he did. These were the people with whom the business of his life was conducted. They were comrades in the cause.

Each of the two men had picked up a pint of kvass on his way in, and they sloshed the glasses down on the table. The younger was tall, with a fine-featured, intelligent face. He had been a medical student until he was expelled several months ago for attending a radical assembly. The other man was stockier and coarser in appearance, although he too had been a student, expelled from the engineering school. He was now employed in the adjacent cotton mill as a cleanup man, but his foremost activity remained that of a radical agitator.

Paul knew the factory man, whose name was Stepniak, and had worked with him at the mill. The ex-medical student was new to the organization. Paul had seen his face but he had never spoken to him. Stepniak made the introductions.

"This is Ivan Remiga," he said to Paul.

Paul nodded. "I'm Pavlikov," he said. He had long since taken on an alias, but since many in the organization knew his real name, he took one close to his own, to avoid confusion.

"I am happy to meet you," said Remiga, in an eager, almost innocent tone that made Paul feel strangely like an old veteran of the movement.

"Why does it take two of you to make the delivery?" asked Paul.

"There is another matter I thought might be of interest to you," said Stepniak. "But first things first."

He surreptitiously slipped a folded paper from his pocket and handed it under the table to Paul. "We will need several hundred copies."

"That should be no problem," said Paul, placing the handbill in the pocket of his own coat.

"We must have them as soon as possible."

"Why?"

"Melikov is pushing the government closer and closer toward a constitution—"

"Which would be disastrous," put in the enthusiastic Remiga. "A constitutional monarchy would pacify the masses just enough to nullify all our efforts."

Paul eyed the two cynically. Did they really think he needed to be told all this?

"Melikov knew what he was doing when he turned the government effort from harassing radicals to pacifying the people," Remiga added.

"A constitutional monarchy would never work in Russia," said Paul disinterestedly, hoping to put an end to this discussion and get on with the immediate business of what had brought them together.

"It wouldn't have to work as long as it *looked* good on paper," said Stepniak. "They are running scared. They will do anything to sway public opinion over to their side."

"Yes, of course," said Paul. "But the three of us do not need to hold a referendum on it. It's been debated already many times, and we all know where we stand. Now get on with it. What's on your mind?"

"The urgency of the situation is why these handbills must be distributed immediately. The truth must be told to the people. The tsar does not intend to fulfill his meatless promises."

"Lower your voice," said Paul quietly, in a tone that lacked the urgency of his comrade. "Even a noisy tavern is not the place for such a discussion."

Remiga, the most inexperienced of the trio, glanced about, his eyes darting hurriedly around the room in sudden panic.

"All right," said Stepniak in a strained whisper. "But will you see to the handbills?"

"I'll talk to Zhelyabov," replied Paul. "It should be no problem."

"But I have something else to discuss," Stepniak said. "This place will have to do."

"Then just keep your enthusiasm quiet," cautioned Paul again.

"You knew Basil Anickin, I believe?"

Paul nodded his head skeptically. "Only vaguely."

"He was a vital part of the university organization," said Stepniak. "It is a travesty that nothing has been done for him all this time."

"What could be done? He has been sealed away, heaven only knows where."

"Don't fool yourself, Pavlikov. Zhelyabov hates him and has refused to give sanction to any efforts on his behalf."

"Those are strong words against our leader."

"They are true. You know it yourself."

"There have been other priorities."

"Bah! What are we if we do not take care of our own?"

Stepniak paused, rubbed his beard thoughtfully, and sipped his kvass. Finally he spoke again, measuring each word.

"I had the impression, Pavlikov, that you and Anickin were close."

"Not at all," replied Paul.

"Did he not defend your friend, Kazan?"

"He did, and Kazan was hanged."

"So, you hold that against him?"

"No. But neither did it make us bosom friends. To tell you the truth, I was always a little afraid of him."

"Weren't we all—a little!"

"What you say is probably true. However, I know that Andrei's fear has nothing to do with being afraid *of* him, rather for the damage one such as he can do to the cause."

"The cause needs more like him!"

Paul did not know how to respond to such a statement, especially from someone he had reason to respect till now. Was this the beginning of a rift between Zhelyabov and Stepniak? The latter could never match either wits or might with his mentor, thought Paul. According to Zhelyabov, the best thing that ever happened to the movement was the arrest of Basil Anickin. Paul sat reflecting on the words, and said nothing.

"Then," Stepniak went on, "you would not be interested in joining a plan to aid his escape?"

"Escape?"

"We have recently developed a connection inside the place they are keeping him—a menial employee who is a sympathizer with our purpose. He has sent word that Anickin will be transferred back to the fortress soon. A transfer would give us the ideal opportunity for a break."

"I don't know..." said Paul hesitantly. It was the last thing he wanted to do, but he deemed it unwise to voice a strong protest now. In this game a man had to watch himself constantly, making sure his alliances were strong. If Stepniak carried enough support, he could one day take over leadership of The People's Will, and then where would that leave Paul? He didn't want to say anything just now that Stepniak might take wrongly and thus suspect Paul of betrayal. "There has been talk of another attempt on Melikov," said Paul evasively. "I wouldn't want anything to—"

"All talk! Zhelyabov has gotten cold feet since the bombing failed and Melikov took power. There are those of us who think it is time we stopped waiting for him to take action. Believe me, things will change once we get Anickin back. They do not scare him."

Paul shrugged. "Nevertheless, to mount such an escape plot would be very time consuming."

"You sound like Zhelyabov! Are you going soft like him? I thought better of you. That's why I asked you to meet me."

"We have more pressing commitments. The organization has already set the agenda for the next—"

"Then you won't go along with us?" interrupted Stepniak.

"I shall talk to Andrei and see what he has to say."

"You leave Zhelyabov out of it! I'm asking *you* to make your choice. Your future in the movement could be at stake, Pavlikov."

It was a moment or two before Paul answered. "I will consider your words," he said. "Give me a few days."

"As you wish. But nothing will wait for your decision."

"We must all make the choices we think are best—best for the cause," said Paul.

The factory man shrugged. "Of course, I understand." In spite of his words, his tone had turned cold. "It seems perhaps

I was unwise to take up your time with a matter that interests you so little." He leaned across the table. "You will keep this talk to yourself, Pavlikov?" It was more command than question.

Paul nodded. "All I can say is that I wish you success. If I can help, I will." He hoped his words would keep from alienating Stepniak.

"I believe you. I always thought you were a bright young man."

Stepniak rose and drained off the last of his drink. "I hope you come out on the right side when all the dust settles. Things are bound to change with Anickin back in the thick of it. Come on, Remiga," he added to his young protege.

The ex-medical student rose and followed his comrade out of the tavern. Paul watched them exit, an unsettled feeling growing within him.

Basil Anickin was a name he had wanted to forget. And short of that, at least he had hoped he'd never see the man's face again. But apparently that was not to be the case if Stepniak had his way.

There remained the possibility that the escape could fail. Anickin was locked up tight, with high security, and even his location had been kept a closely guarded secret these many months. Surely success in getting him out was a slim possibility at best.

But Paul could not help wondering what it would mean if he did escape. For The People's Will, it meant another lunatic to keep in tow. Granted, his very lunacy made him fearless and thus a valuable weapon in the right circumstances—*if* one did not mind carrying around a lighted stick of dynamite in his pocket!

Paul's chief concern, however, had little to do with the cause. Anickin had vowed to destroy the Fedorcenkos, and Paul still remembered the wild look in the lawyer's eyes when he had done so. It had been no idle threat. Paul did not doubt that the moment he was free, Anna would immediately be in danger—and that concerned him no less now than it had months ago when he had tried unsuccessfully to warn his sister.

Yet Paul found himself faced with a dilemma. If he spoke

to Zhelyabov, or otherwise warned anyone, and Stepniak's plan was thwarted, Paul would be known as the traitor at once. Then, when and if Anickin ever *did* get out, he *himself* would become a target for the madman's revenge!

He must try to find some means to solve the problem without foiling the plan. He'd have to keep himself apprised of Stepniak's progress. Maybe there was still a chance he could talk him out of it.

But he'd have to be careful. Whatever he did, he must see to it that Basil Anickin stayed right where he was—behind bars where he belonged!

15

It seemed that every unpleasant odor in the world had been collected and injected into the stifling atmosphere of the Novgorov Asylum. The stench made the senses reel and the stomach lurch; but when the initial nausea passed, the ears were assailed by something far worse.

The sounds of insanity.

Cries, groans, chants of sing-song lunacy, laughter, and mumbled conversations all mingling together into an incomprehensible sound of Babel—many tongues ignorant and unconcerned with one another, speaking of secret agonies and hidden ecstacies that no one even wanted to understand. The sounds droned on, and no soul asked for explanations, for there were no listeners. A handful of beings, scarcely human, cloistered together in the drab, dark, filthy, windowless room . . . but no one to *hear* their voices.

Occasionally one of the residents would stop and glance

around at his fellows as if just noticing them for the first time, triggered by some unseen apparition of a diseased mind to venture forth out of his closed little world. If lucidity did not exactly come at such moments, something in the eyes hinted that he caught a brief glimpse of the reality of his surroundings. Then the laughter and nonsensical chanting turned to cries and groans of horror. For the reality was too awful to face, and the retreat into madness which followed was welcomed as a peaceful sleep.

Basil Anickin had spent his share of moments within the netherworld of reality, oblivious even to the presence of his fellow wanderers. His whole being had been so absorbed in hatred and a thirst for vengeance that the prison physicians had deemed him mentally deranged. But even after removing him to the asylum and applying appropriate "curative measures," his visions continued to be stained with the blood of his enemies. Nothing existed, in reality or lunacy, but hate and blood and violence.

They gave him drugs and treatments until his skin paled, his eyes glazed over, and his body sagged with despair. Finally they concluded that their efforts had succeeded in curing him. His teeth no longer ground out curses. His clenched fists relaxed. His eyes lost their lethal intensity. He became a docile lump of a man. Such was the goal of their methods, and it appeared they had worked.

The confident physicians gradually lessened the treatments until they were discontinued. Slowly, by degrees, Basil remembered why he was there. Gradually came the sense that he was different from the others, that they were crazy but he had only come unhinged. Once, in another world—he could not say if it had been real or not—he had been driven by something. He had felt passion and life. He remembered a purpose, a reason to live.

How had he come to land in this pit of human filth. . . ?

As the effects of the drugs dissipated, from deep inside his bosom came a new feeling to the surface. New, but not new. He began to discover something that felt old and very familiar . . . and slowly the hatred grew.

Somewhere, out there where the air was not filled with

stench or the haunting sounds of agony, was one to whom justice was due—his justice! Someone had wronged him, someone had used him, someone had made a fool of him.

Someone . . . but who could it be. . . ?

Basil struggled to form answers to his half-seen questions. But his numbed mind was still too foggy, too slow. Summoning every effort of the will, he tried to speak clearly and behave with sanity so they would give him no more medicine or—God help him!—take him into that tiny room again. There was something he must remember! But he could not think right when they deadened his mind.

The other inmates in Basil's cubicle were too absorbed in their own shadowy worlds to take notice of the lawyer. They lived and breathed in parallel universes, none ever touching another. But one fellow, an old man who had been in the asylum for years, occasionally included Basil in his unreality. He fancied himself royalty, no less than a grand duke, whose days were taken up with bemoaning the fact that he, rightful heir to the throne, had been banished in exile to this miserable hellhole. How Basil, of all people, fit into his imaginary court was uncertain, except that the fellow commented now and then how much the doctor's son resembled a certain Polish prince he had once known.

One day the "grand duke" sidled up to Basil. "I had a visit from my sister . . . the Grand Duchess Alexandra, you know."

Basil squinted dully at the old man. "What do I care?" he said.

"I think she has taken a fancy to you."

"Me?"

"You may be too modest to admit it, but you are a handsome lad—for a Pole, at any rate."

"Leave me alone."

"You could do worse than win the hand of a grand duchess."

Basil turned away. He didn't have to listen to this fool. But before he could make good his retreat, the old man spoke again.

"She gave me a message for you," he said.

"What are you talking about?" asked Basil, annoyed now.

"Don't be proud, lad," he said, thrusting a crumpled piece

of paper into Basil's face. "Such an alliance between our houses is imperative."

Basil did nothing, said nothing.

Thwarted, the would-be tsar stuffed the paper into Basil's hand and shuffled off for an important audience, in his words, with the foreign minister.

Mechanically Basil lifted his hand and opened the paper with his fingers. The words were as crazy as the deliverer of the note:

The Coronation is set at last, this twenty-ninth day of October in the year of our Lord, eighteen hundred and eighty. The Crown shall make you free.

He shook his head and began to wad the paper up in his hand when suddenly he stopped. A memory from some former time flashed into his mind.

He too had secrets! Secrets from those he hated. He and his comrades had communicated in code to one another. Codes like . . .

This note sounded like some of those back then . . . messages he himself had sent! Gradually images of words, communications, floated back into his consciousness.

"The Coronation . . ." It could mean anything—but almost certainly some major event!

What event? When?

Ah, *when*? That was the interesting part of the code. It was in the numbers—he remembered that much! But not so simply as what it said. No, not October 29, that was the decoy. When the numbers were written out like this, it meant something else. Something about . . .

Yes, *within* the numbers. Twenty-nine . . . *two* and *nine* . . . Two-nine . . .

That was it! The second day of the ninth month! Now he remembered how the code worked. He had thought it up himself! September 2, 1880.

A big event to occur on September 2. When could that be? He hadn't an idea of the date now. He had given little thought to the passage of time. How long had he been here? He didn't even know what season of the year it was!

And *what* was the event?

Could it truly be a coronation? Was the tsar dead? Could the impossible have happened without his hearing about it?

No, that was too obvious. If this code was really a *code*, then it meant something else.

What does it matter, anyway? Basil fumed. *The note is from a crazy old man who imagines himself to be the rightful heir to the Russian throne.*

Or was it?

He studied the piece of paper more closely. The writing was firm and clear. It was obvious the old man's trembling hand could never have produced such script. Someone must be sending him a message.

Someone from the outside!

Basil shook his head several times, trying to get the jumbled pieces of his memory to jog themselves into some order that made sense.

Yes, he had friends out there. He remembered that much. There weren't *only* enemies. He had comrades with the same purpose he had. Comrades and purpose which would not rejoice in a coronation but rather would grieve. What could a coronation mean except that they had failed.

He sighed and reread the note. Struggling to make sense of it, he read the whole thing again, moving past the word *coronation* and on through the words . . .

Suddenly it jumped out at him—the single word that held the substance of the entire message:

. . . shall make you FREE.

Perhaps this message had nothing to do with the tsar at all—but with *him*. Could it be possible?

Did the message concern his *freedom* rather than the tsar's coronation? Perhaps . . . it could not hurt to think about it . . . to wonder . . . to wait. It might be that if he waited long enough, that day would come—September 2—and somehow he would be free.

If only he knew *when*. Perhaps it would even be tomorrow!

But no matter when the time came for freedom or coronations or whatever it was, he had to be ready! He *would* be ready. He had to rid himself of the awful cloud the drugs had drawn over him. He had to force himself to remember all he could . . . to remember everything. He had to remember!

But the momentous event of the message did not occur the next day . . . or the next.

And the waiting gave him time enough, with his determined effort, to clear away most of the remaining cobwebs and replace the muddled, unfocused fog with the clarity of his true insanity.

Memories returned. Hatred swept in to kindle his passions anew. When the keepers of drug cabinets were not looking, his teeth clenched and ground silently, while behind his back his fists tightened. When he lay in his bed, his nostrils stinging with the foul smells around him and his hearing dominated by the babbling of voices that had once included his own, the hatred at last found a name upon which to hang itself—Remizov. And the violence also knew its purpose afresh—Fedorcenko.

Basil Anickin once again had a reason to live.

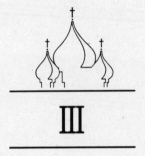

III

A Soldier's Disgrace
(Fall 1880—Winter 1881)

16

Faint though it was, the cool breeze lifting off the southeastern shore of the Caspian Sea was welcome enough. But it was hardly sufficient to dispel the memory of the searing desert heat they had survived over the previous two weeks.

Sergei Fedorcenko lay back on his camp bed, head and shoulders propped against the flimsy wall of the tent, notebook in lap, pen in hand, and tried to make some sense of the whole scorching experience.

The skirmishes with unruly Turkish tribes of the last several days represented only a portion of Sergei's present mental disarray, and he began to write his thoughts:

> I am now back at Krasnovodsk, our fort on the south shore of the Caspian. I never thought I would feel thus about this wretched place, but when I saw its battlements glittering in the desert sun yesterday afternoon as we returned, I found myself actually glad to see it. Anything—*anything!*—is preferable to the desert. Even a place where for the last months I have known my greatest distress.
>
> Certainly I never expected to be happy here, or even close to it. I suppose I did expect to find some modicum of what I have always enjoyed from my peers—respect, camaraderie, acceptance. Perhaps I would not make close friendships here. I saw no reason, however, not to think there would exist between those who shared this duty a certain mutual regard, if not courtesy.
>
> That was not to be the case. I suppose the yunker class of officers likes nothing better than to see their betters debased. Their failure to make it all the way through military or cadet school makes them bitter, whatever their own per-

sonal flaws. They blame it on others, especially those whom they view as privileged, and do not seem to change this attitude even when they work their way up through the ranks. If there is a stigma to their yunker past, it is as much internal as external; and they seem bent on taking out their hostility, especially on one such as myself.

Of course, I see myself as better than no man on a purely class basis. But it will take more convincing rhetoric than my own to impress that upon my present comrades. From the first days of my assignment here, I was the aristocratic prince who had fallen from grace. They seemed to enjoy my plight.

I think what rankles them the most is knowing that at any moment I could be reinstated to my former so-called glory, while they have little hope of rising above their present positions. Actually, I cannot say as I blame them. I hate the system as well that looks to a man's blood above his competence. Many of these men here are good soldiers and deserve more than dusty obscurity in this blasted desert outpost. Unfortunately, like everything else in Russia, the military remains locked in the Dark Ages. General Milutin's recent reforms have taken the army many leagues forward. But there is still so much further to go.

But I digress. I was recounting how miserable I am, and I am loathe to be deterred from that cheery topic!

As gloomy as it may be, I must write down my experiences of the past days. Our assignment was to subdue marauding Turkmen who had lately been preying upon our caravan routes. After General Lomakin's defeat last fall—the worst ever by Russia in Central Asia—the natives had become rebellious and self-assured once more. Lomakin had only himself to blame for his failure, though. He had the defenders of the Geok-Tepe Fortress squeezed in and in a hopeless plight. A few more days of bombardment would have seen a certain surrender of the Turks.

But the general wanted more than mere victory. He sought glory, and the medals and promotions that accompany it. In his lust for more than victory, he ended up with nothing! When the civilians tried to flee the fortress, Lomakin drove them back inside. Accolades from superiors come only when a commander imposes *total* defeat upon his enemies, crushing innocents and army alike. Lomakin took the attempted flight as his opportunity. He would not wait for surrender. He would take the fortress by storm!

He called off the bombardment and gave the order to charge en masse. Nothing could have more perfectly played into the defenders' hands. For though the Turks had little to speak of in the way of weaponry and munitions, they still had men. Their superior numbers gave them the advantage in the hand-to-hand combat that followed. Suddenly the tables of fate were turned. The Turks forced our army into retreat, inflicting heavy casualties. Geok-Tepe remained firmly in Turkish hands, and Lomakin was disgraced.

I had not yet arrived in this torturous hellhole at the time, but the men were still feeling the sting of the defeat months later. I was shocked at the incident, but even more so at the sympathy of the men toward Lomakin in spite of the obvious foolhardiness of his decision. He was summarily relieved of his command. I have the distinct feeling that if he had been successful in his blunder, no matter how many lives it cost, he would have received the Order of St. Andrew instead. But such are the twisted fortunes and obtuse ironies of fate when one's lot is cast with the military of the Motherland!

General Skobelev is now in command, he whom I so admired at Plevna! And still he cannot help but stir my admiration, cynic though I have become. In that white uniform that blazes even more magnificently in the desert sun, he sits upon his gray mount, prancing regally among the troops. I believe the men see him as something of a Zeus.

Curious as it is, since he replaced an already popular leader, he is yet thought of even more highly than was Lomakin. In fact, Skobelev—I do not think I understate it—is nothing less than idolized here, and to criticize the man is at the very least a cardinal sin.

But who can criticize him? Certainly not I! If I had but half his courage, I'd not be in my present predicament. He sits atop his horse the very epitome of daring and charisma. His eyes gleam like the sun in battle. Though of course the Turks have a slightly different impression of the man. They call him *Göz Kanli*, or "bloody eyes." Perhaps they are right. Could it be that what I have always taken as the glow of courage is nothing more than a thirst after blood?

It will not be long before whatever it is that motivates the great general will be satiated. Another offensive is being planned against Akhal-Tekke, that rebellious oasis where Geok-Tepe is situated. It simply would not do for Russian prestige to be undermined here in Central Asia. Last fall's defeat must be vindicated.

Recent events, however, cause me to dread the upcoming battle even more than I might have otherwise. . . .

Sergei paused in his writing.

The pain, confusion, and humiliation of what had transpired over the last few days was still too raw for him to easily transfer the memories onto paper. He realized his ramblings about Lomakin and Skobelev were an all-too-transparent attempt to avoid dredging up the painful incident.

He should have expected what had happened out in the desert. But somehow the expectation did not dull the shock of reality. He had heard stories of Russian exploits here in this outland far from the probing eye of civilization. From his own father, Sergei had learned about the campaign against the town of Khiva in the early 1870s when the order was given and executed: *Give over the Yomud Turkmen settlements, and their families, to complete destruction.* Sergei had believed only half of what he heard. Russian soldiers, like military men everywhere, were given to boasting. What kind of men, he wondered, would *boast* about atrocities against women and children?

Sergei's unit, commanded by Captain Rustaveli, had come surreptitiously upon the nomad village late in the afternoon. They had been scouring the desert for the slippery devils, and to come upon them with their guard down as they had was a delightful surprise after the long march. It was obvious these were the thieving rascals who had been terrorizing caravans, for much of the loot was in plain sight. Reconnaissance revealed no more than a dozen rifles in the entire camp, and the Russians outnumbered the nomads in excess of two to one. The fact that women and children numbered among these was of little import. The orders were, upon encounter, to subdue—by any means possible—the marauders *and all likely accomplices.*

What followed was a grisly nightmare.

The Russian force swooped down upon the unsuspecting Turks, swords glinting in the hot afternoon sun, rifles spitting out a lethal spray of lead. The tough nomads gave heroic defense, but they were no match for the far superior force. The slaughter lasted less than an hour, and at last the order was given to stand back and survey the carnage.

Sergei struck down no women or children in battle—he was innocent of that, at least. But when the dust of the butchery settled, he saw the bodies of the innocents sprawled lifeless over the sandy ground, splattered with their own blood. Sergei was sickened by the sight, so violently that his stomach continued to cramp and heave long after it had emptied itself of its contents.

Captain Rustaveli, a yunker who had twenty years of service and had risen into leadership from the ranks, witnessed the pathetic scene with laughter.

"You call yourself a soldier, Fedorcenko!" he chided as the pale prince stood on wobbly legs. From the first day Sergei had arrived, Rustaveli had held him in disdain, and had taken every opportunity to rail at the pampered aristocrat who had the great misfortune to suddenly find himself under the command of a lowly yunker.

"Pull yourself together, Lieutenant," Rustaveli ordered with a smirk. "We're by no means through yet."

"What do you mean by that?" replied Sergei, his tone defiant despite his quaking insides and trembling hands.

"Look at these murdering scum that are left! They hardly appear *subdued* to me!" Rustaveli jerked his head toward the remnant of the nomads standing at the mercy of the Russian soldiers surrounding them.

The captain was accurate in his assessment. The Turks scowled hatefully at their captors, shouting crude obscenities and spitting on any who chanced to come within range. Even in defeat, they were a savage people and gave every impression that at first chance, they would slit any Russian throat they could get their oily hands on. Even the women were no less contemptuous, although their vulgarities came from veiled faces.

"Lieutenant Fedorcenko, I command you to finish carrying

out our orders!" The captain gloated with an evil smirk toward Sergei.

"Well?" Rustaveli barked after a moment as Sergei only gaped dumbly in response.

Another moment of disobedient silence passed. Then the commander burst out laughing. "I thought as much! You don't have the stomach for it! But I will put you on report for your insubordination!"

Rustaveli himself gave the order. His silent subordinates immediately fell upon the surviving nomads and put them to the sword—all save for a few children who had somehow avoided being slaughtered in the mayhem of battle.

Sergei wanted to turn away, to be sick again. But he did not. He watched the bloody execution dutifully. And he made no protest.

He argued with himself later that all the protest and heroics in the world would not have saved a single Turkish life. Had Sergei raised a hand in defense of the helpless victims, Rustaveli would no doubt have personally taken great pleasure in cutting *him* down with them. But such an excuse hardly justified his silence. Perhaps he *should* have died trying to save the poor creatures.

On every step of the hot dusty ride back to Krasnovodsk, the horrible scene played itself over and over in his brain. It had haunted his dreams every night since. Most horrifying of all was seeing himself standing there *consenting* by his impotent silence.

Whenever Anna chanced to flit her way into his mind, which was often, his anguish of soul deepened and became unbearable. Dear, sweet Anna! What would she think of this man she loved if she knew what a true coward he was? What would she think if she knew the horrible truth about him—that he had watched mothers and their helpless babies slaughtered? And he had raised no hand against it! How could he ever face Anna again, knowing what kind of man he was?

During one of these moments, when the face of his beloved Anna filled the eye of his mind, he made his resolve. He would never allow such a thing to happen again, even if he had to stand up to Skobelev himself to stop it. He would die before he would again witness the cruel slaughter of innocents without raising a hand of objection!

It all seemed so clear now, sitting on his bunk in the relative security of a quiet Russian fort. But he was a seasoned veteran of war, despite his lack of stomach for it. He knew how muddled the lines of reason became under the stress and confusion of battle. Even good men were driven to unspeakable acts, especially in the midst of watching their own comrades being cut down by vicious enemies. He supposed most of all he feared that such a moment would come to him, when he lost his reason altogether. What if circumstances he could not predict, things beyond his control—

His thoughts were suddenly interrupted by the clamor of voices and footsteps entering the barracks. He groaned silently.

"Well, well . . . there's our little prince!" bellowed Rustaveli. "We missed you at dinner, Lieutenant—oh, but I forgot, you haven't had much of an appetite these past few days!" He laughed derisively, joined by two or three of his yunker companions.

"I am off duty, Captain," Sergei replied evenly. "If you don't mind, I would like to be left alone."

"Would you now?" As he spoke the words, drawing them out with a knowing grin, the captain drew closer. He lifted a dirty boot onto Sergei's bunk. "And what does a high and mighty prince do with his free time?" He cocked his head toward the notebook in Sergei's hand. "Writing more of the seditious garbage that landed you here in the first place?"

Sergei swallowed stiffly, but said nothing.

"You know what I think," the captain went on, encouraged by the laughter of his comrades. "I think this stuff should be included in my report of your disobedience."

He snatched the notebook from Sergei's hands. "Hey, Caplja!" he called to one of his cohorts, tossing the notebook to him as he spoke. "Let's hear what the mighty Prince Fedorcenko has to say about our glorious exploits."

"Why don't you read them yourself, Rustaveli?" said Sergei. "Or are you as illiterate as you are ill-mannered?"

Rustaveli only laughed in reply. Even if he was in fact illiterate, he knew he held all the cards. "Go on, Caplja, read."

Lieutenant Caplja began to scan the words that had only just come from Sergei's hand, his eyes coming to rest on the final paragraph. " 'It will not be long,' " he read, " 'before whatever it is that motivates the great general will be satiated. Another offensive is being planned against Akhal-Tekke, that rebellious oasis where Geok-Tepe is situated. It simply would not do for Russian prestige to be undermined here in Central Asia. Last fall's defeat must be vindicated. Recent events, however, cause me to dread—' "

Sergei could stand no more.

"Stop, you lout!" he shouted, jumping from his bed with the intention of retrieving his book.

Rustaveli restrained him. "No, no, Caplja, don't stop—this is very interesting. What is it that our princely lieutenant dreads—the sweat of battle, I'll warrant! The sniveling little coward—"

But his words were ill chosen. Sergei wrested free, spun around, and took a wide swing in the direction of his captain's jaw. But Rustaveli had expected the attack as much as he had invited it, and was too quick for Sergei. He lunged aside and caught Sergei's wrist forcefully in his strong grip.

"What?" railed the captain. "Must we add to your offenses physical attack upon a *superior* officer?" he said, spitting out the word with relish.

Sergei bit down his fury with effort. "What will they do to me, Captain, *demote* me?"

"Ha, ha! Believe it or not, Prince, there *is* still lower for you to fall."

"Perhaps the fall would be worth it."

"Do I consider that a threat?"

"I defied the tsar himself. Do you think I would be daunted by some murderous scum of a yunker?"

"Why you—!" Rustaveli reared back with lethal rage and might have seriously wounded Sergei had not one of the captain's men intervened.

"He's right, Captain," said the man. "I wouldn't test him. He's probably half insane."

"You're not worth it, at any rate!" spat the captain, calming slightly. "But it won't take much, Fedorcenko—not much at all! Consider yourself lucky . . . this time."

"I want no trouble, Captain," replied Sergei. "But whatever you may think of me, I am not afraid to hand it out if provoked. And *that* would not take much either!"

Sergei shoved past the captain and exited the barracks, taking his notebook from the hand of his fellow lieutenant as he departed.

What Sergei had said about not fearing demotion was not exactly true. The only thing that gave him any hope in life these days was the thought of returning to Anna. Somehow, though all seemed against him, he had to survive this heinous place so that he could return to her. Nothing else mattered. But he wondered mordantly if his only chance for promotion hinged on killing women and children, could he do it?

He knew he could not.

Was he doomed here forever then, or at least until his term of service was complete? To a man not yet twenty-five and separated from the woman of his heart, the two seemed identical. Anything could happen—and he feared *would*—if he was forced to remain here much longer.

And what of Anna's God? He had done nothing but ignore his and Anna's prayers.

Not that Sergei had the heart to pray lately. God seemed about as interested in him as his own father had been, loving him—if such it could be called—from a cool distance, unwilling to reach out a rescuing hand when he needed it most.

Why waste his breath praying?

He had little luck with father figures. If he was to make it out of this place, it would be by his own initiative. Somehow, in some way, he'd manage to overcome the oafs like Rustaveli, the incomprehensible, inhumane orders, the stifling heat, and most of all the ever-lurking insanity that would certainly defeat him if ill chance forced him to remain here much longer.

He *would* get away. He would be with Anna again. And until then he would not stop dreaming of the day when once again he would lay eyes on the lovely, peaceful, smiling face of the servant girl he loved.

17

Anna stood back to admire the shimmering Christmas tree. When the candles were lit tonight, it would rival even the trees of the Imperial Court. How her mistress had managed it on the shrunken finances of her new household, Anna could not imagine. But she was glad Princess Katrina had done so, even if they had to trim back someplace else.

The year had been a difficult one. It was time for a festive celebration. The fear and oppression fostered by all the unrest and rebellion was gradually lifting from the city. Residents breathed a little easier and ventured out of their homes with a renewed air of security. That alone gave reason to celebrate.

Misha had told her recently that many ministers and governmental officials were dispensing with their Cossack guards. Anna was glad that the streets of St. Petersburg were safe once more, although Anna could not avoid conflicting feelings over the cause for the change. Governor-general Melikov's relentless crackdown on subversive and revolutionary elements within the city had resulted in many arrests. She could not help worrying about Paul. The news had it that Melikov was primarily after ringleaders rather than rank-and-file followers. But where Paul might fit into the underground hierarchy, she hadn't an idea. All she could do was pray daily that he would escape the government's ever-spreading net long enough to come to his senses.

In spite of her concerns about her brother, the peace and relative tranquility of the city were certainly welcome. It went far to dispel the gloomy atmosphere settling upon Anna's personal world.

For herself, she could and would survive Sergei's absence with tolerable equanimity. She was, after all, more accustomed to his absence than his presence. The change to the new environment of the Remizov household had been more jarring to the daily ups and downs of her life than Sergei's reassignment.

But the occasional letters, which reached her via Misha's hand, were not encouraging. When writing to her, Sergei did his best to put a brave and stoic face on it. But she could tell he was miserable. And not just from their separation, but from the horrible conditions at his new outpost.

Most frustrating of all was her helplessness. All she could do for him was remind him every time she wrote that her prayers were with him.

Katrina's melancholy, so much closer at hand, was more pressing to Anna at the moment. The physician gave his assurance that the princess's moods were nothing more than a natural consequence of her condition. For the most part, Anna supposed he was right. But she knew it went deeper than that.

She could not blame it all on Dmitri. On the other hand, she knew that a change in his present behavior would go far to lift Katrina's spirits. He had continued for months to spend more and more time away from the estate on so-called army business. It was obvious to all that the epithet was no more than a thinly masked way of saying he was out carousing with friends who happened to wear the Russian army uniform. Anna sensed, however, that his unseemly conduct did not mirror whatever was troubling his expertly veiled mind.

He had arrived home very late one night, as had become his habit, early in the month. The princess had long since abandoned the hope of waiting up for him, and had retired. Anna had not been able to sleep, and had finally risen and was on her way to the kitchen to prepare some tea for herself. Crossing the entryway, she heard a fumbling with the latch on the front door. Knowing it to be Dmitri, she quickened her step to avoid an encounter.

But it was too late. The door opened the next moment.

"Anna . . . Anna," she heard behind her. "Is a maid's work never done?" His tone was slurred, the content of his business that night all too apparent.

"No, Your Excellency," replied Anna, turning to face him. "I just could not sleep."

"Well, I am glad it was you I ran into and not . . . someone else." He swayed unsteadily on his feet. "People do talk, you know."

He leaned clumsily toward her and gave her a conspiratorial wink. "You can keep a secret, though, can you not, Anna?" he said.

"Yes, Your Excellency."

He laughed. "Except in life-or-death situations, eh, Anna?"

"I—I don't understand."

"You told Katrina's secret about me, to save her from the clutches of that maniac, remember?"

"Yes, sir, I do."

"You saved her life and you brought us together. We have you alone to thank for our marital bliss. A regular cupid, you are!" His tone, harsh and caustic, gave a sarcastic twist to his words.

"Your Excellency, let me get a footman to help you up the stairs."

"Shame on you, Anna! I'm steady as a rock."

As if to prove his boast, Dmitri lifted a foot and held out an arm in an effort to demonstrate his balance. He reeled backward, toppling over.

Anna stepped quickly forward. She could hardly have kept him from crashing to the floor, but grabbing her shoulder with one hand and bracing the other against the nearby wall, he managed to keep himself upright. Steadying himself, he kept a firm grasp on Anna's shoulder. Then he turned, pressed closer, and attempted to focus his bleary-eyed gaze upon her. Anna's heart thudded uncomfortably within her. Surely the count would not forget common decency in his drunken state!

"You know, Anna," he said, his voice almost earnest, "you are a devilishly pretty girl."

He took her chin in his hand and studied her as if for the first time. "Very beautiful indeed . . . I can see why Sergei fell in love with you."

Anna gaped in stunned silence. Perhaps it should not have been so surprising that Sergei had told his best friend. After all, she had confided in Misha. But for it to come out now, like this, so unexpectedly! She was so taken aback that she could force no response.

Dmitri grinned. There was no maliciousness in the smile, but rather an almost brotherly sympathy.

"I am sorry," he said sincerely. "I didn't mean to . . . well, I see I have embarrassed you. . . . I won't say another word. I don't know what came over me." He let go of her shoulder and fell back against the wall. Then the grin faded, and with it his inebriated joviality. He let out a deep breath. "You must think me a drunken sot—a fool."

"Please, Your Excellency," Anna insisted, "let me call a footman."

"You are a good girl, Anna. You really are. You will always watch over the both of us."

"I will do what I can, Your Excellency."

"Katrina is fortunate to have you. You'll always take care of her for me, won't you?"

"Of course, Your Excellency."

"I am sure she did better in choosing a maid than she did a husband."

"That is not true, Your Excellency."

"Do you dare call your master a liar?" he said, raising one eyebrow. "Ah, but it is true," he sighed. "Sad but true, as they say. I did so want to make her happy, but . . ."

He paused and shook his head. "You know," he went on after a moment, "I once boxed a bear. I really did. For a meager twenty-ruble wager, I climbed into that cage and boxed the hairy creature. I felt not an ounce of trepidation, either. Nor did the fact that I was more than half drunk have anything to do with it. I once rode two stallions together at full trot for half a vesta. And I tottered on the ledge of a third-story window in dead of winter and swallowed a bottle of rum. I—"

He stopped, shaking his head once more. "Anna . . . do you want to know the truth? I have never been afraid of anything in my life, until now . . ."

"Your Excellency—"

"Anna, I am quite drunk. Would you . . . would you point

me in the direction of the stairs? I will be able to make it from there."

"Yes, sir."

Anna did as he had requested, watching him tensely as he made his shaky way to the top of the long flight.

But she found herself unable to relax even when he had reached the top safely. As she continued on her way to the kitchen, she found no small consternation still bubbling about inside her. Except for her talk with him about Basil Anickin prior to the wedding, she had never had any further personal contact with the husband of her mistress. Why had he now suddenly revealed such an intimate and vulnerable side of himself? And why to *her*? She was no confidante. What could it do but cause additional tension in the household?

It set her mind greatly at ease when she encountered the count the following morning. He made no intimation whatever about the previous night's interlude. The look on his face gave not the slightest hint that he even remembered it. He had probably been too drunk to remember.

She knew Katrina was utterly unaware of her husband's insecurities. Any of his acquaintances would have insisted that Count Dmitri Remizov possessed not an insecure bone in his body. The trouble was, very few people ever truly *knew* him.

Anna found herself wishing for Sergei's presence all over again, though for different reasons. He would be capable of helping his sister understand her husband better.

But he was a thousand miles away. It was probably no accident that Dmitri had chosen only a timid maid to receive a brief glimpse of his innermost self. The secret of his vulnerability was safe in the heart where also dwelt the love of his best friend.

18

Katrina had determined to make this Christmas gathering memorable. She had invited about a dozen guests, including her parents. Two days before Christmas, it was not exactly a gala affair, but as much as she felt she could handle, considering her condition. She became tired so easily, but that would not stop her from marking this very special occasion—her and Dmitri's first Christmas as husband and wife.

She supposed she had gone a bit overboard on the tree and garlands and the new gold candlesticks. But Christmas was no time to pinch kopecks. Anyway, she brought enough of her own money into the sparse Remizov coffers to allow herself *some* pleasurable spending.

The princess came downstairs promptly at 7:30 to begin receiving guests. Anna had done marvels with Katrina's costume this evening. Her hair had been swept to one side in a cascade of ringlets with a strand of baby pearls woven in for effect. She wore a gown of emerald velvet that drew out the color of her eyes so vividly that they seemed cut from the same fabric. The dress had been designed especially for her, with its pearl-trimmed hem and delicately scooped neckline. The designer had quite a task trying to contrive a dress around four months of pregnancy. The problem was not the princess's size nearly so much as her self-consciousness. She hardly showed the effects at this point, yet she complained of feeling bloated. She rejected half his ideas as worsening the way she looked.

Anna had done everything in her power—through both persuasion and patience—to make sure that it would turn out perfect. And since Anna did not lie, Katrina was inclined to accept her word, although more than once she swore she would adopt the old practice of women confining themselves from public eye during such a time. She could not have been more joyful about the coming baby. But she would be glad when she could stop worrying about her waistline and again enjoy the opportunity of trying out some of the exquisite new Paris fashions.

Princess Katrina reached the final step just as the parlor clock struck the half hour. The guests would be arriving at any minute. There was one person, however, who should have made his appearance long ago. She stopped a passing footman.

"Alexander, has Count Remizov returned yet?"

"Not that I know of, Your Highness."

"Would you please check the coach house, and perhaps the study also. He may have come in while no one was about."

"Yes, Your Highness."

She swept past the servant and into the parlor where she would receive her guests and where the *zakuska* would be served before dinner.

It should have been easy to maintain her Christmas cheer amid such a festive atmosphere. The tree glittered, the candles sparkled against the delicately tinted crystal ornaments. Bouquets of red roses and holly and chrysanthemums adorned every nook and corner, making the room look like the greenhouse where the flowers had been obtained in the dead of winter. The lovely fragrances, the warmth of the crackling fire in the hearth, the glow of all the candles—surely such an atmosphere would lend to this evening.

But Katrina felt little contentment. She knew it was foolish to think mere Christmas decorations could bring it. With each passing minute, her carefully honed determination dissolved a little more. Dmitri should have been home hours ago! Even one hour ago would have indicated he cared perhaps a little. He knew how special this evening was to Katrina, and all the effort she had put into it. Yet here he was late—*if* he chose to appear at all!

No doubt he preferred to spend his Christmas with his maudlin cronies! It wouldn't surprise her—

No, she would not pursue that line, thought Katrina, breaking off her silently rising temper. She refused to allow Dmitri's behavior to spoil her evening. Perhaps she might be so gracious as not even to get angry at *him*.

He deserved her full wrath, of course. Of that there could be no doubt. Should he walk in the door at this very moment, it would have been rude and grossly inconsiderate to cut his arrival so close. But perhaps she could give him that one Christmas gift, undeserving though it be—to control her anger. At least *one* of them ought to be mature and caring toward the other! No, she positively would not let her anger rise to the surface. She did not want to ruin this Christmas.

She calmed herself and was breathing more easily when a few minutes later the footman announced the first guests at the parlor door.

"Prince Viktor Fedorcenko and Princess Natalia Vasilyovna!" intoned the servant in a grandiose voice fit for the Winter Palace.

Katrina rose and embraced her parents warmly. True, only a day had passed since she had seen them last. But lately they were becoming more dear to her than she would have ever thought possible. She could not help cringing, however, when her father's first words called attention to the very fact she was trying so hard to ignore.

"Your husband is, ah . . . not with you this evening, my dear?" he said in a tone of concern.

"He has been detained on some military business or other," she replied airily. "He'll be along directly."

She hated herself for lying and making excuses for Dmitri. But she hated her husband nearly as much for placing her in the position of having to do so. In years past she might also have been annoyed at her father for asking the question. He knew both military protocol and Dmitri Remizov well enough to recognize the facade without benefit of Katrina's explanation. But he held his tongue and said no more.

Her father did not look particularly good this evening. His eyes seemed tired, and his cheeks a little hollow and drawn. Had he lost weight? Christmas was no time for that. But now that she thought of it, his uniform did seem to fit looser than usual.

She had no more time to reflect. Almost immediately the other guests began to arrive. After a few more awkward references to the absence of the head of the household, the party celebrating the nativity began to flow along more gaily. Besides the beauty of her face, Katrina had inherited from her mother a natural ability to entertain. She found it the most comfortable thing in the world to float easily from guest to guest. She knew all the right things to say, the proper moments to laugh, how much to laugh, when to look concerned, and, in short, all the ways and means to make people feel at ease and welcome and able to enjoy themselves.

The most awkward interchange of the evening did not concern Dmitri at all, but rather Katrina's brother and father. The conversation had turned, as was not surprising, to the current political climate and Russia's military involvement in various parts of the eastern world. Some unkind remarks had been brought up that Great Britain's Disraeli had recently made concerning Russia's activities in Central Asia.

"The British Prime Minister is ever worried about his precious India," offered one of the guests in response.

"As if we would *want* the place, really!" added another.

"I visited Bombay once," commented one of the ladies, "and I wouldn't have it on a wager. A poverty-stricken, backward, smelly, horrid place!"

"Well, my dear," said her husband patiently, "what you must understand is that the tsar and his advisors do not make decisions on the basis of the appeal of the place to visiting Russian noblewomen. It is all a matter of geography, not wealth versus poverty."

"I still hate the place!" rejoined his wife.

"It does have some strategic importance, however," the husband went on, "whether you grasp the reasons for it or not."

"Nevertheless," put in one of the other men, "I might find myself siding with your wife on this, Count. We don't *need* India, certain strategic value, notwithstanding."

"Some would argue," said Viktor dryly, "that we don't *need* Central Asia either. But we are fighting for it as if it were the Crimea itself."

"We certainly needed it during the American civil war."

"I'll never forget how the price of cotton soared," said another of the women. "My goodness! I wouldn't want that to happen again!"

One of the men, only a slight acquaintance, who had come as a guest of Princess Marya Nicolaievna, was unaware of the awkwardness into which he was stumbling.

"Prince Fedorcenko," he asked, "did I not hear that your son was in Central Asia somewhere? How strong is our hold on the area?"

Even as he spoke, he did not notice the tense quiet that suddenly came over all the other close friends who well knew the delicate circumstances surrounding Sergei's transfer. Princess Marya attempted to stop the *faux pas* of her escort in time, but he bumbled on unaware.

Viktor merely stared forward, his eyes looking more hollow and distant than ever, and gave no indication that he had even heard the question, much less intended to answer it. Everyone knew he *had* heard it, however, and waited anxiously for two or three seconds.

The next voice to be heard, however, was not Viktor's at all, but his daughter's.

"Dear me! You know all the secrets the military has!" she exclaimed, fielding the man's questions deftly but lightly. "Why, the family knows less than someone who reads the daily newspaper! I'm an army wife—I ought to know!"

Her bright smile brought on a chorus of amused chuckles from the others, not only for her off-the-point comments but for her ability to save the family prolonged embarrassment. The conversation moved forward smoothly once more.

19

Katrina was so pleased with herself and with the way the evening was progressing that when Dmitri arrived ten minutes later, she was in a tolerant and forgiving mood.

The party was just being seated in the dining room as the master of the house made his appearance.

"Ah, Count Remizov!" said one or two of the men.

"Welcome . . . welcome, all of you!" said Dmitri buoyantly as he swept into the room, shaking hands with the men and giving his compliments to each of the women in turn. "I apologize for my tardy arrival. It is inexcusable, I know. I hope you will all forgive me. I trust my wife has been taking good care of you!"

Katrina's greeting to her husband was almost genuine. Who could stay mad at such a congenial, handsome, gracious personality for more than an instant!

However, as Dmitri bent over where she had just seated herself to place a light kiss on her forehead, the unmistakable odor of rum on his breath caused Katrina to fume. She forced a smile and determinedly shook the irritation from her. She made herself put the best construction on it. It was perfectly understandable for him to enjoy a Christmas *libation* with his Guard Regiment. It had probably been ordered by the commander himself.

But as the evening progressed, it became increasingly obvious that more than a small "libation" had passed his lips before arriving home. He was not obnoxiously drunk, only embarrassingly so—sufficiently tipsy to make a fool of himself more than once. He laughed too loudly and at the wrong times.

His hand was unsteady as he poured the wine out for his guests; he sloshed more than a few drops onto the white linen tablecloth, and once missed his father-in-law's trousers by only a millimeter. His conversation was boring at best, boorish at worst. And he aggravated matters all the more by consuming several more glasses of wine at dinner, followed by two or three snifters of brandy afterward. As her patience wore thin, Katrina stopped even trying to count. Had she married nothing but a common drunkard, after all?

Katrina was exhausted when the last guest finally left sometime after midnight.

Once upstairs in her boudoir, she quickly slipped out of her dress, leaving it in a heap on the floor for Anna to take care of in the morning. She had given Anna the evening to herself and did not want to disturb her now. She had just shrugged into her nightgown when Dmitri knocked on the door.

"Yes?" she said tiredly.

"May I come in, my dear?"

"I am still dressing." Her tone was cool.

"Modest, are you, Katrina?"

"In my condition—"

He didn't wait for her to finish. The door opened and Dmitri strode toward her. "I don't mind your condition a whit," he said. "If I didn't know better, I wouldn't even know you had a condition. You look as lovely as ever." He bent down to kiss her.

Katrina stiffened. The smell of alcohol was nauseating.

"I am really *so* tired, Dmitri." If she hadn't been so tense, Katrina would have been amused at how much she sounded like her mother.

"Come on then, my tired wife. Let us go to bed." He gently took her hand and led her to the bedroom.

He seemed to be making such an effort now to be compatible, and as he helped her into bed he gazed down on her with such a tender expression of love that she almost forgot her irritation. She smiled up at him. Encouraged, he climbed into his side of the bed and drew close to her.

"You made a lovely evening tonight, Katrina," he said. "I am quite proud of my wife."

"I suppose I enjoy having guests and playing the hostess.

Perhaps next year we could have a grand ball."

"And I promise not to be late!" He smiled his sheepish, endearing smile.

"You had better not be!" she replied with a light, teasing tone.

"I was sure I was a doomed man when I came in to find you already gone in to dinner," he chuckled.

"You make me sound like the chief of police."

He laughed. Brushing aside a loose strand of her hair, he kissed her. In spite of the liquor, she could not keep from responding with a gradual warming of her passion.

"I'll warrant Vlasenko could never kiss like that!" He laughed again. "I am so happy you are not vexed with me."

"Oh, Dmitri, it is Christmastime—our first Christmas together. I don't want to be mad."

He recoiled slightly. "Which is as much as to say that I deserved it nonetheless, eh?"

"Of course you deserved it," she replied, still half-playfully. "You can't deny that you were rude and dreadfully inconsiderate."

"Guilty as charged, Madam Gendarme! I am overwhelmed by your great mercy!"

"Do you know what I think, Dmitri?" said Katrina, her irritation now quickly returning at the provocation. "I think you *do* feel guilty, but are too proud to admit it. So instead you want to start a fight in order to vindicate yourself."

"You think all that, do you?"

"And if you weren't so drunk, you'd see your own foolish behavior for what it is!"

"I am drunk—at least I *was* drunk. But pleasantly so. Now I am sobering up very quickly. All your analyzing prattle is enough to sober up a peasant."

"They have nothing on you."

The discussion that had begun playfully enough grew sharper and sharper until not a hint of amusement remained. All the pent-up frustrations, not only of that day but of weeks and months, seemed suddenly to vent themselves. They pulled apart, all hint of passion dissolving in the heated exchange. Katrina sat up on the side of the bed, while Dmitri sat up likewise on the other side and threw his legs over onto the floor.

"I'd sooner be drunk as a peasant than—"

He broke off, unable in his present condition to come up with a suitable conclusion for his intended barb.

Katrina was quick to take up the thought. "Than be a responsible husband!" she spat.

"If I'd known it was going to be little more than a prison, I would have thought twice about the whole thing!" he shot back.

With the acrimonious words still hanging heavily in the air, he lurched out of bed, grabbed his dressing gown, and stormed from the room, slamming the door behind him.

Katrina fell back against the pillows and wept. The whole stupid mess had happened so quickly. Her mind was reeling. She didn't even understand what had gone wrong. She thought she had been trying so hard to be understanding. Was her marriage ruined after only eight short months?

Overwhelmed by fatigue and distress, she did not at first hear the knock at the door. Then it came again, a little louder.

Had he come back to apologize?

She rose and went to the door. "Dmitri," she said, opening it. "I—" She stopped. Anna stood in the doorway.

"Forgive my intrusion, Your Highness," she said. "I heard a crashing sound and was concerned."

"Oh, Anna!" cried Katrina, breaking into a fresh flood of tears. She threw her arms around her maid. "I've ruined everything, Anna! My marriage is over! I—I . . ." Sobs choked out whatever additional words of self-recrimination were on her lips.

Anna held her mistress like a child, then led her back to the bed. They sat down together arm in arm, and remained in silence for some time.

At length, Anna rose, then helped her mistress back into bed, adjusting her pillows and making the blankets as comfortable as possible. She pulled the silken coverlet up around Katrina's shoulders and neck, then stooped down, gave her a final motherly embrace, kissed her on the cheek, and rose to return to her own bedroom.

Quietly weeping, Katrina was asleep before Anna's head even touched her own pillow.

20

Some days later, in a section of town far removed from the fashionable Remizov home, a vastly different meeting of friends was occurring.

Few citizens of the capital who were not residents of Grafsky Lane ventured there, even by light of day. This poverty-ridden Tartar district of the city was so infested with crime that black-coated gendarmes walked their beats only in pairs, praying for an ordinance then under discussion to pass, permitting them to carry sidearms for their protection. As it was, they had only their bare hands and a solid hardwood stick to keep a very tenuous peace.

The ragged Tartar children and gaunt-eyed veiled women on the scene that particular afternoon, poor and disreputable as they may have appeared, hardly seemed to merit such police vigilance. The real threat, especially at that early hour, was holed up behind closed doors, in dark, rat-infested corners—the thieves and owners of prostitutes and dealers in opium. Any of them would have killed for half a hopec's worth of food.

With them, in these shadowy recesses of St. Petersburg, were criminals of a different sort—men driven to crime by the extremity of their passionate ideals. These St. Petersburg slums held the only sanctuary possible for beleaguered revolutionaries and terrorists.

Throughout the closing months of 1880 and into the new year, the tsar's appointee had indeed achieved both his and the tsar's objective. Loris-Melikov had, if not quite put the revolutionaries to flight, certainly subdued them and given them cause for considering their peril before instigating any further incidents.

In the panic of the previous year, many citizens had believed the rebels and malcontents to be so vast in numbers that they might flood the city at any moment with revolution. That could well come later. But as 1880 drew to a close, Melikov believed the troublemakers to be relatively small in number and, with some good sense and stoic persistence, easily contained. Taking this practical approach, he had made great strides in curtailing the threat, and, he believed, eliminating the terrorist hold on the city. Indeed, the government's enemies had been driven deeply underground; some in their fear of arrest had fled the city, even deserted the cause. But the tenacious few that remained were as much to be feared as earlier. For they were the unbending, unshakable elite of the sacred cause.

There were as many hidden and personal reasons for their staunch loyalty as there were insurrectionists. Among this select class of criminals, motives were seldom discussed. It was taken for granted that each had his own motive, and it was enough.

One of those gathered that afternoon in the back room of a grimy Grafsky Lane tavern, however, possessed motives so sinister, so evil in intent, that even his very comrades would have shuddered at a full revelation of his heart. Basil Anickin's hatred was uncompromised by human compassion, so purely personal that it had long ago driven out any vestige of humanitarianism. He sometimes *spoke* of the oppressed masses and the corruption of the government, but these words and causes had become for him only a tool to achieve the one goal that mattered to him.

After he had received his first contact in the mental hospital, Basil had labored like the devil himself upon a struggling soul to force his drug and depression-dulled brain back into focus. He had gradually, by degrees, regained his lucidity, and even managed to convince his keepers that he had recovered. Basil Anickin's mental state was, perhaps, normal for him. But it was by no means *sane*.

In mid-November, months after the originally envisioned date, he had been finally transferred from the asylum back to the Peter and Paul fortress, and his friends had effected a successful escape. Anickin would not quibble about the timing. He was a free man now, and little else mattered.

Even Basil, in one of his more philosophical moods, might have seen the irony of using such a term to describe him. *Free* was a euphemistic word to describe the hunted life of a fugitive.

From the high-society son of a wealthy physician, to a criminal sitting in a dilapidated tenement in Grafsky Lane—a man could hardly descend lower socially. Even imprisonment in the fortress held a certain twisted sort of prestige in these low circles. Now he had only filth and squalor and near starvation to boast of. Yet the comforts of his past life meant nothing to a man consumed by hatred and vengeance.

Basil sat on the floor listening to the proceedings around him with aloof interest. His eyes narrowed keenly when the discussion chanced to probe something that might possibly be of use in fulfilling his driving purpose in life. The others in the room, especially those who did not know him from before, tended to avoid him.

Basil Anickin did indeed present a most forbidding figure these days. His once strong physique had grown wasted and hollow. His face, at one time so strikingly handsome that it nearly won the heart of a proud princess, wore a ghostly look, the eyes ringed with cavernous circles, his cheeks sunken and skeletal. This cadaverous appearance was enhanced by his hair. It had been cropped by his captors, and now he chose to keep it so as some statement of principle or badge of imprisoned honor. Only his eyes belied the sense of death about him. They shone and glinted with passion, with hatred, and with a brutal strength of will as they never had previously.

His presence at this clandestine gathering, however, was not primarily for the benefit of his companions, nor was it strictly for the cause he had espoused years ago. If by his presence some strides could be made in destroying the detested government and Romanov regime, so much the better. But more than anything, he had taken up with his former comrades because he knew in all likelihood he would never be able to achieve his goal without them.

During his weeks in the asylum, while he contemplated his proposed rescue, he had also begun to formulate a purposeful plan for his desired revenge upon the young Count Remizov and his foolish new bride. And it so happened that his scheme seemed to fit very nicely around the designs of The People's Will. He reasoned that after the tsar was assassinated, there would follow a spontaneous rising of the people, with naturally resulting mass violence—peasant risings, general strikes, street fighting, *and* many isolated incidents of physical violence against aristocrats by their servants and others of the peasant classes. The murder of Count Remizov and his wife would raise no untoward questions, and Basil would walk away a free man. He would then travel to Switzerland or England, and live out the remainder of his life in fulfilled peace.

On the far side of the room, another younger man sat quietly contemplating his own future. Paul had not been successful in foiling Anickin's escape. He regretted that fact more and more deeply as he watched the man that afternoon. Anickin looked like a hungry animal—of some dark species that thrived on blood.

Paul's only recourse now was to stick as close to the man as possible. Better to have a mad bear in your sights than crouching unseen behind you.

But the thought of being in that lunatic's company for even a second made his skin crawl! Moreover, if Anickin's purposes began to run against the organization's, Paul might find himself caught in a ticklish—and dangerous!—situation.

Perhaps he was inflating the potential risks all out of proportion. It had been over a year since Anickin's attack against Princess Fedorcenko and Count Remizov. More than likely, thought Paul, the malice that had precipitated those acts of violence had long since dissolved.

Or had it? Paul wondered morosely.

One would have to be blind to truly believe *that*! But perhaps it was possible that at least Anickin intended to concentrate his malice against the tsar and not some inconsequential noble family. Why else would Anickin be present at this meeting? No doubt he was sane enough to recognize priorities, and that the death of the tsar must certainly take precedence over personal objectives of revenge.

But about his own personal motives? Paul rebuked himself. He needed to heed his own counsel and remain single-mindedly set upon the program of The People's Will! Anna was capable of taking care of herself, after all. She had done so very well in the several years she had been on her own in the big city. It would do no one any good for him to try to assuage his own guilt by maintaining this false sense of protectiveness toward her. He'd be worthless to the cause if he continued worrying more about his sister than the larger drama of their destiny to reshape Russian society. He could not fail his comrades now. They were so close to success.

He glanced again toward Anickin, who had suddenly leaned forward with intense interest as Zhelyabov was describing some tunneling procedures they were using in order to mine a street that lay within one of the tsar's oft-traveled routes. The insane lawyer was surely no longer a threat to Anna or her mistress. He had more important enemies to worry about than a mere ex-lover.

Paul turned his attention also toward Zhelyabov. *This* was where their future purpose lay—with the designs and schemes he was now describing! And it might have surprised Paul that the glow in his own eyes looked strangely like a reflection of the expression worn by the mad lawyer, Basil Anickin.

Then again, perhaps it would not have surprised him, for hadn't he suspected all along that they were all a little insane, separated not by leagues, but only by tiny degrees?

21

A thousand miles away, another kind of insanity reigned.

Incessant bursts of artillery fire had been shattering the torpid desert air for what seemed endless hours. It was a cruel nightmare, the siege of Plevna all over again. And Sergei found himself once more, against his will, right in the thick of it.

This time the besieged town was Geok-Tepe, sitting upon a desert oasis.

As if it were indeed Plevna in the Caucasus being played out for a second time, there again sat the White General upon his mighty steed, leading his troops with the same fiery zeal he had three years ago.

Sergei, however, beheld the scene this time with far different eyes. He had lost his grip on patriotic idealism back then. This present conflict was causing him to lose his grip on reality altogether. The book that had gotten him exiled to this hell for its so-called sedition seemed but idealistic prattle now, after eight months on the very edge of civilization. Nothing he had learned in cadet school or in the Balkans could have prepared him for the animalistic horror of *this* place.

The army had been given *carte blanche* to destroy everything. No one cared to look too closely at the details of how the specifics of the assignment were carried out, especially where infidel Tartars were concerned. General Skobelev made no bones about his ruthless military policy.

"I hold it a principle," he had been quoted, "that in Asia the duration of peace is in direct proportion to the slaughter you inflict upon the enemy. Strike hard and keep on striking till resistance fails. Then form ranks, cease slaughter, and be kind and humane to the prostrate enemy."

Simple enough, really. Kill and keep killing until there are so few left alive they can do you no harm. And then be kind and humane to them.

Kind and humane, thought Sergei caustically. Who was anyone trying to fool with such contradictory words!

Why couldn't he accept the policy like everyone else? He was a soldier. He had been trained to fight, to conquer, to kill. Why had *he* changed, but no one else had?

The killing now seemed so senseless, so avoidable ... so wrong. Why couldn't they see the lunacy in it all? Or why couldn't *he* close his eyes and merely endure? Why did he feel as if every fallen innocent had been cut through with his own sword?

Was he the only man of conscience in all of Asia?

No. He had more than once observed one or another of his fellow Russian soldiers comforting a child they had themselves orphaned. Yet Sergei had a problem most of his fellows did not seem to share. He was unable to accept authority that had no reason behind its commands. His father had pointed out this flaw many times. It was a mortal flaw when it rose up in the heart of a soldier, where blind obedience was the mortar that held the entire structure of the military together. And his propensity to fall prey to this fatal weakness of character was more than half the reason Sergei had attained only the rank of lieutenant after five years in the army.

All at once a voice shattered his thoughts, its sound more disconcerting than any artillery blast.

"Lieutenant Fedorcenko!" shouted Captain Rustaveli. "We don't have all day. Prepare to move your men forward."

"Yes, sir!"

Rustaveli made certain Sergei noted his satisfied grin at the word *sir* before pushing on. Sergei made an equally pointed effort to ignore it. He had a job to do, orders to follow. He *had* to stop *thinking*! That's how the others must do it. Think of nothing but orders and the job to be done. Ignore the numbing stench and cries of death. Close off your mind to the horrifying—

No! He was thinking again! He must stop before he went

mad! With a swift motion he spun around to the handful of troops under his command.

"You heard the captain. It's time. Ready yourselves to march!" he shouted with more volume than enthusiasm.

Two months ago, Skobelev had laid siege to the desert fortress after the Turks had taken refuge inside its walls. The White General's forces numbered less than eight thousand. There were upwards of twenty thousand Turks, but the best estimates placed only eight thousand firearms in their possession, along with assorted knives, swords, and pikes. And again, as they had done last year, they held on stubbornly. The Turks attempted many fierce sorties out of the fortress, but always Skobelev's forces drove them back.

The Cossack general, however, was determined not to suffer the doom of his predecessor of the 1879 campaign. He kept his head and commanded a siege that easily put the Grand Duke Nicholas's bungled attack on Plevna to shame. He had ordered tunnels to be dug, by which the walls of the fortress would be mined. He'd not waste good soldiers in senseless heroics; Russian lives were too precious. Not that he had anything against heroics—he all but thrived on them. But he preferred them served up with assured victory.

The mines were now in place and ready to detonate. The troops were forming ranks by which to move on the vanquished Tekke fortress.

Sergei mounted his coal-black gelding and felt a knot tighten in his stomach. Even now, at this late hour, he tried to convince himself that what he had witnessed in small skirmishes were but isolated acts of brutality. This was a full-scale battle, with the general himself overseeing the action. He must certainly have meant the word *slaughter* only in its broadest, almost figurative sense.

But even as he mounted, Sergei remembered his resolve. He would not stand idly by again. He would not give even the White General blind obedience that silently condoned the murder of innocents.

Deafening blasts suddenly rent the air.

Great columns of smoke and dust rose at intervals around Geok-Tepe. The ground shook tremendously as the mines exploded, bringing down first one, then another section of the fortress walls. Sergei's horse snorted and stamped restively.

"Whoa . . . easy, boy," Sergei murmured, rubbing the animal's taut neck. A moment later the general gave the order. Eight thousand Russians surged forward with wild war cries and shouts.

A few of the Turks met the attacking army in an attempt to fight them off long enough to allow others to retreat somewhere to safety. It was a hopeless attempt. The clash of swords and bursting gunfire and artillery now rose to match the dying echoes from the mines. The Russians surged forward to engage the Tartars in combat hand to hand. This was the kind of fighting Sergei had been trained for. As long as they were battling enemy soldiers for control of the battlefield, he could perform his duty and keep his manhood intact.

He was parrying blows from a Tartar scimitar when Rustaveli rode up and hacked the nomad down from behind.

"I had him!" shouted Sergei.

"From that look of cowardice in your eye, I think he would have killed you instead! I cannot wait for you, Lieutenant. We have orders to pursue the retreating infidels!"

Sergei hesitated.

He balked at any assignment with Rustaveli. And something inside told him he was better off right where he was.

He should have refused to follow. Maybe he was no braver than Rustaveli had said. Maybe he was not as much the cynic as he feared. Part of him still believed in the Russian army and its purpose. At least part of him desperately wanted to. Whatever the cause, without further thought, Sergei reined his horse around and galloped off behind the captain.

Thousands upon thousands of Tekke refugees fled their destroyed fortress. Men, women, and children had taken refuge in Geok-Tepe when the Russians had first arrived. Now they had to find another haven, for they knew what lay in store for them if they were caught.

The ruthless Russian soldiers cut down all they caught, without regard for age, sex, or occupation. All previous skirmishes with the nomad thieves paled in comparison to the unrelenting carnage now underway.

"Stop . . . stop!" Sergei found himself screaming, not knowing when he had started. His voice was but a whisper in the midst of the rampaging Russians and the screams of the terrified, fleeing Tekkes. The men under his own command were heedless of his cries as well, caught up in the frenzy of the attack.

Somehow he kept riding. He had to keep on; if he attempted to turn back now, he would find himself trampled under thousands of his fellow Russians' feet. He would ride and ride and never turn back. He would ride beyond the burning, smoking fortress, beyond the mountains. He would escape! He would find his way back to Anna. They would escape this horror together!

He urged his horse on across the rocky terrain, not even noticing as it trampled over a mound of fallen bodies. Suddenly a woman sprang up in front of him, as if out of the very ground. He had seen nothing, and all at once there she was in his path.

"Have mercy!" she wailed, with arms outstretched toward him. His horse reared, whinnying wildly.

Perhaps its master's panic had seized the horse also. But for whatever reason, the animal was out of control. Its sharp hooves crashed down upon the pleading woman, killing her instantly with a vicious blow to the head.

The horse reared again, throwing Sergei off its back. His fall was cushioned by two bodies alongside the path. He lay stunned for a moment. When he tried to move off the corpse that had undoubtedly saved him from a broken neck, he saw that it was a young boy, perhaps eleven. Blood still oozed from the fatal wound to his chest, but Sergei was too numb to feel sick.

He crawled from the boy to the woman. He knew in an instant that she was dead also, her eyes still wide with terror, her final scream still etched upon her lips and in Sergei's seared consciousness.

He rose to his feet. The uniform he had once been so proud of was stained with blood—blood that poured just as red from the bodies of Turks as from any Russian aristocrat. He felt no gratitude that it was not his own blood spilling out upon him. Would to God it *was* his blood! He would willingly, gladly die

Travail and Triumph

to be spared the sights before him!

His horse had fled. If he could not be dead with the heaps of Turks on the ground, Sergei regretted only that he was not still on the gelding, riding . . . racing away from this nightmare. But he could neither escape nor die. He had to stumble along through the slain by foot.

It seemed he walked for hours, but it could have been only minutes. The mayham of pursuit and slaughter still continued around him. His vision, blurred with sweat and dirt and tears, spared him the full impact of the horror. But what he had already seen was enough to burn the memory of this day into his mind forever.

Then Sergei came unexpectedly upon Captain Rustaveli and two other yunker officers. They had rounded up a dozen or so refugees of both sexes and varying ages. Rustaveli was about to give the command to execute the whole group.

Suddenly the sickening pain and disgust overwhelmed Sergei. He could not watch another senseless death. In some rational recess of his mind, he knew that to stand by and watch such a crime was as despicable in its own way as actually committing it. At that moment, however, he held rationality by a slender, unraveling thread. His confused and fragile mind did not stop to debate philosophy, but instead repeated silently, *This must stop . . . stop . . . stop!*

Rustaveli stood in front of him. Sergei could not still the impulses, the voice that had echoed inside him sounded forth from his lips, although his ears could not hear it. He ran forward, unaware of having made the decision to attack.

"Stop . . . stop!" he shouted, rushing toward the captain. "Stop, Rustaveli . . . do you hear!" His voice was hoarse, and his body shook. Suddenly he stopped, finding himself standing in the midst of the condemned Turks, half of whom were women.

The yunker captain's eyes glowed with the passion of hatred. Then slowly his mouth widened in an evil grin as he kept his rifle trained on the refugees.

"So, Lieutenant *Prince*," he said derisively. "You would put an end to my command, is that it?" He followed the words with a snort of laughter.

"There has been enough killing!" cried Sergei, feeling whatever control he still possessed slipping quickly away.

"Bah! You're a fool, Fedorcenko. We are only obeying orders," sneered the captain. "Now out of the way before you are killed along with them! I *will* have you tried for treason. Do not add to my pleasure by forcing me to kill you."

Rustaveli cocked his rifle.

Sergei swiftly drew his own pistol. Even with trembling hands, he had a sure bead on his commander before the captain could respond. Any of the yunkers might yet turn their weapons on Sergei, but none of them would be able to fire before he sent a bullet into Rustaveli's head.

"I will kill you before I watch another innocent life taken," said Sergei. His voice shook as he sputtered out the words, and the captain laughed in his face.

"You don't have the guts!" growled Rustaveli through his laughter. He fired. An old man beside Sergei fell to the ground. The small crowd of Turks screamed in panic and tried to scatter.

Sergei discharged his pistol, but at the same instant the captain's horse reared back on its hind legs. The bullet from Sergei's gun missed its mark and crashed instead into the captain's shoulder, spitting out blood and pieces of the shattered bone.

The double shock from the bucking mount and the errant shot sent Rustaveli over backward, the last words on his lips a violent imprecation against the cursed aristocrat. He fell hard against a rock and lay motionless in the dust.

Sergei was only dully aware of all that happened next. There were more shots, more screams, more running. He was aware of doing nothing himself but standing where he was, pistol still in hand. He wondered vaguely why the other two yunkers did not immediately cut him down. But they were too shocked at what they had seen to respond. Killing Turks was a far cry from shooting down one's own commanding officer.

Sergei heard horses approach. Then he heard the voice of the regimental colonel. Nothing registered clearly in his mind. He continued standing stock still, his hand down at his side, the pistol hanging from it loosely.

"What is going on here?" barked the colonel. The scene must have presented itself clearly enough. Sergei's pistol in plain view.

The yunkers came to themselves quickly in the presence of a colonel. "He went berserk!" answered one.

"Who?"

"The lieutenant there. He came up bellowing and shouting. Before we knew it he had thrown himself in front of the prisoners and threatened the captain."

"Shot him right off his horse!" added another.

"Without provocation?" asked the colonel.

"The captain told him to stand aside so that the orders could be carried out. Then the lieutenant fired on him."

"Is this true, Lieutenant?" asked the colonel, casting his eyes on Sergei. Sergei turned slowly toward the officer as if noticing him for the first time. He opened his mouth and tried to speak, but no words would come.

"Answer me!" persisted the colonel.

Sergei felt his head nodding.

"All right, men, take him into custody," ordered the colonel.

"What now?" asked one of the witnesses. "A firing squad is too good for the likes of him!"

"There'll be an inquiry. No doubt a court-martial," said the colonel. Then he turned and again addressed himself to Sergei.

"Do you understand that you are in a great deal of trouble, boy?"

But Sergei understood nothing just then, except that his loathing of killing had turned *him* into a murderer. That he himself was a victim did not occur to him.

He let the soldiers bind his hands as if he needed restraint, and they led him away without the slightest struggle.

At last he had brought the ultimate shame upon his father's name. He had debased himself beyond all hope of restitution. He could never face his father again, never face Anna again. How could either of them ever look upon him again with anything but reproach?

A firing squad would be the supreme blessing—the fitting end to a life of failed dreams and visions, a life marked with only one joy—the love of a young woman who would now look upon him with as much disgust as he had felt for the captain he had tried to kill.

Whether he had succeeded or not hardly seemed to matter. The result would probably be the same regardless.

22

Katrina mounted the stairs of her home with heavy step. A footman opened the front door, and a valet inside immediately took her thick fur coat and hat. But she hardly noticed the servants. Her mind was still dazed from the shocking interview with her father.

The thing still seemed impossible. It could not have happened! Not to Sergei . . . not to her dear, sensitive, gentle brother Sergei!

It had to be a mistake!

She had been angry at first. She had fumed and stormed. Finally she had cried as the reality began to sink in. Her father, of course, had all the facts straight. That was the kind of man he was. And the facts were all too clear-cut. Viktor himself had gone to the Russian fort on the Caspian to verify them. The tragic news was unalterable.

She climbed the winding stairway to the first floor, her white-knuckled hand gripping the rail more for the sense of something solid in her careening world than for the physical support it offered, though her weak knees alone needed that as well. She sought her room—she had to be alone.

Alone . . . no, being alone was the worst thing! She needed someone. Where was Dmitri? Gone, of course—who knew where?

The thought of her husband made Katrina realize anew how alone she felt. She entered her room and closed the door behind her, then broke down in tears.

It was quiet and still. There was no one to comfort her—not father, not mother, not brother. And now even her own husband had deserted her. She sat down on the divan in her sitting room and wept—as much for herself as for her dear brother. There was nothing else to do.

Anna found her in this state ten minutes later.

"Oh, Princess . . . what is it?" she said with deep compassion, hurrying toward her mistress. She laid a hand on Katrina's arm and knelt beside her.

Katrina felt a sudden rush of relief at the welcome sight of her maid. "Oh, Anna . . . Anna!" she said, starting to cry all over again. "It's my brother . . . Sergei—" she sobbed, unable to get any more words past her lips.

Anna let out a gasp. She felt her face go white as she jerked her hand to her mouth and fell back from the divan.

Dear God! she breathed to herself.

She had feared the worst for so long, dreamed about it in her most terrifying nightmares. She had imagined the horrifying scenes of battle: the blood, terrible gaping wounds . . . a bullet, a sword, a dreadful slashing bayonet finding its way straight to the heart of . . .

Anna breathed in deeply to calm herself. All the thoughts and images which had flitted unsought through her waking and dreaming consciousness for so long suddenly assailed her with their full force. As the color had drained from her face, the blood now drained from her head.

She tried to rise to her feet. The room reeled, her legs went to rubber, and she nearly fell.

Katrina had been crushed too, but she hardly expected such a response from her maid. Seeing that Anna was about to faint, she jumped to her feet, her own tears forgotten for a moment. She took two quick steps and braced Anna just as she was about to topple to the floor. She put an arm around Anna and guided her to the divan, where they both sat down.

"It's . . . it's my fault," Anna moaned softly.

"Anna . . . what can you mean?" said Katrina, bewildered

by Anna's words. Suddenly the comforted had become the comforter.

"I pushed him away," said Anna, heedless in her grief of divulging more than she should. "I told him he should follow his orders. He wanted to desert the army. It's my fault! If he had not listened to me, he might be a fugitive, but he would still be alive!"

"Anna . . . what do you mean, *if*? When did you talk with Sergei?"

"Before he left. Oh, Princess—what have I done?"

"I don't know what you're saying, Anna," answered Katrina, more bewildered than ever by her maid's cryptic replies.

"How will you—how will any of you forgive me?" Anna went on. "With Sergei gone, your father will—" Anna began to cry.

"*Gone?*" repeated Katrina. "We may yet hope that *something* will be done to bring him back."

Anna's head shot up and her cheeks flushed.

"Princess!" she said, with confused hopefulness. "Are you saying . . . do you mean that Prince Sergei . . . he is not—" She could not bring herself to say the dreadful word.

"*Dead*, Anna?"

Anna nodded, her eyes wide as they stared into Katrina's face for an answer.

"Oh no, Anna—he is not dead . . . not yet, at least."

Anna closed her eyes and struggled for a breath. The weight of her misunderstanding took a moment to sink in. At length she covered her face with her hands, unable to stop the tears.

The intensity of Anna's reaction temporarily took Katrina's focus off her brother's troubles. The truth had begun to dawn on her.

"I must admit to feeling a bit foolish in the midst of my bewilderment," she said, with her arm still around Anna's shoulder. "Your tears are not only in sympathy for *my* grief over Sergei's plight, are they?"

Further deception was useless now. Everything had all but been revealed. Even if nothing was said, Katrina divined the full extent of Anna's heartache in a moment.

She smiled. "I cannot believe I didn't know before," she

said, almost reflecting to herself. "I suppose I was too heartsick over Dmitri to see much of anything else."

"Forgive me," said Anna, looking up and meeting her gaze. "I did not know what to do."

"You could have told me," said Katrina tenderly.

"Oh, Princess, I thought . . . I didn't know what you might think! You might have sent me away!"

"Never, Anna."

"It was so confusing at first—a nobleman . . . and me, just a servant. I was frightened."

"How . . . how long?" said Katrina.

"Almost since I first came," admitted Anna.

"All this time, and you said nothing." The princess laughed lightly. "How could I not have known it!"

"I'm so sorry, Princess. Now I wish I had told you."

"Did my brother swear you to secrecy?"

"No. He was ready to give up everything—his name, his position, his wealth. He was ready for us to leave the country together."

"That does sound exactly like Sergei," reflected Katrina. "He never was one to make distinctions based on his noble blood. Sometimes I think he despised it."

"Oh, but Princess!" exclaimed Anna, suddenly remembering the cause of her grief. "What of the prince? If he is safe, then. . . ?"

Katrina sighed. "He may be alive, Anna," she said, "but hardly safe."

"Has he been wounded?" exclaimed Anna.

"I am afraid it is even worse than that," replied Katrina. "He—" She stopped, but only briefly. "I can hardly say the words, they seem so preposterous in regard to Sergei. But it is true. He even admits to it."

"Admits to what?" said Anna frantically.

"He attacked his commanding officer, Anna. He actually fired on him, and may have killed him."

"No, it can't be true. Sergei would never . . . he *could* not do such a thing!"

"My father himself has just returned from the outpost. It has all been verified. It is true, Anna, as much as I cannot believe it myself. Sergei pointed his pistol straight at a Russian captain . . . and fired." She went on to describe the entire affair, at least as much as her father had related to her. It was a reasonably fair accounting of the incident as it had occurred, omitting, of course, the terrible atrocities that had led to Sergei's loss of control.

"My father believes something has happened to his mind," Katrina went on, starting to cry herself once more. "A breakdown of his mental faculties. Sergei refused even to see him. Father only laid eyes on him during the court-martial proceedings. Even then poor Sergei said nothing in his own defense. Father says he seemed bent on condemning *himself*, as if nothing would satisfy him other than to be put in front of a firing squad."

"Oh, Princess, don't even say it!" exclaimed Anna. "Is the man he shot . . . dead?"

"Not yet. He is in a military hospital, but is not expected to live."

"But he was court-martialed even before?"

"Whether the man lives or dies hardly matters," replied Katrina. "The treason is equal either way. Sergei defied a direct command, then shot his superior."

"Princess," Anna said at length, "after what I have done in keeping this from you, I have no right to make any further request, but—"

"Anna," Katrina broke in firmly despite her still shaky voice, "I believe I know you well enough to understand why you wanted to keep your feelings about Sergei quiet."

"It was more for him than myself I was concerned. A servant loving a great prince is probably not so unusual, but a prince condescending to—"

She found it impossible to say the words *to love a maid*.

"Of course," said Katrina sympathetically. "It must have been awkward for you both. To think—two of those I love most in the world . . . in love with each other. And I knew nothing of it!"

Again they were quiet.

"I would have helped you any way I could," said Katrina at length.

"But I am your *maid* . . . a servant, a peasant."

"Oh, Anna," said Katrina almost in disbelief, "do you think that matters to me now . . . after all we have been to each other?"

"I'm sorry, Princess. Sometimes I still find myself confused . . . and don't know what to think. Now that you are married, I have wondered—"

"Anna, Anna," interrupted Katrina. "Say no more. Don't you know how deeply I love you and care for you, as no friend I have ever had? Your being a servant and my being married changes none of that."

"Forgive me, Princess. But class attitudes are so common. I do not know what Count Remizov thinks of me. And judging from your father's reaction—"

"My father knew . . . about you and Sergei?"

Anna nodded. "He discovered us together before Sergei left for Asia."

"And took it none too well, if I know my father?"

"Not where Sergei was concerned. But I will say he was very kind to me. He did not dismiss me, and even spoke graciously to me, although he did make it clear he expected me to 'right the unfortunate situation,' as he put it."

Katrina smiled. "I can hear my father saying those exact words."

"As Sergei was bound for Asia," Anna continued, "there seemed no reason on either of our parts to do anything drastic. So he allowed me to stay until you returned, and I saw no benefit to be had from making any change. Nothing could make me leave you, Princess."

"Oh, thank you, Anna. You are so loyal—I don't deserve you for a moment!"

"But neither will I desert your brother, Princess. Now that it is all in the open and he has been sentenced, I must go to him."

"Is that the request you spoke of?"

"Yes, Princess, I must see him!"

"Anna, I would send you there this instant if I could—if I thought it would do the slightest good. But I have not yet told you everything."

"If he is to be executed, I *must* see him first. Who could deny us a few last moments together?"

"You would have a more likely time of seeing him if that were the case," replied Katrina, letting out a ragged sigh.

Anna looked at her with a confused expression.

"He is not to be executed."

At the words, Anna's face brightened with hope. But the princess continued.

"Because of what they call extenuating circumstances—by which they mean his mental state, specifically . . . I don't know what Father's position may have to do with it, if anything—the court agreed upon leniency."

This wonderful news hardly seemed reflected in the downcast tone of Katrina's voice. Still Anna gazed at her mistress expectantly.

"He's been remanded to hard labor . . ." Katrina paused. "In Siberia."

Anna gasped. "A life sentence, Anna!" said Katrina, then broke down and wept.

They were hardly the most worldly-wise or politically astute of women in Russia, from any class. But both had a fair idea of what such a sentence meant.

This was no political exile where wives and family often followed loved ones.

Hard labor meant prison. The *worst* of prisons! Incarceration with Russia's vilest criminals. There were innocents there too, of course, for the imperial legal system had never been known for its justice. Yet if innocents were sent to the mines in the frigid eastern reaches of the empire along with the guilty, it was an incontestable fact that few ever returned from there innocent, if they returned at all—which few did.

Sergei had been condemned to a living death. And a death it was—just as surely as if the firing squad had been ordered instead.

23

Viktor Fedorcenko came for a visit later in the afternoon.

Katrina had taken to her bed in grief. Anna had attempted to set aside her own misery by burying herself in work, washing and ironing until every piece of laundry in the house was clean. Then she had begun attacking duties normally assigned to the other servants—polishing silver, dusting, sweeping, and whatever else she could find to distract her from the pain of the news about Sergei.

She was near the front of the house when Katrina's father arrived. She went to the door and opened it, beckoning him to enter.

"The princess is resting, Your Excellency," she said, speaking in the hollow tone of one who has spent hours crying and yet remains still on the verge of tears.

"Please, do not disturb her, Anna," Viktor replied. "It is you I have come to see."

"Yes, sir?" said Anna, her voice registering neither surprise nor any other kind of emotion. She had no energy left even to wonder that he would come to see her, rather than summoning her to him.

"Let us go into my daughter's parlor where we may speak privately," he said.

He led the way as if they were in his own home, giving instructions to the other servants not to disturb them. No one questioned his authority. Not only was he the father of the princess, Viktor was the kind of man who exercised a commanding presence wherever he was.

Anna took a seat, as indicated by Katrina's father, on the

settee. He sat opposite her in a brocaded Louis XVII armchair. As Anna looked over at him, Prince Fedorcenko seemed more weighed down than he wanted to let on. His eyes seemed tired. His shoulders occasionally stooped slightly as well, very uncharacteristic of the tall soldier and ruler of men who was accustomed to walking with the leaders of the land.

"It is not difficult to see, Anna Yevnovna," Viktor began, "that you have heard the news concerning my son."

"Yes, Your Excellency," she said, glancing down into her lap. Anna's reddened, ringed eyes, the pallor of her skin, and lips that trembled at every word she tried to utter were evidence enough. She did not want to cry in front of the nobleman. If she said any more, it might be impossible not to.

"I felt compelled to speak to you personally regarding this matter," he said.

Anna said nothing. Viktor took a deep breath before beginning again.

"I want you to know I did everything humanly possible to aid in my son's defense," he went on. "I traveled to Krasnovodsk, where he was stationed, the moment the news reached me. I took with me the best legal counsel in all of Russia. I hounded the prosecution day and night, and did everything short of outright bribery—however, I must admit that I even attempted to go to *those* extremes. Except for my position in the government and the extremity of my desperation, I would likely have been arrested myself. All my efforts, I am sorry to say, proved to no avail."

"I . . . I do not understand why you are telling me these things, Your Highness," said Anna, at length braving the use of her voice.

Fedorcenko sighed—a long, ragged, melancholy sigh.

"I almost do not know the answer myself," he said with a humorless chuckle. "Perhaps, whatever our past differences, we yet shared something in our concern over my son that drew us together in this moment of travail. I only know that I found myself thinking of you, Anna, and felt perhaps you deserved a more full explanation."

"I am a mere servant, Your Highness. I deserve nothing."

"My son apparently thought you deserving of his love."

"But you did not," rejoined Anna, almost the same instant clasping her hand over her mouth, shocked at her own bold statement. "Forgive me, Your Highness!" she exclaimed immediately. "I did not mean . . ."

"Think nothing of it, Anna. I deserved it entirely."

Anna looked over and caught a glimpse of the deep pain he was suffering.

"Do not think that I have not rebuked myself a hundred times since first learning of Sergei's terrible fate," he said. "Every day I blame myself for turning my back on him. I hardly sleep at night. I—" He stopped abruptly.

Anna wondered if his voice had been caught on the edge of emotion. But Viktor rose immediately from his seat and strode across the room, his back conveniently toward her. He paused at a small liquor cabinet and poured himself a glass of brandy from a crystal decanter. Anna had the impression his movements were more for something to do, some diversion with which to occupy his hands, than from sudden thirst.

"I don't imagine you take brandy, do you, Anna?" he asked at length, still facing the bar so she could not see his face.

"No, sir."

He took a slow sip from his glass, then even more slowly began speaking to her again.

"I am convinced," he said after swallowing, "that nothing could have saved Sergei. He was guilty, by his own admission and that of several eyewitnesses. His insubordination reached beyond the limits of what can be tolerated, especially in battlefield conditions. He not only defied orders, he shot his commander. It was premeditated—a deliberate act—as the prosecution was all too successful in proving."

"You cannot believe your own son to be a murderer?"

"Not when we last saw him, no, I do not believe he was. But things can happen to a man. Things no one can predict may drive a man to do most anything, even murder."

"Not Sergei," said Anna with firm assurance.

"Anna, I am his father. I want to believe that just as strongly as you do yourself. But you are a young girl who thinks she loves him. I am a military man who has seen what the stress of battle can do. My eyes have been opened many times to the cruelties that life can inflict."

"I could never believe—"

"I know how you must feel, Anna. But I was also there, and therefore cannot contest what happened. I heard his confession with my own ears, although it was not spoken directly to me. It was about the only thing he said during the entire trial. But I did not, even then, give up on him."

"Why should you care that I know?"

"It is my way," Viktor said reflectively, "of continuing to try to find some way to believe in my son. Now . . . perhaps . . . you are the closest thing I have left to him, knowing . . . how he said he felt about you. Although he hardly spoke to me, I did not give up on him. I suppose that is what I wanted you to know."

"Yet you are giving up on him now . . . now that the trial is over?" There was more pleading than accusation in Anna's tone.

"What more can be done?" His steady voice now broke momentarily into frustration. "It is over! Sergei has . . . Sergei is lost to us."

He absently brought his glass to his lips and tossed back the remaining brandy.

"Do you think that it doesn't kill me daily that I failed with him? Can you imagine the anguish of knowing that because of your failure, your *own* son must spend the rest of his life in . . . in a living hell! I do not need your rebukes. I have discovered my own living hell, Anna—if that is any consolation to you!"

His hand trembled as he set the glass back on the sideboard. Anna rose and rushed to him. She could no longer bear talking to his back, even if looking upon his emotion shamed him.

She grasped his arm and turned to face him with pleading eyes. "I am sorry, Your Highness!" she said, tears obscuring her vision. "I would never think to rebuke you. I had no right to say what I did."

He flipped the back of his hand toward her as if to indicate it had been a mere trifle.

"I selfishly saw only my own pain," Anna went on, suddenly seeing the human side of the stoic Prince Fedorcenko. "I had no right to forget that you did—you *do* love your son. Please forgive me!"

He did not reply verbally. Silence was his only remaining protection against complete humiliation in front of this servant girl. He had come to see her on a whim, hardly knowing what compelled him to seek her out. But Anna could detect in his eyes that her apology was appreciated.

Anna continued speaking, to spare him. As she spoke, she temporarily forgot how far beneath him she was, and discovered a renewed inner strength to keep from breaking down herself.

"Maybe Sergei's plight is hopeless," she said, "although I am not ready to fully accept that. I cannot helplessly let go of him. I must do something for him."

"Forgive me for saying so, Anna, but if there is nothing *I* can do, what could a poor servant girl hope to accomplish?"

"I don't know, but I must see him."

"I do not see what—"

"Please, Prince Fedorcenko . . . I must go to him!"

"Anna, I fear that would be impossible."

"You would, even now, deny us—"

"No, Anna," he interrupted, "you misunderstand me. It has nothing to do with *my* objections now." Gradually the prince was gathering back his self-control. "Anna," he said, taking her hands in his, looking in her face, and speaking with deep earnestness, "I have given this a great deal of thought since my son's trouble came upon him. Perhaps, I was . . . too hasty before he left. If there were some way I could atone for past mistakes and bring the two of you together, I would be prepared to do that now, believe me. I would give up my proud, foolish notions of class responsibility. If only I could turn back the time to that moment when I first saw the two of you in the garden . . . if only I could have realized that Sergei's happiness means more to me than I could have believed possible. For so many years, all I could think of was my own—"

He stopped, pulled away his hands from hers, and turned quickly away. She saw him breathe in deeply, then try to continue.

"*I* held the power," he said, "to permit that happiness. But instead I heaped misery, perhaps even death, upon him—" His voice broke.

Anna moved around to face him. Tears had welled up in his eyes and threatened to spill over. But he did not turn away from her.

"It is a hollow statement now, Anna," he said, his tone tentative, "but if I were given the chance again, you two would have my blessing."

"Thank you, Your Highness," Anna murmured, unable to say more.

"And not merely because it would make my son happy," Viktor added, "but because I see so clearly now that he made a wise choice as to where to place his affections."

Anna glanced down.

"None of us, however, will be granted a second chance," he said, trying to bring resolve to his voice. "We . . . we have lost Sergei, Anna. We must *both* accept that painful reality."

"I can go to Siberia," pleaded Anna.

"It is no use."

"Even if I cannot *see* him, he would know that I was near, and that I love him. I cannot desert him!" she cried in desperation, bursting into fresh tears.

Prince Viktor Fedorcenko had never been one to feel altogether comfortable in such situations. The complex mystery of crying women was an arena of life far removed from the offices and situation rooms and battlefields where he had always been at his best. Yet all that past life of being a nationally important figure and advisor to the tsar was beginning to fade. Alexander was losing faith in him. Whatever influence he might once have enjoyed now rested upon the shoulders of Loris-Melikov. And Viktor's son was considered a traitor to the very empire to which he had given his life.

In light of all these factors, somehow the pleading and loving voice of a servant girl and the heart of a son who had been estranged from him for years seemed more *real* and tangible than all the prestige he had once enjoyed, the glory which now was gradually crumbling away.

And the simple fact was, however discomforting he had always found the shedding of tears—his or his wife's or anyone's, for that matter—he could not refuse to comfort *this* young woman who, but for his arrogance, might well have been his daughter-in-law.

Thus, the tall, tired, proud, stoic military officer and Minister of the Empire slowly bent his arms and stretched them stiffly and tentatively into new and unexplored regions of intimacy. As his arms closed around Anna's small shoulders, his hands drew her tenuously toward him. The gesture broke down Anna's reservations completely in love for the man out of whose being her Sergei had come, and she cried out her tears freely against the rough wool of his uniform tunic.

Several minutes passed.

When Viktor gradually began to sense the flood of her tears subsiding, he spoke again. The tone was fatherly, yet sad and serious.

"There is something you must see," he said, loosening her from his embrace and leading her gently back to the settee. When Anna was seated he took a folded paper from his pocket.

"It is from Sergei," he said. "He gave it to me for you. It is not much, I grant you, and if you read between the lines it would seem even more hopeless than it does on the surface. But you will understand from it his state of mind."

She took the paper from his hand, opened it, and read:

Farewell, Anna. I am dead. You must accept that. It is the only way I can prevent myself from going completely insane. Grieve for me as you must. Then go on with your life without me. I am buried in a deep grave. Light a candle for me, pray for my lost soul, but do not—DO NOT—hope for resurrection. I do not want it. And there can be none. Forget about me, Anna—for your own sake, and for mine. Forget I exist. For by the time you read this, I will exist no longer.

Anna quietly made the sign of the cross over her chest as tears streamed once more down her face.

Although the note was unsigned, the handwriting was Sergei's. She knew it well. But the words sounded as though they had come from a stranger. She could almost *hear* the terse, cold, cynical brevity as if the message had been spoken.

How could Sergei have sunk to such hopelessness and despair? She ached inside, searching to find some hint that his humanity remained, some trace of the Sergei she knew. Over and over she read the words, almost frantic to locate a clue of desperation that said he was calling out for help in spite of the finality of the words themselves.

But it was not there. Sergei had given up on his country, on his family, on her . . . and most of all on himself. Worse, he seemed to have given up on God as well.

Was that not all the more reason for her to go to him? Her very presence, the love she could give him, even if only for the briefest of minutes, might be the only thing that would rekindle his hope. Her papa had always said, "A little love in the tea is sweeter than a copper's worth of sugar." She could visualize her father's smiling countenance as he uttered the words, while she, on the other hand, doubted she would ever be able to smile again.

Oh, Papa, Papa . . . she thought, *what would you say? How I need your wise, understanding words, your simple, loving embrace!*

"I know what you are thinking, Anna," came a gentle voice in the midst of her quiet reflections of home. Anna glanced up, realizing suddenly that Sergei's father was the closest person she had to her own papa just then. "You think that your going to Sergei may be his only hope, is that it?" said Viktor.

"I can think of nothing else."

"Even if you were able to obtain permission to visit him," Viktor said, "he is already on his way, I have no doubt, to that land from which few return. You would never find him. Even if you and I both went, we could never find him. And even if, by some miracle, you *were* able to reach him, and see him and speak to him and give him that hope you want to give him, even then, Anna, it still would not change the fact that Sergei is facing an imprisonment that will last for the rest of . . . his life."

Viktor's voice broke over the final word. "You will never be able to be together, Anna. You must understand that. By law he is considered legally dead once he is in Siberia. Even if you were now married, his sentence carries the same weight as death. You would be free to remarry. My son was right when he said that you must go on with your life."

The hard words pounded over Anna's head like stones tumbling down a raging mountain torrent, carried by water so powerful that nothing could stop them.

"I know I must sound coldhearted to you," Viktor went on. "I know it will take time for you to adjust to this change in your life. But it is the only thing you can do. Imagine how much more it would grieve Sergei to know you were wasting your life away—your entire life, Anna, for you are so young—waiting for the impossible."

He paused, drew in a long breath, and once again tried to assume a steady businesslike countenance.

"At any rate," he said, "that is my counsel to you. I realize I have hardly earned the right to offer you, of all people, advice. But I was your master for some time, hopefully a fair and compassionate one. And I doubt you'll hear different counsel from another."

"I take it you are saying there is nothing *anyone* can do?" said Anna. "Neither myself, nor you . . . nor anyone." The firmness of her conviction was clearly dissolving.

"There was a time," answered Viktor, "when I could have wielded my authority on Sergei's behalf. But my influence at the court is nearly gone. There are ways for the son of a man in my position to avoid prosecution for a crime even as terrible as Sergei's. But I no longer occupy the position I once did. I have fallen from imperial favor. I was already on shaky ground in the changing political climate that keeps Russian aristocrats fearful for their heads. And Sergei certainly did not help his own cause on my behalf with that book of his. The tsar took it very personally. And this latest treasonous incident, especially committed as it was in battle! Ah, Anna—all of it has reflected woefully on me."

He paused, then shook his head slowly. "It is not entirely Sergei's doing, I must admit that in all fairness. The erosion, as I said, began long before that. I was never much good at groveling to obtain the tsar's favor. I always believed somehow that honesty would win out. But how miserably I was wrong! I would march straight to the Winter Palace this minute and kiss the tsar's feet if I thought it would bring back my son. But it is too late for that. The tsar is angry with me because of Sergei. He says I have made him look doubly foolish, especially in these times when radicals are saying all manner of falsehoods against him. He is in no mood for being ridiculed from *within* the ranks of his own circle of advisors, which is his perception of what I have allowed to happen. He refused to see me when I attempted to obtain an Imperial decree in Sergei's defense. I doubt I could fight a warrant against me for spitting on the street!"

The room fell silent. There seemed little more to be said. A moment or two more passed; then Prince Fedorcenko bade Anna farewell, turned, and departed, leaving her alone in the parlor.

Anna's mind was numb. No single thought would remain focused within her mind. One moment she was thinking of the first day she had seen Prince Sergei as they watched the skaters on the river. The next she was thinking of their walk in the garden. Then her mind raced back to Katyk, and filled with images of the joy she and Sergei had shared there together—walking by the stream with a stiff autumn breeze at their backs, sitting under the willow talking for hours, or resting before the hearth in the cozy *izba*, with children on Sergei's knee shrieking with laughter as he told them his lively, animated tales. The most precious memory of all was that of working in her father's field together to bring in the grain before the coming of the rain.

But within a short space of time, these pleasant images faded, to be replaced by one unfamiliar to her senses and therefore all the more dreadful in her imagination. In the eye of her anguished mind, Sergei lay dejected, alone, half starving. The surroundings were dark, as of a deep, cold, dank prison cell—without life, without hope, without sight of sun or any other human being. And there lay Sergei—silent, thin, in rags, his heart broken, his mind deadened by the stupefying numbness of aloneness, what little life there was left in him pouring slowly and invisibly out onto the damp, cold stone floor as if his tortured body were a sieve.

Oh, but for me, she thought in the agony of her distress, *we would still be in Katyk. But for me, none of this nightmare would be happening!*

Anna buried her face once more in her hands. No answers came to her distraught mind . . . and no prayers came to her lips. Only the depth of her heart could open itself to the Father, although as it did she neither knew it nor felt it.

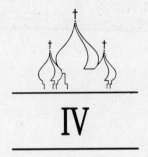

IV

A NATION'S TRAVAIL
(January—March 1881)

24

Winter in Russia was as cold as it was hard.

There were no exceptions—at least in his lifetime Yevno remembered none. Changes, yes. But no exceptions. Youth felt the cold not nearly so deeply, and was innocent enough to delight in the frozen white powdery manna from above. The young did not feel the cold in their bones, and their cares were few. The weight of provision did not yet rest on the unburdened shoulders of guileless childhood.

He had been young once, too. He had not felt the burden or the cold then as he did now.

Perhaps it did grow colder each year, thought Yevno. He certainly felt its bitter sting through every bone, in every fiber of his tired body. To young Tanya and Vera and Ilya, whose shouts and laughter even now greeted his ears as he lay in bed, the snow meant exuberance and life and joy—with a thousand new possibilities for play and happiness every morning. That their fingers and toes were frozen beyond feeling mattered nothing.

But the snow was no life-giving manna to one like Yevno. It was, rather, the powder of death—killing the ground, taking from it the power to give life, killing the bones, killing the fingers, numbing legs and arms and even brain. Spring always came, they said. Indeed, he had found it so. Yet every year he doubted the fact anew. Every year it seemed longer in coming. One year, he was all but certain, it would not come at all. They would wait and wait and look and look outside. But snow . . . more snow . . . drifting higher and higher until everything was covered—cottages, fields, barns, even trees. The whiteness would remain . . . forever.

Perhaps then would come death—the final winter, and the soft frozen flakes would indeed bring life ... of a new kind.

"Your tea, Yevno," said a soft voice, interrupting his drifting thoughts.

"Ah, Sophia," smiled Yevno, turning to face her and stretching out his hand. "You take such care of this tired old husband!"

"No more than you would do for me if I lay in bed," she said, lovingly caressing his forehead and stroking back his gray hair.

"Alas, I never seem to be given such an opportunity," chuckled Yevno, "for I am always the one lying here. You still possess the youth and vitality of a forty-year-old, Sophia."

"Bah, Yevno, I am as old as you!"

"Why, then, does age not creep up on you?"

"Perhaps because I am so full of love for you," she said with a smile. She stooped down to the bed and kissed him.

Yevno sipped from the strong, hot brew. It felt good to the tongue and stomach as he swallowed, but was powerless to send its warmth to his benumbed extremities under the blankets at the far end of the bed. No matter how much tea he consumed, he could not seem to make his feet aware of it.

"The children sound so happy," said Sophia after a moment.

"They do not need food to make them laugh. They know we will take care of them," said Yevno seriously. "But how long will we be able to, Sophia?"

"There is yet much wheat and rye in the bins in the barn."

"Thanks to Anna and her prince, and my good health last fall. But as you yourself can see, that health has failed again."

"We have grain enough to last until this year's *stradnya pora* and beyond, Yevno, my dear husband. You can lie right here all winter, through all the snow our God chooses to send us, though it bury us alive, and we will have bread in plenty! For one time, Yevno, put aside your fretting over your family. You are the best husband a woman could have hoped to have. Look at me—I am old, and still plump! You have fed me well all the days of my life ... yes, and through all the winters, too!"

Yevno sighed and tried to force a smile. "Ah, wife, you ever lavish me with your kind words. But the reality of the cold is that the earth is frozen, and I lie here and slowly we eat the grain, and the bins will grow empty, and then how will I replace their stores? With what will I make provision for my family then?"

"You are anxious over a mirage, my husband," replied Sophia. "We have grain enough to last ten blizzards, if our tiny *izba* were full of ten children!"

"Ah, but next year, wife . . . what of next year? Do we have wheat to last *two* winters . . . or three? What if no miracle comes next time from the city? What if there is no Anna . . . no prince? Were it not for them, you would even now be sweeping the kernels of wheat from the bottom of the bin, mixing more dirt into your bread than grain itself. Last year's harvest was meager, and had we not had much left over, we would now have none."

Sophia nodded. She could hardly deny it, for she knew it was true. But the fact was, Anna and the prince *had* come, and this year the elder prince had hired a helper, and they *did* have wheat and rye in abundance. Next winter at this time, she had every confidence they would yet be eating bread from grain cut from this year's *stradnya pora*. It was all in the cycle of life. Winter did not make poor people like them die; it taught them to endure. Even buried under a blanket of whiteness, life in Russia went on. Thus it had been for centuries.

"You are a good man, my Yevno," said Sophia at length. "You have but one fault. You are *too* anxious over your duty."

"How can a man be too anxious over his family? It *is* his duty to feed them. He must do it, though his bones ache and his fingers and toes be frozen."

"If he forgets by whose hand the provision comes," said Sophia, "then perhaps he is too anxious. Would you not say the same thing if you were telling your own sons of their duty?"

Yevno was silent. His wife had spoken the truth. But his silence was only partially due to the conviction her words brought his soul. There was also the reminder of Paul. What did *he* think of duty? And would he ever again listen to his father speak words of truth? The thought of their eldest son was not a pleasant one these days. They knew nothing of the depths of his troubling rebellion; and yet in their ignorance, how could they not grieve?

They knew nothing. Therefore they did not speak of him. They only sighed, looked at each other with expressions of shared pain of the kind only loving parents can know, and silently offered up what prayers and petitions were yet left within them.

"No more word from Anna?" said Yevno at length. He knew well enough there had been no letter. It was only a way to offer comment about Paul without saying his name.

"Not since her Christmas greeting."

"She remains busy in her new home."

"And with the princess in her way, Anna will have to care for her more and more."

"Will the child be born before *stradnya pora*?" asked Yevno.

"Long before."

"Then perhaps, if I am yet ill—God forbid!—she might again be able to help us."

"Are you fretting again, Yevno?"

"Only thinking ahead, wife," smiled Yevno.

"Ah, Yevno," said Sophia with a knowing and maternal look. "How little you men know of childbirth and the babies that follow it! Anna will not leave the princess's side for months. No, we will not see her this summer or autumn. She too must attend to her duty."

"Perhaps her prince . . ." said Yevno, letting his voice trail away.

"Yevno, what are you saying? That a prince of Russia would come to our *izba* by himself, *without* Anna—merely to help us?"

Yevno did not answer immediately. He had not told Sophia the substance of the conversation he had with Sergei the night late after the celebration at Ivan Ivanovich's. He had probably already said too much. He was still not ready to tell his wife that the young Prince Fedorcenko had that night asked for their daughter's hand in marriage. If it was bold for him to think of the prince lending his muscular frame to the gathering in of another harvest, it was no less preposterous than that same prince considering it an honor to call him his future father-in-law. If the prince had spoken truly from his heart, and was a true man—which Yevno believed he was—then he was certain to come. By then the conflict where he had been sent to fight was sure to be over and his troubles with the tsar resolved.

Yevno sighed deeply, with as much satisfaction as he could feel during the biting chill of winter. He took another long swallow of the tea, now scarcely more than lukewarm. Thoughts of the prince and the memory of his time in Katyk gave Yevno a secure feeling. Yet he was still not ready to divulge to Sophia the reason for the smile that now accompanied her tea to warm his spirits.

"You are right, wife," he said at length. "It is beyond a doubt a foolhardy notion to have even entered my tired old brain. But I will heed your exhortations, and will fret no more over my duty."

There was indeed a change of heart that went along with his words, for thoughts of Prince Fedorcenko had reminded Yevno of his own words of faith in God's provision that he had spoken so confidently that night as they had walked back from the tavern to the cottage. If it was still too soon to speak of the prince returning to Katyk, it was not too soon to speak again the words Yevno had said to him: *From inside comes a gratefulness to my Father in heaven for watching over old Yevno with such kindness.* Even though almost in the next breath Yevno had confessed to Sergei his constant anxiety over the harvest, perhaps the memory of God's provision last year through the prince could sustain him to have faith in this year's provision, from whatever source. He could at least try.

"I am glad to hear it," replied Sophia. "If I have no anxiety over where the grain will come from to make my bread, then you need have no anxiety over me or the children."

Yevno nodded, and finished the remainder of his tea.

He laid his head back on his bed, thoughts of Anna and the prince mingling with those of Paul, as he silently asked the God of provision to watch over them all just as carefully as He did the supply of wheat in the wooden bins out in his cold, snow-surrounded barn.

25

The blizzard lasted for hours into the night, not abating until well into the morning. By the time the storm tapered off sometime before noon, huge drifts of fresh whiteness had covered every conceivable nook and alleyway and close in St. Petersburg. Even the slums, for a time, wore a clean look.

As Prince Viktor Fedorcenko rode in his troika across one of the city's broad avenues, he absently watched workmen, hefting spades and brooms, strenuously clearing the street and walkways, packing the snow into thick walls to be hauled away by great horse-driven lorries.

Viktor was no melancholic. He well knew that the machinery of life moved inexorably forward, paying no heed to the private travails of men's and women's hearts. The principle was an ingrained part of his character. It was not something he would have said he *believed*, but rather an expression of the man he *was*. Nevertheless, on this particular day it had taken every grain of self-will he possessed to make him leave his house and force himself back into the mainstream of his work. He desperately wanted to cloister himself within the four walls of his home and never have to face another living soul again. He had never experienced such feelings, such self-awareness, such self-preoccupation, in his life.

But these were new times. Besides the guilt that gnawed at his soul, he knew well enough what people were thinking: *Oh, poor Fedorcenko . . . his son broke down . . . stress of battle . . . shot his commander.*

He remembered thinking the same kinds of things about Dr. Anickin and his lunatic of a son. Now it had all come to rest on him, and he could hardly bear to be the object of such pity and questioning criticism himself.

But Viktor was not so trivial a man that this was the full extent of his despondency. True, he could not deny the natural sense of humiliation caused by all that had happened. Yet it cut much deeper than that. The fact was, he could not face his peers. He could not look them in the eye, stand tall, and return their gaze with confidence. Even less could he face himself. His belief in his own stature as a man had been shaken to the core.

Every pitiful glance and well-meaning word of condolence bit deeply, making him painfully aware of the undeniable fact that he, and he alone, was responsible for Sergei's terrible fate. The book might have been written regardless, but he wished he had found some way to communicate more personally with his son earlier, years ago. Perhaps those turbulent emotions that had prompted the book might have been stemmed, moderated, not felt so caustically when Sergei had joined the Guard Regiment. But even when the book *had* been written, if only Viktor hadn't turned Sergei away, the lad might have endured the misery of the Asian assignment without breaking.

But it was too late for such thoughts! He *had* turned him away, and Sergei *had* broken under the stress. He *had* lost control, he *had* been court-martialed, and now he had been exiled to Siberia!

It was over. There was nothing to do but accept it. He had to heed the advice his own lips had given to the young Burenin girl.

Natalia had urged him to return to work. It would distract him from his sorrow, she said. It was a prescription she could have made good use of herself if she had any "work" to return to. The eyes of the princess were perennially red-rimmed these days, and her pale skin seemed almost ghostly. She had never been the most zestful and energetic woman. And now the pallor of her skin and lethargy of her movements were almost eerily wraithlike. She had withdrawn completely from the whirlwind round of parties and balls and theater and ballet engagements that marked St. Petersburg's winter social season during these months. She slept or lounged in her bed most days, rousing occasionally for meals, but more often than not taking them in her room. Her thinning frame indicated that she did not eat enough. She visited her daughter on occasion. But the two Fedorcenko women ignited each other's sorrow to such a degree that they both began to avoid the frequent visits that had become habitual between them.

The prince and princess also seemed to avoid each other's company more these days, although that was probably more Viktor's doing than hers. Natalia's grieving countenance served as a constant reminder to him that *he* had doomed her son to life in a freezing hell.

That Natalia rose from her own misery to show concern for him was touching. But it only increased his torment. In the end, however, it did have the effect of forcing him to heed her recommendation. Better to absorb himself in a day's work than to face the dear wife who so mirrored his own pain day after weary day.

Viktor soon found that the so-called cure for his depression was almost as deadly as the problem itself. He discovered that he himself had little meaningful work to return to. His duties seemed to be evaporating as rapidly as was his Imperial standing.

Not only was there little for him to do, but his colleagues and former friends maintained a chilly distance. Most of the other ministers and officials had received the message clear enough, albeit unofficially. There had been no orders; it was merely "understood" how things stood between Viktor and the tsar. Prince Viktor Fedorcenko was under an unspoken interdictive ban. His peers were obviously uncomfortable in his presence, and he was given only the most inconsequential of tasks.

The childhood friend of the tsar, the man who had such a short time ago been one of Alexander's most trusted advisors and confidants, was relegated to a status less vital than that of a minor civil servant stationed in some distant and insignificant outpost of the empire.

Three days of this pathetic routine had driven Viktor all but to distraction. If the avoidance of eyes and the subduing of voices when he walked into a room did not combine to drive him insane, surely the tedious monotony of nothing to do would finish the job! He had always thrived on activity. This was a living death—in its own way, perhaps not unlike his son's.

Why he kept enduring it, facing the humiliation day after day, he did not know. Viktor had never been a quitter. Although everything in his life seemed to have suddenly gone sour, he could not give up easily.

Sometimes, though, he felt but a hairsbreadth away from succumbing to the tormenting call of madness that now hounded him.

26

There was one, however, who did not seem to mind the censure of Viktor Fedorcenko, and who himself paid not much attention to it. Remarkably, that was the most powerful man in Russia other than the tsar himself.

As Viktor was walking through the Winter Palace to his office a week after the blizzard, he ran into Michael Loris-Melikov midway through one of the long corridors. The governor-general of St. Petersburg was in exceptionally high spirits and greeted Viktor as if nothing had happened. They fell into stride together, chatting amiably. Viktor was so shocked by the other's friendly good cheer that he stumbled with the interchange for a few moments. He had almost forgotten what it was like to carry on a normal political discussion!

He had not seen Melikov since before Sergei's trouble. It was impossible that the man did not know of the incident. Yet he treated Viktor with the same camaraderie of spirit as before—as a respected peer and confidant. He invited Viktor into his office, which was nearby, and as he handed his guest a brandy, Melikov continued to talk enthusiastically.

"Ah, Viktor, we have them on the run now!" he said, eagerly rubbing his hands together and speaking as if Viktor were privy to an ongoing conversation that had preceded their meeting in the hall and the small talk that had followed.

"Them. . . ?" asked Viktor distractedly. Fortunately Melikov was too caught up in his good news to notice.

"Those cursed terrorists! I've made major arrests, Viktor! I'm on my way now to report the good news to Alexander—"

The mere mention of the tsar's name sent a brief chill through Viktor's spine—a chill of mingled pleasure to be so close again to the center of power, and terror lest he misspeak himself with one who had the tsar's ear.

"I've got leaders this time—the real core of the foul bloody movement!" Melikov had gone on.

"Can you be certain?" said Viktor. The question seemed a safe one he could not do wrong in asking.

"Without a doubt. I've finally laid my hands on the brute Andrei Zhelyabov."

"I have heard of him."

"One of the top men. The slippery miscreant has given me a merry chase for some time, but I have him now."

"You mean you've located where he is hiding—"

"No—*got* him, I tell you, Viktor! In custody—right in the fortress."

"Has he talked?"

"No, and to tell you the truth, I doubt he will. The man is a fanatic. Just like them all—no value for his own life."

"Will his arrest be of any lasting impact, then?"

"With the radicals leaderless, the rest of them won't last for long. Zhelyabov was the catalyst, the brains, the voice. Without him, they will disband—I am sure of it. Whichever ones don't run away in fear, we will catch eventually because of their stupidity."

"It is good news," said Viktor. At any other time he would have meant the words enthusiastically. Today, however, even the conflict between the Crown and the radicals had little power to touch him deeply. "I am sure this report will be welcome by the tsar," he went on methodically. "Perhaps he will be able once again to walk the streets in safety."

"That scum Zhelyabov continues to rant and rave that the tsar is a doomed man. He insists his own arrest means little. Bah—I don't believe him!"

"What does he say?"

"He wants us to believe they have created an organism that will survive without its head."

"Could it be true?" asked Viktor, showing a hint of concern.

"He is a liar if he is anything. He will say whatever seems expedient at the moment."

"Perhaps caution is still advised in any case."

"That, of course, is up to the tsar. But I hope, Viktor, that he has more confidence in my judgment than you appear to have."

Viktor winced. It would not do to offend *anyone* these days. He had only loosened his guard for an instant. He had to watch himself.

"Fortunately my opinion is of little import," he said dryly, "so you hardly need worry what I think."

Melikov grunted. "Wretched shame that is too, Viktor. And I want you to know I am on your side."

In spite of himself, a glimmer of hope shot through Viktor. If someone like Melikov would speak for him to the tsar! But the vain hope was dashed as quickly as it had arisen as Melikov continued.

"If things were not so touchy right now, Viktor," he said, "I want you to know I would tell Alexander what a mistake he is making in snubbing you. How responsible can a man be for the actions of his son, anyway? A man has to be judged on his own merits, if you ask me."

Viktor nodded slightly, vouchsafing no smile but at least acknowledging the other's words of support.

"But I find myself in a rather precarious balancing act at the moment myself," he went on. "Life around Alexander—given the climate and turmoil in the capital during this past year—is a cloudy and turbulent affair. What with the Dolgoruky woman and her brood, the tsarevich and his reactionary friends opposing me at every turn with the constitution. Then there is Pobedonostev, and Orlov and his bunch. *And* on top of it all that plebeian boor Vlasenko lurking in the wings waiting none too patiently for it all to cave in on me—"

Another involuntary shudder ran through Viktor's being. That would be all he'd need—for Melikov to discover that Cyril Vlasenko had obtained his appointment through *Viktor* because of his wife's bloodline. He'd be joining Sergei in Siberia if he wasn't careful!

"And with the constitution in the balance," Melikov continued, "I tell you, Viktor, these are perilous times for us all. I simply cannot risk my own standing."

"I would not dream of your speaking on my behalf, Michael," said Viktor. "We all must bear our own political burdens like the men we claim to be." More than a hint of Viktor's stoic pride accompanied his words.

"It is a sorry pass, Viktor, when good men are left standing in the corridors, while fools and nincompoops are invited through the hallowed doors to sup at the king's table."

He paused as if to allow the sage wisdom of his words to sink in. Then he continued in a different vein.

"I could certainly use your experience and input now more than ever, Viktor," he said. "The tsar has set a task before me that I fear even I will be hard pressed to conquer." He paused and gave a coy smile, but made no attempt to modestly downplay his boast.

Viktor did not fault him his immodesty, for Melikov was one of the few men in the capital he truly admired. Yes, he could be pompous at times. And he was an adept conniver. But he was highly intelligent, and not without a good deal of common sense—a commodity in far too short supply in the Winter Palace.

Michael Loris-Melikov had already done what many would have considered impossible. Not only had he won Alexander's favor, he had managed to keep from being destroyed by the bickering and divisive factions of Russian politics. Viktor would not rate him brilliant, but his pragmatic wisdom went far beyond the commonplace. He had juggled all the various factions of the Imperial Court, had pushed a far-reaching program of historic foresight tenaciously through the maze of imperial and political red tape, and had emerged largely unscathed—with his reputation and his head still in place. Whatever new obstacle the tsar had set in his path, it could hardly be insurmountable to such a skillful politician and shrewd strategist.

"Surely, Michael," said Viktor, "you have gone too far now to allow anything to impede you." Viktor's words, coming as they did from a man who *had* all but given up, were rather hollow. He meant them, but he had not the fortitude left to heed them for himself.

"Besides my news of the arrest of Zhelyabov," Melikov replied, "I will also be delivering to the tsar the first draft of my proposed constitution."

"That *is* good news!"

Viktor rose momentarily from his emotional lethargy to speak with deep sincerity. The constitution was everything—what moderates like him had been hoping for. The constitution was the only hope, as he saw it, for suppressing the radical movement and bringing the nation into the twentieth century. He might even go so far as to say this news superseded even his personal grief. If they could make a success of it, the Russia he dearly loved might still have a chance to survive.

"Unfortunately," Melikov added almost drearily, "what I will hand to His Majesty is little more than a glorified extension of the *zemstrovs*. And we all know what a pitiful failure they have been."

"That was local government, Michael. There was never a sufficiently broad base of experience on the local, especially the rural, level to make those so-called self-governing bodies work effectively. That factor alone should change the impact dramatically on the national level."

"I would have expected you to be above such self-deception, Viktor."

"Perhaps I am deluding myself," sighed Viktor, "but *something* in the way of democratic change is better than nothing, is it not?"

"In my opinion, what the tsar expects is equivalent to *nothing*. The other day he said to me, 'There is one thing in this country that I hold sacred and inviolate—that is the Russian monarchy. Have your reforms if you must, and your constitution too. But I will not rob my heir of his rightful due.' "

"It sounds as though he is giving you power to change the government with one hand, and yet taking it away from you with the other," observed Viktor.

"That, my friend, is *precisely* Alexander's game. He wants me to change the system without changing the system."

"Now I see why you called it a task you didn't know if you could conquer."

"Listen to what else he said," Melikov went on. "He wrote it for me, in an official letter, presumably so that I would not forget the boundaries of this position he created for me."

He took a sheet of paper from his desk, looked at it for a moment, then began reading. "Here are Alexander's words:

'My father, for all his difficulties—a reign that began with mutinous rebellion and ended with a humiliating defeat at the hands of the British—passed on to me a throne completely intact. I received from him the power and majesty of the Russian autocracy as he received it from his father and had been passed down through the Romanov line for nearly three hundred years. I fully intend to do the same with my son and heir. I suppose we must have this constitution, but, mark my words, I will be able to approve it in clear conscience only if it preserves the autocracy of the Russian throne.' "

Melikov stopped, put the paper back on his desk, then looked back toward Viktor. "Believe me, Viktor," he went on rather sharply, "I have marked his words, in that I will not forget them. But fulfilling his wishes is quite another matter."

"I suppose whatever else Alexander is, he is a Romanov above all," commented Viktor.

"Exactly! And by his stiff-necked clinging to the cursed autocracy, he may well lose everything. Then he would have nothing to pass on to Alexander."

Melikov's bold critiques were gradually loosening Viktor's tongue. He could scarcely believe one so close to the tsar could be so free with such denouncing words. "It is rather curious," he said, "that the future tsar's throne should be of such overpowering concern to him. He and the tsarevich have had almost as many differences as I have with my son."

"Everything about the tsar is curious these days, Viktor. There is not much that makes sense. One thing I do know, that is if the tsarevich's reactionary policies hold sway over the tsar rather than his former bent toward reform, you may mark *my* words, there will be revolution in this land of ours one day."

"Despite your earlier confidence that Zhelyabov's arrest will put a stop to the violence?"

Melikov nodded thoughtfully. "Yes, Viktor, you see through the charade of my optimism." He sighed. "Deep down I do fear the movement is much larger than Zhelyabov himself. That is why the constitution is so vital. I tell you, Viktor, the people—specifically the troublemakers—will not stand to be merely appeased. I have done what I could to stave off open rebellion and violence. But all my efforts have been built on the premise that we give the people what they are clamoring for and thus knock the wind out of their radical sails. Failing that, I fear in the end the masses of people who are now neutral will eventually throw their support to the other side."

"I believe it was de Tocqueville who said that the most dangerous moment for a bad government is usually when it begins to reform itself."

"I should like to remind His Majesty of that."

"Then I will soon have company where I stand *outside* the palace door," added Viktor with attempted humor. It felt good to crack a wry smile again.

Melikov shrugged. "I wouldn't mind your company, Viktor. But I am not quite ready to commit political suicide *yet*. I hold my tongue as well as I juggle."

He smiled grimly. "Time is of the essence, Viktor. Now that the terrorist threat has abated for a season, I fear Alexander will waver even more in his support of reform. What he began he is already shrinking back from."

He eyed Fedorcenko with an inquisitive eye. "You were close to him back when the reforms of his early reign were effected," he said after a moment. "How is it, do you think, that so much was accomplished back then?"

"Alexander is not the same man he was twenty years ago," replied Viktor.

"In what way, do you think?"

"Back in 1861, he could badger and cajole even the most hardheaded of nobles. Otherwise he would never have succeeded in abolishing serfdom. But his base of support eroded and has fragmented since then."

"Not to mention that he lacks the essential drive these days," added Melikov.

"Even back then, it took years of debate and study before we were able to bring about the fruition of emancipation."

"We don't have years now, Viktor. We can only hold the flood at bay so long." Melikov stopped abruptly. "And speaking of the time," he said, rising, "I must be off."

Viktor rose also, while Melikov gathered up some papers on his desk and slipped them into a leather portfolio. He walked around the desk and gave Viktor a brisk handshake.

"It was good to talk with you, Michael. I wish I could be of more help."

"Your day will come again, Viktor—if this government has any sense at all. Be patient, and circumspect. Don't give up yet. Good day."

When Viktor and Melikov parted, Viktor continued on to his own office. But there was no more for him to do there than there had been the day before, or the day before that.

Alone again, the mounting oppression began to weigh heavily down upon him once more. The conversation with Loris-Melikov had lightened the burden temporarily, but only accentuated his present impotence to be of any substantive help—to the governor-general, to the tsar, to anyone! Now, when the Motherland needed him most, he was useless.

He must live with the awful burden not only of having failed his son but his beloved homeland as well. He had done with his life just what Melikov feared the tsar would do to his throne. In a vain attempt to save a tiny stone, the whole fortress was in danger of crumbling.

Viktor poured himself a drink, downed it in a single swallow, and poured another. "Perhaps I should set myself as an example to His Majesty," he thought mordantly. "Perhaps, come what will, I should speak to him."

He had nothing to lose anymore. For the first time in his

life he could abandon all caution and say exactly what he felt. Yet as much as he mourned his nation's woes and his own impotence, what Viktor felt more than anything else was apathy.

Indeed, he had nothing to lose. But if he did chance to gain liberty for his country, what even did *that* matter? It could not bring back his son. And what was life or freedom or a constitution or anything else without that? Nothing else was anything to Viktor Fedorcenko.

He was a lost soul, as lost as his son in the faraway icebound reaches of Siberian Russia.

27

It had been only two months since his sentencing. It might as well have been two years . . . or two centuries.

What did time matter now? Time for Sergei Viktorovich Fedorcenko no longer existed. Time was a weight, an invisible ball chained to him, heavier than any burden that clung to his arms and legs to keep him from escape.

It seemed that he had been trudging northward forever. Already in flashing visions of insanity, as he desperately tried to recall her face, he found himself unable to remember what Anna looked like. He could see her body, her form, even her hair and hands and simple servant's dress. But the beautiful, wonderful, loving face would not come into focus in his brain, sending him into deliriums of panic and frantic, maddening frustration. The other faces of his former life, even those he loved so dearly, looked at him from a distance, receding from view into the fog of his past, a life he would never know again.

With every step northward and eastward he trudged, their faces grew smaller, their voices and laughter more faint.

Laughter . . . would he ever hear its sound again? Would he ever hope again . . . would he ever dream again . . . would he ever love again, except in the bitterness of his own past?

The same destiny overtakes all. The hearts of men are full of evil, and there is madness in their hearts while they live, and afterward they join the dead. Their love, their hate, and their jealousy have long since vanished; never again will they have a part in anything that happens under the sun.

Onward and upward he forced his weary feet, blindly following those ahead, heedless of those who came after him, condemned men all. Northward across the plains, upward through the snow-covered Urals, and downward into the great immensity of Russian Asia. Now he was separated from his past not merely by his crime, nor by the huge mountains rising from out of the lowlands as if to the very sky itself.

He was separated by an entire continent. He had left behind him the westernmost reaches of Europe, and with it the finest of Russian culture and history. Before him now lay only emptiness and desolation . . . ten thousand kilometers, from one end to the other, of Asian Siberia.

This was now his home . . . and would be until God showed mercy upon him and took life from him.

I saw the tears of the oppressed—and they have no comforter; power was on the side of their oppressors. And I declared that the dead, who had already died, are happier than the living, who are still alive. But better than both is he who has not yet been, who has not seen the evil that is done under the sun. And I saw a man all alone; he had neither son nor father nor mother nor brother. There was no end to his toil . . . and all was meaningless under the sun. . . .

What was there now to hope for, to fight for? The invisible tide of fate had quelled all hope, sweeping over him like a flood, drowning every dream. He was not only a prisoner of the state, but also a captive within the depths of his own being. For how can a man with no vision continue his struggle on the battleground of life without in the end becoming prisoner to his own lifelessness, bound on all sides by thoughts that have no escape?

How cruel are the scales and balances of life, tipping in favor of those whose only goal is to satisfy their greed and selfish ambition to get whatever they can, while others—provoked by deep yearnings of the human spirit to resist the injustices of life—find themselves grinding out their steps toward exile in a labor camp.

I have seen evil under the sun, and it weighs heavily on men. God gives a man wealth, possessions, and honor, so that he lacks nothing his heart desires, but God does not enable him to enjoy them. He snatches it away from him, and sets his feet to toil and labor and meaninglessness. What does a man get for all the toil and striving with which he labors under the sun? All his days his work is pain and grief; even at night his mind does not rest. All is meaningless, a chasing after the wind. Man's fate is like that of the animals; the same fate awaits them both: As one dies, so dies the other. Everything is meaningless. All go to the same place; all come from dust, and to dust they return. As a man comes, so he departs, and what does he gain, since he toils for the wind? All his days he spends in darkness. . . .

Sergei thought little about the options awaiting him. The mines of *Nerchinsk* near the Mongolian border—the Siberia of Siberia, where perennial ice freezes the landscape, even during the summer months—or *Kolyma*, the uttermost place of exile in the arctic netherworld of isolation. What matter to him where he went, or even if he survived past Tiumen or to the next holding prison at Tomsk? What matter to him whether he even lived to see a single speck of gold, silver, lead, or Siberian snow? If he prayed now, it was only that merciful death might take him while he was still young.

In the scant moments when his brain tried stiffly to function as it once had, he could not concentrate long enough on any one thought to make sense of it. His head hurt dreadfully, and in spite of the frigid temperatures, his body was hot and aching. He could not eat, although the taxing daily march depleted him of all stamina. Twice yesterday he had dropped to the ground. The first time brought a beating at the hands of a nearby guard until he again regained his feet. The second time he had gone unconscious before hitting the ground, and did not awaken for several hours, when he groggily became aware that he was bumping along on the bed of a rough wooden cart.

Whether he would make it through this day, he neither knew nor cared. He had managed to hold down a cupful of the foul gruel he had been given last night. He had slept tolerably and had awakened, if not with renewed energy, at least capable of holding his feet under him. But he could not keep from shaking with chills one minute, and burning from heat the next. And to make matters worse, he had picked up an irritating and itching rash all over his back and chest, and was starting to cough. Tiumen could only be a day or two away. All he needed was a few days rest. Not that it mattered how he felt. But this was misery itself.

Again the heat seized him and his brain began to spin. He shook himself, trying to clear his sight, but lights flashed before him.

Fleeting images whirled about through his head . . . sights that had no meaning, nonsense sounds . . . memories that stung his heart but whose features his mind could not fit into sequence.

Emotion swelled within him. Suddenly, for a brief instant, the visage of his beloved Anna came into view and stood indistinctly before him! He gasped, and his chest surged full. The face . . . he could just faintly make it out!

Deliriously he lunged forward, his arms outstretched. She was so close! If he could just clutch her for an instant . . . to shelter his bruised and beaten body in the warmth and innocent comfort of her precious embrace!

He stumbled toward her. *Anna . . . Anna!* he cried. But he could not even hear his own voice . . . *Anna!*

No! Her face . . . she was fading farther from him . . . *No, God . . . no! Anna!*

His hallucinating brain had deceived him! His heart wrenched in agony as he realized he was the victim of a wretched mirage. A thief had come to destroy the last remaining fragment of hope he possessed—sending the final weight of chaotic confusion against the fragile veil of reality that stood between him and insanity.

With a deafening, guttural wail of remorse, he threw himself to the ground, his arms still stretched toward the empty wilderness, begging to die.

"Hey, you blackguard!" yelled a nearby guard, leaping toward him. "None of your insolent sloth!" Without sympathy, and in cold-blooded determination to silence Sergei's pleas, he sent a cruel boot into the young prince's side, followed by several whacks with the club in his hand. "On your feet, you miserable scum!"

Sergei pulled his legs up under him and covered his head with his hands and arms, but otherwise surrendered to the would-be courier of death. Waves of nausea engulfed him in his last moments of coherence. As darkness closed over him, his final thought was that perhaps now this horror would finally come to an end.

When he next came to himself, he was on his feet, tramping wearily and listlessly forward as if the incident had never occurred. How or when he had again begun the death march, he could not imagine, nor did he even pause to conjecture.

His head pounded horribly within his skull. And try as he might, he could see Anna's face no more.

28

The little cheese shop on the Maly Sadovaya was doing a meager business that chilly Sunday morning.

The shop had opened for business only a few weeks previously and could hardly be expected to have much trade built up in such a short time. But, nevertheless, the proprietor could not have been expected to establish any business or handle the requests should customers begin coming his way. The shelves were but sparsely supplied with goods; three quarters of the rough planks were altogether empty.

The man's customary response to the few potential customers who stopped in to inquire after this or that was, "Ah, you know how it is to get on one's feet. But we will increase our stock very soon."

In truth, every kopeck of the strained budget was going to pay the rent on the shop. It was not likely any time in the near future that the quantity of cheeses on hand would increase. Supplying the people of the neighborhood with food was not the reason the store had been opened, nor did its owners care if it ever made a profit. They would not be in business that long.

The People's Will still had but one driving ambition. It had not changed in the year and a half since that summer in Voronezh. It had not been altered with Andrei Zhelyabov's imprisonment. *Tsar Alexander Nicolaivich Romanov must die!*

Rather than curtail their efforts with Zhelyabov in jail, the remaining leadership of The People's Will only resolved to intensify their labors, for Andrei's sake as well as for the cause. Toward that end they had procured a lease on the Maly Sadovaya storefront. They had no intention of becoming well-known cheese merchants. The location had attracted them for altogether different reasons. It lay along a route frequently traveled by the emperor when coming or going from the Winter Palace, in a relatively deserted area alongside one of St. Petersburg's broad and well-traveled avenues. In addition, it boasted a fine basement which, notwithstanding the sluggish trade above, had become a beehive of subterranean activity.

For some time the insurrectionists had been working in shifts, digging and burrowing like industrious moles. Zhelyabov himself had inspired the plan some time before. Now since his untimely arrest, his lover Sophia Perovskaya was carrying on his vision with fervor and determination. From the basement of the cheese shop, they had tunneled under the street, then dug a shaft straight up to within two feet or the surface itself, just wide enough to plant a powerful mine to be detonated at the precise moment the tsar's carriage came atop the shaft.

But Perovskaya had devised a backup plan to go along with the dynamite. She did not lack faith in Zhelyabov's idea, but there had been too many ironic twists of fate in the past to give her much faith in anything. This time, she determined to make sure. She was prepared to do it herself, if need be, although two or three others who knew of her resolve had already begged her to allow them to martyr themselves instead. The movement needed her, they insisted, to carry on until Andrei's release.

Perovskaya peered into the dark tunnel, the glow of a single lantern at the other end her only light. She shivered, not because of the cold—for it was many degrees warmer here underground than on the icy street above—but because she felt so very close to her long-cherished goal.

"How is it going?" she asked as she approached a figure crouched over a wooden crate.

Paul looked up, the lamp casting eerie shadows over his fine-featured face. "Very well, Sophia," he answered.

"Will there be enough explosives?"

"Not enough if we want to bring down the Admiralty, the Winter Palace, and Tsarskoe Selo. But it will do nicely for our purposes." Paul allowed a dry half-smile to accompany his mild attempt at humor.

"He attends the Mounting of the Guard every Sunday. He is sure to use this route within a few hours." She did not have to specify to whom she referred by *he*. They well knew the object of their labors.

"I am ready for him."

Sophia bent over and inspected the bomb as Paul tinkered here and there with the final wires and connectors.

"Andrei has taught you well, Pavlikov."

"It is a shame he won't be here for our final triumph."

"It may well be that before long we will be able to tell him all about it—*in person*." She straightened up, rubbing the small of her back as she did so. "I only hope that if I am arrested the charge will be *murder*. I could not bear to hang merely for the *attempt*."

"If this mine detonates anywhere near the tsar, it will kill him," said Paul. He did not mention, nor did he even pause to consider the fact, that it would also kill anyone else within a stone's throw of the blast.

Paul glanced over his work one final time.

"It is ready," he said. "All that remains is for me to raise it up into the shaft. Believe me, Sophia, it will blow the entire street apart from side to side!"

29

In spite of his innately melancholic nature, Alexander Romanov, tsar of Russia, found himself beginning to catch some of Loris-Melikov's optimism.

He was approaching his sixty-third birthday. He was in relatively sound health, except for his cursed asthma. He was at long last married to the woman he loved, and, if he had his way, she would be crowned empress before the year was out. His government was at last on a sure footing. Melikov had seen to that with his sweeping reforms. Some, of course, were more apt to refer to the governor-general's program as radical insanity. But it had gotten the job done. He'd known what he was doing by making the appointment, even if Melikov had been a bit pushy about the constitution. The city was safer than it had been in two years.

It had been a year, almost to date, since that dreadful explosion at the palace. And it had been that long since any attempt had been made on his person. Perhaps he was justified in breathing easier, lifting his head, and . . . well, he wasn't quite sure what he might do next. But surely it was time to begin enjoying life again.

A stray glance toward Melikov's draft of the constitution nearly dulled some of the gleam in his eye. He still was not completely resolved to the idea of being the ruler known for stripping the House of Romanov of its power, nor of being the first Russian *figurehead* monarch.

He hated the thought! The very word left an acrid taste in his mouth, especially when applied to him. He could not tolerate the possibility. He preferred the epithet that had been given to him twenty years ago—the *Tsar-Liberator*.

No, he would be no mere figurehead. He had insisted upon that proviso before giving the governor-general *carte blanche* to initiate reforms last year. In that vein, Melikov had devised a system by which the throne retained its essential power. Alexander hated to admit it, but that Armenian was a genius.

What the tsar refused to admit was that the new system did not even come close to the sweeping reform Russia needed, and needed desperately, if it were to survive. The very thing, in fact, that the radicals were crying out for. *That* would be going much further than Alexander would have been willing. He might be optimistic, but Melikov questioned how much good it would ultimately accomplish.

The proposed constitution broadened the powers of the *zemstvos*, but they remained local in structure, without any power to unify or, as elected bodies, to form any sort of national parliament. Melikov's scheme did include a provision for each local *zemstvo* to send a delegate to a national council, the *Gosudarstvenny Soviet*. But that body would be deliberative in nature, lacking any executive power.

Actually, from the tsar's point of view, the system was ideal. It provided the *form* of self-government, certainly as much or more than the Russian people could manage at that time in their history, but it kept the autocracy intact. Russia could never return to the days of Peter the Great, or even the iron rule of Nicholas I. Alexander was forward enough in his thinking to realize that. These were modern times requiring contemporary solutions to the problems of governing a complex assortment of people. Melikov's plan seemed to take all this into account, acting as a sort of bridge between the old ways and the new.

When Melikov entered his office later that morning, Tsar Alexander was thus in an unusually high-spirited mood.

"Good morning, General!" he said. "I trust you are well."

"Thank you, Your Majesty. Yes, I am. I am happy to see that you appear very well also."

"I am indeed, General! This is a momentous day for our country's future. You are here to deliver the Manifesto you have prepared, are you not, General?"

"Yes, Your Highness. I have it here."

Alexander took the paper from the general, gave it a brief glance, and laid it on the desk.

"Tomorrow," the tsar went on, "with all due ceremony, I shall sign it, making public our intention of presenting a constitution to the people." He smiled. "This *is* a grand day. It will put the rabble-rousers to rest once and for all."

"It is a great day indeed, Your Highness!" Melikov spoke with enthusiastic tone, giving no hint of his pessimism toward a plan which he still viewed as almost completely ineffectual.

"Now, I am afraid I must cut this audience short," Alexander said, "for I am expected at the parade grounds to review the Mounting of the Guard."

"You plan to go out today, Your Majesty?"

"I attend the Guard's ceremony every Sunday."

"It has always been advisable for you to deviate from fixed routines as much as possible, Your Majesty."

"I thought that was no longer necessary, as you had the most dangerous culprits in custody. Is the danger not past?"

"That is, ah . . . partially true. Yes, we have made significant arrests. Still, until the Manifesto is made public and the people are solidly behind us, I think caution would still be wise."

"I never took you for the fainthearted sort, General. I can understand my wife urging me to stay indoors. But coming from you, it sounds ludicrous."

"The princess has requested you to curb your activities?"

"Only this morning," answered the tsar. "But she worries unduly. Now, if you will excuse me."

"Your Majesty, I really feel I must urge you to—"

"Please, General—" The tsar cut him off sharply, though not angrily. He was in too good a mood to be easily upset. "I simply must go. Be here at nine tomorrow morning for the presentation of the Manifesto."

"Yes, Your Majesty." Melikov bowed and backed obediently out of the room. Alexander shook his head and shrugged. This was a new and promising day. No longer would he skulk about within the borders of his own realm.

He was the *tsar*, after all, ruler of the mightiest nation on earth! He called in Totiev and ordered up his carriage.

30

Michael Loris-Melikov, governor-general of Russia, second only to the tsar, walked away from Alexander's study with a heavy step and a heavier feeling in the pit of his stomach.

He had not been completely honest with the emperor about the successes with the revolutionaries.

Yes, he had captured Zhelyabov. He and several other members of The People's Will were behind bars. Zhelyabov had not talked. But Melikov, nevertheless, knew far more about the terrorists' movements than he admitted to the tsar. For others *had* talked. What they revealed was enough to put Melikov in deeper disgrace, if events conspired against him, even than Fedorcenko.

He had learned that they were mining the streets—the very streets of St. Petersburg! He did not have to guess how *that* would make him look in the eyes of the Crown! Even if no danger came of it, the very fact that he had allowed it to go on under their noses would reduce his standing in imperial favor.

He also knew that another dangerous leader was still at large—a woman by the name of Sophia Perovskaya.

Melikov needed time. A few days would do. He had to locate those mines and, more importantly, track down the Perovskaya woman. He had played down the danger to the tsar because he was so close to wrecking the entire ring of radicals. Yet he knew close was often not good enough.

Well, he *had* tried to warn Alexander.

What more could he do, short of admitting to his own deficiencies and the inadequacies of his police network, of course? At this delicate time, the less the tsar knew of any man's blunders or mishaps, the better off that man was. He did *not* want to end up like poor Viktor!

31

Sophia Perovskaya had placed a series of lookouts along the tsar's route to the parade grounds. Each was accompanied by a runner who would relay information of the tsar's movements as necessary. In some cases they signaled one another with flashes of light from mirrors.

She also had her backup plan in effect. At intervals she had posted men trained to deliver hand-thrown bombs if the underground explosion, for some reason, failed to kill the tsar.

Zhelyabov, assisted most capably by Paul, had adopted a new explosive compound using a purer form of nitroglycerine. It was far more dangerous than mere dynamite, and could be contained in a much smaller package. A parcel no bigger than a snowball could be concealed most effectively and do more damage than ten sticks of dynamite.

Each of Sophia's volunteers today carried such a tiny lethal package, prepared to use it if necessary. They all knew that the likelihood of the bomber himself surviving the blast was almost nil. But each was prepared to make the supreme sacrifice for the cause.

Sophia returned to the cheese shop. Paul was sitting in the

back room savoring the warmth of a glass of tea cupped between his hands. His calm demeanor should have reassured her, but it irritated her instead.

"How can you drink tea at a time like this?" she railed.

"Because I have been breathing the fetid air of that cold, damp, dirty tunnel for hours," replied Paul, "and I could not put my teeth together without grinding them like sandpaper."

If he had seemed calm to Sophia, it was only a momentary reaction to the one pleasant moment he had spent all day. Her remark had perturbed him, and the tone of his response did not hide the fact. His nerves were as taut as hers, and any calm produced by the tea quickly evaporated in the tense air between them.

"And everything is finished?"

"Yes."

"The fuse is where I told you to place it?"

"Of course. I know what I am doing, Sophia."

"I am only making sure."

"Zhelyabov and I went over it many times."

"You can see the lookout?"

"Everything is in order," he said flatly, then pointedly took a long drink from his glass.

"This *must* be the day, Pavlikov. Our time is running out."

"Andrei will never betray us."

"I know that. But we cannot be so sure of the others. Stepniak was also arrested, and he knows nearly as many details as Andrei. I feel in my bones that the police are closing in."

"We are still safe."

"I did not want to tell you this, Pavlikov, but yesterday they raided one of our flats where we have secreted supplies. They confiscated several kilograms of explosives. Thank God no one was there."

"Were there clues for them to find?"

"I hope not. But you and I have both been there many times, and it won't be long before the neighbors give descriptions and either Melikov's men or Vlasenko begin to piece together our movements."

This was not shocking news, at least in the sense that it was unexpected. But it did serve to cast their current efforts in a more final light. They could not fail today. It might well be their last opportunity.

"Then we must make certain nothing goes wrong today," said Paul, his previous calm returning to his tone.

32

At quarter to one in the afternoon, that second Sunday in March, Alexander Romanov prepared to leave the Winter Palace of St. Petersburg.

He kissed his new wife warmly, and asked her to be prepared upon his return for their customary Sunday stroll in the gardens. She tried once more to dissuade him from going out, but he merely shrugged off her words with light banter.

"Don't try to dampen my mood, my dear wife."

He took her hands in his and focused his eyes lovingly upon her for a brief instant, heedless of all the city's gossip and revulsion at his open love for her. "I am so happy at present, Catherine, that it almost frightens me."

Outside he was greeted by a pleasant winter's day. Frost hung in the air, and snow packed the ground. There had been no fresh snowfall for days, and he would thus be able to travel in the wheeled carriage rather than the sleigh.

A guard detail of six mounted Cossacks accompanied the carriage, with a seventh, Lieutenant Grigorov, standing on the coachman's box, rifle in hand, keeping vigilant watch. Two sledges followed the royal carriage. And the tsar's brother, the Grand Duke Michael, rode alongside on horseback.

The ride to the parade grounds proved uneventful. The ensuing hour of viewing the precision exercises of the Guard passed quickly.

Misha found himself wondering at the royal fascination with military drills. He supposed it gave an impression of security, however false, to know one's army could perform so well in ranks. If it only bore out with the same efficiency upon the battlefield!

The Cossack resumed his position in the carriage.

True, this was no battlefield, but agonizing experience had too often proved that even a peaceful St. Petersburg street could erupt into violence at any unexpected moment. He had saved the tsar's life once. He hoped he never had another such opportunity, but he could take no risks.

He gripped his rifle as if readying to meet a heathen Turk, and the carriage lurched into motion to begin the return journey through the streets to the Winter Palace.

As the carriage clattered steadily along, its wheels occasionally crunching across remaining patches of hardened snow, Misha kept his head roving slowly in all directions.

Peering into the distance, suddenly a flash of light caught his eye, then disappeared. He shouted at the driver to slow a moment. He squinted ahead, studying the area carefully. It must have only been the sun glinting momentarily off a window.

"Go on!" he called. Perhaps he was *too* vigilant, he thought. Yet these days, one never knew. He couldn't afford to let his guard down for an instant.

Even though it had proved to be nothing, Misha found himself still nervous after the incident. He therefore felt an unaccountable sense of relief when the tsar signaled the driver that he had decided not to go straight back to the palace.

Instead, he wanted to make a brief stop at his cousin's, the Grand Duchess Catherine's.

The carriage rumbled on through another long block, then veered sharply left along the new route. Misha Grigorov, Cossack guard to the emperor, immediately found himself breathing much easier.

His roving eye, however, continued scanning the street ahead.

33

Paul uttered a frustrated curse and leaped up.

He had slammed down the detonator the moment the lookout had signaled him of the approach of the royal entourage. Only silence had met his ears.

He spun around and flew down the stairs to the basement and toward the tunnel, heedless of the wires strung out along the floor.

Everything had been perfect. He had checked it only moments before!

There could not have been sabotage in such a short time! Only he and one or two others who were completely trustworthy had come near the bomb.

Just as he reached the tunnel entrance, suddenly a cat flew out of the dark, between his legs, and past him into the store basement. Paul groaned but hurried on. A moment or two's quick investigation revealed that a wire had been pulled loose from the bomb lodging above him in the shaft, whose bare end now lay exposed and useless on the tunnel floor.

Of all the idiotic luck! He had never given a thought to the cat that had wandered into the store one day and adopted the place as his home. Paul had been sympathetic toward the ragged, homeless creature and began feeding it from the meager scraps available. The miserable beast!

He spun around again. Was there still time to make a hasty repair? He bounded back up the stairs after the cat and ran to the window.

Mounted Cossacks rode even with the storefront, following the carriage that had already rumbled past. The prime opportunity had been missed! It was too late now to recapture it!

Angrily Paul kicked at the animal, then grabbed it roughly by the scruff of the neck, opened the door, and tossed it rudely into the street.

He closed the door, sat down for a moment, his face in his hands, dejectedly contemplating his failure. But he did not have long to wallow in his despair.

Shortly, the door opened, then slammed shut after a moment. There stood Sophia Perovskaya glowering at him.

"What happened!" she demanded.

Glumly Paul told her that their itinerant houseguest had tangled itself in the tunnel wires.

"Perhaps they will return by this way later, since it has proved safe," he said hopefully.

"Forget it, Pavlikov. They will not be back by here this day. Just clean up and lock the basement—it may be of use another day."

"Next Sunday?"

"Perhaps."

"But why wait?" said Paul excitedly. "Sophia, let me take one of the nitro bombs! There is still time for me to take up a position."

"Don't be a fool, Pavlikov. With Zhelyabov gone, I need you for more important assignments than getting your brains blown out. If today's attempt fails, the mines will need to be manned by someone who knows what he is doing."

"After such a miserable failure, how can you still say such a thing about me?" exclaimed Paul mournfully. "I let a stupid cat—"

"Don't worry about it," she said, her angry tone softening slightly. "It's passed. What's done is done. If we fail today, then we all share the failure."

Paul nodded in gloomy appreciation.

"And," she added, "if we succeed . . . then we all share that as well."

34

The imperial coach stopped at the Michaelovsky Palace, where the tsar called on his cousin Catherine.

He did not stay long. He only wanted to tell her personally about the Manifesto he planned to sign the next day.

It was half past two in the afternoon when the tsar's covered carriage and entourage began its return journey to the Winter Palace. Not many people were out along the street as they went. No one, not even the vigilant Cossack Lieutenant Grigorov, noticed the woman on the street corner near the *Ekaterinski*, otherwise known as the Catherine Canal. Neither did they notice as she raised the handkerchief in her hand, and instead of applying it to her eyes or nose, waved it up and down with two or three quick motions, then stopped.

Sophia Perovskaya herself had come to oversee this vital final leg of the tsar's journey, following the carriage as best she could from the cheese shop, and then waiting. She tucked the handkerchief into her pocket as she watched her volunteer assassins take up their positions. The street was uncommonly quiet and deserted. That concerned Sophia, for one of her colleagues, a long-haired student of geology, stood out dangerously. She hoped no one noticed the small parcel he clutched in his hand.

Without warning the imperial carriage sped up and hastened past the critical juncture. The geology scholar had just been ready to make his move, but the unexpected lurch of the carriage threw off his timing the second it took for him to miss his mark.

He hurled the bomb in his hand an instant too late for it to strike the imperial coach. It exploded instead in the midst of the trailing Cossack guards. Horses reared in the deafening explosion amid panicked whinnying. Several of the guards were flung broken and bleeding to the ground.

The force of the blast caught the royal carriage from behind. In the mayhem of the rocking earth and the wildly spooked horses, the carriage's back wheels splintered and it toppled over sideways, screams coming from within. The driver was thrown clear, uninjured. Misha, likewise, was thrown off his perch, but his head struck the icy street below and he lay unconscious.

Miraculously, with the help of the driver's assistant, the tsar climbed from the wreck unscathed. That he had once more defied the assassin's hand seemed unbelievable, yet clearly apparent. The grand duke likewise bore only a few bruises.

Only a moment later police sledges skidded to a stop at the scene and the hapless student was immediately seized.

"Come with me, Your Highness!" cried one of the gendarmes, running to the tsar and urging him to board his undamaged sled in order to rush him safely back to the palace.

"No, I will not leave until I have ascertained the condition of my poor wounded Cossacks."

He began making his way on with uneasy step back toward the site of the blast.

"Are you unhurt, Your Highness?" called out someone in the gathering crowd of bystanders that was pressing closer and closer.

"Thank God, yes I am," replied the tsar.

"Thank God?" repeated a sharp voice. It was a voice full of malice and derision. The tsar turned to see the man who had spoken as he broke free of the crowd and was now running toward him.

Alexander never saw the face of his assassin. The bitter words were no sooner out of the killer's mouth than he sprinted forward, pitching something toward the object of his hatred. It could have been a child's snowball, but it carried enough lethal power to shake the world.

The violent blast blew the martyr to bits. But his life was not given in vain. Even before the echo died away, the tsar of

Russia lay shattered beside him, stretched out in a pool of his own blood on the snowy St. Petersburg avenue.

The grand duke rushed forward and knelt down in the blood-stained snow. The tsar had just enough breath left to whisper a handful of words to his brother.

"Home to the palace, Michael . . . must die there . . ."

His final Imperial command was hastily followed. His broken body was carefully transferred to one of the waiting police sledges and rushed to the Winter Palace.

Less than an hour later, the last sacrament was administered. And in the bastion of the Romanovs, Tsar Alexander II of Russia went to join the tsars that had gone before him.

35

Black-shrouded carriages, in red and gold royal equipage, wound their way along the river embankment from the Winter Palace. The procession would creep for hours through the streets of Russia's capital before at length crossing the Troitsky Bridge. There it would reach its destination at the cathedral of the Peter and Paul Fortress, where Alexander's predecessors, all the tsars of the Romanovs, were buried.

The crowds of mourners along the street were silent, lulled, by the forlorn tattoo of drumbeats and the dolorous tolling of church bells.

Russia's "Little Father" was dead, felled by the assassin's hand. It was perhaps shock more than grief that darkened the faces watching the cortege. Alexander had never been immensely popular, and even what approbation he had enjoyed had waned considerably in later years. Perhaps it was true after all, what so many conservatives were now saying in guarded whispers, that what Russia needed, and really *wanted*, was a strong, firm leader.

The people of this huge land were children who required the security of firm discipline. They simply did not know how to follow a man like Alexander II, whose benevolence had appeared as weakness and whose attempts at despotism bordered on the laughable.

But this late ill-starred monarch, notwithstanding his deficiencies, was still the "Tsar-Liberator." Thus he *would* be remembered, though even that singularly supreme act of his reign was also marred by strife and imperfection. One French diplomat lamented at the funeral, "Oh, a liberator's task is a dangerous job!" Perhaps Alexander's major fault was that unlike his contempory and fellow liberator, Abraham Lincoln, he had outlived the glory of his grand deed.

Viktor stood on the fringes of the crowd with his friend Alexander Baklanov. Baklanov had commented that the general grief of the people was not perhaps as profound as it should have been for a dead monarch, and one of the half dozen or so most powerful men in all Europe.

"At least you have good reason, Viktor," said Baklanov sympathetically, "not to be pained by his passing. He could have interceded on behalf of your son. He could have granted him clemency. After all, you and he were friends for years. But instead, he turned his back not only on Sergei but on you, the most loyal friend a man could have."

"You are right, Alex," said Viktor pensively. "And perhaps that is why I am unable to conjure up enough outward show of anguish. But it has little to do with my son. You see, I have already grieved for Alexander long before this. It began, I suppose, with his destructive relationship with that woman. And after the war when he fell so low in public esteem."

Viktor paused and sighed. "It all changed him, Alex," he went on slowly. "He could have been a great man, a great tsar. But he sacrificed it all to personal whim. It seems to me that God might have in this way spared him from losing still more of his dignity and self-respect. His death can only be regarded as a blessing, Alex, if only the circumstances had not been so horrible."

Viktor Fedorcenko felt no bitterness for Alexander Nicolaivich, though he knew that his death sealed forever any hope of reprieve for Sergei. The new tsar was a stiff reactionary with whom Viktor himself had been at odds on many occasions. Alexander Alexandrovich, no matter how much he had himself argued with the former tsar, would not be favorably disposed toward the idea of leniency toward one who had wronged his murdered father.

Even worse, the *entire* royal family, the new Alexander III included, had been shown in a negative light in the scuttled writings of would-be author Sergei Viktorovich Fedorcenko. The new tsar had his *own* reasons for despising the author of *A Soldier's Glory*.

36

If Viktor Fedorcenko was in no position to make appeals to the new Tsar Alexander III, there were others who made attempts on behalf of their own causes.

The dead tsar's body was still fresh in its grave, and mourning still draped the Winter Palace, when Michael Loris-Melikov approached the tsar about the status of the constitution that had been so close to becoming reality. Melikov was no favorite of Alexander Alexandrovich, for the governor-general had gone too far in trying to curry the favor of Catherine Dolgoruky in order to wheedle his way further into the good graces of Alexander II.

Another obstacle faced Melikov in the person of Pobedonostev, who had long been tutor and close advisor to the tsarevich. Now, with his protege's ascension to the throne, he himself rose to great power. Melikov had tried in the past to win over Pobedonostev with cunning and manipulation, but never with much success. Now the past was about to blow up in his face. For it was Pobedonostev who answered Melikov's inquiry.

The tutor listened patiently to the governor-general's question, then rose in indignation, declaring that a constitution would signify the very collapse of Russia. His belief in the holy imperative of the monarchy was well known throughout St. Petersburg. But his angry passion this day far exceeded political orientation.

As Melikov stood by silently, the tutor pointed an aged finger out the window toward the Peter and Paul Fortress, where the dead tsar's body lay, and fervently cried, "It would be nothing less than desecration to reward the murderers of the late emperor in such a way. The action would shame all who would stand as men in this council!"

Even Melikov realized that Pobedonostev's words spelled the kiss of death for the governor-general's reforms. The new tsar was as conservative as he was dull and unimaginative. He was, if nothing else, a loyal pupil of his longtime tutor.

Pobedonostev spun around from the window, then snatched up a sheet of paper from a nearby desk.

"Listen to this, Melikov!" he cried. "These are the people you would give in to. Those cursed maniacs who call themselves by the absurd name The People's Will—this is what they have written to Alexander when his father's body is scarcely cold in its tomb. We received this yesterday."

He looked down for a moment, and then began reading.

> The tragedy enacted on the Ekaterinski Canal was not a mere casualty, nor was it unexpected. After all that had happened in the course of the previous decade, it was absolutely inevitable, and in that fact consists its deep significance for a man who has been placed by fate at the head of governmental authority.
>
> You are aware, Your Majesty, that the government of the late emperor could not be accused of a lack of energy. It hanged the innocent and the guilty, and filled prisons and remote provinces with exiles. But the revolutionary move-

ment did not cease—on the contrary, it grew and strengthened.

Whence proceeds this lamentable necessity for bloody conflict? It arises, Your Majesty, from the lack in Russia of a real government in the true sense of the word. The Imperial Government subjected the people to serfdom, put the masses into the power of the nobility, and is now openly creating the most injurious class of spectators. All of its reforms result merely in a more perfect enslavement and a more complete exploitation of the people.

From such a state of affairs there can be only two exits: either a revolution, absolutely inevitable and not to be averted by any punishments, or a voluntary turning of the Supreme Power over to the people.

And now, Your Majesty, decide! Before you are two courses, and you are to make your choice between them.

Pobedonostev paused, then added, "It is signed *The Executive Committee of The People's Will*."

He laid the paper back on the desk and glared at Melikov. "And you would have us bow to their ultimatum? No . . . no, my friend. That will not be my recommendation to Alexander!"

"Will you at least give me an audience with the new tsar," asked Melikov humbly, trying to hide his annoyance at the tutor's narrow viewpoint, "so that I might lay out my proposals in greater detail for His Majesty?"

"I will tell him of your request," Pobedonostev replied. "I can promise you nothing."

Indeed, nothing was promised, and nothing came of the interview. Less than two months after Alexander II's death, the new emperor published his own Manifesto, declaring a new course for his reign.

Pobedonostev's mark was clearly stamped throughout the document that amounted to a wholesale regression to Russia's commitment to Slavophilism, a determined refusal to accept any European form of constitutional government. It affirmed renewed dedication to all of what it termed the "old traditions," and carried a distinct undertone of Orthodox fervor.

The autocracy, with the supreme sanction of Almighty God, would continue to flourish in the Motherland of Russia.

As for Melikov, he had no delusions about his own continued longevity in the Imperial Court. Liberal thinkers would follow the same path as their liberal ideas—into the waste bins and onto the dust-laden shelves of obscurity and ignominy. Michael Loris-Melikov was slowly being forced into a position where he would have no choice ultimately but to resign.

His thoughts were consumed with irony. If he had been given but a few days he would have been a hero. If Alexander II had lived but one day longer, the Constitutional Manifesto would have been made public, and the whole history of Russia might have been changed.

There was another in the empire who also had a hope of altering history, but his way was perhaps even more impossible for the new tsar to fathom than Melikov's. Even while the young Prince Fedorcenko found himself in exile for his writings, the man whom he looked to as his mentor was attempting to wield his pen to speak for moderation and reason.

Count Leo Tolstoy wrote to the new tsar imploring him, for the good of the nation, to forgive the murderers of his father.

> Monarch! If you were to do this: were to call these people and give them money, and send them away somewhere to America, and write a manifesto headed with the words, "But I say, Love your enemies," I do not know how others would feel, but I, poor subject, would be your dog and your slave! I should weep with emotion every time I heard your name, as I am now weeping. . . . At those words, kindliness and love would pour forth like a flood over Russia. All revolutionary struggles will melt away before the man-tsar who fulfills the law of Christ.

The imperial response to this heartfelt, if euphemistic, plea was to lower the heavy fist of repression even harder than before upon the Russian people, especially those the dreamy author would have him forgive.

As for the murderers of the tsar's father, he would deal with them swiftly and certainly with no manifesto of goodwill. The woman with the handkerchief *was* noticed after the explosion, and as her eyes glowed in triumph from across the street, she had been taken into custody by two watchful gendarmes. Andrei Zhelyabov was taken from prison to join his lover Sophia Perovskaya and two surviving would-be bombers.

All four were condemned to the gallows.

37

Eighty thousand spectators gathered in the public square to view the hanging.

None of them knew that it was to be the last public hanging in Russia. They only knew that the prisoners to be executed were criminals of the vilest sort, for they had violently cut down their blessed tsar.

The irony utterly escaped them that these very criminals had fought for, cried out for, and indeed given their lives to free from autocratic oppression those throngs that now cheered their death. It mattered not to these masses that Alexander was less of a monarch than they might have wanted, or that he had been killed for opposing freedom.

He was the tsar! He deserved all reverence and homage, for he ruled by the very edict of God. Hanging itself was too kind a punishment for such evil emissaries of the devil as would take his life!

Scattered throughout the crowd were those who remained as a remnant of The People's Will. They had escaped the hangman's noose, but still lived in fear of arrest. Alexander and Pobedonostev had initiated purges that were now sweeping St. Petersburg. Only a few were willing to risk exposure this once in order to bid their brave and heroic leaders one final farewell.

For Paul Yevnovich Burenin—now cast adrift with neither mentor nor purpose—the pain of witnessing the tragic end of his comrades was a continuation of that awful ache that had never diminished from the day he had seen the neck of his friend Kazan snap. His mind had become so dulled with pain and loss that he could no longer distinguish who the real murderers were.

Yes, Andrei had planned it; Sophia had signaled to Yazkov, who had been blown senseless along with the tsar, and Remiga and Griggovski had been arrested at the scene. But if *they* had killed the tsar—so had *he*, although fate had prevented him from the honor of actually being present at the moment the blood had been spilled.

But they were not killers ... *murderers*! This was a war. Alexander Romanov was merely a casualty of the conflict. Perhaps Kazan and Zhelyabov and Sophia were also casualties.

If by such thoughts he justified the government along with his rebel brothers, then so be it. In this struggle, each side had its moral agenda and could equally defend its motives and courses of action. The revolutionaries said they must destroy the perpetrators of oppression and injustice. The government declared that it must ruthlessly punish treason and sedition in order to maintain peace and tranquility.

The arguments reminded Paul of the age-old proverb of origins, whether the chicken or its egg had come first. To Paul's mind—and he thought the same conclusion must be drawn by any objective and rational man—there would be no need of treason or sedition if a government handed out liberty and justice instead of slavery and corruption.

Thus, the government could defend its case all it wanted. But it would always reduce to the simple fact that there would be no revolutionaries if the government acted on behalf of the people instead of itself.

In the end, if this horrible struggle ever did have an end, the true heroes of the conflict for freedom would be those like Kazan and Zhelyabov and Perovskaya, not Alexander II of Russia. The heinous history of imperial atrocities would surely indict the monarchy and elevate the memory of all those who had fought against it.

At this moment, however, as Paul glanced nervously around him, it was all too clear that no one in this pressing throng would extol the praises of those dangling from the ropes in front of them. The vacillating mood of the people had swung back in favor of the monarchy, whether the emperor be Alexander II or Alexander III. Paul had no doubt that if it became known that he too was a member of The People's Will, those around him in the crowd would scourge him senseless and carry him forward to hang with his comrades, rejoicing in having done their patriotic duty.

The spontaneous uprisings of the people predicted by many radicals had not occurred. Nor would they. It had been wishful thinking from the beginning to believe the masses would fall in behind their loud outcries for change.

The imperial regime possessed a frightfully strong, almost hypnotic hold on the people. Many in Paul's circle blamed this on the Church. Orthodoxy and the mechanics of empire were so tightly interwoven as to be indistinguishable. And the people were so bound to the traditions of the Church that they could not, or were afraid to, separate the two. They were equally afraid to think for themselves. The priests and the tsar told them what to think, what to believe, and what to do. Theirs was not to question . . . only to think what they were told, and to obey.

It was becoming more and more apparent that it would take far more than killing the tsar to bring about radical change in Russia.

Those revolutionaries who had opposed the populist movement ten years before in the early 1870s had claimed that the people were not ready for any form of self-rule. Perhaps they had been right, after all. Not only were the masses not ready to govern themselves, it seemed they didn't even want such liberating change. Would the Russian people ever be ready?

In any event, it would take a long time—too long, perhaps years. In the meantime, the imperialist government would be free to run rampant, to add to its ever-lengthening list of atrocities, to further delude and enslave the weak-minded masses.

But change *must* come, whether the people were ready,

whether the people even wanted it or not! A new form of government must replace the rule of the Romanov tyranny—a new government unshackled by bondage to tsardom and the Church. A government committed to freedom for the masses, freedom and the right and power to rule themselves!

There had been times since the assassination that Paul was almost consumed with guilt over his miraculous escape from arrest. He had been nearby, but was not apprehended. He had even gone back to the cheese shop, and left only minutes before Vlasenko's thugs burst down its doors. Why ... why had he not been seen and arrested that day?

Not only had he been spared the rope, but he had also managed to slip through the tightening net of blanket purges carried out by the Third Section. And as he watched his comrades breathe their last that day, his guilt began to dissolve, giving way to a renewed sense of purpose.

He had been spared for a reason. Change must come! The people had to be made ready! The throwing off of oppression must not wait years!

The revolutionary movement could not die out, even with this massacre of its finest leaders! Someone must continue to carry the torch, to stir the people from their sleep!

He must not give up. If he could endure and hold on to the vision of freedom and change, perhaps all would not be lost. In time there would come renewed revolutionary fervor.

He and the few who survived must be ready!

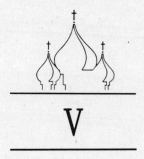

V

AFTERMATH OF DEATH
(Late March—Early April 1881)

38

Dull, blurry lights . . . muted moans . . . foul smells of bodies, urine, and sickness. Hot, cold, pain, and heaviness . . .

Then again the blackness.

Not the blissful blackness of peaceful sleep. It was the live blackness, the darkness visible, fire without light, the black flame that consumes not and cannot be quenched.

Again the voices . . . thin, vapory lights . . . groans of suffering . . . words that seemed familiar but had no meaning . . . names . . . sounds close by . . . hands touching him, lifting his head, pouring something down his throat . . .

In the pitiful conditions of a prison ward—with minimal medical supplies, meager rations, cramped, cold, dank conditions, and men huddled together on makeshift cots—Sergei endured the deathlike agony of his fever. Hardly alive enough to pray for death, not dead enough to escape the prolonged and inescapable suffering, he merely existed, scarcely human at all.

The bright uniform of the prestigious Guard Regiment unit that he had once worn with such dignity had long since turned to rags and been replaced by drab gray. The light in his eyes and the noble bearing of his countenance and stature had disappeared. The fire of passion had gone out. The broad, straight shoulders had become slumped and thin. The manly body now lay feverish, shrunken, and wasted. The virile brain of author, thinker, and lover was scorched and void.

Around him were thieves, murderers, and insurrectionists, on their way—like him, if they survived—to the mines and prisons of the east. Attempting to purge the land of troublemakers and treasonous notions, the government of the Alexanders was unwittingly throwing into a cauldron of apprenticeship the anarchistic ideas that would ultimately seal its doom. The prisons and work camps of Siberia were, in fact, training an entire new generation of revolutionaries, and many of the forerunners now awaited their transport in the cells or sick wards of Tiumen.

Already in the east, listening for the first cuckoos of spring to send their calls through the desolate snow-enshrouded forests, convicts throughout Siberia were making ready to join "General Cuckoo's Army," the yearly migration west of escapees. Those clever enough to bribe, kill, or con their way out of the mines, over or under the prison walls, or through the gates manned by unscrupulous guards, were lucky if they remained alive long enough to enjoy their freedom. Without provisions, and thousands of kilometers from friendly faces and hospitable climates, most died along the way. Yet every spring thousands more made the attempt.

Those just on their way, however, were watched more closely, and few would swell the Cuckoo's ranks this spring, especially those ensnared by the rampant epidemic of fever. Men, women, rebels, and robbers alike were struck down and now lay prostrate, thinking of no escape other than sleep ... or death.

If sleep cannot be had for the fever, thought Sergei as gradual sensations of semi-reality and blurry consciousness began to return to him, *perhaps death might be accomplished by taking eternity into one's own hands.*

Sergei's mind filled with the ecclesiastical broodings of Solomon, the despairing son of David whose great wisdom, like this prince's own attempted writings, had left him desolate, alone, and full of meaninglessness: *For the living know that they shall die; but the dead know not any thing, neither have they anymore a reward, for the memory of them is forgotten. Meaningless! Meaningless ... Everything is meaningless!*

What was life but meaninglessness, a chasing after the wind ... futility and folly? Yes, there was a time for everything. A time for war, a time to speak, a time to weep, a time to kill. He had done them all. They had brought him here. For him there would be no time for peace, no time to laugh, no time for healing. There was only a time to live ... and now to die. What could life be, when to recover meant only a doomed existence of backbreaking servitude? Better to end it now. To think of a future commission in the Cuckoo's army was a futile hope. Why wait? Escape—a complete escape, a glorious escape from this cesspool of stench and cold and vermin infestation—could be had ... now! All it would take would be a moment or two when the fellow dressed in white had his back turned....

Sergei struggled to lift his aching head two or three centimeters off the filthy mattress and rolled his eyes to the left and right, trying to make some sense of his surroundings.

If only his opportunity would come before the hot spells and shaking and delirium returned. It was suddenly all so clear! His brain was functioning again. How long had he been in this vile place? How could he have forgotten everything? He had even forgotten who he was ... how long had it been since he had remembered?

But now he *did* remember! His focus was back. And with it the clearheaded determination of what he must do.

If only he could get to that table on the other side of the room where the man's instruments lay. There he was sure to find something sharp enough. If only he had the needed strength to plunge it deep into his flesh!

His head fell back, his breath coming in short gasps now. Sitting up had been exhausting. The flashes were coming back ... he blinked several times, trying to regain the clarity of vision.

The fever was coming upon him again! It had to be now, or who could tell when another opportunity might come! He was only seconds away from the table where he could leave his suffering forever ... only seconds away from bliss and comfort and rest!

With a mighty gargantuan effort he hoisted himself to a sitting position, sweating from the effort and anticipation. His lungs gasped for air. He glanced around. The room, the ceiling, the lights, the man's white uniform—all spun in mingled disarray. Frantically he shook his head and blinked again, trying to keep them still.

He lifted his feet over the side of the cot. As the skin of his bare feet touched the dirt floor, he felt as though he were standing on a glacier. But his head was on fire . . . and he could not stop himself from shaking.

There was the man . . . his back still turned . . . or was it his back? He was still dressed in white . . . he was wearing a robe . . . a robe of white . . . now he was coming closer . . . it must be an angel come to welcome him!

Sergei had not stood for weeks. His knees shook, but he would steady them . . . the table was only five meters away . . . five meters to escape . . . to peaceful sleep!

He lurched forward . . . one step, two, three . . . heedless of the buckling of his knees . . . conscious only of flashing, spinning lights and figures and shapes, all now blurring into dreamy confusion and distortion.

Voices . . . shouts . . . that name he no longer recognized as his own . . . Hands grasped at his shoulders . . . unfriendly hands . . . tugging and pulling . . . hands of ice and fire.

He shoved, and with one last summoning of some memory of the energy of his former life, he pushed the intruding angel from him, then stumbled forward, crashing onto the table. Even as his legs gave way beneath him, he felt his hands close upon the instrument of death.

He collapsed onto the floor, breaking the table. Wood, instruments, tools, and a pitcher of water shattered around him in a great din of chaotic clatter.

Unaware of the shouts now filling the room, or of the approach of still more white-robed angels, or of the blood now running freely from the hands clutching the surgically honed steel blade on the wrong end, he groped with fading strength to bring the wicked knife in one fatal blow into his chest.

And still there were calls . . . and shouts . . . and grabbing, pulling, unwelcome hands . . . until the spinning lights slowly dimmed . . . and the voices dissolved. . . .

His head fell against the blood-muddied floor . . . blackness engulfed him . . . and he knew no more.

39

Basil Anickin cursed the inept failure of The People's Will. How naive they all had been! The death of the tsar meant nothing. If anything it signified a regression, and put them in an even weaker position than before. Whatever support they might have had from the people, they had all but lost now. And the new tsar's repressive reaction had decimated their numbers to but a fraction of what they had been two years ago.

All this, however, was only a small part of Basil's frustration in the aftermath of the tsar's assassination. Anickin had not fallen in with The People's Will after his escape from prison primarily because of shared vision for revolution, but merely out of expediency. His objectives were then, and remained now, entirely personal. What did the tsar matter to him? What did revolution matter to him? Revenge tormented his sinister mind.

The only thing that did matter is that his previous plan calling for the demise of the House of Remizov would have to be altered. The masses would not rise to follow the rebels. The tsar had been killed, there had been four hangings and a city-wide purge of the radical element, and that was that. No riots. No bombings. No mass attacks on the aristocracy. St. Petersburg slept.

He would not have the convenient cover of a popular and mass uprising to shield his murderous activity. He would have to find some other way. The risk to himself would be greater. And he would also have a much more difficult time enlisting anyone from the organization to help him.

Basil ground his teeth to admit that he was going to need

help at all. What pleasure it would give him to feel the noble whelp's neck between his fingers, squeezing the life out of him, until he gave it a final, lethal snap! But a frontal, man-to-man assault would never work. He had learned that lesson too well last time. He was not willing to risk getting his *own* neck snapped, and the coward was of unnatural strength.

However, if he could find no one, if forced to that extreme, he would brave the consequences even of exposing himself to such peril. He would not take him on frontally this time. He would attack with stealth. The element of surprise would be his ally.

He fully intended to survive and gloat with satisfaction over the demise of both the hated Remizovs!

The plan he would use to achieve the greatest appeasement of his hunger for revenge was simple.

First he would kill the princess. Katrina's beautiful face still haunted his waking and dreaming memories. With an acrid bitterness her rejection still stung the deepest core of his being. But she would pay for what she had done!

And then he would watch her blackguard of a husband suffer, and suffer cruelly, at her loss. He might even let Remizov know he had taken Katrina's life himself. He would attend the funeral, and show himself more frequently, perhaps enticing Remizov into the attack.

He rubbed his hands together and grinned at the thought of Dmitri's bloodshot eyes and anguished countenance. He would tip his hat and smile knowingly at him from afar, steadily driving Remizov insane at the loss of his true love!

And then, when Count Remizov had suffered sufficiently—not that any amount of suffering would make up for what *he* had been through!—then, but not before, Basil would find him alone in some black recess of the city, on his way home late one night. He would strangle the life out of him, whispering the hateful venom of his bitterness in his ear until finally would come the moment of supreme satisfaction when he would break the blackguard's neck and drop him in the darkened alleyway—dead like the snarling, mongrel outcast of a cur he was!

But as satisfying as it would be to kill them both with his

bare hands, he would rather sacrifice a bit of the satisfaction in order to be assured of success. The logistics of the plan were going to require care. A bomb was the safest and surest way. He needed someone adept with explosives to assist him.

The first candidate that came to Basil's warped mind was Zhelyabov's young protege, the fellow named Pavlikov. As far as Basil knew, the man had survived the post-assassination purge. But whether he would be willing to take the risk under the current conditions, Basil didn't know. What Basil did know of the young Pavlikov was only that he was something of an idealist. There would thus have to be some ulterior motivation to lure the young man into the web of Basil's scheme.

Fedorcenko might prove useful in that regard. It would be but a small matter to imply that the death of an imperial minister would benefit their cause. He would merely have to strike at a time when Katrina was known to be visiting her father's house.

Notwithstanding its simplicity, there were many inherent difficulties with the plan. But he would surmount them. Basil had come too far to fail now. He had only to approach the shining objective of his eventual triumph step by step. He must not allow emotion to cloud his logic.

His first task, therefore, was to locate Pavlikov, if he was still in the capital.

40

Several days after the hanging, Anickin found Paul in one of the dark and disreputable taverns on Maly Prospect on Vassily Island.

The young protege had not been easy to locate. He had changed his name again and was living—if such it could be called—in alleyways mostly, or almshouses when he had been fortunate enough to find such accommodations.

Anickin's own lodgings were hardly better now since there were fewer citizens sympathetic enough to assist fugitive radicals. But he had lately found a woman of low repute who agreed to keep him in her tenement apartment. He was certainly faring much better than Pavlikov.

The younger man had a drawn, hungry look about his features. Anickin wondered when the man had last eaten. A starving revolutionary would be a definite asset to his purpose, but he could not have the man fainting on him in the midst of their important task. Therefore, as Anickin slipped onto the rough bench opposite Paul at a table in a dark corner, he called a drab-looking servant girl over and ordered a copper's worth of brown bread to accompany their kvass.

"I have no money," said Paul flatly.

"We are brothers, Pavlikov," said Anickin. "You need no money when you are with me."

"You don't look much better off."

"What I have I share."

"Why?" It was the first time Basil had shown the slightest interest in, much less friendship for, Paul. His suspicion was natural.

Basil smiled—not a handsome smile, for it suffered greatly from disuse and evil intent.

"Caution is our greatest ally in these dangerous times," he said cryptically, then paused as the girl brought their bread and drink to the table. He shoved the plate of bread toward Paul, who hesitated only a moment before grabbing up a chunk. He would worry about his suspicions later. It had been days since he had eaten something not pilfered from a garbage bin.

"Of course you must wonder if I have some purpose in seeking you out," Basil went on after a moment's silence.

"I do."

Basil glanced furtively around, then lowered his voice. "You must know that our task is not finished," he said. "We may have killed the tsar, but it is clear that we failed to elicit the public response we desired. There was a reason for that, Pavlikov—because a new tsar was at the ready to step in."

He looked at Paul with deep furrows etched into the lines of his forehead. Paul said nothing.

"Surely you see what I mean—the reins of government only slackened. We will never succeed until we interrupt the entire process of the governmental system."

"Are you saying we must kill the new tsar?"

"That, of course, should be our long-range goal. But we are far from ready for that now. It will take months, perhaps years, to build our strength back enough to undertake another attack on the emperor. In the meantime, we must strike where we can. Wasn't it Zhelyabov who said we must do whatever we have the strength to do?"

Paul nodded, thinking to himself how clever it was of Anickin to bring Zhelyabov's name into the conversation. It lent, if nothing else, a certain nobility to whatever point he was about to make.

"What are you proposing?" asked Paul, not even bothering to mask his innate suspicion.

"We must continue to mount terrorist attacks upon government officials. The death of the tsar only garnered public sympathy for the Crown. But the loss of a few aristocrats and government officials will not. That's where The People's Will made its mistake, Pavlikov. We rushed the assassination. The masses are not yet sufficiently educated to accept the necessity of doing away with the Crown altogether."

"Then perhaps we should concentrate our efforts on education—printing the pamphlets necessary to continue getting this message out," suggested Paul.

"No, we must forget the people altogether—for now. Terror is the only effective commodity of revolution. It was that and that alone that finally brought Alexander to the point of approving a constitution."

"But we don't want a constitutional monarchy."

"True. But the point is, terror is the only effective tool by which to achieve change, to achieve our ends—whatever they may be. And it is a tool we must continue to wield."

"I take it you want to enlist my services?"

Anickin nodded.

"And others?"

"Of course. But I believe you are the key. You learned all Zhelyabov's techniques, and that is what we need just now. I know nothing about explosives, wires, fuses, charges, detonators. You do."

"What you are saying rings with a certain clarity," mused Paul. Even to himself he had to admit that it did, despite the fact that it came from a man who had proven himself a lunatic. For that very reason, it was extremely unlikely that he would ever see his way clear to join forces with Anickin. But it couldn't hurt to hear him out.

"Then you will join me?"

"I don't mind taking a few risks," answered Paul. "But I doubt we would get very far in the present atmosphere in St. Petersburg."

"That's the genius of it! Now is the perfect time. Everyone's guard is down. The last thing they will suspect is more violence with the police vigilance at such a high peak just now."

"With good reason!"

"We will strike first on a low-risk subject."

"And who would that be?"

"Prince Viktor Fedorcenko."

Of course! Suddenly everything came clear to Paul in an instant. He had suspected some devious motive behind Anickin's sermonizing, and here it was as plain as day—his old vendetta against the Fedorcenkos. It was pure chance that he had been drawn into his scheme. But now that he had, he must consider carefully his response. It was sure to affect lives, and could even touch his sister.

For now, he would appear to go along with the man, if for no other reason than to keep fully apprised of his movements and thus keep Anna out of danger. But he'd have to watch himself. If Anickin suspected him of mixed motives, no doubt he'd end up floating in the Neva.

"Yes . . . that does seem a logical choice," said Paul after a pause, during which he had covered his deliberations with renewed interest in the food. He finished off the last of the bread, not even thinking to offer the last morsel to Basil. "I'll help out as long as we don't hurry the job," he added. "I want to come out of it alive, if possible."

"Good. That is a reasonable request."

"When do we start?"

"Soon."

"I'll have to get supplies, and that won't be easy. Also, we may need one or two others to help. Explosives are a complicated business."

"I'll take care of that."

"How shall I contact you?"

"We will meet in two days at that tavern we used to use on Grafsky Lane."

The two conspirators rose from their seats. As they did so, Paul caught a troubling glint in Anickin's eye.

He was treading dangerous ground associating with this man. He'd heard stories. Some said he was still crazy. If Paul was smart, he'd quit him as quickly as possible.

In any event, he must warn Anna immediately, even if it endangered his own life.

And he had no delusions as to his own safety if he foiled Anickin's plans. Only a miracle, if he still believed in such things, would be able to save him from the madman's wrath then.

41

The boy could not have been more than ten. He was filthy, lean, and ragged, with an expression not altogether innocent.

He would have been an object of pity anywhere. But in the

fashionable South Side, his raggedness stood out all the more against the clean and spotless backdrop of wealthy homes and estates. He received more than one piteous glance from passersby, although one man soundly boxed his ears when he tried to stop him to ask directions.

He found the Remizov home regardless.

The cook received him with the kind of welcome one might reserve for a common thief. On the street she might have given him a copper if she had one to spare. But it was unseemly for such a ragamuffin to approach her master's door, even if it was the *back* door.

Visibly perturbed, she told him to wait while she fetched Anna. For on top of everything else, the boy's message had to be delivered verbally and directly to Anna and no one else.

The message was puzzling, if simple.

The boy told Anna he had been instructed to tell her to come to St. Andrew's on Vassily Island at four o'clock that afternoon. He could not tell her who it was from because he did not know.

Anna told Katrina about the odd messenger and his mysterious message when she asked the princess permission to leave later in the afternoon.

"I think it must be from my brother," Anna said none too enthusiastically.

"Aren't you glad? Isn't it well over a year since you last saw him?"

"Yes, Princess, and that is why I am worried. The note is secretive. He doesn't leave his name, though I am certain it is from him. What can it mean but that he is in trouble?"

"Where is your faith, Anna?" Katrina spoke gently, in a tone of entreaty. "Even if he is in trouble, isn't it a hopeful sign that he chose to meet you at a church?"

"I hadn't thought of that, Princess."

Anna attempted a smile, although these days they did not come as easily as they once did. It faded just as quickly, however. "I don't think I can bear any more troubling news just now about young men I happen to love."

Katrina took Anna's hand in hers and gave it a firm squeeze. She needed to say no more to express her sympathy. The last weeks had been difficult for both of them. A few more details had filtered in regarding Sergei's sentence.

He had been sentenced to twenty years of hard labor, followed by life in exile—that is, *if* he was fortunate enough to survive the labor camp, which many did not. Gradually, over the dreary days and weeks, both young women had reluctantly been forced to accept the inevitable. Neither of them would ever see Sergei again.

The thought that now there might be some tragedy involving her brother was a burden that Anna doubted she had strength to endure.

"Would you like me to go with you, Anna?" asked Katrina at length.

"Thank you, Princess, but I think I had better go alone. I do not think he would want any undue attention drawn to him. If someone were with me, he might leave without ever talking to me."

Katrina nodded. "I understand. I will be praying for you while you are gone."

Anna smiled. More than ever she was thankful for her mistress. She had matured with the prospect of becoming a mother. And the faith of the princess, the inner calm that had gradually become part of her bearing, was a marvel all its own. She hardly knew it, but by her newfound inner strength, the princess helped to sustain Anna through this dark time.

"If nothing else," Anna said, "I will be able to light a candle for him while I am at the church."

42

The days grew longer as April spring progressed.

It was still light when Anna made her way through the market near Maly Prospect. Dusk would soon descend upon the city, however, and she clutched her cloth-wrapped parcel tightly to her. She hoped her errand did not take her past dark. She had a few kopecks with her for a *droshky*, but in this part of the city they were not always readily available.

She began to feel some comfort when she caught sight of the drab old walls of the cathedral on the other side of the market. The church was busy that afternoon. Many were still offering prayers for both the dead tsar and his successor. She found herself hoping, for her brother's sake, that there were some benevolent voices interceding for the revolutionaries as well.

The light from many burning candles helped her eyes adjust quickly to the dimness as she walked inside. Thirty or forty worshipers knelt at the altar, their subdued voices filling the vacuous building with a low chanting hum. A score of others milled about the great high-vaulted room, some conversing quietly with one of the priests, others standing with their own thoughts and prayers. Some seemed to have wandered in merely to seek a few moment's respite from the chilly winds outside. One shabbily garbed man lay in a corner, propped against the stone wall, sound asleep, his snores blending almost harmoniously with the prayerful intonations coming from the front of the church.

Anna glanced about, hoping to see a familiar face. The church bells had tolled the hour about ten minutes ago as she made her way across the street. She knew the time was right. But she saw no one who reminded her of her brother.

Slowly she began to wander through the church, looking about inconspicuously every now and then.

The sound that jarred her from her inward thoughts was no more than a whisper.

"Anna . . . please—do not be startled."

She turned toward the voice.

"Oh, Paul! I so hoped it would be you!"

She threw her one free arm around him. He did not retreat from her, nor rebuke her affection. Rather, he seemed for a moment to want nothing more than to melt into her—desperate, hungry for the sisterly love she had to offer, for *any* kind of love.

The tender mood between them lasted but a moment. He appeared to catch himself and then withdrew abruptly from her.

As he stepped away, Anna focused more fully on her brother. His appearance had deteriorated noticeably since the last time she had seen him. His clothes were threadbare; the long wool overcoat could barely warm a man even in the milder spring weather that would soon be on the way. Paul was thin and gaunt, and the dark circles under his eyes hinted at too many nights spent on the hard cobbles of dirty alleyways.

Anna's initial joy at seeing him was replaced with a terrible ache. Tears welled up in her eyes. Even if she had wanted to show restraint for his sake, her emotions these days were too close to the surface to command much control. She could not keep from crying.

"Paul . . . how have you been?" She wiped her eyes hastily, thankful for the darkness of the church. Paul would not appreciate being pitied! "I have thought so much about you and prayed you'd come to see me. Are you well? Can I do anything for you?"

Her words poured out in a rush, as if it would be possible to make up for a year's absence in a few moments. Paul detected her nervousness and knew she was uncomfortable with how he looked.

"Anna," he said, "there is no time for pleasantries." His

voice was strained and hard around the edges, as if he were battling with his own ambivalence at the reunion.

"Please, Paul, don't do this to me! You are my brother, and I love you. You can't expect to ask to see me and then think I will not care about you." Frustration and hurt were more evident in her tone than irritation.

"I can tell you nothing about myself," replied Paul, still distantly. "You wouldn't want to hear it even if I were at liberty to tell you. As far as how I am—I couldn't lie if I wanted to. You can see for yourself, can't you?"

"Let me help you, Paul."

"It is too late for that," he replied bitterly. "I didn't send for you to beg for help—"

"You never have to beg, Paul. I am your sister."

He shrugged but said nothing, obviously unwilling to open himself further to the risk of her generosity. He took her arm lightly in hand and directed her to a more private corner.

They came to a little alcove no larger than a small stall in a barn. Paul stopped, then led her inside. It was open on the side that faced the interior of the church, but there was no one nearby, so they could talk in relative seclusion, though they still kept their voices in whispers.

"Anna," he began, "I asked to see you for one reason only..."

He hesitated, as if he regretted saying the word. But he did not correct himself.

"I have certain connections in this city, Anna," he went on. "People from whom I hear things and obtain information—things that are unknown to most people."

Again he paused. Anna stared deeply into his face, waiting.

"Recently I heard something I felt I ought to pass on to you. It regards your employers—I believe your mistress is now Princess Remizov."

Anna nodded, a perplexed look on her face.

"Do you know the name Basil Anickin?"

Anna's shocked gasp was answer enough.

"I see you do, and undoubtedly understand the danger this man represents."

"But how do you know all about this, Paul?"

"I cannot answer your questions, Anna. I do know, and that is enough. Suffice it to say that I know of this man, and I know of his cause against Princess Remizov and her husband. But what you may not be aware of, Anna, is that Anickin recently escaped from prison—"

"No! Paul . . . is this true?"

"It is true," Paul replied, almost evasively. It was clear to Anna that he wasn't saying all he knew. But she also realized the futility of trying to get information from him that he was unwilling to give. "You must also know," he went on, "the danger this implies to your employers."

"But surely, after all this time . . ."

"Oh, Anna! Your naivete is both your greatest virtue and your greatest fault. Time does not heal all wounds, especially where a man like Anickin is concerned. His wounds have only festered and become all the more virulent and dangerous in the time that has passed. He is, I believe, consumed with a passion for revenge."

"How do you know all this, Paul?"

"Do you not believe me?"

"No, Pavushka, it's not that." Anna shook her head. She *was* naive. It was simply unimaginable for her to conceive of such destructive animosity.

"Anna, I tell you the truth—this man means to harm, even to *kill* your mistress and her husband—"

Anna could not keep from sucking in a breath of air at the shocking words, but Paul continued.

"I am telling you this because . . ."

He faltered momentarily. When he spoke again, his lips trembled slightly. "I tell you because you are my sister."

"Is . . . is there nothing to do?" said Anna, still in disbelief.

"I suggest you warn Remizov."

"I will tell the princess," Anna replied.

"I . . . I may be able to keep somewhat apprised of his movements, and can possibly let you know should the danger become imminent. But I can promise nothing. They must take great care."

"If we knew where he was, perhaps the count could have him arrested now before there is worse danger."

"I don't know how to find him. He too is a fugitive."

"He . . . *too*? What does that mean, Paul?" said Anna with fearful tone.

Only then did Paul realize his error. He closed his eyes and shook his head. "No questions, remember?"

"Paul," implored Anna, "you warn me of others' danger, but what of your own? Do you not trust me, that you are so secretive?"

"Trust, Anna? Trust has nothing to do with it."

"Then what *does*, Pavushka?"

"Oh, Anna, you are so sheltered from the real world. My dear sister, don't you even realize what you are saying? You call me *Pavushka*, but I am not that boy any longer. You don't even realize that merely *talking* to me as you are now could land you, and perhaps our whole family, in a Siberian prison. I isolate myself because I must."

"But—"

"There can be no argument. I am an exile without even leaving Russia—"

At the word *exile*, Anna's eyes involuntarily closed and a shudder coursed through her frame. One beloved exile was intolerable. Two, and she would break in half from sorrow!

"This is how it must be," Paul was saying, "how I have chosen it to be."

Anna drew in a deep breath and tried to compose herself. "These things you believe must be very important to you," she said, "if you would forsake everything for them."

"They are," he answered emphatically.

"Then I appreciate all the more the risk you have taken to warn Princess Katrina and her husband."

"Please understand me, Anna. One aristocrat more or less means nothing to me. But because you are involved, I feel duty bound to speak to you."

Again Anna closed her eyes at the cruelty of his words. But only for an instant. She opened them again and did her best to say nothing that would offend him. "I understand, Paul . . . thank you."

But did she understand? No, how could she ever understand such a change in one she cared for! *Oh, dear Paul . . . how hard-*

ened you have become! Yet I see the pain and sorrow in your eyes. There is still a deep vulnerability in you; all my heart can do is weep for you. You want to be loved just as I do, but you have closed your heart off to everyone! Why do you need to protect yourself with such a hard shell, when we—

"I must go now," said Paul abruptly, breaking into Anna's thoughts. "We have already been together too long."

"When . . . When will . . . ?" Anna tried to form the question.

"With the police stalking Anickin, he has plenty on his mind. I think your count and princess have time to prepare themselves."

"What should they do, Paul?"

"The count is a Guard. Let him figure out best how to protect himself. Now listen to me, Anna. If I think you must act quickly, I will get a coded message to you. It will say, *The harvest is ripe*. If you hear that, you must be especially vigilant. Anickin will probably be on the loose and prowling around getting ready to make his move."

"I will look for it, but hope it never comes."

Paul turned to leave. But Anna caught his arm. "Wait, Paul . . . I almost forgot. This is for you." She handed him the package she had been holding.

He frowned. "What is it?"

"Some spare things from the pantry—"

"I need no aristocratic handouts!"

Finally Anna's sadness for Paul reached its limit. "Don't be so stubborn!" she snapped. "You hardly look in the position to turn away a little food."

Their eyes met for a moment or two in a brief battle of wills. Anna's frustration with Paul's intractability, now that it had spilled over, put her immediately in the stronger position of older sister she had always occupied with him when he was younger. Neither would ever know to what extent she was prepared to stand up to him now, for it only took another second or two for the gnawing hunger in Paul's stomach to make him give in.

He reached out and took the parcel.

"Thank you, Anna," he said, not exactly with a smile, but at least with a serious look of gratitude.

She smiled. Their hands touched as he laid hold of the parcel, and her fingers lingered on his for a brief moment.

He turned to go once more, then paused again. He opened his mouth to speak, but it seemed to take a moment before he could master his rising emotions enough to utter the words that were trying to get out of his heart.

"Anna," he said, "how is . . . Papa?"

"He is better, Paul," she answered. "He needs to rest much more, but he has a helper who comes during the sowing and harvest."

"How is that possible?"

"Prince Fedorcenko has made it possible. After I was home a year and a half ago and the prince learned of Papa's troubles, he said he wanted to do something for my father. So Papa had help last harvest." Anna hoped her answer did not sound smug and would show Paul that not all the nobility were evil and selfish.

Paul nodded. He seemed to have understood. "Thank you for telling me," he said quietly, somehow implying without words that he knew he did not deserve her patience. "Goodbye, Anna."

"Godspeed, Paul!"

No more was said. Anna desperately wanted to hug him. But Paul turned and hurried away. With tears in her eyes, Anna watched him go, wondering when, or *if*, she would ever see him again.

43

Paul dashed the back of his hand across his eyes as he hastily made his retreat from St. Andrew's Church.

The same thoughts that at the moment were in his sister's mind were crossing his also. But he knew they'd both be better off if this were their last meeting.

What he'd said about the police arresting her and the family because of *his* revolutionary activities was a real enough danger. He had spoken a true fear, and that was sufficient reason in itself for avoiding all future contact. He had known that very thing to happen to the innocent families of others.

There was more than that, of course.

It tore him apart every time he thought of, much less laid eyes on his sister. It stirred too many longings in him that were best forgotten. The warm security of being surrounded by a loving family was not to be his lot in life. It was absurd to put himself through such torture.

Thus he put as much distance as he could between him and Anna, and did so quickly, walking away from the church as if the devil himself were on his tail.

He was panting freely by the time he reached Maly Prospect. His exhaustion came as much from lack of nourishment as from the swiftness of his pace. He continued on for a few more blocks, then stopped for a rest. He found a small courtyard between two dilapidated tenements, slipped inside, and sat down next to a pile of garbage. A rat scurried past, but he hardly noticed. He had long ago become accustomed to their inevitable presence.

Paul tore open Anna's bundle and silently applauded his

concession in taking it. Inside, neatly wrapped, were a large loaf of stout brown bread, a rich hunk of cheese, and several plump red apples. He finished off half the contents in less than ten minutes. The rest he put in his pockets for later. He rose and started again on his way.

He walked another hour or two, until well past dark. Roaming the city streets seemed to be his chief occupation of late. There was little else for a homeless fugitive to do. He could stop for a while here or there. But remaining too long in one place could get him arrested just as easily for vagrancy as sedition.

Mostly he frequented back streets and poor neighborhoods where his presence would go unnoticed. He seldom went to the same place twice if he could help it, at least not on successive days, and never showed his face anywhere he had lived prior to the assassination.

When he had first come to the city he lived just this sort of aimless, homeless existence. He had known so little then! Had it not been for Kazan, it was doubtless he would have survived at all that first winter. But now he knew the ropes, and it was a good thing. For his life depended on his experience in a far more profound way than it did back then. Then, cold and starvation were his only enemies. Now, there were a thousand enemy eyes that might be peering out of the dark, waiting to snatch him! He had to scrounge food, keep away frostbite, and watch out for all those unknown lurking eyes at the same time.

Sometimes all the wariness in the world was not enough. And on that particular evening, Paul's mind was cluttered with things other than his own safety. He had not been able to rid his heart and mind of his encounter with Anna.

When he walked into the little tavern on the Eighteenth Line of Vassily Island, his thoughts were too preoccupied to remember that he had been there the day before with Basil, or to think that he had come this way and stopped in at this very place on too many occasions in the previous months. All he wanted was a strong glass of kvass, and this place had the best for the money.

He ordered the glass, laid down his last few coins, and took not the slightest note of the peculiar glare in the proprietor's eyes as he served him. Nor did he grasp the veiled and furtive attempts by the barmaid, who seemed to have taken a liking to him, to convey signals of warning.

"That's him!" cried the tavern owner.

Glancing up almost distractedly, Paul suddenly realized that it was he himself the man was pointing to. It was too late! The gendarmes had already pushed their way into the tavern and were making their way toward him.

They grabbed hold of Paul's arms roughly, knocking over the kvass, and dragging him from his seat.

"I knew he'd be back," gloated the owner, "the way my bar girl was flirting with him the other day."

"What's this all about?" said Paul.

"You've been involved in secret meetings and passing out seditious literature—that's what!" said one of the policemen.

"That's ridiculous!" protested Paul. Oddly, the lie sounded discordant in his mouth, no doubt because Anna was still so fresh in his mind.

"Don't believe him," put in the owner. "I've seen him. He was here just yesterday with another of them, talking all hidden and quietlike."

"Come along peaceful if you know what's good for you, you rotten scum. You'll see what happens to murderers and traitors."

Suddenly, in the passage of just a minute or two of time, what Paul had feared for so long was upon him. The likelihood of capture had been a constant part of his existence for months, yet the reality came as a shocking, terrifying surprise.

Later, as he sat in a cold, dark cell in some city gaol, he realized he would never be able to deliver another message to Anna.

Basil Anickin was running loose, and there was no one to stop him.

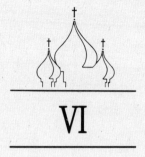

VI

DOWN THE DARK ROAD
(Spring 1881)

44

They called it the journey of the dead.

On the road outside Tiumen the snow had belatedly begun to give way to the pressures of spring, a season in these regions sometimes so short that it seemed to last but a few brief weeks. But winter's ice and snow might have been preferable to trudging through the knee-deep sludge and mud.

Or thus Paul had concluded as he lifted his *kati* one more time from the endless mire. The government-issued shoes were expected to last him for months of travel by foot; but it had been only a week since they were issued, and they were already beginning to pull apart at the seams. And the journey had only just begun.

After his arrest he had spent some days in jail before his sentence—without benefit of a trial—was passed: two years of penal servitude, followed by life exile in Siberia. The sentence was less severe than for some political criminals, but no less than he expected.

He was transported from the capital eastward, across the frigid, snowy Urals, and still farther eastward, ever eastward, to Tiumen. The prison had been such a hell that even under these conditions, Paul actually found himself glad to be starting out on the journey which would last weeks, if not months, before reaching his destination.

A convict party of some four hundred prisoners had been organized to embark that week. Such parties set out almost at a weekly rate in any and all seasons of the year. They were given an allotment of several kopecks a day for provisions, and were expected to buy food from local peasants along the way.

Noblemen sometimes received an extra kopeck or two. But no other distinction existed between prisoners, either by severity of crime or by sex or age. Women, children, political antagonists, and hardened murderers all traveled together. All wore drab convict gray uniforms, visorless caps, and long overcoats. Those destined for hard labor—as distinguished from the politicals—also wore two-kilo leg fetters and had half their heads shaven, both measures intended to discourage escape.

Paul marveled that already the detail had organized itself into a kind of self-governing unit, quite hidden from the scrutiny of the captain in charge of the guard. The convict body, known as an *artel*, was headed by the strongest member of the party, in their case a huge murderer that none of the others would dare cross. He collected contributions that went by the droll name of *dues*. Everyone was expected to pay his share, and with the proceeds, he and his fellow leaders of the *artel* bribed guards, bought illicit tobacco, helped the sick, hired wagons on which they sold the right to ride, sometimes facilitated escapes, and occasionally—when they thought they could get away with it—lined their own pockets as well.

The pathetic gathering looked like the poorest and most destitute assemblage of peasants that could have been gathered from throughout all Russia. Yet Paul knew that many of his fellow sojourners were men of culture and intellect who had lived lives of comfort and ease in Russia. Their only crime was political dissent—a crime that in Russia ranked among the worst.

One man in particular caught Paul's attention as they had readied to leave Tiumen. His leg fetters and partly shaven head immediately marked him as a hard-labor convict. Yet he had a look about him completely incongruent with such a designation. He was emotionally beaten, with a look of utter desolation in the vacant staring of his eyes. But in spite of it, he wore a quality of gentility that rags and filth could not hide. Paul wondered what heinous crime such a man could have committed to warrant irons bound to his legs. Probably the writing of a poem that sang the praises of freedom.

Paul's pensive observations of his fellow prisoners were cut short.

"*Gatova!* . . . Ready!" cried one of the guards, and the convicts all began to form ranks.

Following the prisoners came a procession of *telega*, small one-horse wagons on which the sick were to ride along with the privileged nobles. A cordon of Cossack guards on horseback hemmed in the entire procession along both sides, and the captain brought up the rear.

When the diverse assembly was ready, the captain turned in the direction of the prison church, bowed, crossed himself, then gave the order to march. They would be expected to cover about thirty versts (approximately thirty kilometers, or twenty miles) a day, a difficult enough distance over primitive roads for a healthy man, but near torture for a malnourished prisoner in leg irons. Paul had not eaten a decent meal in weeks, but he was not chained and was able to manage well enough. Nevertheless, he was exhausted when the party took their first rest at noon after a grueling fifteen versts.

At the rest stop the convict party was met by a dozen or so peasant women and girls selling food and refreshments. Paul bought a small jug of milk and loaf of black bread from a girl who looked like his little sister Vera. The resemblance was no doubt just a trick of his distraught mind, but it put him in a melancholy mood.

He noticed the prisoner with the genteel bearing some thirty meters away. The young man, who appeared only a few years older than Paul, was sitting with his back up against a tree, too exhausted to care about the muddy earth under him. He had purchased no food, but had rather collapsed almost where he had halted.

Paul walked toward him. "The girls will be leaving soon," he said. "If you are too tired, I can buy you something."

The gentleman turned his head slowly, as if with effort, toward the intrusive voice. As he focused momentarily on Paul, something like interest, even the briefest hint of astonishment, seemed to flicker across his otherwise passive countenance. He rubbed his eyes, shook his head with disbelief, then glanced away again.

"You look as though you could use something to eat," Paul pressed once more.

Still there was no verbal response.

A voice spoke from behind Paul. "You're wasting your time with that one."

"What do you mean?" Paul asked, turning around.

"Why, he's been—" The newcomer suddenly broke off his response as recognition dawned on him. At the same moment Paul also realized that the man was no stranger.

"Stepniak!" Paul exclaimed.

"Well, Pavlikov, they got you too, did they?"

"Yes, but where have you been . . . why have I not seen you?"

"Up in front of the lines. You've been back here, I take it?"

Paul nodded.

"So—what happened?"

"Nothing but what was bound to come to us all eventually."

"Recently?"

"A couple of months."

"Then tell me, are the rumors we hear true?"

"What rumors?"

"The tsar . . . is the tsar dead?"

"It is true," answered Paul.

"Then we have succeeded! Why so downcast, Pavlikov? Our imprisonment is a small price to pay."

"Because Zhelyabov, Perovskaya, Remiga, and Griggovski were all hanged for it."

Stepniak grimaced. "Poor Remiga," he said. "He was so young."

Paul did not comment on the fact that the martyred medical student was at least three years older than himself. But Stepniak continued. "If I had not been arrested, it would have been me instead of him. How did you escape the noose, Pavlikov?"

All their previous differences over the leadership and direction of The People's Will grew pale in light of the tsar's assassination, their friends' deaths, and their own banishment. For whatever good it would do them, they were comrades again.

"Only luck, I suppose," answered Paul.

"How so?"

"Wrong place, wrong time . . . right place, right time—however you want to look at it. But why are you only now being transported? You were arrested months ago?"

"True," replied Stepniak. "I should by now be more than halfway to the mines. But fate—or as you put it, dumb luck—interceded. A typhus epidemic struck the prison back there. That's how I came to be acquainted with that one—"

He jerked his head toward the man sitting against the tree who had shown no interest whatever in the little reunion taking place only a few paces away from him. He continued to stare vacantly into space, absorbed in his own morose and silent world.

"Does he ever talk?" asked Paul.

"He knows how, if that's what you mean. I heard him talk enough in his delirium."

"Delirium?"

"He caught typhus also. We were in the hospital together. He almost didn't make it. Even before he got the typhus, he was in pretty bad shape."

"From the journey here?"

"No. He'd attempted suicide."

"What a tragedy. He looks as if he was once a fine man."

"I feel sorry for him too. But then I have to remind myself that he is an aristocrat. Or rather, *was*. He is a dead man now, just like all of us. Though I suppose it is worse for those who have something in the first place to have had their rights and property and positions taken from them."

"No more than most of them deserve," said Paul, the bitterness of his political leanings showing through again.

"Maybe you're right. Now the miserable fellow doesn't even exist except as chattel on a convict gang. Poetic justice, I'd say."

"Come on, let's move away from him," said Paul, feeling awkward talking about the man as if he truly *were* already dead. Aristocrat or not, the fellow was indeed a pitiful specimen of humanity. Feeling something akin to compassion even for one of the hated nobility, Paul broke off half his hunk of bread and laid it down at the man's side.

He and Stepniak moved slowly away. The other man took no more notice of their leaving than he had of their arrival.

Travail and Triumph

Neither did he seem to note the food that had been laid beside his leg.

"You say he is an aristocrat," Paul said at length.

"A prince—from St. Petersburg."

"Do you know who he is?"

"Fedorcenko's his name."

Paul's surprise registered in his sharply raised brow.

"You've no doubt heard of him," said Stepniak.

"One of the capital's important families—of course I have." Paul deemed it best even now to say nothing about his sister's relationship with the Fedorcenko household. "What could he have done that even his family could not have interceded for him?" he added.

"A good question. I've known noblemen to murder their brothers and not even be jailed. The entire family must be out of imperial favor."

"Do you know what he did?"

"Shot his commanding officer—in battle. I know no details. He says nothing about it. Most of what I heard is nothing more than rumor. You know how the low-lifes in a place like this love to spread gossip about one of higher rank than themselves. Not to mention rebels like you and me. Everyone loves to see a high, proud man fall. It's not often we get someone of his stature in the midst of a convict gang, his legs in irons, his head shaved, and bound for a life in exile."

"Ironic in a way," mused Paul.

"But like you said, probably no more than he deserves."

Paul glanced back at the pitiful object of their conversation. He still hadn't moved, other than to pick up the piece of bread Paul had left. At least he still knew how to eat, although he chewed on the hard crust so absently that it seemed he hardly knew what he was doing, nor cared.

After the brief hint of recognition when Paul had spoken to him, the face had shown no more sign of life. Paul recalled one or two of Anna's letters mentioning the prince. He must have known Anna, even if only in passing. And now here they were, sharing bread together a thousand miles away en route to Siberia. Paul, however, gave no consideration to reasons beyond *coincidence*. Even if, in some dormant corner of his being, the faith of his father still resided, Paul could never have imagined that someone's prayers could have drawn the two unlikely rebel brothers together. The very notion would strike him as ludicrous that he could be a tool in the hand of that Higher Power he had, in his rebellion, repudiated.

His interest in the poor nobleman who might at one time have known his sister was suddenly diverted. The convicts were roused by the guards from their short rest, followed by the shout of the captain: *"March!"*

Paul and Stepniak fell in stride together. The crisp air of the budding spring meadow was filled with groans and curses and the rattling of chains. The party heaved forward slowly once more, and for the rest of the day, and indeed most of the rest of that first week, he lost sight of the condemned prince of the House of Fedorcenko. Sometimes it was all he could do to keep himself going, sloshing and trudging through the grass and mud and what snow yet remained.

Days passed, then a week, then two weeks. They would be many months on the road together. There would be plenty of time to resolve any further curiosity Paul may have had about the son of his sister's employer. The fact that he was here, and in chains, meant that he was as powerless as Paul himself to help in the danger that even now might be drawing its net closer and closer to the sisters of them both.

What did it matter that they were here together? They could not help the princess or Anna. Neither could they help each other.

What did anything matter now?

45

There seemed no end to the heartbreak and loss coming to the St. Petersburg House of Fedorcenko. Whatever the reasons, fate seemed to possess cruel designs of destruction, bent on claiming both generations of princes.

Anna had read the scriptures in which King Solomon wrote: *To everything there is a season.* She knew there must be wisdom in the words, because God himself had spoken them through his king. However, as she read on, it was more difficult to understand: *. . . a time to mourn and a time to dance . . .*

She would never cease grieving for Sergei. How could she ever put aside her mourning to dance again with joy? There would always be an empty ache in her heart that could only heal itself by his nearness. How could she ever be loved, or feel love so deeply again?

Despite such feelings within the quietness of her own breast, she could not help being glad when the princess and her parents began to emerge from the grief over Sergei's exile and enter back into the routine of their lives. There would, after all, very soon be a new member of the family, and no one wanted Katrina's baby to be born into a somber house of mourning.

The Princesses Fedorcenko and Remizov gradually began to socialize again. Though their spirits were halfhearted in the attempt at first, with increasing frequency they began to appear in the circles of the nobility as St. Petersburg society celebrated spring and the coming of summer. A new tsar was on the throne. The troublemakers had been hanged. And once again the streets of the city were safe and, as if life and the world existed merely for the pleasures of the nobility, its ballrooms festive.

Katrina's father, however, was considerably slower to take up the social duties of his position. He used his declining position at the court of the Winter Palace as an excuse. Whatever disfavor he had sunk to with the old tsar, his esteem was even lower in the eyes of Alexander III. And yet it was clear that this was not the true source of Viktor's trouble. His was a man's most bitter sorrow—finding himself rejected by his only son, then finding the convictions of fatherhood coming upon him too late. Now his son was bound for Siberia, having written seditious treason against the Crown, and having shot his regimental commander. Everything he had given his life to preserve—the authority of the tsar and his military—Sergei had tried to destroy. And yet . . . and yet . . . for the first time, Viktor realized that he *loved* his son!

He should hate him for what he had done. But he could not. He had been proud and high too long. At last his heart was ready to love. But the very one upon whom that love now yearned to expend itself was gone . . . exiled . . . never to be seen again!

The mortification he felt over the loss of Sergei was dreadful enough to drive him to the bottle more than was good for him. Yet the outer humiliation and disgrace were nearly as painful. He had to walk among his colleagues knowing that the very name Fedorcenko had brought a double mark against the throne, and that Sergei *Viktorovich* was viewed by many as no better than the scum that had been hanged for Alexander's assassination.

With the gossiping tongues of St. Petersburg wagging against him, and the demon of guilt gnawing and scraping against the inner cavities of his soul, it was little wonder that Viktor Fedorcenko shrank from the peering eyes and probing questions of his fellows. No longer could he walk among them with his head held high. He was plagued with tormenting visions of his own ineptitude, for which repentance had now come too late and for which restitution would never be possible. The man who had walked beside the tsar had shrunk to a tragic shadow of his former self.

Even Katrina, who had loved her father as had no other, said he seemed to lack vitality. In truth, he had lost more than vitality—he had lost the very heart to live. His uniform hung loosely upon his shoulders, just as the pale and thinning skin sagged from his high and once-majestic cheekbones.

When he drank, which he did more and more, he tended toward a surly sullenness, quiet and morose, apt to burst out in a temper at any moment. No longer was he the stable rock of a man that both Natalia and Katrina had always known and depended upon.

When Viktor agreed to accompany his wife and daughter to the ballet, therefore, the whole family rejoiced. Perhaps, they hoped, he was at last taking the final steps through the dark passage of his guilt-stricken grief, and was ready to begin living his life once more.

46

The carriage came around for Prince and Princess Fedorcenko at five minutes before six in the evening.

Viktor had braced himself for the outing with two or three glasses of Scotch. Or had it been four? He had lost count. The strong amber brew made from the barley in the north of the despised British Isles was one of his chief comforts of late. It helped dull the harsh realities that pressed upon him wherever he turned. He had almost come to feel as though the only way life *could* go on was by maintaining a low-level stupor, a condition of mind and spirit considerably facilitated by the golden whiskey. And if nothing else, at least a little drunkenness now and then provided a convenient reason for his mood swings and for the temper that, along with the silence, dominated his personality.

The fact of the matter was, Viktor was angry with no one but himself—angry, and possessed by self-reproach and remorse. But even when directed inwardly, anger and guilt are the red-hot fuels for passionate outbursts of indignation; combined with alcohol they turn rancorous and hostile. Viktor knew the truth, even if he would not acknowledge it—he had come to hate himself, and thus it was impossible for him not to treat others with the kind of abuse he believed he himself deserved.

He should have known it had gone too far the other day when he actually flared up at Natalia. He had nearly struck her, in fact, for nothing more than misplacing a book he had been dabbling in, pretending to read. Oddly, he hadn't been drinking excessively at the time. The incident should have revealed to him that the problem went deeper than the bottom of the crystal decanter on the sideboard. But he ignored his relative sobriety, and in fact considered the entire incident as a fluke of temperamental vicissitude.

The look of horror and shock and hurt on poor Natalia's face was difficult to ignore. But a few glasses of Scotch from the nearby decanter dimmed the ugly vision in his mind well enough.

Making amends to Natalia, though he had hardly summoned the gumption to admit to having wronged her, had been the motivation behind his sudden desire to attend the ballet. She was not the kind of woman to be cooped up in her misery for long. Melancholy was too weighty a burden for her lovely, simple mind. She might not be able to hold her own in a ponderous drawing room discussion; but, perhaps now, in this dark hour of their family's travail, her true strength could at last rise to the fore and see her husband through. The flighty personality which seemed made for the social rounds that had so bored Viktor in the past now gave him something outside himself to hold on to.

Thus, in his despondent state, she pulled him up and—as she danced and laughed and breezed through one crowded room after another, delighting everyone with her coquettish banter—added to his reason to live. Though neither of them realized it, Natalia was gradually transferring an inner strength to her husband that neither had known she possessed. On the surface of it, Viktor told himself that *for her sake* he would force himself to face the merry St. Petersburg society. But he could not do it cold sober.

When a footman announced that the carriage was ready, Viktor helped his wife on with her fur wrap, slipped his arm around hers, even managing a smile of sorts, and escorted her to their waiting carriage. She made no comment about the strong fumes on his breath. But then Natalia, with all her strengths *and* weaknesses, was too self-absorbed to be a nag. Besides, she had grown used to it, and loved Viktor too much to say anything. If she did not apprehend the full depth of his mental turmoil, she was at least cognizant enough of his suffering to know she did not want to annoy him by adding herself to his list of burdens.

"Good evening, Your Highnesses!" said the coachman as he opened the carriage door.

"Where is Vanka?" asked Viktor gruffly. "Or what about Moskalev?" he added, nettled that a new man had been assigned to drive him instead of the head coachman or his experienced assistant.

"Many pardons, Your Excellency," apologized the driver effusively. "I know it is an honor too high for one such as myself to drive you, sir, but Vanka felt I warranted the experience. If you are dissatisfied, I will fetch—"

"Never mind," interrupted Viktor, still crusty but somewhat placated, "we'll be late. But next time I expect to be notified about such changes. Do you know the route?"

"Very well, Your Highness. I have traveled it many times."

"Then let us be gone." Viktor followed Natalia into the carriage and sat down with a grunt.

"Now, dear," said Natalia, "I am certain the man will do just fine. How difficult can it be to drive to the Maryinsky?"

"That's not the point. New drivers can drive the servants."

"Oh, let's not talk of it now. We don't want the evening spoiled over such a triviality. But if anyone has a right to be miffed, Viktor, it's I. You haven't even mentioned my new gown!"

Isn't it delightful? The color is all the rage this season in Paris. They say it's the color of peaches. Do you think it suits me?"

"I've never seen a peach of exactly *that* hue," replied Viktor, making a fumbling effort to show some interest in his wife's dress, even if the words came out more like a criticism than anything else.

Natalia giggled. She was not particular. He had said something, anyway. "Well, fashion designers can't be expected to be greengrocers! But it's a delicious shade, whatever it's called."

The carriage lurched into motion and the prince and princess settled back into their seats.

"Cantaloupe," Viktor observed after a few moments silence.

"What?"

"The dress looks more like a ripe cantaloupe."

"Really!"

"In my opinion, at least."

"If you say so, dear. Hmmm . . . what an interesting idea!"

In fifteen minutes they arrived at the Remizov home. Katrina greeted her parents with a warm kiss. A brief frown crossed her brow when she caught a whiff of her father's breath, but she said nothing. She was so weary of remonstrating with Dmitri over the subject of his drinking—she did not call it nagging, though he often did—that she had no desire to start in on her father. She had, however, noticed him taking to the bottle more frequently. Next thing, she thought peevishly, her father and husband were likely to become drinking cronies.

But like her parents, she was determined to make this a successful and enjoyable outing. She pushed all gloomy thoughts from her mind. They would have a good time no matter how much effort it required. It had already gotten off to a rocky start when Dmitri announced earlier in the day that he had other plans for the evening. Katrina had wanted this to be a special evening for all *four* of them. But she would not let even Dmitri's absence spoil it!

She led her parents into the parlor, where refreshments had been set out. There proved to be precious little, even in the way of trivial banter, for them to talk about that did not strike some tender nerve. Dmitri's scarcity around the place, or anything pertaining to their marriage, could not be mentioned for Katrina's sake. Politics, current events, and the new tsar's reign had to be avoided for Viktor's sake. All three, by mutual avoidance, would not come within a furlong of alluding to the one unnamed member of their family not present with them that evening. That would have been more painful than all the other subjects put together.

They managed to chat innocuously about plans for the coming birth of the new Count Remizov, as Dmitri called the child. He was certain it would be a boy. But even this subject had to be approached cautiously, if for no other reason than for propriety's sake. Social custom required that Viktor not appear to notice, much less refer to his daughter's advancing condition.

The subject of names had come up before. Out of desperation they turned to it again as a relatively safe arena of discourse. But even that had its pitfalls.

"Well," offered Natalia, "you may choose what pleases you, dear, but I suppose I shall always regret that I could not name a child for my mother—Mariana. It is such a lovely name."

Katrina nodded and uttered a few pleasantries in response.

"But we named you for your father's grandmother," the princess went on, "and then there were no more children." Natalia's voice began to waver slightly as hidden emotions stirred.

Katrina jumped in quickly to rescue the precarious conversation. "It seems to me risky naming children after ancestors," she said. "You're always going to run out of children before relatives. Then someone is bound to get hurt. Besides, I want something unique—like Ekaterina, if it is a girl. And perhaps Mark, if we have a son."

"Mark!" exclaimed Viktor, taking momentary leave from the refuge of his sherry to register his distaste for his daughter's outlandish ideas. "Where in heaven's name did you come up with a name like that?"

"Anna and I have been reading a delightful book called *The Adventures of Tom Sawyer* by an American named Mark Twain," answered Katrina.

"Why not Tom, then," rejoined Viktor with sour expression, "if you want an American name for your *Russian* son?"

"Hmmm . . . not a bad suggestion." Katrina was trying to

be playful, and had no idea what her little tease was stirring.

"I thought you had more respect than that for your heritage. As if I don't already look bad enough. My reputation in this city is all but gone. You are starting to sound like your—"

Whether it was the startled looks of his wife and daughter, or his own realization that he had nearly blundered into forbidden conversational territory, Viktor stopped abruptly. The pause was awkward, but only lasted a moment or two.

"Oh, who cares about a silly name anyway!" he growled, grabbing up his glass and tossing back the remainder of his sherry with both relish and relief. He then lurched, rather unsteadily, to his feet and walked toward the sideboard in search of a decanter full of something stronger.

"Well," said Natalia, with a trace of nervousness in her voice, "I suppose Dmitri will want some say in the matter . . . of names, you know."

"I doubt he will concern himself with it much one way or another—" Katrina stopped suddenly. The bitter tone of her comment surprised her; she was about to flounder into an unpleasant discussion about her marriage, and she did *not* want to open that door.

This could go on no longer. Somebody was going to say something they would all regret if they didn't put an end to it. "Well, I think we ought to be off," Katrina said, abruptly changing the course of what she had been saying before. She set down her glass and wiggled to her feet. "We don't want to miss the first act, do we?"

No one protested. The diversion of the imperial ballet would last the rest of the evening. They would not have to speak or even look at one another for several hours.

47

Viktor, Natalia, and their daughter, Katrina, all loved one another deeply. But all were inept at expressing those deep feelings of the heart. The art had not been learned, the skills of intimacy had not been practiced. All Katrina knew of open-hearted communication and affection had come since Anna's entry into her life. And although the changes within her had opened deep wells out of which springs of living water flowed into her being, she still did not fully know how to let those streams pour into that man and that woman who had brought her into this world. The past was an overpowering obstacle to change between them. They needed one another, but the pain of being together was too overwhelming.

They walked from Katrina's house to the *droshky*.

Viktor swayed on his feet a few times. Katrina tried not to show her embarrassment when the footman had to steady the prince. Natalia either pretended, or did not notice. Katrina groaned inwardly at the spectacle. It was going to be a splendid evening . . . *if* they survived.

They reached the carriage. The footman hastened ahead a few steps, and then stood at the ready to open the door and assist his charges in stepping up to board.

Katrina was hoisted in first. Though the man did his best, she felt as much like an unwieldy bundle as a woman nearly full-term advanced with child would naturally feel. When the young princess was reasonably settled, the footman turned and offered his hand to Princess Natalia.

The moment her foot touched the step, the carriage lurched unexpectedly. Something seemed to have spooked the horses, and Natalia was thrown off balance and backward. Had it not been for the swift intercession of the footman catching her with his strong arms, she would have sprawled flat on her back.

She gasped amid the clattering noises of the wheels and horseshoes on the cobbles. The fidgety horses, however, did not have a chance to settle down before Viktor's voice rose above the confusion.

"What in blazes!" he cried, swinging around to aim his displeasure at the idiot of a driver sitting up on the box with the reins in his hands.

"I—I don't know what happened, Your Excellency," the man stammered. "Please accept my—"

"You incompetent fool!" interrupted Viktor. "Moskalev would never allow such a thing!"

"It was the horses. They—"

"Don't give me excuses!" he yelled. Both alcohol and his rising blood pressure turned Viktor's countenance bright red. A mere verbal tirade was not about to appease his fury.

Before the driver knew what was happening, Viktor had jumped unceremoniously up on the step, reached up and wrested the buggy whip out of his hand, thrashing him wildly.

"You fool . . . idiot!" he shrieked, now stepping back and venting his wrath with the full length of the wicked leather lash.

Holding his hands protectively over his face, the inexperienced coachman let loose the reins and desperately attempted to stumble off the box while warding off Viktor's blows. But Viktor, caught up in the uncontrollable loosing of a legion of inner demons, did not relent. Nor did he realize that half his wild blows were falling dangerously close to the flesh of the already skittish horses.

"Viktor!" cried a frightened Natalia. "There has been no harm . . . I am safe. It was but an accident." She had been standing next to the still-open door of the coach. As she spoke, she rushed around it and toward her husband at the front of the droshky where the coachman was struggling down and Viktor was beating him as one crazed. Katrina beheld it all from inside with horror.

"Viktor . . . Viktor, please!" cried Natalia.

But Viktor heard nothing. He continued whipping the coachman as the symbolic embodiment of his every failure and frustration, as if he could exorcise the guilt from his own soul by castigating another into senseless oblivion. But as his victim at last stumbled to the ground, his hands fell against the harnesses to keep himself from tumbling over. At the same instant the wicked tip of the scourge snapped the rump of one of the animals. It let out a sharp whinny of pain and reared up dangerously.

The coachman jumped clear even as Viktor hesitated momentarily and took a step backward. The only one who did not react in time to the wildly rearing horses was Princess Natalia.

In one terrible moment of shrill frightened whinnies, Katrina's screaming voice, the clattering of hooves, and terrified shouts of warning from the footman, Natalia was knocked to the ground with the first terrible jerks of the carriage against her.

"Mama!" screamed Katrina, half-leaning out of the carriage, heedless of her own danger should the carriage sway suddenly. She felt the heavy iron wheel bump once, then suddenly jerk back in the reverse direction.

The footman had by now gathered his wits about him enough to grab the front harnesses, but the horses continued to rear, their great powerful hooves crashing down frantically.

Within seconds the man had the horses standing again, though quivering with fright, and the carriage still.

No more than thirty or forty seconds had passed since Viktor had grabbed the fatal whip into his hand. Everything had happened in a blur of drunken passion. Only now did his benumbed senses begin to take in the awful sight of his wife lying pale and motionless on the granite cobblestones under the harnesses between the skittish horses and the droshky.

The whip fell from his hand as he made his way forward. Oddly, he first noticed the lovely flounces of peach satin, soiled and torn, on the stones.

Pale from the shock, and fearful of the result, Katrina slowly emerged from the carriage and with great effort stepped to the ground. In mute anguish she moved slowly around to the front of the carriage, a sickening dread seizing her as she beheld the poignant scene before her.

"I've ruined your lovely new dress, my dear," said Viktor, kneeling down beside the motionless form. His voice was soft, childlike, pathetic. "I will buy you two new ones . . . I will go to every ballet, and you shall have a new dress for every one, with all the Paris colors."

His hand reached down and tenderly stroked the warm, white cheek. "Natalia," he said, even more softly now. "Natalia . . . open your eyes . . . please tell me you forgive me . . . Natalia . . ."

Only Katrina, as she drew nearer, saw the bright red from under her mother's head staining the fashionable gown she had been so proud of.

When her eyes fell again upon her father, something of the truth seemed beginning to dawn on him. He too had grown silent as he bent over and laid his proud soldier's head upon his wife's breast.

From behind, Katrina could not see his face but only his shoulders, heaving with wretched, silent sobs of bitterest anguish.

48

In another dark corner of still one more grimy St. Petersburg tavern, three conspirators at one of the back tables far from the window were thankful there were so many such disreputable places in the Russian capital for them to carry on their diabolic business away from curious and prying eyes.

"Fools!" rasped Basil Anickin in a voice no less menacing for all that it was a whisper.

"How was I to know that maniac would attack me?" came the defensive reply from one of the men opposite him.

"Do you know what I went through to get you hired on at the Fedorcenko estate?" shot back Anickin. "And you couldn't even carry out the simple assignment of driving a carriage!"

"I tell you it was an accident!"

"That was *not* the 'accident' I had planned!"

"It was not my fault."

"And if you were going to kill one of the women, why couldn't it have been the other one?"

"Other one . . . what in the—"

"No, of course . . . we could not have that, could we?" Basil went on as if talking to himself. "What am I thinking—not some freak accident . . . not for *her*."

"What are you talking about?"

With effort Basil forced his attention back to his comrades. "She must *know*," he said, answering both the question and his own evil thoughts with the same words. "She must be fully cognizant . . . at the moment she realizes she is about to die . . . she must know *why*."

"What do you mean *she*? I thought we were after the prince."

"I want the whole family. I thought I made that clear."

The other, who had not yet spoken, grinned, showing rotting teeth and malicious intent. "Well, we got one, then— what's the problem?"

"You imbecile—moron! I don't want to pick them off like ducks on a pond."

"As I see it, dead is dead."

"Ah . . . spoken like the fool you are! And if they begin to suspect and raise their guard?"

"They will suspect nothing," argued the first man. "Nothing will arouse suspicion. It was an accident, I tell you." He was beginning to regret signing on with this Anickin. He'd heard the man was crazy. At the time he had been willing to join anyone still brave enough to strike against the government. But he was having doubts now, especially since the other fellow had joined them. Anickin and he had been inmates together— they *said* in prison, but there were rumors of a mental hospital.

And now he had begun to believe the latter. He was glad he had been fired by the prince after the accident. It provided him with a convenient excuse for quitting the operation.

"He's right there," said the other. "Why, I hear the prince blames himself for—"

"As well he should," put in the ex-coachman. "He attacked me like a wild man. "Look—" He pulled down his collar, revealing raw lash marks on his bare neck. "We are free men, yet they still treat us like chattel!"

"So, Anickin," said the other cohort coolly, ignoring the erstwhile coachman's outburst, "what do you want us to do next? You can be certain it will be more difficult to get at them now that the family is in seclusion."

"Yes," mumbled Anickin, rubbing at the unkempt stubble on his chin. For all its lurking insanity, his mind was still as sharp as when he had served on the bar. And he used the ensuing moments, while a serving girl refilled their glasses with cheap brew, to analyze the possibilities before him. He wasn't going to be able to get another man inside either house—he had been lucky enough to be able to contrive it in the first place.

So the avenue of inside staff help was no doubt closed. The seclusion of the family was another problem. If they were not going to come *out*, he would somehow have to get *in*.

If only I had been able to get some competent help in the first place! he thought, taking a sip from his glass and looking over its rim at his two bungling associates. Nothing from his eyes or expression gave evidence to his thoughts. These two were numbskulls. What made him think he was ever going to get the thing accomplished to his satisfaction with the likes of them? But most of the good men had either been arrested or fled the city. It had been a boon to find that Pavlikov fellow still around. But with his sudden arrest, Basil had grown impatient and had been forced to accept the aid of an inept fool and a lunatic more bloodthirsty than himself.

It had all been a mistake. He should not have lost his patience. It would have been better to wait a while and just see to everything himself if need be.

The more he turned the situation over in his mind, the more clearly he began to see that perhaps all these setbacks were but the interceding hand of fate. Forces beyond his control seemed propelling him inexorably toward the one scheme mere logic had caused him to avoid. Yet it was the one scenario that his evil heart cherished.

Katrina Remizov could not die by the hand of *hirelings*. Nor could the deed be accomplished by means of some impersonal happenstance or device, such as a bomb or tiny bullet of lead.

No. It was only right that she die by his own hand. He had been a fool to think it could be carried out otherwise.

Somehow he had to get to her. *He* himself—get to her alone. The fact that she was in mourning might even work to his advantage. She would be vulnerable and weak. He would use her vulnerability as she had used his. He would kill her, then—at the proper time—kill the count also.

But Katrina must be the first to die. She must look into his very eyes . . . and know who . . . and why.

This time nothing would be left to chance. Nor to the incompetence of others. The success of his mission—his *holy* mission—would rest entirely upon his own shoulders.

Again Basil took a sip from his glass, but this time let a smile part his lips as he swallowed. He felt confident of his success!

And also in the surety that he would survive to fully relish the moment of his triumph.

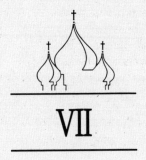

VII

BROTHERS IN EXILE
(Summer 1881)

49

Summer would make as abrupt an exit from the wastes of southeastern Siberia as its appearance only a short time before. September would not depart before the wind would again moan cold and stiff. But for now, for a blessed few weeks, the days were long and almost warm.

Not a cloud was to be seen in the sky on most days. Even though a quarter of Siberia lay within the Arctic circle, in these regions farther to the south, for all their bitter cold, not much snow, or even rain, fell throughout the year. Pity the poor travelers whose route took them north where nothing but white was to be seen year-round. At least down here, greenery covered much of the frigid landscape.

This was an arid region, despite the fact that through it flowed some of the largest rivers in the world. Dense taiga forests covered the unrelenting land, giving way only to empty high-desert plains where the forests ended. Without a wall, without span of barbed wire, without so much as a single watchtower, it formed the most perfect prison in existence. Where was an escapee to go? How could he survive alone, when the very soil under his feet remained mostly frozen eleven months of the year?

The imperial government, of course, was not inclined to leave security merely in the hands of the elements. It constructed man-made prisons as well, manned their towers and reinforced their walls. Yet with all this, regimes of Russian tsars had for centuries steadily perfected an even more insidious deterrent to escape and rebellion than any prison, than any wilderness, than any punishment could afford.

Stronger than any wall was the rampart of *despair*.

The mines of Kara lay at the eastern extremity of the Trans-Baikal region of southern Siberia, some four hundred fifty versts from its capital of Chita. Bounded by the Shilka River on the south, the mines themselves were scattered along the Kara River valley for a distance of twenty miles. Accessible only by boat in the summer and sledge across the ice-locked rivers in the winter, there were several weeks in autumn and spring, during which the ice was either forming or breaking up, when the mines were totally isolated from all access to the outside world. No traversable overland route connected Kara in any direction to anywhere.

The mines were the tsar's personal real estate, worked entirely for the benefit of his purse. Arguably, the operating expenses greatly outdistanced whatever profit came to the emperor. But the mines yet continued in operation. The name *Kara* was derived from the Tartar word "black," in reference to the gold-laden black sands of the river. The uses made of the place by the emperor had long since given the appellation a darker meaning.

The Lower Diggings, one of the first settlements along the river, had the appearance of a typical Siberian village. However, the whitewashed tin-roofed officers' quarters and log barracks of the Cossack guards contrasted harshly with the dilapidated, gloomy prison block. The government buildings had been arranged with some order, intersected by a few broad streets, furthering the village-like impression. On the outskirts of a cluster of buildings scattered along the road leading to the next settlement sat a score or more of poor shanties—ramshackle wooden houses occupied by the convicts of free-command. Those politicals who had completed the hard-labor portion of their sentences resided away from the prison cells themselves. If such an existence could be called "freedom," the hardy ones who endured their years of toil were *free* to continue their labor on the tsar's behalf.

As the sun dropped behind the western hills bordering the mines, the little nondescript village stirred with activity as its residents returned from their labors. From the mines a few walked alone or in groups of two or three in the direction of their own personal hovels. The rest formed a long, drab line of humanity along the road, shuffling listlessly toward the prison enclave—apathetic, unsmiling, unfeeling. The gall of their despair weighed down their spirits more heavily than the day's work had tired their muscles or the chains dragged down their legs as they walked. The gates of the compound swung wide for them, but they responded not with a shout of relief at returning home, but with a rusty groan as from a floundering ship about to break on the shoals of despond. Awaiting them was only a vermin-infested barracks and a meal of doughy black bread, watered-down soup with a sliver of discolored meat, and tea if they were fortunate. This sparsity they ate on their bare-boarded bunks, after which most fell quickly into an exhausted sleep without blanket or pillow or even so much as a layer of straw for a mattress.

Onetime Prince Sergei Viktorovich Fedorcenko chewed on his broken life with little more enthusiasm than he showed the bland, rubbery hunk of bread. Since the beginning of their journey, the *artel* had been broken and its original members sent in two or three diverse directions to different destinations. By the time Sergei's senses finally began to come back to him, Paul was on his way farther northward. He never knew whose hand had fed him, or how close he had been to one he once had loved.

Sergei's senses *had* gradually returned as he had trekked with the others of his party across the lowlands north of Mongolia. Thoughts came back. He remembered. But he had allowed no hint of former dreams to clutter his desolation. He wore his bitterness like his tattered gray coat, hugged to his body against the late-evening chill. He wore it as a badge, more vivid than the convict tattoo on his forehead. To the others of the *artel* he had come to be known as *Pokoinik*, the dead one, an epithet once applied to none other than Dostoyevsky during his own sojourn in Siberia, and thus especially fitting to the young prince who had once dreamed of spending his days, like the great novelist before him, weaving stories of Russian life. Sergei no longer dreamed of writing stories, for all the hopes that gave rise to tales had grown more bitter than bile. The name his fellow travelers had given him held fast.

Shifting his wracked frame on the hard, cold boards, he found it difficult to even dredge up hope enough for recriminations. Whom could he blame for his plight? A government whose injustice and irresponsibility had driven him to the extremities of violence, madness, and suicide? A war whose atrocities still revolted him, even at the very memory? A moment of insanity that had made of him the animal he had hated in his commander?

No. What was the use in blame? Blame was a luxury only for those who hoped for some vindication.

In a moment of blind and desperate frenzy, caught in the horrifying battle-slaughter where mothers and children were being cut down along with warriors, his reason had snapped like a dry twig. Unable to witness one more death, although the battlefield was already strewn with thousands, he had made himself an instrument of death as well. He had thought nothing of the consequences. He had not considered right or wrong. His numbed mind was still too crazed with guilt over the woman his own horse had trampled to death.

He had not thought . . . he had only acted. And with his act, his very power of thought had seemingly been taken from him.

Suddenly he was bound and chained and imprisoned and tried and sentenced and sent on a march that now seemed like the only life he had ever known. Time had lost all meaning. He had no idea how long he had been gone, only that somewhere in the journey he had been deathly sick. They told him he had tried to take his own life, but he remembered nothing of it. In truth, he remembered little of anything. Most of the time he had not even remembered Anna. Faint sensations fluttered at his heart upon occasion, but the one who seemed to be calling to him never came into focus.

But as he had walked, gradually the effects of the typhus lessened. And in spite of the exhausting regimen, by degrees his bodily strength began to come back. With soundness of limb, once again his mind slowly began to function. Sights, sounds, memories began to intrude where had been only a void for so many months.

His arrival at Kara had snapped his mind from the trap of insanity. As thought processes slowly took hold, the reality of his situation dawned all too clear. There would be no blame, no recriminations, no vengeance. Perhaps he would never write again, never see civilization again. And perhaps he was indeed a *pokoinik*. But he would not attempt again to achieve that end by his own hand. If dead he must be, it would not be by the tsar's guards at this hellish place. It would not be from his own doing, nor would he ever again carry a weapon on a battlefield to die fighting innocent enemies of the great Russian state. If he was to die, he would die with purpose.

His was a life beset with ironies. He blamed neither himself, nor his father, nor Rustaveli, nor the tsar, nor anyone. If he was going to be called "the dead one," at least he would earn the name.

He could not—*would* not—stay here enduring a living death for all his days. He would drown in the river, freeze in the bitter wastelands, or starve in the taiga wilderness.

But he would not stay . . . never to die, and yet never to live.

50

The light of dawn pierced the grimy, heavily grated windows of the barracks with a bent, turbid light. It was welcomed with the groans and mutterings of dried-up voices, and the clank of chains as the inhabitants pried their stiff bodies from hard beds.

Sergei did not move immediately. He wondered, as if it were a surprise, why the cheerless beams of light slanting over his prostrate body did nothing to warm his frozen limbs. The others had been here a year, two years . . . ten years. They were used to the unwarming sun. But the incongruity now struck him for the first time. He glared at the pale rays as if to intimidate them into doing their job. But all they did was illuminate the dirty walls, splattered with the blood of countless bedbugs that had met their end with the cold slap of a convict's hand. Sergei had killed a few himself, although he noticed that those who had been here longest no longer bothered, but let the pests share their beds of hopelessness. The realization further nurtured his budding resolve not to allow himself to become one of such hopelessness.

Sergei's vacant stare fell on the yellowed placards nailed to the wall across the room. *Come unto me all ye that labor and are heavy laden and I will give you rest*, one read. Some benevolent warden had thought to install a measure of hope into his charges. But the words blared out like a bad joke. Maybe the warden had not been so benevolent after all. Perhaps it was just another form of punishment, planting the seeds of hope within the hearts of inmates for whom there *was* no hope.

Sergei had tried faith. Some time long ago, deep in his past, he remembered actually thinking there might be a Being who could give him rest, peace. But that was long ago, before he became the dead one. Such ideas belonged to that insanity whose comfort he could not afford.

He could not believe. He could not hope for *life*. He could only hope to give the death that had already come to him some meaning. To grasp after the unattainable would only lead again to devastating despair. The catalyst of pain and suffering drove him away from hope rather than toward it.

Instead of the words of Jesus, Dante's words should have been nailed to the kamera wall: *Abandon hope, all ye who enter here*. The warden would have done better with this saying than to mock them all with drivel about rest for the heavy laden. Even if some Father in heaven existed to whom one might go, what would it matter? The harsh truth of this living hell would not change one iota. If there were some heavenly Savior, He would do better to expend His saving energies elsewhere.

Sergei would hope . . . but not for *life* as he had once known it, neither for eternal life. He would hope only to be away from this place so that he might die in peace. Not peace with God, but perhaps a modicum of peace with himself.

With a sudden, violent jerk, Sergei swung his feet off his bed. Such morose thinking was dangerous. He had to keep his wits sharp. He couldn't fade off again into the emptiness . . . the fathomless black pit. He would be better off not to think at all. Better to concern himself with only matters of survival until the day came—and he would be sure it was soon!

The other inmates were already attacking the tray of bread and bucket of warm tea left by the guard. Sergei shouldered his way through the mob. The men gave way to him. There was some advantage to being a quiet newcomer, with a reputation that had grown over the course of the journey. Some said he was a murderer, others that he was dangerous for other reasons. The faraway look in his eyes gave evidence of a strangeness that separated him from most convicts at Kara, and Sergei did nothing to dismiss any of the speculations one way or another. He let them think what they would. Let the rumors spread and fester. If it got him a bigger crust of bread, what did it matter?

He grabbed one of the hunks left on the tray, then dipped his dirty tin cup into the bucket twice, draining off the first cup in a few seconds before going back for another. A reputation could not hurt in this place where men killed for little more than a morsel of food. Survival was the only liturgy worth heeding in this house of the dead.

A few moments later the inmates shuffled outside for the verification inspection that preceded the day's toil. Everyone was present except those who had died during the night—the lucky ones.

"One more day, eh, Kaplan?" said the guard to one of the older prisoners—one who had befriended Sergei his second night at Kara.

Kaplan grinned garishly. "Just make sure you have the key to unlock these chains tomorrow at this time," he said.

Sergei wondered if he should feel happiness or remorse for him. In a few months winter would be beating against the thin walls of his shanty in the free-command edge of the village. The old convict would doubtless die long before General Kukushka rallied his army of escapes next spring. Sergei didn't want to have to wait so long. Perhaps his old friend's release might afford him an opportunity somehow. He would be alert today and try to make his brain think more than it had of late.

Then they were off, herded like beasts to another day in the unending drudgery of pick and shovel and mine carts.

If only Dmitri were here, thought Sergei. *He* would be able to devise some way out of this godforsaken and hideous place!

51

Another day's toil behind him.

It was only his eighth since arriving at Kara. Some of these men had been here twenty years . . . even thirty. How did they keep from insanity? He had not been here two weeks, but he would not last many more days.

The black bread grew more tasteless and the soup more watery with each passing evening. Tonight there was no tea.

Sergei lay down on his bunk with a wearisome groan and stared straight up at the dark ceiling.

A dull, scraping sound drew near Sergei's bed, but he made no response to it until a voice like the scrape of fetters on the plank floor rasped in his ear.

"Hey, Pokoinik," said the man called Kaplan. His visage appeared ancient and his face as gray and creased as the Siberian landscape. "Don't tell me you are asleep."

"Why not?" Sergei answered in a frayed voice that still revealed the effects of the typhus.

"Tomorrow I go into free-command."

"I am happy for you, Kaplan. But your good fortune will not help me."

"They say I am reformed," replied the other, seeming to

ignore the young prince's comment. He chortled a sound that was supposed to resemble laughter. The glint in his squinting eyes hinted that he had pulled a great joke on his keepers. "You can join me, Pokoinik," he added, in a low, nefarious voice that hinted at some undisclosed scheme.

Stiffly Sergei rolled over in his bunk and eyed the old man.

"You told me you did not intend to remain here as long as I," Kaplan went on. "Perhaps I might assist you."

"Why should you help me?" Sergei asked. He had already developed the skepticism that permeated such prison camps and kept most of the convicts within self-made walls even thicker than those around the perimeter of the compound. His words sounded like a challenge.

"Pokoinik! Did I not befriend you and take care of you when you arrived? I saw in you a friend. Now that my big chance has come, I am offering you the chance not to have to wait twenty years as I have. You need me, Pokoinik, if you are to get away from this place."

"It is fatal to need someone, Kaplan."

Kaplan lowered his voice still further, to little more than a raw whisper. He ignored Sergei's skepticism. "In the spring I will answer the call of the cuckoo," he said. "From the free-command village, it will be much easier."

The first songs of the cuckoo in the spring gave the signal that the taiga would once more be warm enough to be hospitable to potential escapees. Even then, however, an escape was considered foolhardy, for without food, weapons, or allies, the wilderness at any season was not a friendly place, and the majority of Siberian peasants would sooner kill a convict than help him. Nevertheless, hordes of prisoners attempted to join General Kukushka's army each spring. Few made it out of Siberia.

"You are a fool, Kaplan. You will never make it."

"That is why I need you as much as you need me, my friend."

"You expect me to repay a week's friendship by risking my life to get you out of Siberia?"

"And you out too. We help each other, eh?"

"What makes you think I want to escape?"

"You have told me so, Pokoinik."

"Even supposing you are right, I have no intention of waiting until spring."

"To leave now would be certain death. We would scarcely be away from here before winter would freeze us in our tracks."

"I would sooner die in the attempt than spend the winter here waiting for Kukushka."

Kaplan paused, thinking. After fifteen years of living like an animal, chained like some wild and dangerous beast, he knew no other life. Once he had hid the death of one of his fellow inmates for two days so he could get the man's ration of food. They had chained him to a wheelbarrow for three days for that horrendous crime. They had attached the barrow to his leg fetters and he dragged it behind him morning till night and even while he slept, as if it were some millstone of sin. Once, by some unknown fluke, a book had found its way into the kamera. A young man, a new inmate, had somehow smuggled it past the inspectors. Kaplan vaguely recalled that in the past books had meant something to him, just as they had to his new friend, the condemned seditious author. In the night, he had stolen that book—and thrown it into the brick oven for fuel against the bitter cold.

He had learned to survive, but in so doing he had allowed himself to become like his surroundings. Perhaps that was why he had befriended the young new fellow in the next bunk, the one he called Pokoinik. The young man seemed to symbolize something to him, something of what he had once been.

Escape. The very thought sent floods of anticipation mingled with the nausea of terror through his body.

The thought that he would at last be free of these cursed chains told him he ought to dismiss the notion of escape. Yet . . . how could he not long to be completely free? Perhaps the young one was right.

His physical condition was a repulsive wraith of his former self. His pale hair was riddled with lice and stained with dank strands of gray. His weathered, mottled skin made him look as if *he* should be called the dead one, not the young prince. His once tender and sensitive eyes had turned hard and cold in their dark sockets, like the waters of a bubbling brook frozen by implacable winter. The gaunt, hollow aspect of his ghastly pale face made him look twenty years older than he was.

Why should he wait till spring? He could be dead by then. The young one was right—why not die trying to make good the attempt? He had been listening to his comrades for years, listening to their plans, taking ideas from one, now another, carefully formulating a strategy of his own. The young Pokoinik could probably help him make it work. He had already begun bribing one of the guards, who, when he escaped, would continue to receive an allowance by keeping him on the books as under his charge. It was a common practice, and Kaplan had been slyly keeping watch on how the process worked for some time. It was a daring plan; if they could get far enough through the mountain passes before the onslaught of winter, they could survive. His scheme did not call for a northern or western route through the wild wastes of Siberia, but rather southward ... toward lands of the far east and peoples unknown.

As Kaplan pondered his future, on the bunk next to him Sergei, too, was considering what to make of the old man's words.

His few months of imprisonment were nothing in comparison to Kaplan's, but it might as well have been years for what it had made of him. He had long forgotten the genteel ways of his youth, the essence of polite conversation, how to hold silver, how even to relieve himself with propriety. Kindness and mercy and faith had become as foreign to him as ... the loving touch of a woman.

Yes, he desperately wanted away from this vile place. If he died, it was no more than he had sought at Tiumen. Why not do as Kaplan had suggested? Perhaps he was right; perhaps they did need each other. And if either of them chanced to make it, would not it have been worth the risk?

52

The route followed by Paul Yevnovich Burenin took a more northerly direction than those whose destination was the mines of Kara. With others of a revolutionary bent, Paul found himself bound for Kolyma, in the distant regions where snow and ice prevailed.

The longer the journey and the smaller dwindled their band, the more somber they all became. Even one-time comrade Stepniak had grown distant. More and more Paul found his thoughts skipping backward through time and painful circumstances to happier and more pleasant memories. Faces and images, sights and smells, from Katyk and his father's *izba* crowded into his mind. For so long he had banished them from his thoughts, as if he could will that former part of his being into nonexistence. Now, however, with his own exile and banishment for crimes against the tsar, he no longer had the mental strength to keep them at bay. With every passing day they intruded closer and closer toward that innermost region of his heart, the heart he had kept hidden and walled up since the day he left Katyk. He now found himself regretting that he had not spoken to the young Prince Fedorcenko and identified himself as Anna's brother. Such a connection, however slight, would have meant a touch, even if distant, with a sister he had always loved.

Now the prince was gone, Anna was gone . . . they were all gone. He would never see them again.

All the things he had believed in now seemed hollow. It had once seemed so important to oppose the aristocratic league of the tsar and his government. Their goal had been to overthrow the oppressors, thinking it would rid society of all its evils. They had killed the tsar, but what had really changed? Were the rebels really any different from the nobles, down deep where the foundations of life pulsed within them? As they left Tiumen, what could be said to have distinguised him from the young Prince Fedorcenko?

Fragmentary conversations and memories flooded him as he made his way toward a future of empty meaninglessness at Kolyma: happy childhood play in Katyk, walking silently with his father away from the jail in Akulin, his father's enthusiasm over Paul's education. He supposed they would always represent the former carefree days of his youth. Even when he thought back to his first introduction to political ideas at the feet of his martyred friend, Kazan, he could not do so without a sense of pleasant nostalgia.

His papa's hearty laugh . . . Mama's bustling energy . . . his little brother constantly tagging after him . . . Kazan's passionate idealism . . .

Anna had always spoken of God in a way that, try as he might, Paul could not understand. She had trusted Him as an all-loving, all-sovereign Father who only wanted good for His children. His ways, she said, were truly beyond understanding, but when we did trust Him, the understanding of His nature grew with it. Paul had not been able to grasp the reality of Anna's personal God. He had always considered such faith something only for people like Anna and their father, people he thought of as weak and ineffectual.

So many times as he was growing up he had come upon Anna somewhere alone—in a corner of the *izba* when the weather was cold, out under the willow tree during the warm season, sometimes just walking along through the solitary fields. She always had a smile for him, and was usually either reading or carrying the small Bible of their papa's. She had read to him occasionally from some favorite passage. She had spoken to him of wisdom.

He could not deny that he yearned for those sweet days now as he trudged along in filth and despair to an uncertain future, exiled to permanent sorrow and loneliness—his life cut short and essentially ended in its very prime. All his ideas, all his passions—where had they left him in the end? Broken and empty, drained of direction and purpose. Even his final act of rebellion, the assassination attempts of the tsar, had been for nothing. The people had responded by spitting in the faces of the heroic assassins, and a new tsar was cheered on to his throne. And the hand of tyranny and repression fell harder upon them, though none seemed to care.

Why should *he* care anymore?

He had given his life to bring freedom to a people who didn't want freedom. He had suffered and fought and even murdered for them, but all he had to show for his efforts was . . . nothing. He had watched his friends die for an illusion. How could they have been so foolish? He used to call Anna naive, but she was far less so than he and his comrades who actually *believed* they could change the world and make a difference. They were all gone, dead, exiled, or simply deserted, and yet the world on as if they had never existed. Nothing changed.

If he could, he'd forget it all and go back to Katyk and till his papa's meager patch of earth, milk the scrawny cow, and try to prod some life out of that ancient horse Lukiv. He'd marry and have children and break his back every day to try to keep them all from starvation. If the peasants liked that life so much, perhaps there was something to it that he had missed seeing.

Well, he couldn't go back now even if he did want to, which in all truth he did not. Not, however, because he was afraid of labor or poverty—God only knew he had worked harder and starved more in the city than he ever had at his papa's—but because he could never look with respect upon those simple peasants again who had refused a chance for a better life.

All he had ever wanted to do was help. What was so terrible in that? What more could a feeling man do when he saw need and injustice?

But it was all over now. Exiled for life. Completely isolated. Even after his hard-labor sentence was over, he would be remanded to some tiny village where he would live out his days as an "enforced resident." Perhaps since he could read and figure, he could earn a little money as a clerk and find a way to survive. But what good would it do? What good could *he* do? His life was over.

But even in the midst of his despair, from out of the distant past came Kazan's words back to him. What was it he had once called Siberia . . . *the University of Revolution*.

Perhaps . . . just perhaps . . . there *might* be something more than nothingness and ignominy ahead of him. Kazan himself had escaped exile.

Was it possible that his life might not be over? Regardless, he was *not* alone. There were still others who believed as he did. Perhaps together, even here in the isolated wastes of Siberia, they might yet have an impact upon the government and the ambivalent masses.

It was something to think about anyway. Something to warm his bones and soothe the hungry ache in his stomach as he marched onward toward whatever destiny lay before him in this empty, desolate land.

53

For three days Kaplan had enjoyed the fetterless freedom and solitary nights of free-command as a Kara convict.

One of the best-kept secrets of the Russian Siberian prison system was the fact that escape was not nearly so impossible as the St. Petersburg government would have its people believe. It all depended upon what one meant by *escape*. If getting outside the walls of one of the prisons sufficed in itself, then so-called "escape" was not altogether uncommon. If escape meant a successful and healthy return to Russian life and society in the cities and temperate climes west of the Urals, then it was indeed *impossible*. The distances were so huge, and the terrain and weather so fierce and inhospitable that the land simply could not be traversed by one traveling alone. Scattered throughout the sparsely populated regions of far eastern Russia, however, lived any number of former convicts who had managed to escape from the various prisons and labor camps and had been content to carve out some life of poverty in the nearby environs, free of their chains. Whether it was a "freedom" worth risking one's life for, each man had to resolve for himself. Hundreds made the attempt every year. Most continued the futile effort to cross the Siberian plains before winter, the vast majority dying before catching a distant glimpse of the Urals. The wise ones did not try, but set their sights nearer at hand. Without help, without transportation, without food, escape usually meant a hasty death. So most of the convicts remained where they were, weighing the risks of escape against the possibility of pardon or release at some distant future time.

But for those intent on getting free from their shackles, ways could be found, and usually the guards did not stand in the way. Half the guards and wardens were paroled onetime prisoners themselves and were cut out of the same breed of humanity as their charges. If they could discover a means whereby to profit themselves from a prisoner's escape, they would allow it and line their own pockets in the process. Scruples, integrity, and morals were not common in Siberia, on *either* side of the fence.

Of course it wouldn't do to have the prisons emptying. The guards had to keep some semblance of order. But they all had their favorites, even those they might be inclined to help or encourage—the old and the infirm particularly, whose loss would scarcely be felt in the daily tally of gold, and whose chances of survival in the wilderness was slim. If they looked the other way, and a few escaped and died, so much the better for everyone. It was an effective means of weeding out the aged, the troublemakers, the malcontents. And if they remained on the roll, the governmental allowances continued to come in for total head count, and their reputation did not suffer from having to report escapees.

Kaplan was one such who would not be missed; he had not one chance in a thousand of making it fifty versts beyond the mines. At least that was the opinion of the guard whose friendship the old convict had been cultivating for five years—especially once Kaplan divulged his plan to follow the treacherous Shilka River to Nerchinsk, thence to embark southward over the Khingah mountains into Mongolia. It was suicide, the guard thought as he chuckled to himself over the prospect. But if the old fellow wanted to try it, who was he to stand in his way? Maybe he would even make it. He would never see Moscow or St. Petersburg again, and what harm if some Mongolian or Tartar tribesman ran him through with a scimitar.

It was late afternoon. A relentless, tiring sun beat down upon the mines of Kara. During the last of the five-minute water breaks, Kaplan sauntered over to the guard to engage him in conversation, while Sergei, by prearrangement, eased his way inconspicuously to the crude privy at the back of a short line of his fellows. The area was halfway enclosed, though hardly private.

Sergei delayed until all the others were through and the place empty. Kaplan may have been old and insignificant in the eyes of the authorities, but not Sergei. He was young and was accompanied by a reputation. It would take ingenuity and daring for him to escape the watchful gaze of the guards.

Kaplan had thought of this too, although when he first proposed it to his young accomplice, Sergei had laughed with disgust and revulsion. Only later as he pondered his hideous fate did he realize the genius of the plan. As Kaplan had said, it was his only chance. There was no other place to hide. Inspection would not reveal him missing until the morning. And by then the two of them would be many kilometers downriver—if his chains didn't drag him to the bottom and permanently entomb him under thirty meters of icy water pouring down out of the Mongolian highlands.

The thought of freedom had nearly been outweighed by the disgusting horror of the plan. Sergei's stomach had been churning all day in morbid anticipation. He would sooner face an entire battalion of Turks singlehandedly!

"That is exactly why it will work, my squeamish young friend!" said Kaplan the night before, with a grin of pleasure at Sergei's discomfort. "Not the most suspicious, not the most wicked, not the most alert guard in all of Siberia would suspect such a thing! You will be safe until I come for you after the night is well dark and everyone in free-command well asleep."

Safe! thought Sergei with abhorrence. His stomach would be empty within two minutes! He would then have to lie in his own vomit besides!

When the last of his fellows had left the walled-off area, Sergei knew the moment of his greatest earthly trial had come. To do what now was set before him would take more courage than it had for him to step in front of Rustaveli's loaded gun. He inched forward, dragging his chains slowly across the dirt, knowing that the nauseating reek all about him was only the beginning. New latrines were dug only every several months, and this one was nearly full.

He crept to the edge of the ditch, casting a quick glance behind him through the opening in the privy barricade. At the edge of the pit he was shielded from the view of both convicts and guards. He slid to a sitting position, dangling his legs over into the foul hole of refuse. Then, closing his eyes and grimacing as though facing a firing squad, he slid over and lowered himself into the pit.

His feet oozed their way deep into the noxious human dung, covering the tops of his boots and going halfway to his knees before feeling the slightest resistance. His stomach retched violently from the stench—once . . . twice . . . and was empty in less time than he had predicted.

But he had to hide himself out of sight in case another prisoner should enter to make use of the place. He had known that when he began the descent, and now, without pausing for further reflection, he slowly lay down on his back, allowing the vile muck to close over his legs and body. He might faint a half dozen separate times before nightfall from the rank stench and the mere realization of what he was doing. But for now he was out of sight—just as a heavy-footed guard walked in, glanced hurriedly around for malingerers, and then exited again, leaving the onetime prince of Russia in the most hideous of self-dug living graves.

The seven-hour wait seemed like seven years, but at last Sergei heard the raspy whispering voice of his savior above him. He reached up a hand he had kept free of the muck. Kaplan took it and, with great effort, pulled his young accomplice from the hideous pit.

Without pausing to comment on his condition, Kaplan motioned him to follow. Sergei did so, and, following a circuitous route so as to avoid being seen, they arrived two or three hours before dawn at the entrance to the great Shilka, a kilometer and a half beyond the free-command border of the Kara settlement.

"The water will clean the stench from you, my young friend," Kaplan said. "But it will also bury you if you allow your chains to drag you out into its depths. The river is rapid and treacherous. Stay near the side or you will be pokoinik, indeed!"

Sergei nodded. Right now, death itself seemed a pleasant thought alongside how he had spent the last nine hours!

Kaplan looked at him once more. "After this I will call you *Pokoinik* no longer, for we shall be free men indeed!" Then he turned toward the river and leaped into the turbulent blackness below.

Sergei hesitated only a moment, then followed.

He plunged in, sank down, and knew instantly the water was well in excess of his own height in depth. His chained feet hit the bottom in a moment; and from the tumbling along of the rocks beneath him, he knew he was already being carried along quickly by the fierce, icy current.

The only other creature out at that midnight hour was a solitary owl, circling above the taiga in search of field mice and wood rats. Its keen eyesight instantly discerned the two creatures at the river's edge. But even as it swooped down for a closer look, two faint splashes sounded and then were quickly swallowed up by the rush and roar of the river itself.

The great night bird glided down with outstretched wings and floated along the water's surface, turning its head this way and that. There would be no dinner for it to pluck out of the water, however. Far in the distance, downriver, the owl could just barely make out the form of a single head bobbing up and down in the swirling flow.

But the current was swift, and had already borne whatever it was well beyond its reach.

Part VIII

VENGEANCE UNLEASHED
(Summer 1881)

54

A light rain splattered the branches of the great elm outside Anna's window. She sat at her little desk, her mind distracted for the hundredth time from the book she had been trying to read. She watched as the beads of water gathered on the fresh green leaves of the tree, their weight bending the slender shoots steadily downward until the moment when each fell with a tiny silent splash to the damp earth below. One after another the drops fell from the tree—dozens, hundreds, thousands—in the infinite dance of a Russian summer rain.

Lately their own lives mirrored the simple patterns of nature.

This family, to whom she had pledged not only her loyalty as a servant but also the love of her heart, once seemed unassailable, as strong as the thick trunk of the mighty elm where it emerged from the ground. Now the family resembled instead the elm's higher regions, where willowy new sprigs of growth were not able to bear up under the weight of the tragedies falling so rapidly upon them.

Her own mistress, Princess Katrina, was clearly holding up the best. Her faith had become stronger than any of the others in the household in recent years, and yet with half the small family now gone, even the princess was approaching the limits of her deep inner strength.

What would happen if she did reach the end of it, Anna did not know. She had never seen Katrina weak since she had known her. Vulnerable upon occasion, but never *weak*.

She had been praying for them all, masters and servants alike, so often that her knees ached with the strain. She tried to pray and then lay her anxieties aside, as her papa would tell her to do. But she could not deny that the family's travail continued to worry her. Considering her own personal grief, she could not help comparing *herself* with the fragile leaves that seemed so weak, and wondering if *she* could hold up indefinitely under the cascade of hurtful circumstances.

Such a state of mind had driven her on this dreary day to seek consolation by escaping to her books. Dostoyevsky's newest, *The Brothers Karamazov*, had caught her eye on her shelf and she had taken it down and begun reading only a short time ago. She would rather read about the problems of others than think about her own. And somehow the selection seemed a fitting honor to the great writer, who had died only three months before.

A few years ago, at Sergei's urging, she had read *Crime and Punishment*, although it had taken her forever. They had a lengthy discussion of the book afterward, which had brought to the surface widely differing opinions on the motives and innocence or culpability of the protagonist. She wondered what a similar discussion would reveal now. They both had changed so much since then. What would Sergei say now to the plight of the fictional student murderer Raskolnikov? She shuddered at the comparison.

Back then Sergei had also urged her to read *Memoirs From the House of the Dead*. She hadn't, even though he said it would help her understand Raskolnikov's plight better. Since Sergei's arrest she had tried once again to read it, hoping Dostoyevsky's portrayal of life in Siberian prisons would help her feel closer to Katrina's brother. But she could only wade through two or three pages before snapping the little volume shut in utter despair. In this case, the truth neither set her free from her fears nor consoled her. It was simply better not to know.

Perhaps that was in part why Prince Fedorcenko had taken Sergei's exile as such a devastating blow. He had visited the labor camps years ago as an emissary of the tsar. He had seen firsthand all that Dostoyevsky had described in his book. He *did* know.

The thought of Sergei's father drew Anna's attention once more from her reading. The man who had suffered over the sentencing of his son was utterly inconsolable since the death of his wife. Within the span of a few short months, half his family had been cruelly snatched from him—the tsar had been assassinated, and his own career and reputation shattered. The shock to his mental and emotional state had been debilitating. He was a man whose whole life was crumbling into ruins at his feet.

For all her frivolous, even childlike mannerisms, Princess Natalia had lent a peculiar and invisible stability to the family. No one would have acknowledged it, least of all Natalia herself. Yet now, since her death, even stouthearted, feisty Katrina had shown shaky moments of insecurity. In Prince Fedorcenko's case, he had always derived his reason for being from having someone to protect and care for—and not only his frail wife. In a brotherly sort of way he had considered the tsar at least in part an object of his care as well.

Now suddenly both objects of his patronage were gone. The very underpinnings of his mode of existence were no longer there. Son exiled, daughter married, wife dead, Alexander dead. Nothing was left to him but the cold, empty silence of a huge house that once rang with laughter and activity.

At every turn tragedy seemed his lot. And in combination with his guilt over the plight of his son, the bizarre accumulation of events seemed to be gathering sufficient momentum to push the once mighty prince over the edge of sanity itself.

55

The visit to the Remizov home by Mrs. Remington, while unexpected, was not altogether surprising.

"I would not think to trouble you at such a time, Princess Katrina," said the faithful Fedorcenko housekeeper, "if I did not think it to be extremely important."

"Please, Mrs. Remington," said Katrina, "think nothing of it. It is good to see you, here in my home. Won't you come into the parlor and sit down."

"Oh, Princess, I should not bother you for so long as—"

"Nonsense, come in and visit," persisted Katrina, heedless of the other's hesitation. "I will order us tea."

Although Mrs. Remington had known Katrina from infancy, now that she was married and mistress of a home of her own, the difference between their stations had exerted itself, causing her to defer to the daughter of her master. The little girl had become a nobleman's wife and an aristocrat in her own right. And she would be a mother herself—almost any day now.

The Englishwoman followed Katrina into the parlor without further argument, and received tea from the hand of one of Katrina's servants. As Mrs. Remington spoke, the awful realization had dawned on Katrina that she might well soon be the only viable head of the House of Fedorcenko. Unaccustomed feelings of mingled pain and unsought maturity flooded through Katrina's heart as she listened. Even as new life beat strongly within her, Katrina ached the way only a sensitive child can for an aging parent, wondering if her new son or daughter would ever know as grandfather the man she had loved as father.

"I have come concerning your father, Princess—"

Mrs. Remington hesitated and looked away for a moment. "May I speak frankly?"

Katrina nodded her assent, "Please go on, Mrs. Remington."

"You know, I am certain, how much difficulty he has had accepting your mother's death?"

"Of course," answered Katrina slowly.

"But I had hoped that after the funeral, reality would settle upon him."

"Yes. It has taken us all some time to adjust," replied Katrina.

Mrs. Remington grimly shook her head. "It is now some time since the funeral, and I fear the situation is growing worse."

"How so?" said Katrina.

Mrs. Remington paused again, hesitant to intrude into areas too familial and too personal, yet compelled for the sake of love not to keep silent.

Katrina read her ambivalence. "Please, Mrs. Remington," she said with almost a hint of impatience, "you said you wanted to speak frankly."

"Forgive me, Princess. It is difficult to speak so about the prince. I am very fond of my master. He and your mother have been more kind to me than I deserve all these years. I—"

She turned away and hastily brushed a tear from her eye. Katrina pressed no further, and waited for her to continue.

"Often in the night," Mrs. Remington went on after a moment, "your father is heard roaming the corridors of the house. I hear the sounds of doors opening and closing. And then comes his voice, low and soft, calling for your mother. Oh, Princess, I am so sorry to tell you such things, but his voice sounds so pathetic when he calls, 'Natalia . . . Natalia, where are you?' It makes my heart break for him! Over and over he calls her name. More than once I have had to send for the menservants to try to coax him back to his room and bed, but sometimes he becomes violent if they try to come near him."

The housekeeper stopped, wringing her hands together in

obvious distress over the man she had always respected and admired.

"Why have you come only now to tell me of this?" asked Katrina straightforwardly.

"I did not want to trouble you. And I hoped it would subside. But an incident only yesterday finally has driven me to come to you."

"What was it that happened?"

"You know that poor Nina has taken the loss of her mistress as hard as anyone. She devoted her entire life in service to your mother, and loved her deeply."

"I do know. I truly believe Mother considered Nina her closest friend," said Katrina, her thoughts flitting momentarily to Anna.

"Yesterday, Princess, your father, the prince, happened upon Nina cleaning Princess Natalia's rooms. He approached her roughly and yelled at her as if addressing a stranger, 'What have you done with my wife, you Lithuanian hag?'"

"Poor Nina!" said Katrina.

"Fortunately, one of the men was nearby and heard the uproar. His approach calmed the prince down. I honestly do not know what would have happened otherwise."

"I must talk with Nina as soon as possible," replied Katrina. "Hopefully I will be able to set her mind at ease."

"I am afraid it is too late," Mrs. Remington went on. "She resigned her position immediately after the incident. Not in anger, mind you, but because she felt that her presence as one so closely associated with the princess would be too painful for the prince."

"I suppose there is truth to that."

"I think, as well, that she was having difficulty coping with her own grief. In the midst of a lifetime of memories, she could not help feeling an emptiness deep inside her soul. She packed her things and was gone by evening."

"Did . . . did you say anything to her?" asked Katrina, moved by the sad turn of circumstances.

"I took the liberty of sending a favorable recommendation along with her, and I believe she will have no difficulty finding a new position." Mrs. Remington punctuated her words with a heavy sigh. Her natural British reserve was holding her in good stead, but her control was strained with every word, and the tears which had thus far come only in ones and twos threatened to break into a flood.

Katrina, however, who did not have the benefit of English stoicism, found herself weeping freely. Her tears fell not only for dear Nina having come to such a sad end but also for her father.

"There is more, Princess," Mrs. Remington went on reluctantly after a pause.

No words would come, but Katrina nodded for her to continue. It was best to get it all out in one painful revelation.

"Later in the day, I went to your father's study, hoping to perhaps divert his grief by interesting him once more in a few matters concerning the household's affairs. He bade me enter when I knocked. But what I saw when I walked into the room shocked me so terribly, Princess, that I knew I must come to you at my earliest convenience."

The fear apparent in the housekeeper's voice dried Katrina's tears instantly. "Go on," she said soberly.

"He sat at his desk staring blankly ahead as if I did not exist. And lying before him on the desk was a pistol, which he was absently stroking with one hand. I am sorry, Princess Katrina, if I have overstepped my bounds in making my own conjectures—"

"Mrs. Remington, you cannot think—"

Katrina could not even verbalize the horrifying thought. It could not be possible. Not her father!

"Princess, I believe he has lost all will to live."

A stunned silence settled over the room the moment the words left her lips. "I—I cannot imagine he could actually consider such a thing," said Katrina at length.

"It is difficult for me to believe it also. In God's name, Princess, I pray I am wrong. But nevertheless I took the precaution of assigning some of the more faithful men to take turns in keeping a watch on him. I hope I did not err too badly in taking such a great liberty."

"No, Mrs. Remington, it was very wise of you. Whatever my father may think, I at least thank you for your concern." The practicality of the housekeeper's action struck a responsive chord in Katrina's brain.

"I fear your father did *not* react well. This morning, when it dawned on him what they were doing, he flew into a rage. He attacked the poor servant whose watch it was. 'Imperial spies!' he screamed. 'I knew they were out to get me!'"

Again Katrina's tentative reserve crumbled. She sent a hand up to cover her trembling lips.

"Oh, Papa!"

The loss of the inexplicable security that Natalia had provided her family was difficult enough. But the impregnability of her father's unmovable presence had long dominated even that. *He* had always been the weighty foundation stone, the family's rock, the rudder giving direction and purpose to the ship called Fedorcenko. Sergei may have chafed under it. Katrina may have wished for deeper fatherly intimacy from him. But the stability and force of his bearing could never have been assailed. He had ruled the home—occasionally with an iron fist, often with a hand of gentleness. But whatever the circumstances, whatever the method by which he displayed it, Viktor's authority had been unquestioned.

Now suddenly that rock seemed crumbling to powder. Katrina wondered with despair how she could manage life without him.

The same afternoon, after relating these things to Anna, and a good share of cleansing tears, Katrina arrived at the decision to return to her father's home. Whether her father's life was truly in danger or not, it was certain that his self-command was nearly at an end, and she desperately hoped that her presence might encourage him out of his despondency. She quickly made arrangements for a message to be sent to Dmitri's regimental commander.

Then she and Anna packed a few belongings, had the *droshky* brought around, and departed.

56

Katrina knew the stalwart Mrs. Remington well enough to be certain she wasn't one to exaggerate. Yet she was still shocked to observe her father's condition with her own eyes.

The picture she would always hold in her mind's eye was her father as a trim scion of military perfection. His uniform jacket, with its neat rows of medals and the blue sash of his Order of St. Andrew, never showed a wrinkle no matter how long he had been wearing it. His broad shoulders and fine military bearing, the gold buttons on his coat and his high leather boots polished to a glossy finish . . . *that* was her father.

She hardly recognized the figure that greeted her that evening at dinner. Her father looked more like a dissolute street vagrant than a Russian prince. He had discarded his uniform jacket altogether. The white shirt he wore and the uniform trousers were creased and wrinkled and had not been washed in days. His hair was disheveled, and his beard untrimmed and shaggy.

Most remarkably, Katrina noted more gray in his hair and beard than had existed there the last time she had seen him. She had heard that emotional distress caused people to go prematurely—and sometimes quickly—gray. But never had she seen it demonstrated so dramatically. She decided it must be a trick of her imagination.

But one thing *was* certain. He *had* aged, either physically or in some deeper, unseen way. No doubt a bath, a shave, and a good night's sleep would remedy the surface haggard look. But it was clear from his eyes that the change went beyond anything that could so quickly be mitigated. And although she did her best to hide it, Katrina was shocked.

When he came near her he reeked like a distillery. She was thankful at least that he didn't flare up at the sight of her. She had hoped he would not question her impromptu appearance just before the dinner hour. Perhaps, this once, Mrs. Remington was exaggerating after all.

"Ah, Katrina! What a pleasure to see you!" he said expansively. He took her hands in his, and except for the outward appearance and the smell of alcohol, she might have begun to doubt the housekeeper's morbid speculations.

"Hello, Papa. I hope you don't mind a visit just now."

"Of course not," he replied. "You are just in time to join us for dinner."

"Thank you."

"It is only a pity your mother is away," Viktor went on. "What a time for her to visit Lividia! But you know how she hates the coming of summer here in the capital. I would join her, but duty calls, you know!"

"It's . . . it's you I came to see anyway, Papa."

"How nice . . ."

His words trailed away as if some thought were trying to divert his attention. His eyes seemed to glaze over and momentarily lose their focus. "Uh . . . what . . . what were you saying?" he mumbled at length.

"We were talking about why I had come."

"Ah yes . . . why *have* you come?" he said, turning toward her more forcefully. His eyes narrowed and he suddenly became suspicious.

"To see you, Papa."

"Ha! That's a good one!" He said the words as though they made perfect sense. Then he turned and walked away toward his chair at the dining table.

"Well," he said sharply, "you are going to eat?"

"I . . . if you want me to, Papa," she answered hesitantly, following him.

"You may as well. That's why you've come—that's all you really want anyway, is it not?"

"I don't understand, Papa. I just want to see you. I heard you weren't well and—"

"Ah! So *that's* it! My own daughter!" he roared. "I thought I could expect some loyalty from you, at least. But I see this plot is wider than I had imagined. You are no better than Orlov and Baklanov conspiring against me . . . trying to be rid of me once and for all!"

"No, Papa!" Katrina said in a pleading tone, trying with little success to hold back her tears. "I want to help you!"

Almost expecting an explosive outburst from her father, Katrina was surprised at the brief moment of silence that followed. The next words were not those of a madman, but seemed to grope for some reality of relationship from out of the past to latch onto.

"You have known me better than any other human being, Katrina. Don't you realize yet, daughter of mine, that I am beyond help?" For a single instant he appeared focused and sane.

It lasted but a few seconds. Suddenly he let out a sharp, humorless laugh, then strode toward the door, forgetting altogether about the meal, appearing not even to see the maid approaching with platter in hand.

"All the good brandy is in the parlor," he said. "I must tell Natalia to have the servants begin serving Scotch at dinner— I don't care how ill-mannered it is."

He walked through the door and left the room, leaving his daughter staring dumbfounded after him. For a fleeting moment she wondered if she should go after him and make some continued attempts to find something to talk about that would distract him. But she thought better of it. She dismissed the maid, then left the dining room with heavy step.

In despair she dragged herself back upstairs to her old quarters. Anna had been busy freshening up the rooms, although they had been fairly well kept up during the year of Katrina's absence. Even the warmth of Anna's presence, however, could not console the princess. For Viktor Fedorcenko to lose the grip on his sanity was tantamount to nothing in this life being strong and sure enough to trust in or depend upon. If a man with his fortitude could break, then what else in life could be relied upon to stand?

Anna placed an arm around her mistress and tried to offer her what comfort she could.

"Oh, Anna, it's awful to see him so weak. It takes my very heart away."

"You must not give up, Princess, even if it seems that is what your father has done."

"But it is destroying him, Anna!" wailed Katrina softly and tearfully. Anna sighed deeply, softly stroking Katrina's hair. "I mean no disrespect, Your Highness," she said after a moment, "for I know how painful your father's losses are. But it would seem to me that he is making a choice not to face reality."

The words hung in the air a moment; then Katrina turned to face her maid with a serious expression on her face.

"What are you saying, Anna?" she asked.

"Only that no matter how terrible the circumstances that come upon us, we still must choose what will be our response. I must admit sometimes I do not think I am doing well in the matter of your brother. But I nevertheless realize I cannot lose heart, and must go on living, and serving you as well as I am able."

"And you think my father *has* given up?"

"That is not for me to say, Princess. I only know that *you* mustn't—no matter what grief you feel for him. You have too much to live for."

Even as the words fell upon Katrina's ear, the unborn infant within her gave a vigorous kick. The present physical reminder jarred Katrina's natural resiliency back toward the surface.

Of course she couldn't lose heart. And not only for herself, but also for the sake of the next generation she was carrying in her womb. Besides, giving in to adversity wasn't her way.

Even if that part of her nature had come from her father, she could not deny it or hide from it as he now seemed to be doing. Even if mother, brother, *and* father were taken from her, somehow she had to face what life was left to her with head held high.

There was no other way to triumph over painful circumstances in the end.

57

Alone later in the evening, Katrina's despair began again to sweep over her spirit.

It was only about seven in the evening and early, by her normal custom, for retiring. Yet she was exhausted.

Anna had gone to the other wing of the house to visit her former friends and acquaintances, particularly in the kitchen. Katrina undressed and got herself ready for bed. She was sitting at her dressing table brushing out her hair when a knock sounded on the door of the sitting room.

"Come in, Anna," she said without looking up.

She heard the door open, and at last she finally glanced toward it. "Dmitri!"

As Dmitri approached, Katrina felt a thrill of joy and yearning almost like she had before their marriage. She *needed* him just then—perhaps more than she had for months, even if just the feel of his strong arms around her. Oddly, she hadn't thought much about her husband throughout most of the very difficult day. But now that he was at her side, she wondered how she could have survived it without him. She dropped her brush on the table, jumped up, and went quickly to meet him.

"I came as soon as I got your message," he said, embracing her.

"I am so glad . . . thank you."

"I would have been here sooner, but I was in Tsarskoye Selo, and the message was long in reaching me."

"Oh, I don't mind how long it took. Just that you are here means so much to me."

"I saw Anna downstairs," Dmitri went on. "She told me you and your father argued."

"You did not see him when you came in?"

"No, he had retired to his rooms."

"He looks awful, Dmitri. He is drinking heavily, carrying on as if my mother is still alive, and ready to fly off angrily if anyone crosses him. He actually struck one of the servants."

"I am sorry, dear," he said tenderly, running his hand through her hair.

"What am I going to do, Dmitri?" said Katrina, sobbing again. "He has become like a stranger."

He continued to hold her tight, as if for now the only answer he had to give was his embrace. After a moment, suddenly she winced slightly as the hilt of his sabre jabbed her side. He pulled away quickly.

"I'm sorry—how thoughtless of me," he said. His voice displayed a deeper concern than she had heard from him in what seemed many months. For the first time she realized there was no odor of alcohol about him.

She smiled through her tears. "There's the army," she said, "coming between us again."

He chuckled, and they both felt the healing touch of the brief moment of levity between them.

Dmitri unfastened his sabre, slipped off the belt, and rested it against the wall in a corner. He then stripped off his jacket before taking his still-weeping wife into his arms once more.

"My poor Katrina," he said in her ear. "How I wish I could make all this pain go away for you. Don't forget, Sergei was my best friend, and I miss him, too. If I could, I would bring him and your mother back. And I will try to talk to your father if you think it might help. But—"

"Just hold me, Dmitri. Just now I need nothing more. Father would not listen to me or anyone else right now."

He smoothed back her hair and gently kissed her forehead, then eased her gently toward her own bed. He set her down, then lay beside her on top of the coverlet, cradling her head on his shoulder. Katrina received his tender affection eagerly. Soon her tears were gone and they were talking freely. In one respect Katrina was very much like her mother. She was not made for the somber existence of perpetual mourning. Ongoing grief wore her down as much as whatever heartbreaking circumstance had caused it in the first place.

For the first time in weeks Katrina felt truly relaxed, and a few hints of a carefree spark returned to her tone. More than that, she felt in loving harmony with Dmitri for the first time in a long while. For months a tension had hung in the air between them. Yet now, emerging out of the desolation and loss the day's events had brought so close, here they were talking spontaneously and unreservedly as they hadn't during all the months of her pregnancy.

Was it possible their marriage still had a chance to be everything she had always dreamed it would be? Perhaps the birth of their child would be the key to unlocking their future as a family together.

58

Another knock came to the sitting room door.

Both Dmitri and Katrina would like to have ignored it. But with Viktor's unstable condition they could not take the chance.

Dmitri gently pulled his arm out from under Katrina's head, stood beside the bed, then strode into the sitting room and opened the door to find his valet. Their conversation drifted into the other room, where Katrina continued to lie dreamily on the bed.

"This had better be important, Andrei."

"Forgive me, Your Excellency. I would not think of disturbing you, but the lieutenant seemed most urgent."

"The lieutenant?"

"Yes, sir. Lieutenant Plaksa has come from the barracks

with a message for you. It seems there has been trouble."

"What trouble? Tell him to come back tomorrow. There is trouble here too, and my wife and family need me now."

"What shall I tell him, sir?"

"Tell him exactly what I said—no, wait," Dmitri added quickly. "Go downstairs, Andrei, and bring him here. I shall tell him myself." Dmitri's voice revealed his clear annoyance at being disturbed like this. For the first time in a long while, he did not want his professional life to intrude upon his personal one.

The valet turned and disappeared. Dmitri walked slowly back into the bedroom, apologized to Katrina for the interruption, kissed her lightly, and assured her he would take care of it as quickly as possible. The valet was just returning with Dmitri's fellow officer when the prince made his way back through the sitting room to the still-open door.

"What's this all about, Plaksa?"

"It wasn't my fault, Dmitri!" responded the lieutenant in an excited, agitated voice.

"Whoever's to blame, it looks as if you got the worst of it. I would think you'd been through a war!" Dmitri scanned his eyes up and down the man's bedraggled uniform.

"You've got to believe me—he asked for it, and that's all there—"

"Hold on, Plaksa," interrupted Dmitri. "What are you talking about?"

"The captain, sir. Sajachmetev."

"I suppose from your appearance there's hardly much need for me to ask what happened." Dmitri sighed. "Well, I suppose you'd better tell me about it, Lieutenant."

Plaksa took a breath so ragged Katrina heard it in the bedroom.

"I took all I could from the captain, sir," he said. "Then I thrashed him. That's all there is to it."

"By heavens, man! You didn't strike the first blow? He's your superior officer!"

"You know as well as I do that the man's a snake and deserves whatever he gets."

"That may well be, Plaksa. But it will be you who suffers

in the end. I told you not to let him goad you."

"He went too far, I tell you!"

"I am surprised he let you go afterward," observed Dmitri, knowing all too well the callous reputation of the captain in question.

"He didn't exactly *let* me go . . ."

"Don't tell me you bolted!"

When the miserable lieutenant nodded, Dmitri added, "Desertion will go all the worse for you, man! He could have you sent to fight the Turks, or even to Siberia for this!"

"You've got to help me, Dmitri," pleaded the lieutenant.

The two young men had entered the regiment together. But even with all Dmitri's close calls, scrapes, and foolish escapades, he had fared better than Plaksa, who lacked the count's wit and intelligence. Sergei, too, had known the lieutenant, but had long since made it a practice to keep clear of him, warning Dmitri that his friend's hot head and ready fists would be the undoing of him in the end. Now at last Sergei's prophetic word—though he had gotten himself into far deeper trouble in the meantime—seemed about to be fulfilled. Plaksa was the illegitimate son of an ambassador, and only his family name had kept him from the stockade, or worse, till now. But even that protection seemed about to lose any remaining effectiveness to prevent him from facing the consequences of his temper.

"You'll have to turn yourself in, Plaksa."

"They'll drum me out of the regiment. My father swore he'd not bail me out again."

"You should have thought of that before you lost your senses."

"Please, Dmitri!"

"Turning yourself in and losing your commission would be better than the stockade . . . or Siberia—one of which you're sure to get if they catch you on the run and the captain brings you up on charges."

"What am I going to do?" said the lieutenant in the forlorn tone almost of a wail.

"If you give yourself up and plead insanity or something, they will more than likely go easy on you. Maybe a demotion to ranks for a short while, but no worse."

"I couldn't stand prison!"

"If you keep your wits, you won't have to worry about it."

"I'd kill myself."

"You aren't going to Siberia, I tell you. Just keep your head!"

"You might be able to talk your way out of a mess like this, Dmitri, but I'd fumble it for certain."

"It is your only chance."

"Would you come with me—speak for me . . . explain what happened?" asked Plaksa hopefully.

"Look, I'd help you if I could. But I have problems of my own. That's why I left the barracks and hurried here earlier."

"I am a dead man if you do not help me!"

"Was it *really* so bad? Perhaps you are overreacting."

"You know Sajachmetev as well as I do. He hates me and is out for blood."

Dmitri scratched his head in deliberation, then gave a quick glance back toward the bedroom.

He had to admit, the lieutenant was right. If he did not have help, he could only hope for the worst. Yet, Dmitri wondered, how much help could he truly offer? Captain Sajachmetev didn't care that much for him either—as a man, at least, although he had always showed him the utmost respect as a soldier. Actually, as hard as it was to understand, the captain had from time to time displayed something like a regard for Dmitri. Perhaps it had to do with the fact that they had fought together in the Balkans and had forged a distant sort of mutual respect. Might that alone be enough to save Plaksa's skin? Perhaps . . . though if it didn't, he might be jeopardizing his own hide in standing up for him.

Even if he could help, was it worth abandoning Katrina again, just when she needed him? He had not done well by her. He knew that. And now, just when he had the opportunity to help in this new crisis within her family, was he going to leave her again?

Perhaps if he was gone only for an hour, just long enough to accompany Plaksa back to the barracks and convince the commander to hear his story tomorrow when everything had cooled down, then he could return to Katrina. He would spend the night here, offering what protection and solace his presence could to the deteriorating spirits within the Fedorcenko home. It was his duty as the man's son-in-law and as Katrina's husband. He would take care of his friend's trouble, then hurry back.

Resolved, he told his valet and the lieutenant to wait for him in the parlor downstairs. He closed the door and returned to Katrina.

"There has been some trouble at the regiment—" he began.

"I heard, Dmitri."

"I'm sorry, but I have to—" he began, sitting down on the side of the bed and taking her hand. But she interrupted him.

"I know. You need to help your friend."

"I would not leave under any other circumstances, believe me."

"I understand, dear," she said.

"Do you . . . do you *really*?"

Dmitri found himself almost surprised by his young wife's sincere response, but he tried not to let it show. He did not deserve her patience and understanding after all he had put her through.

"Yes, of course I do, Dmitri," Katrina said softly.

"I won't be long."

"I shall have a nap while you are gone. But promise you'll wake me when you return."

"I promise."

He bent over and touched his lips to hers in a long and heartfelt expression of his love. Slowly he rose.

"Look," he said, grabbing up his jacket from the chair where he had tossed it, "I'll be gone such a short time that I'm going to leave my sword right there." He paused a second longer, blew Katrina a parting kiss, and added, "I'll be back before you know it." He turned again and disappeared.

Katrina lay contentedly on her bed, staring up at the ceiling, so happy at the brief interlude with Dmitri that she did not even question what change might have caused it. She did not stop to ask herself why his sudden departure had not angered her, nor what change in Dmitri made him so apparently reluctant to leave her. It might need analyzing later, but in the meantime she did not want the encumbrance of logic to intrude upon the contented warmth within her heart. If her father was not doing well, it made all the difference in the world that Dmitri now seemed ready to share the heartache with her.

Her eyelids grew gradually heavy, and within moments she was dozing peacefully. She dreamed sweetly of Dmitri, and only once did the ugly figure of an insane man, who uncannily resembled her own father, wander across the otherwise blissful fields of her mind. But even this attempt to mar her happiness was unsuccessful, for when he was gone, there was Dmitri again, in the full brilliance of his uniform, a glowing smile upon his face, running toward her, ever closer, with arms outstretched. The only incongruity in the phantasm of her husband was that his sabre was missing from his side.

When she returned from the kitchen, Anna looked in upon her mistress. Katrina was sleeping peacefully, so she tiptoed in, retrieved a tray of tea things and left with only one final parting glance down at the dreaming lady on her bed.

It was wonderful, Anna thought, to see the princess wearing a smile again, especially in her sleep.

59

Basil Anickin had been watching the Remizov house for over a month. He had analyzed every movement of the servants, for they were chiefly the ones who came and went. The count himself was gone most days, and Katrina—both because of grieving for her mother and her physical condition—remained unseen behind high walls and closed doors.

Then had come the sudden moment of uncertainty when,

shortly after a visit by the woman he recognized as the Fedorcenko housekeeper, Katrina and that servant girl of hers had boarded a carriage with their luggage tied to the back.

They could not be leaving town! Where would they be going . . . for what purpose? He had even cultivated a spy or two in the household, and he had heard no such rumors from them.

He had actually been hoping for some such activity. As soon as the carriage had pulled away from the house, he jumped into his own nearby rig and followed at a safe distance.

Considering the luggage, he was surprised when the carriage pulled into the drive of the Fedorcenko estate. He stopped, tied his horse a hundred meters from the entrance, and hurriedly followed on foot. He saw the bags being unloaded and carried inside. Was Katrina in the process of moving back into her old home? With a child nearly due, was she running away from her husband? The very thought was too delicious to be true!

No, it must be something else. He had picked up other vague rumors since Princess Natalia's death. Her husband, Katrina's father, had been unwell, said some. Others hinted at darker troubles afflicting the house and mind of the prince. No one had been specific, but speculations and hints gave rise to the intimation that he had taken leave of his senses. Perhaps his daughter had returned home to tend him.

It made sense, thought Basil. And perhaps this sudden change could work to his advantage after all.

One thing that had greatly hampered his plans was an unfamiliarity with Katrina's new home. He had never been inside it, and his so-called spies were not in point of fact wholly *his*. He had befriended a coachman and a gardener, who worked by day in the Remizov home, and had been able to wheedle bits and pieces of information from them. But when once he had attempted to approach the topic of the lay of the house, he had met with dangerous questioning.

Thus he had abandoned that pathway for the time being, hoping a more trustworthy source would come along.

So this move to the old house was propitious, indeed. He knew the place well—not only from courting Katrina two years ago, but from his visits as a child. His father's traitorous selling out to society would at last serve some noble purpose!

He wondered how long this move, or visit, or whatever it was, might last. Was it merely for the night? That was unlikely, judging from the quantity of luggage.

But did it really matter? He had already waited as long as was tolerable for his revenge—months . . . years! And people said he was out of his mind. Ha! Only a deadly sane man could exercise such patience, such single-minded devotion to a noble purpose.

But his equanimity was wearing thin. The recent setbacks and delays had eroded it almost to oblivion. He had to get the thing done! He could not run the risk of being arrested again. It had been pure luck that he had survived this long as a fugitive in this city. He was tired of living in dark, scummy holes, coming out only at night for fear of being recognized. He was tired of living like a rat, grateful for the sympathy of a filthy street woman.

"Another debt to reconcile with that Fedorcenko hussy!" he hissed to himself. He pressed back into the shadows out of sight across from the Fedorcenko home.

Except for Katrina's cruel rejection, he'd still be a man of worth, a barrister defending a cause that had all but faded from his vision in the overwhelming glare of his hatred. Except for her, he would not have had to endure prison and that nightmarish asylum.

It was her fault—she was entirely to blame.

And now he would exact his revenge. She would pay . . . she and all those she cared for!

Her husband—oh, how he would relish that task!—and that brat she was expecting. Why should he leave out any of them? As she had snatched life's happiness from him, he would take life itself from them. It was perfectly fitting and just.

He would not wait another day. He would strike this very night!

Somehow he'd gain entrance to the house. A little reconnoitering ought to suffice his purpose. Of course half the servants would recognize him. He'd have to sneak his way, but that shouldn't be too difficult in a house where the order seemed slipping into chaos. He no longer cared about a finely

honed plan, not even the possibility of capture. After the deed
... well, he'd make a run for it as best he could. If he was
apprehended, he doubted he'd hang for the offense. At worst
he'd be sentenced to hard labor, a horrendous prospect, but
one from which escape was always possible for a resourceful
man.

To survive, however, and later look the count in the eye,
knowing that he *knew*, and then to end his life as he had his
young wife's—that would bring the crowning sweetness to the
taste of his revenge!

Carefully Basil stepped from his hiding place. The evening
was gradually drawing to a close, and even with the summer
twilight, a semblance of the dark clouds overhead would bring
night on even sooner than usual. He should have no trouble
with his evil work. The moon was thin. It should be dark
enough.

He inched back to the street; then, hugging the wall encircling the estate, he made his way south around toward that
flank of the huge house. Katrina had mentioned once that her
rooms faced the Neva, and that on clear days she could see the
green-blue water, and make out ships and pleasure craft sailing
on the river.

He himself had never been close to her rooms. But he had
once observed Katrina's shadowed form through a window he
was certain was her bedroom. He had made sufficient mental
calculations about its position relative to the rest of the place,
and its direction from the various possible entrances, to be
confident that he could locate that very room once inside the
familiar corridors. With the brother gone, and the father daft,
what danger could there be? The place was probably like a
tomb inside, and nobody would pay the least attention to him.

It would not be difficult. This was a St. Petersburg town
estate, after all, not a fortress. And the family—what was left
of them—were so wrapped up in their own troubles, they
would never expect a visitor from out of the past.

60

As evening shadows enshrouded Katrina's room, wakefulness began to creep upon her.

How long had it been since Dmitri had left? She had dozed off the minute he was gone and had no idea of the time. Only a little light from a sliver of a moon showing between the clouds filtered through a crack in the closed drapes. The only movement she detected as she turned her awkward body on the bed was a slight billowing in the drapery in front of the open window.

Katrina stretched out her arms to their full extent. She kept her eyes closed a moment or two longer. She still wasn't entirely ready to give herself over to wakefulness yet. The rest had been good, and she wasn't sure she was ready to face the new crisis of her father's state just yet.

Her thoughts turned to her husband. Might she have overslept his return? Perhaps he was out in her sitting room dozing on the settee, reluctant to wake her. A smile flickered across her lips as she recalled the pleasant interlude that had passed between them only a short while before.

A sound came to her ears.

"Dmitri?" she murmured, opening her eyes, and lifting her head slightly to scan the room. Nobody was there. When the sound repeated itself, she realized it was only a breeze rustling the tree branches outside the window.

She lifted the little silver bell at her bedside and gave it a quick shake. A moment later Anna knocked and opened the door.

"Anna, has Count Remizov returned?"

"No, Princess."

"Hmm . . . I thought he might have," replied Katrina, with a long, disappointed sigh.

"Did you have a good rest, Your Highness?"

"Yes, I suppose I did."

"Might I get you something? Some tea, perhaps?"

"I don't know . . . maybe I shall rest a bit longer. But come tell me the moment Dmitri comes back. Even if I'm sleeping."

"Yes, Princess."

"That's all, Anna. Thank you."

Anna left the room, and Katrina turned over on her side and tried to sleep again. But her waking had apparently awakened the baby as well. The unborn child kicked and squirmed in her womb, and Katrina smiled.

She wasn't really sleepy now anyway. But the bed felt cozy, and she didn't want to get up, not until Dmitri was with her again. She continued to lie in the darkness, gradually dozing off again.

Suddenly she was startled awake by a sharp sound. Before she could open her eyes, a hot, sweaty hand closed tightly over her mouth. A scream shuddered mutely through her body. She could not see the form lurking in the shadows at her back, but the flash of cold steel was unmistakable as his free hand jerked a long dagger up toward her throat.

"My patience is finally rewarded!" rasped a voice as hard and cold as the weapon it held.

Basil! Katrina's heart leaped into her throat. But only muffled grunts could escape the vise grip hand on her mouth.

"I am fortunate indeed to find you in bed . . . and *alone.*" The ominous emphasis on the final word only deepened Katrina's dismay. "Do you not agree, Princess? Am I not immensely lucky?"

Katrina struggled all the harder against his hold. "You want to speak, Your Highness?" he mocked. "How rude of me. I do not know my manners. I am, you know, merely the lowly son of an ex-serf."

All the rumors she had heard about Basil Anickin rushed in upon Katrina. Most of them she hadn't believed. But suddenly the truth was all too clear, and fear overwhelmed her.

He sensed her terror. "Yes, Katrina! I am going to kill you. I am going to kill you this very night!"

He let out a deep, horrifying, sickening laugh. "But I am in a quandary, my love," he went on after a moment. "You see, I have spent months dreaming of nothing but this moment. Yet now that it is here, I cannot decide if I will slit your throat or rend your heart in two as you did mine. Do you not see my perplexity? And . . . should it be a quick death, or shall I watch you suffer as I have suffered these many months?"

He paused and, without loosening his hold over her mouth, wrenched Katrina's body up into a sitting position. A slight wincing scream escaped her lips.

"Silence, you hussy!" he cried in a demonic whisper, "or I will end it immediately!"

He slid in behind her on the bed, holding her trembling frame in his wiry, muscular arms.

"I had hoped," he went on, calming again, "that the passion of the moment would dictate my method. But all at once I feel no passion. My loathing has somehow surpassed such emotion. In a way, I regret that, for it dulls some of the enjoyment."

He sighed. "But," he continued, as if debating within his twisted self, "perhaps the relish I had anticipated will return as I watch you suffer—there! My decision has been made. A long, painful death for you, Princess!"

Katrina attempted to squirm, ignoring the sharp stab of pain in her abdomen. But Basil was too strong for her.

"It is useless to struggle, Princess. Now, do you have some final words?" he asked maliciously. "I will remove my hand. But speak only in a whisper, or I will have to kill you quickly."

"Why. . . ?" she said.

"That you would even ask such a thing is reason enough!" he cried, his own vexed voice rising dangerously above a whisper.

"You will never get away with it. There are servants . . . my hus—"

His grip tightened about her again with a harsh jerk, almost choking the air from her lungs.

"Don't talk to me about *him*!" he said with icy command. "Only be comforted to know that he will die also, after he suffers enough from your loss—just as I did!"

"Basil, please . . . this is insane—"

His laughter, a mirthless, cold, hollow sound interrupted her. "Don't you know that I *am* insane, Katrina? That is what this is all about, isn't it? The lovely princess could not taint herself with the doctor's lunatic son. It was fine to *use* me to achieve your ends. He's so crazy, it won't matter to him . . . and then to get him arrested . . . very convenient for your purposes, I must say."

As he spoke, Katrina could feel the knife trembling slightly in his hand. "Do you know what they did to me, Princess?" he went on. "Can you imagine waking every day to the screams and pathetic groans of human beasts? Breathing the fetid air, eating what was not even fit for the rats. Then having my mind insidiously robbed by numbing drugs." Basil's eyes flamed and glinted with hatred as he spoke. "They took from me my very humanity! All so the fair little princess could play the fickle socialite!"

"Basil . . . I'm sorry. I never meant—"

"Sorry now! Now that you are about to die! Ha! Your foolish apologies mean nothing now! How could I have ever thought I loved the likes of you!"

"Please listen, Basil . . . I beg—"

"Ah, the princess *begs*, does she? It is more than I could have hoped for!"

His eyes narrowed and his lips twitched into a brief smile as an evil inspiration stole over him.

"Out of the bed, Princess!" he ordered.

Katrina obeyed, moving awkwardly, both from her girth and Basil's painful grip on her arm. At least for a moment the awful knife was lowered from her throat.

Another abdominal pain shot through her body as she moved. Again she ignored it. Even had she recognized it for what it was, she could have done nothing about it. Her life was now in the hands of a madman.

Basil maneuvered around so that he could face his victim. At last Katrina saw the face, so changed from when she had known it, and the wildly demented glow in his eyes.

"On your knees, Princess!" he rasped. His voice shook and

scraped, hardly able to maintain a subdued quiet in the still house.

Katrina slid to the floor, wincing with another sudden pain and letting out an audible gasp.

"Ah, yes, your *delicate* condition," he said with evil humor. He moved the knife until its lethal tip rested on Katrina's protruding stomach. "Poetic justice, wouldn't you say? Two for the price of one, as the saying goes." He broke out into another low deranged chuckle.

Without thinking what she was doing, suddenly Katrina lurched backward and sideways, hoping the surprise of her movement would throw him off balance long enough for her to make it to the door. But as she tried to scramble away, another pain seized her.

Before she was two feet away, she heard the *zing* of the dagger flying toward her. It struck the carpeted floor only a centimeter or two from where her hand braced the floor for support. In an instant Basil was at her side. He grabbed up the weapon, flung his free arm around her, and pressed the blade once more to her throat.

"You foolish girl!" he seethed. "You cannot escape from me! Do you still not realize that you are as good as dead? Even if you were to escape, I would find you. There is no place you can hide from me. You are a dead woman. Your filthy husband is a dead man. Your unborn brat will never live to draw a single breath of this world's air!"

"Please!" Katrina screamed, her fright overcoming her silence. But the sharp edge of wicked steel stopped her from saying more.

"Silence! I do not plan to go to prison, or to see the inside of that asylum again because of you!"

"Then kill me quickly!" she cried, though more softly.

Basil began to chuckle again, but his laugh was cut short by a sound at the door. He tensed suddenly. Katrina felt the tip of the blade break skin. Curiously she felt no pain, only the warm wetness of her own blood.

"Tell whoever it—" he whispered into her ear, but stopped again. The door opened.

"Your Highness . . . did you call?" came a welcome, familiar voice.

61

Anna rarely entered her mistress's room unbidden. But as she returned from the kitchen with tea, she had heard a voice from the bedroom.

It might have been the princess calling her, though it sounded too sharp and unnatural for that. Thinking immediately of the princess's condition, she went straight to the door.

She pushed it open with one hand, still holding the tray balanced in the other.

No lamps had been lit in the room, and she could not immediately make sense of the perilous situation. She glanced first toward the bed. Finding it empty, she stepped farther inside. As her eyes began to adjust to the dim light, she discerned two figures, one standing, one kneeling on the floor midway between the bed and dressing table.

"Princess!" she exclaimed.

"Anna, get out of here this instant—" shouted Katrina, her momentary relief at hearing Anna's voice overcome with dread for the danger to her maid. But it was too late.

"Shut up!" Basil yelled. "You . . . shut the door—quickly!" he barked at Anna, "or your princess will die this second!"

Anna obeyed, taking in the whole scene in one awful moment of realization. She remembered her brother's warning, but hardly paused to wonder why Paul had failed to deliver his promised message.

"Oh, Princess!" exclaimed Anna.

"Anna, why did you have to come now—I am so sorry!"

"Quiet, both of you!" cried Basil, his mind spinning rapidly. This did complicate his plan. Now he would have to resort to the pistol he had tucked in his belt to get rid of the two of them at once.

A moment of tense silence ensued. At last Katrina's voice broke it. "I . . . I think I am about to faint . . . Anna," she said in a weak, breathless tone.

Without even considering what she was doing, Anna found herself moving toward them across the room.

"Stop where you are!" ordered Basil.

But Anna ignored him. She moved to Katrina's side, knelt down, and set the tray on the floor.

"Get back on your feet, I tell you!" Basil shrieked.

"Can't you see the princess is ill?" said Anna boldly, clutching the teapot and pouring out a cupful of the steaming liquid. "I'm only going to give her some tea to revive her."

Suddenly finding himself on the defensive, Basil hesitated in the face of the lowly maid's brash fearlessness. Within seconds Katrina was sipping from the steaming cup, and Anna was rising to her feet and backing away.

"Don't move!" Basil yelled.

Anna stopped. But she had already taken several steps backward through the dim light toward the door. As she stopped, her hands behind her felt a cold, thin object leaning against the wall. Her fingers closed around it.

"Get on your feet!" Basil ordered Katrina. He clutched at her arm and yanked her upward. "Get over there with your fool of a maid while I decide how to kill the both of you!" He had been prepared to slit Katrina's throat and be gone. But now he had two of them to contend with. Not that he harbored the slightest qualms about killing them both with either knife or gun. But doing so, and then effecting a successful escape, had suddenly become more complicated.

Basil's predicament need not have concerned him, however. His final moment of indecision gave the captive women the opportunity they needed.

As Katrina struggled to her feet, with a sudden lurch, she turned and with a quick upward jerk emptied the hot tea directly into Basil's face.

The same instant, Anna leaped forward, pulling Dmitri's sabre from behind her back and raising the sheathed blade over her head as if it were her father's sickle and the murderer before her was a stalk of grain. Even as he cried out from the scalding tea, Anna brought the sword crashing down onto Basil's right shoulder.

He cried out in mingled shock and pain. But to Anna's dismay his hand now went fumbling for the pistol. She lifted the heavy sword into the air again, but before she could bring it down, a cracking explosion from the gun shattered through the room. Basil had fired wildly in the darkness. The bullet found nothing but the wall opposite the door.

As Katrina screamed, Anna brought down the sword again in a second mighty blow. As she did, the sheath and belt flew off. The flat of the bare steel blade struck Basil's right arm once more.

Katrina was standing now, and from her dressing table whisked a hair brush into her hand. It was hardly a weapon to be feared, but she would not let Anna do battle with the enemy alone! No assailant liked the idea of a two-front battle, and Basil leaped away and out of Katrina's reach. But the momentary distraction of the brush and Katrina's mounting fury was enough. Anna raised her weapon overhead.

Whack!

Down came the sword upon him again. Lighter now without the sheath, and her whole frame filled with the passionate energy of defending one she loved, Anna wielded the sabre with all the stout vigor of an ancient Scandinavian warrior. It crashed down upon him again, the flat of the blade stunning the strong man against the side of his head. Another blow came, followed by two or three more in rapid succession.

From where Katrina stood, Anna looked like a goddess of war doing battle in the night against the demon interloper. Again she struck with the righteous instrument of salvation, the sounds of battle mingled with cries of pain.

Again Basil tried to take aim with the pistol, this time directly toward Katrina. But a shriek of pain came from his mouth even as the deafening report of gunfire blasted again.

The sharpened edge of the sword smashed against his outstretched wrist. The shot went wild, the gun fell with a crash to the floor, and blood spurted from the deep, gashing wound.

Katrina leaped toward the gun, kicking it across the room, while Basil staggered backward, stunned and grabbing at his wrist in pain.

The battle belonged to the tigress of a servant girl!

Anna had raised the sword again above her head. Basil glanced upward, and seeing the blade poised to come full upon him, razor edge first, at last he apprehended his defeat. Already outside he could hear footsteps and voices and the tramp of heavy boots in the corridor.

He leaped backward onto the sill of the window, which still stood open from his entry.

"I'll be back!" he screamed, then turned and jumped down to a ledge, and the next moment had disappeared into the rainy night.

62

Within minutes every male servant in the Fedorcenko household had been dispatched to search the grounds for the intruder. Only Ivan and Peter did not join the hunt. Anna sent them on other errands.

Prince Fedorcenko, as titular head of the house, was one of the last to arrive on the scene. Altogether unable to take in the gravity of what had occurred, he turned away mumbling something to himself about needing to establish greater discipline among the servants about the place. By that time, although she did not realize it, the other servants were looking to Anna for direction about what was to be done.

Once the search was underway, and with two of the men stationed in the princess's sitting room, Anna sent one of the women for tea. She herself would not leave Katrina's side for a second. She settled her mistress into bed, soothing and speaking softly to her, and gradually the premature labor pains subsided.

Twenty minutes later it was clear that Basil Anickin had made good his escape. Forty-five minutes after the attack, Dmitri returned with Peter.

He rushed into the room in dismay.

Katrina conjured up her best smile for him. "I am fine, dear," she said to his frantic questioning. "But you should have seen Anna! She ought to be given a commission in the guards."

"Was the burglar caught?"

Katrina gave a glance toward Anna as she moved toward the door.

"I didn't know, Princess, how much you would want the other servants to know," said Anna, explaining Dmitri's ignorance of the details of the ordeal.

"Do you promise not to do something rash?" said Katrina, looking back toward Dmitri.

"Rash . . . what do you mean? I'll do nothing more than anyone should do. I will notify the police and make sure the rascal is caught."

He stopped short with sudden realization. "Katrina, did this scoundrel touch you!"

Katrina took a breath and glanced once more toward Anna, perhaps hoping she might rescue her yet another time. But as much as she feared Dmitri's response to the truth, she knew he must be told.

"Dmitri," she said, "it was Basil Anickin who broke in and tried to kill me."

"Dear God!" he breathed tightly.

As Katrina attempted to relate what had happened, her lips and hands trembled and her throat went dry in reliving the horror again. Dmitri responded exactly as she had feared.

"I will kill him!" he cried, jumping up from the side of the bed. "I will kill the no good—"

"Dmitri, please," Katrina stopped him, desperately grabbing his hand. "Please let the police take care of him."

"What can they do! Lock him up again? Send him to Siberia

where he will escape? It did not work before, and it will never work with the likes of him! We will not be safe from his hatred until he is dead!"

"But I am afraid for you."

"And we will always live in fear until he is dead!"

Suddenly Dmitri turned on Anna. "What do you know of this, Anna?" he demanded. "You said your brother was involved, did you not?" His tone was far from friendly.

"Dmitri!" said Katrina from the bed.

"By her own admission, her brother knew of Basil's movements. And he was supposed to inform us of any danger! Whatever became of the warning, Anna? And what a coincidence that *your* brother should be the one—"

"Stop it at once, Dmitri!" cried Katrina. "Anna risked her own life to save mine and the child's. She could have been killed along with me if it hadn't been for her use of your sabre."

"I don't know how my brother knew these things," said Anna, tears brimming in her eyes. "But I know he could not have had anything to do with it. He spoke to me at great risk to himself. You must believe me."

"We do, Anna!" replied Katrina firmly.

Dmitri rubbed his hands across his face. An awkward two or three seconds passed; then a knock sounded on the sitting room door. Relieved at the reprieve, Anna went quickly to answer it.

There stood Ivan. "The lieutenant is here, Your Excellency," he said as Dmitri walked up behind Anna at the door.

"The lieutenant . . . what lieutenant, for heaven's sake? I have no wish to be disturbed!"

"The Cossack, sir," replied Ivan cautiously, casting Anna a quick glance.

"Your Excellency," said Anna, turning to face Katrina's husband, "I took the liberty of sending for a trusted friend."

"You seem to be well in control of my father-in-law's house," said Dmitri with irritation.

"I thought the princess should have protection . . . in case you could not be reached," said Anna. "Forgive me if I have acted unwisely."

Dmitri winced slightly at her words, but said nothing further. "Who is this friend?" he asked. "A Cossack, you say?"

"Lieutenant Grigorov. You may not remember, but he once helped me—"

"I remember," said Dmitri. Anna could not tell if the sharpness in his tone was from present tensions or past ones. He turned back toward Ivan. "Bring him up. I don't want to leave the princess just now."

Dmitri dismissed the other two men who had been standing by, instructing them to remain in the corridor. When the door closed behind them, he turned to Anna. The anger that had been so etched on his face before subsided momentarily.

"Forgive my harsh words before, Anna," he said. "I don't know what I could have been thinking. You have never been anything but faithful to your mistress."

"Thank you, Your Excellency."

"Sometimes I think you have loved Katrina better than I."

"Oh, Count Remizov, that is not true!"

"*You* were here to save her when I was not. I cannot even bear to think what might have happened had you not—"

The emotion of his anger and fear and sense of failure all suddenly seized him at once, and his voice cracked momentarily. He swallowed hard and tried to continue.

"I should never have left her tonight," he went on. "I don't ever seem to do the right thing by her!"

"But, Your Excellency, you had no idea this would happen," argued Anna, her sympathies now coming out in favor of the one who had upbraided her only moments before. "And the princess told me you did not want to go, but had no choice other than to help your comrade."

"Katrina defended me?" said Dmitri in amazement. Then he sighed and shook his head dismally.

Dmitri did not reveal the true cause of his present misery. He well knew that he could have been home sooner that night.

After Lieutenant Plaska had been taken into custody, Dmitri had made an attempt to establish a favorable rapport with the offended Captain Sajachmetev. The two officers had gone to Dauphins. There Dmitri had proceeded to ply the captain with vodka while the count made sure the offended officer won enough at faro to mitigate his annoyance over the incident with Plaska.

The line between helping a friend and having a good time, however, had been thin at best. And Dmitri knew it.

Now he found himself hardly able to look Anna in the eye. And to face Katrina, knowing that she had supported him, would be all the more difficult as well. Once again, he had let her down!

Dmitri was spared any further self-recriminations when a moment later, Misha Grigorov appeared at the door.

63

The Cossack and the count shook hands stiffly.

Dmitri could not help resenting Grigorov's presence, all the more that it emphasized the fact that he had not been present to protect his wife. He could sense Grigorov's coolness, although the Cossack *said* nothing, and that rankled the count. He was a Russian nobleman, of an old and respected family—this man was a mere Cossack! And there was enough vodka in Dmitri's brain to make him resent the fact.

Yet Dmitri was man enough and practical enough to recognize that he had to swallow what pride his deeper sense of failure left him. For right now he needed this man.

"Thank you for coming, Lieutenant Grigorov," he said.

"Anna said she needed help," Misha replied. He might not have fully intended his words in that way, but it was plain to Dmitri that Grigorov's loyalties were clearly attached more to his wife's servant girl than to the Remizov family.

Momentarily, Dmitri allowed his vanity to distract him.

"Well, everything seems to be under control—" he began, then stopped. Who was he trying to fool? Nothing was under control. "Listen, Lieutenant," he said. Every word was an effort in humility, a quality with which he was not greatly experienced. "What I said is not exactly true. We could use some help—if you are willing . . . for Anna's sake, and her mistress's, if not for mine."

"I am willing, Count Remizov. What would you like me to do?"

"The man who broke in here tonight *must* be found. Our lives will be in danger as long as he is on the loose."

"Have you made a report yet?"

"No. I will see the police in the morning."

"I know of some places where thieves and brigands often congregate—places where even gendarmes are reluctant to enter."

"We are not looking for a thief," Dmitri went on, "but a madman." He went on briefly to clarify the situation to the Cossack, not failing to mention Anna's heroic part in the drama, during which the lieutenant cast a look of high esteem in Anna's direction. "Because of the man's demented character," Dmitri concluded, "he will be unpredictable and difficult to find. But I have no doubt he *will* be found. In fact, under the right conditions, he will probably make it easy."

"I don't understand."

"He will make it easy for *me*, I should say. I am certain it is his intention to do away with me as well, and I think he will come after me if the opportunity affords itself."

"You do not mean to say you intend to use yourself as bait, Count?"

"Perhaps in a way, yes. But I will not hang limp from the line. I will be a hunter also. I intend to find Anickin before he finds me. But to do so, perhaps I will need to lure him out of the dark holes where he keeps himself."

"Please, Your Excellency," said Anna, interrupting the conversation she had been listening to, "I am concerned for the safety of the princess."

"Are you insinuating that I am not?" Dmitri rejoined, spinning around.

"No, Excellency, only that perhaps it would be best for you to remain here with her for a time before leaving again. The baby will come very soon, and she will need you—"

"Now you presume to tell me what to do in the matter of my wife and child!" he shot back. Guilt and anger rose up in him, a lethal combination. The Cossack's appearance and Anna's cool demeanor annoyed him, pricking his pride and manhood at their most vulnerable spots. Within seconds he had forgotten his kind words to both and how much he already owed each of them.

"Forgive me, Count Remizov," said Anna. "I was only thinking of the princess."

"There is only one way my wife will be safe from that lunatic, and that is after I have killed him!"

Dmitri strode into the bedroom and picked up his sword, which still showed traces of Basil's dried blood. He retrieved its sheath, stooped down to kiss Katrina, then turned to leave, red-faced and trembling from the rush of a hundred emotions.

"Dmitri . . . please, don't leave me now!" sobbed Katrina after him.

"It's the only way," he said, pausing to glance back. "You have Anna, Ivan, Peter . . . the whole household. I'm sure Lieutenant Grigorov will stay if *Anna* asks him to. I can do no good here! The one thing to be done that will insure our safety is something only I can do! You don't need me. You never needed me. I've brought you nothing but heartache! Now is my chance to redeem all that!"

He turned again, strode back through the sitting room without another word to either Misha or Anna, and was gone.

The only sound once his footsteps retreated down the corridor and the door closed behind him was that of Katrina's soft weeping from her bedroom.

Anna went to her, sat down on the bedside, and gently touched her hand to her mistress's head.

"Anna, I am frightened," said Katrina, turning to face her.

"He will be back soon, Princess. I am sure of it."

"No, Anna. Not when he is like this."

"Like what?"

"He had been drinking, Anna. Didn't you smell it? When he

is angry, especially at himself, and it is mixed with vodka, I do not see him for days. He will not be back until, I am afraid, something terrible happens!"

"I'm certain he will calm down. He was angered by what I said. But he will come to himself."

"You do not know him as I do, Anna," wailed Katrina. "I am afraid, Anna, not only about him, but about Basil. He might still be lurking about somewhere, and with Dmitri in such a fury—oh, Anna, you have to get me out of here, away, someplace where we will be safe!"

"With the other men, your father, and Misha here with us, Princess, no harm could possibly—"

"No, Anna!" objected Katrina. "I tell you, nothing can insure our safety here. Basil would not be beyond bombing the entire house. My father is in no position to help. I am as concerned for *his* safety as my own! No, we must get out of here."

"Back to your home, Princess?"

"No, no—that won't do either! Basil will be watching it too. The estate at the Crimea . . ." Katrina said, thinking to herself. "No, it is too far! But we *must* get out of St. Petersburg without delay!"

"But the child, Princess. It is nearly time. A journey of any kind—"

"I know it is not without risk, Anna. But if we all die at Basil's hand anyway, then how much better off are we? No, it must be done."

"Perhaps you should see the doctor beforehand," suggested Anna.

"Ugh!" exclaimed Katrina with a shudder. "I do not think I could see faithful old Dr. Anickin again after tonight without thinking of his son! No, Anna, you will have to take care of me yourself—you and your faithful Cossack—until I am situated someplace safe and we can find another—"

Suddenly she stopped, and her eyes widened. "What is it, Princess?" asked Anna in alarm.

"I was thinking of Dmitri's mother's place in Moscow," replied Katrina. "But even there Basil would be able to find me. And the woman would no doubt turn me out anyway. And then a new thought struck me." She stopped, her face animated with anticipation. "Anna . . . take me to your own father's!"

"In Katyk?" exclaimed Anna.

"It is perfect, Anna! Basil Pyotrovich would never be able to pursue us there!"

"It is but a cottage, Princess—a peasant *izba*!"

"It is your home, Anna. What more could a princess wish for?"

"I . . . I know my mother and father would make you as welcome as they could . . . they would consider it a great honor . . . but what about your father, Princess?"

"Right now it would not appear that I can be of any help to him. No, I'm afraid my father must not know. I'll tell him I'm going home until the baby is born, and afterward plan to spend some months in Lividia. If that word spreads about the city, it may protect Father from Basil's evil schemes. No one else must know . . . that is, do you think your Lieutenant Grigorov will help us?"

"I am certain he will do whatever I ask."

"Then we must be off without delay!"

"You are certain, Princess?"

"Yes . . . yes, Anna! It is the only way I and my child will be safe. Now go—talk to your Cossack. I want to be out of here before morning!"

In a flurry of emotion and rapidly tumbling thoughts, Anna ran into the sitting room where Misha was still waiting patiently.

64

Misha was quickly able to convince the princess not to attempt a midnight flight from St. Petersburg.

"If by chance the man is still spying on the house, or worse, if he has friends inside the estate reporting to him, it will be much easier to conceal our moves in broad daylight."

Katrina shuddered at the thought of a spy for Basil Anickin living under her father's roof.

"I still do not understand you, Lieutenant," she said.

"If we drive away now, through quiet and deserted streets, our presence will be as visible to anyone watching as the tsar himself walking through the city at midafternoon. Believe me, once the sun is high and the day's bustle has begun, you will cause less of a stir by your movements, and the secrecy of your departure will be protected."

"I trust your discretion, Lieutenant."

"Try to get some sleep during what remains of the night, Princess, and I will make the necessary arrangements."

The sun had fully risen the next morning and the dew was mostly evaporated from the grass and new summer's foliage. The air carried a hint of warmth and the fragrance of a true June day. Anna stood at one of the front upstairs windows watching the placid scene below. She had already been busy making her share of the in-house arrangements for Misha's charade, and was now making final preparations to depart with the princess. Only a handful of faithful servants had been taken into their confidence, and the rest, although they thought they were aware of Anna's and the princess's movements, were in fact only cognizant of what Misha *wanted* them to see. If there was talk about the events of the previous night and this morning, he was confident it would all point exactly in the direction he wanted it to—straight toward the Remizov home.

Only Polya, whom Anna trusted more than anyone in the house, was privy to the entire plan, although even she would not be told their final destination. Mrs. Remington herself, whose chief task would be to act as liaison to Prince Viktor, would assume Katrina safe in her own bed across town. Katrina's father was not in the least aware of what was transpiring, and for everyone's sake it seemed best to keep it that way. As of that morning he hardly even remembered that his daughter had come for a visit at all! Mrs. Remington especially wanted to keep from him a realization of the truth of the attack.

Word quickly spread that morning that Anna had asked Polya to return to the Remizov home with her to act as the lady's maid, do laundry, and help her in whatever ways necessary to wait on the princess, bringing tea to her rooms, trays of food at mealtimes, and perhaps even attend the delivery of the baby. With great enthusiasm she scurried about the kitchen that morning, telling everyone of her new assignment, keeping to herself that she would in fact be ministering to an empty house.

Not long thereafter, Princess Katrina's personal carriage pulled to the front door of the house. Enclosed as it was, nothing could be seen of the occupants. Lieutenant Grigorov had helped them inside, he said, before Leo Moskalev, whom the princess had asked for instead of her own driver, had mounted the box outside.

"Anna told me to ask you, from the princess," Misha said, "if you would take them to the rear door of the princess's home, and make certain no one sees them as they disembark. Her condition is of some embarrassment to her just now."

"I understand, sir," replied Leo. "No one shall lay an eye on the princess, including me."

"Anna assured me you could be trusted. Take good care of your mistress, Anna!" he shouted into the carriage, then signaled for Leo to drive on to the front, where Polya would join them.

Travail and Triumph

With fanfare and animation, Polya opened the door and climbed inside the carriage herself, talking inside to Anna the whole time, with now and then a motherly word to Princess Katrina. A few other servants watched from a distance. Polya closed the door from inside, then Leo urged the two horses forward, and the carriage moved down the drive and onto the street, toward the Remizov home.

A few minutes later, two Cossack guards made their appearance. Misha met them, stationing one at the front door and one at the rear of the house. "The princess has just left for her own home," he said in a loud enough voice for the house servants to hear. "But we must be on our guard here against any further attacks by housebreakers. I will be on my way over to the other house shortly to make certain the princess is well protected and safe there as well."

While this ruse was being carried out, the final and most difficult phase of the subterfuge had to be implemented.

About nine that same morning, ten minutes after the departure of the princess's carriage with Moskalev and Polya, the servant's droshky pulled up to the back quarters of the house. Misha had made sure the area was deserted from observing eyes both inside and out. Two servants, simply dressed, exited from the kitchen entry. The gardener on the far side of the lawn glanced up. Olga sent out for produce and other needful items almost daily. He saw nothing so unusual in the scene and went back to his work without another thought about it. One of the two was rather heavyset, and wore a thick babushka about her head that shadowed her face from view. Each carried a basket, and by all appearances were bound for market. The driver, an old man whose wits had more than half left him years ago, sat behind the horses, staring straight ahead, oblivious. He knew horses, and he knew the way to the market, which was all he needed to know, on this or any other day.

Misha paid no heed as the small, rickety carriage bumped and clattered its way toward the street. He did send a quick glance in its direction just as it left the grounds, but no one was close enough to detect the light in his eye, and he quickly brought his gaze back to his duties closer at hand.

65

Katrina had never before ridden in the servant's droshky, with its hard wooden seats and straw-strewn floor.

It was not comfortable, but her forbearance would have raised her greatly in the esteem of many of the servants, especially those who remembered the spoiled young girl of a few years earlier.

It was equally difficult for Anna, who had to behave as an equal to her mistress. Once they were on their way, however, she was able to resume her usual demeanor.

"Do you wish a blanket, Princess?" she asked.

"To *sit* on, perhaps, but not to put over my legs. The day is already warming up."

"I wonder if all this sneaking about is too much," said Anna as she helped Katrina arrange a blanket where it would do the most good. "I do not like to see you so uncomfortable."

"But you do have implicit faith in your Cossack, do you not?"

"Of course. I suppose I must remind myself of Basil Anickin's face to remember how important it is that no one knows your whereabouts."

"Otherwise, it would be quite a lark, wouldn't it, Anna?" Katrina's eyes swept over her attire. "Wearing disguises like fugitives in a melodrama! Passwords and codes and Polya talking away to an empty carriage."

Anna smiled. "There is one good thing to come of all this. I will at last be able to share my home with you, Princess. How I have wanted my mama and papa to meet you!"

"If I make it that far," added Katrina, placing a hand on

her stomach. "I fear I am already past my time, Anna."

"Perhaps we *should* remain at your home," said Anna nervously.

"No, no—my mind is made up. I would not be able to relax for a wink of sleep while in the city. We will just pray it will delay another few days."

Anna sighed. She didn't like the sound of Katrina's feigned confidence.

"I am looking forward to seeing your Katyk," Katrina went on. "I suppose as I grow older, some of the glamour of St. Petersburg society begins to dim somewhat. There is much to be said of the quiet country life. My papa always extolled it, though he never did anything about it beyond hiring servants from the country. Maybe he would have been better off if he had. Perhaps the terrible pressures of court life would not have . . . have brought him to this unhappy end."

"End, Princess? You see no hope for him?"

"What hope can there be, Anna? Will Mother come back? And Sergei? Papa will always carry his guilt with him. And now even I have to sneak from the city without telling him!"

Katrina sighed. "He might have been helped," she went on after a moment, "if he still had his work. It would give his life some purpose. But even that has been taken from him. I wonder if our tsar ever knew the full results of his vindictiveness. I wonder if he cared!"

"Perhaps if he had lived . . ."

"The assassins' bomb created more casualties than Alexander himself. But I can't necessarily hate them, Anna. The tsar's power *is* too great, and too corrupt. My father was always a loyal servant, yet look what happened to him and those he loved. His loyalty could not spare Sergei from his fate, nor could it rise above court intrigues and vendettas. Even if Sergei hadn't been caught in the imperial web, my father would still have fallen from favor eventually. He was too honest, too forthright. He hung on in the previous reign because Alexander II was a human enough man to appreciate—for a time at least— a man like my father. But the new tsar and that regent of his would have sent him packing in posthaste even had it not been for Sergei's trouble."

She let out a long, melancholy sigh.

"No, Anna," she went on, "your little Katyk seems a paradise to me now. I'm sure we will find it difficult to return to the city. That is, if—"

She crossed herself suddenly and said no more. She did not want to risk her melancholy mood bringing more calamity upon them. No sense in voicing any additional fears.

"What is it, Princess?"

"Oh nothing. Do you think, Anna, we will ever be happy again as we used to be?"

"Yes, Princess. I'm sure everything will turn out happily—just as God intends."

"He does not always make things turn out happy, does He, Anna?"

"No, I suppose not . . . but when we trust Him, I think they do turn out as He intends."

"Well, at least we shall be happy in Katyk. I only hope Dmitri will come quickly. I'm not so well acquainted as you are with Polya, Anna . . . are you certain—"

"I gave her your sealed envelope with strict instructions to hide it in a safe place in your house, and to give it to the count the moment he appeared."

Katrina seemed satisfied and leaned back against the hard seat and closed her eyes, at peace for the moment.

Her brief rest was soon interrupted.

The *droshky* stopped a short distance from the market at the door of a little tea shop on Vladimir Avenue, off Nevsky Prospect. The street was lined with antique stores and several bookshops, with many outdoor stalls crowding the sidewalk. At that time in the morning, the street was buzzing with activity, and one more poor droshky more or less caused no notice.

"What are we doing, Anna?" asked Katrina, opening her eyes.

"We are going to have some tea, Princess . . . and wait," replied Anna, stepping down to the street. Suddenly, to her great surprise, there stood Misha at her side just in time to help down Anna's mistress. Like a child living out her part in a strange fairy tale, Katrina obeyed without further question.

Feeling a little pale and faint, she took Anna's arm as Misha led them inside.

"But . . . how did you get here?" asked Anna incredulously.

"Who do you think has been driving your droshky all this time?" smiled Misha.

"But what became of the other man, the old servant?"

"He is waiting at the market to take the carriage back to the house. He is none the wiser about any of it. Now, the two of you have some tea and I will be back for you inside an hour. I must first change back into my uniform, pay a visit to the police station, and arrange for a leave from my duties at the palace."

For the first time it dawned on Anna why Misha looked so different. She had never before seen him out of his stunning red and black uniform of the Imperial Cossack Guard. Now he wore the royal blue servants' livery of the Fedorcenko house. But nothing could make his appearance less striking and handsome. That, and his fierce Cossack visage, should have told even the most casual observer that this fellow could be no mere humble coachman.

The two women went into the tea shop, ordered a pot of tea, and found seats at a wobbly little table. The proprietor had no sooner brought their steaming pot and cups before the Fedorcenko *droshky*, still parked in front, was boarded by two women, one somewhat thinner than the one who had exited a short time before. But no one on that busy avenue noticed. The royal blue liveried driver on the box called to the horses, and the carriage jerked away at a leisurely pace.

They drank their tea slowly, talking softly. Anna was concerned for her mistress. It was clear she was tired already, and their journey had not yet even begun.

Fifty minutes later, Misha appeared again, entering through the back door, garbed in a red peasant's tunic, brown homespun trousers, and worn lapti laced to his knee. He paid the owner. Anna thought he gave the man more rubles than a mere pot of tea was worth, but this day had already contained enough twists and surprises that she was not about to question her friend. She willingly placed her life and that of her mistress in the Cossack's capable hands. Sergei had done the same before he left for Central Asia. And though no one had thought that debt would ever be called upon, Misha now seemed bent on carrying out the promise he had made with painstaking dedication.

The two women rose and followed Misha through the tea shop and out the back door.

In the back of the shop, another droshky waited, one of considerably higher luxury than the carriage they had recently left. Misha helped Anna and Katrina inside. He leaped into the driver's box and urged the horses forward.

How he had arranged everything, Anna could not guess. But she was confident that not a soul in all of St. Petersburg could possibly know that Princess Katrina was leaving the city in a plain droshky, dressed as a servant, and traveling upon dusty highways and rutted wagon roads south to Gatchina. There they would spend the night in a comfortable inn, and, if the princess was able, board the southern train in the morning. Dressed as peasants, no one would pay the least attention to three travelers bound for Pskov.

After a second night at a local inn, Misha would hire another carriage, this time to complete the journey to the village of Anna's birth.

66

The chief of police watched the back of the man's uniform with a placid expression as the guard exited his office. But when the door closed, slowly a thin smile of satisfaction spread across his face.

He looked down at the report he had just hastily filled out

at the man's request, then leaned back in his chair. Gradually the smile turned to a chuckle, which led in turn to outright laughter.

Cyril Vlasenko could not have scripted a more perfect scenario had he tried! The demise of the House of Fedorcenko was nearly complete!

He had followed the case of the young prince with quiet glee—his banishment to the Asian campaign, his trouble with his superiors, his trial, and his exile. He had sent all the perfunctory condolences at Natalia's death. His own wife had truly grieved, but his attentions had been on Viktor's pain and suffering.

And now this—to learn that an attempt had been made on the daughter's life! How could it be that tragedy would strike so perfectly all in the same place!

He would do just as he told the fellow—initiate a search for Anickin, keep a close watch on the estate, everything his official position demanded. He would not search with *too* much diligence. It wouldn't do to find Anickin *before* he had finished with his business. But to round up one more revolutionary, and a murderer besides, would be a fine addition to his dossier in the eyes of the new tsar.

Of course he understood the gravity of the danger, he had nodded seriously as Grigorov explained Viktor's "unstable" condition. The prince was not well just now, and every precaution must be exercised. Yes . . . yes . . . he grasped the situation perfectly. He would do everything possible to use discretion in the protection of the former tsar's trusted minister.

Ha, ha! laughed Vlasenko. *So it was true, after all! Viktor had at last slipped over the edge! It was too delicious! Ha, ha, ha!*

He had heard rumors, but he had never allowed himself to believe they could actually be based on fact.

What the Cossack's position was in the whole thing remained unclear. A friend of the family, he had said. Cyril thought he knew everyone who was connected with the Fedorcenko estate, and he had never seen or heard of this fellow. But he wore the uniform of the tsar's personal retinue at the Winter Palace, so it would hardly be wise to question him too scrupulously. Probably some friend of the girl's ne'er-do-well count of a husband.

"Where is the count?" Vlasenko had asked the Cossack, eying his reaction with sly circumspection.

"Away on matters pertaining to his position," the guard had answered without hesitation.

It was vague, Cyril thought, but the man's unflinching expression gave him no reason to doubt its veracity.

"And the young princess?"

"No harm from the attack, though shaken. She is well along with child," Grigorov had answered. "Were you aware of that fact?"

Cyril had nodded gravely, even though he wasn't sure whether he had heard it or not.

"She had been at her father's only for the evening when the attack occurred," the Cossack said, "and has now been removed back to her own house, where she will remain in isolation for the remainder of her time. The child is due any day, and the princess is well attended to. We should take precautions to have gendarmes positioned to watch both the Fedorcenko and the Remizov estates."

"Yes, yes," Vlasenko agreed. "I shall put the full might of my position behind their protection."

Cyril chuckled again as he remembered the brief conversation, then tossed the report on top of a stack of other papers on one corner of his desk. He would inform a few of his men of the situation . . . but not until next week.

That should give Anickin time to see to his business.

PART IX

TRAVAIL AND FAREWELL
(June 1881)

67

Anna stretched cozily in the bed, a shaft of light from the narrow window slanting across the blankets. If it did not exactly warm her, it at least gave the impression of comfort.

Her first moments of wakefulness were dreamy ones of semiconsciousness during which the last five years of her life suddenly no longer existed. She was a young girl again, enjoying the early country morning of a summer day. Her father would be out in the barn by now, tending to faithful old Lukiv, and her mother would be fixing breakfast, or tending the little ones. Paul was probably—

Gradually her dream began to fade.

The brightness of the light meant that it was much later than she usually arose. And she had left Katyk long ago. She now lived in St. Petersburg with her mistress. But . . . this was not St. Petersburg!

She *was* in Katyk!

Now she remembered as reality began to flood in upon her.

They had been traveling for three days—a seedy roadside inn . . . the long train ride during which the princess had fainted once from abdominal pains . . . Anna's fear that the birth would come before they reached home . . . Misha's calm . . . Katrina's noble fortitude in spite of her misery . . . the night in Pskov . . . the rain between there and Katyk . . . the frequent stops for the princess to rest.

Now all of yesterday came back vividly. They had not reached the shabby cluster of *izbas* until the scant moon had risen through the clouds in the evening sky. The carriage had sprung a number of leaks. Misha, on top, had been drenched to the skin most of the day, and even she and Katrina inside were wet and shivering with cold when they welcomed the first sight of Katyk.

Greetings and embraces and explanations and laughter and questions were exchanged, although Anna could scarce recall a single word that was said. The fire was stoked with fresh wood. Wet garments were exchanged for dry. A soft bed was made for Katrina in a corner of the house, while Misha was led to Paul's old bed in the barn.

The minute her friends were settled and she was certain the princess was comfortable for the night, Anna tumbled into the family bed, hardly stopping to think how long it had been since she had felt the warm closeness of her mother and father and brother and sisters.

Now she was home! Oh, how good it felt!

But immediately upon the heels of her wakefulness and the realization of her surroundings came also the remembrance of the fearful events that had brought them there.

At last she was fully awake. Her eyelids snapped open with a start. Where was Princess Katrina? Her gaze shot toward the bed Katrina had occupied. It was empty! Then she heard friendly voices from across the room.

Katrina sat at the table, a glass of steaming tea in her hand, chatting easily with Anna's mother, who was alternately kneading bread, stirring at a kettle of kasha, and keeping up her end of the conversation all the while.

Anna relaxed where she lay, and could not help smiling. Katrina appeared more relaxed and content than she had for days. And had it not been for her protruding belly, no one could have guessed that she was already several days overdue. The tense lines of anxiety and fear around her mouth were gone, and even some of her high color seemed ready to return.

They had been there but a few hours, and already Katyk was sending forth its balm-like healing into her soul. What was it about this rough little *izba* that seemed to catch up troubled spirits—as it had Sergei's—as if they were soft clouds on the clear horizon?

Her eyes swept over the scene in the kitchen once more, pausing as they reached her mother. Her open, uncomplicated face, the thick, work-strengthened arms and busy hands, the broad, plain smile and coarse country speech that knew no fancy words but spoke unceasing wisdom in simplicity—where were such women to be found in a city like St. Petersburg? No wonder Katrina sat listening as one enthralled. She was a grown woman and about to be a mother, yet here was a quality of simple humanity she had never met in all the parlors and drawing rooms and social gatherings of her youth.

Mama and Papa *themselves* must be the calming and healing and settling and gentle influence, Anna thought. It wasn't the village or the *izba*, or even the country. From *them* exuded the peace that brought contentment to lives caught up in turmoil. Those tossed and buffeted by the harsh realities and dangers and pressures of life might not be able to escape from that world altogether. But this place could offer at least a temporary haven.

For that Anna was truly thankful. Katrina needed that now more than ever. *And so do I*, thought Anna to herself.

How she wished Sergei could be here now to share in this moment of brief respite. But it was too difficult for her to think of him just now. She had been so intent on getting home that she had not considered until now all the painful memories of her happiness here with Sergei. She wondered if the joy of this place and being again at home with her papa and mama would forever be marred with sadness.

She sighed, then rose, quietly dressed in a secluded corner of the room, and went to join her mama and Katrina in the kitchen.

"So, here is my sleepy daughter, come to join us at last!" said Sophia, her eyes twinkling playfully.

"A well-earned rest, Sophia Ilyanovna!" Katrina's gratitude was clear as she spoke. "She has hardly slept for three nights, for saving my life and tending my needs."

Sophia beamed her pride at her daughter, then gave the dough a final slap before laying it on a board to rise. "Then she will sit today, and I will wait on *her* this morning!"

"Perhaps I shall also!" rejoined Katrina.

"Not in my house, Princess!" Sophia threw up her hands as if the very thought was beyond comprehension.

"I have heard my brother was permitted to work here."

"He was a man, and we were in no position to argue with him at the time. My husband was deathly ill. Should he come again, he will be given all the honor his position deserves."

Knowing nothing of Sergei's fate, Sophia spoke innocently. The sudden shadows over both girls' faces puzzled Anna's mother, but she did not understand and gave their darkness of expression other cause.

"And he was not in your delicate condition, Princess!" Sophia went on. "No, no! You will do nothing but let us wait on you in this house! Now, Anna, you sit down with your princess, and I will bring you some tea. The others have already eaten, except for your Cossack, who seems as great a sleeper as you—but I am sure with good cause also, eh?"

"True enough," replied Anna. "But, Mama, I am able to get my own tea—"

"No, no," interrupted Sophia. "You too are our guest, Anna—and an honored one as much as if *you* were a princess! And since when do you argue with your matushka?"

Anna complied, feeling a certain awkwardness at sitting down at the table *with* her mistress and finding *herself* being served along with the princess.

She did not have long to reflect upon it, however, for nearly the next moment the door burst open, and in walked her father preceded by his own rumbling laughter.

"Ha, ha! Misha, that is a funny story!" It was clear in a moment that his health was stronger than the last time Anna was here. The years had aged him, but something of his old vitality of spirit and vigor of expression had returned.

Misha walked in close on Yevno's heels, and the old Russian turned and gave the Cossack a friendly thump on the shoulder. Misha responded with a hearty chuckle.

"Do you mind if I tell it to my friends?"

"Of course not, Yevno Pavlovich," replied Misha. "The thing truly happened just as I have told it."

"Better still," Yevno added, "you will tell it yourself in the village later today, eh? You come as my guest."

Yevno slammed the door, crossed himself at the icon, then turned his attention to his wife and the scene in the kitchen area, where the two younger women were seated at the table as Sophia was in the midst of setting wooden bowls down before them.

"Ah . . . see, you are not too late, my Cossack friend!" Then to Sophia he added, "Have you enough to feed another hungry traveler, wife?"

"I have never fed a brawny Cossack before," replied Sophia, scanning Misha somewhat skeptically. "And this one will no doubt take considerable filling! But no guest has ever yet left my table with his hunger unsatisfied."

"Truly spoken!" laughed Yevno. "And you know what the legend tells of the mysterious Cossack rider of long ago. We of this family have a duty to take good care of our Cossack guests, especially those who risk their lives to protect our safety!"

"What is this legend?" asked Misha with great interest.

"You are not the first Cossack to visit our fair land here," rejoined Yevno. "The rider many years ago was, like you, on a mission of saving lives. We owe your wild breed a great deal."

"Misha is hardly of a *wild breed*, Papa," interjected Anna. "Never will you find a gentler, kinder man. Wouldn't you agree, Princess?"

"From what I understand, he saved the tsar's life once," said Katrina, "and now I consider my own safety the result of his care as well. Yes, Anna is quite right."

Misha could not help laughing at all the praise.

"I meant nothing other than that the name *Cossack* is a wild-sounding name with great traditions of fierceness and violence."

"I admit to being guilty of the name, and of the blood," said Misha, still chuckling. "But I hope my character will stand me in good stead notwithstanding the reputation of my people."

"I have no doubt of it!" said Yevno. "Now, come and fill your hardy Cossack frame with my wife's hearty kasha!"

"Agreed, but I want to hear about the old Cossack you spoke of."

"He spent time here when he was injured attempting to warn the Jews of Poland of an attack by his own ruthless people. He gave the old peasants who nursed him back to health his own Bible, which has passed down in our family ever since. It is in Anna's possession now."

Misha glanced at Anna as Yevno spoke, then sat down on a bench alongside Yevno, while Sophia handed them each a bowl.

The next thirty minutes were spent in warm conversation, and enjoying Sophia's simple but delicious fare. Temporarily, at least, all the troubles they had fled remained far behind in St. Petersburg, vanquished momentarily by Yevno's boisterous laughter and Sophia's cheerful hospitality and pleasant countenance.

68

The happy, peaceful country respite was all too short in duration. The wonderful day was full with relaxation, pleasant conversation, tea, dozing off, laughter—all that a reunion with loved ones should be—and of course abundant simple food from Sophia's hand. Yevno took to Misha immediately, and, his energy back to former levels, showed him everything about his small farm, and took him to meet the men of the village. Misha, for his part, made his host proud of his daughter's friend. "This is the man that saved the tsar's life!" he told everyone he met, not mentioning the fact that the revolutionary forces had proved victorious over Alexander in the end. Neither did anyone throughout the day mention Paul. There was no need to mar the day with such reminders.

But reality intruded upon the life of the simple Burenin cottage soon enough, and it came with a sudden scream of pain in the middle of their second night in Katyk.

Anna shot up out of bed, forgetting for an instant all her family slumbering around it. The cry from the princess's corner of the room had awakened her to full alertness before it had fully left her lips. Anna's bare feet were on the hard dirt floor within two seconds, and she hurried through the darkness to her mistress.

"Oh, Anna," cried Katrina, "there was never such pain! I'm so sorry to have wakened you."

"Princess, Princess . . . don't even think of it! Is it time?"

"I don't know . . . the pains started waking me up an hour ago. I thought they might go away, as they did back at my father's. But they became more painful until I couldn't help myself, and I cried out."

Anna smoothed back her hair, smiled, then kissed her on the forehead. Katrina reached out and took her maid's hand. The grip was not vigorous, as was Katrina's natural way, and Anna knew immediately that some of her strength had already left her.

Sophia approached and stood at Anna's side. She took Katrina's other hand just at the moment the princess lurched up slightly and winced from another pain. Both peasant women's hands were nearly crushed as Katrina's squeezed them involuntarily before letting go again and sagging back into the bed. It was all the confirmation an experienced mother of five required.

"It is time," declared Sophia softly. "We will do our best for you, Princess Katrina," she added, giving Katrina a motherly smile. Then she turned and left the bedside. This was no time to delay. There was much to be done!

In minutes the whole house was astir. Sophia lit the lamp and stirred the banked fire back to blazing warmth, while Yevno dressed and lumbered sleepily outside to fetch water for the great iron kettle that hung above the coals. Boiling water and calm leadership were the two chief ingredients for a successful delivery. Yevno went after the former, while Sophia, steadily now issuing instructions, provided the latter. Anna for the present sat at her mistress's side, one hand cradling Katrina's head, the other holding a cool wet cloth over her cheeks and forehead.

Vera, now a thirteen-year-old, was told to take herself and Tanya and Ilya to Aunt Polya's.

"The birth of a baby is no sight for children," said Sophia.

"Aunt Polya will want to come over, Mama," said Vera.

"Tell her we will send for her, and perhaps you too, when we need her. But tell her not to come yet."

When the door had closed behind the three younger ones, Sophia added, with a smile to Anna, "What your princess needs now is quiet and calm, *not* dear Aunt Polya!"

Sophia had delivered many more babies than had come from her own body. Nevertheless, she was noticeably shaken when, after all preliminary preparations had been completed, she approached the bed for her first detailed examination of the princess. A frown creased her brow. Then she slowly folded the blanket back over Katrina and motioned Anna to follow her to the other side of the room.

"The child seems far too large," she whispered, "and your princess's womb is small. How long has it been, Anna?"

"I don't know, Mama," answered Anna. "I think the princess has expected the birth for a week or two."

"If I did not know better, I would say it has already been *ten* months, although that is impossible. I am worried for the safety of the baby."

"What should we do, Mama?" asked Anna, sensing the fears her mother was reluctant to voice.

Sophia thought for a moment, then answered. "We must send Yevno to Akulin."

"It is a great distance, Mama. And it is night."

"Yes, but the labor could be a lengthy one. And the longer it lasts, the more need we will have of the doctor."

By the time Yevno had Lukiv hitched to the cart, Misha also was dressed and anxiously wondering what he could do.

"The fire will need more wood soon," Anna told him, then explained where it was to be found.

The pains, although still far enough apart to cause no anxiety, had become regular, and Katrina's cries gave evidence of their severity. The doctor in Akulin was the only physician for many versts, and the chances of Yevno locating him were slim at best. As he left he declared himself prepared to travel all the way to Pskov if he had to.

Sophia sighed at hearing his words. She knew that by the time her husband returned from such a distance, the outcome, whatever it was, would already have long been decided. If he did not find the doctor in Akulin, and quickly, she and Anna would have to do whatever they could for the princess . . . alone.

Half an hour later, Sophia and Anna sat by the bedside, doing their best to make Katrina comfortable, while outside—wanting to remain available yet not in the way—Misha paced back and forth in front of the izba, as if it were his duty to stand in for the missing father.

"Anna, where is he . . . where is Dmitri?" Katrina cried.

"I'm certain he has received your message by now, Princess."

"I need him . . . I want him here!" sobbed Katrina.

"I'm sure he is on his way already, Princess. He will be here soon."

Unfortunately, Anna's encouraging words had no basis on fact. Had she known the truth, her heart would no doubt have failed her for her mistress's sake.

69

Four fruitless and nearly sleepless nights had passed for Dmitri Gregorovich Remizov—count, regimental guard in the tsar's army, and now self-reproaching, vengeful husband.

He had consumed far more vodka and kvass than even his system was used to, but had succeeded in drowning neither his guilt nor his enmity. By day he had hounded the police, and by night had stalked every low-life rat hole he knew of, beginning on Vassily Island, but eventually spreading out to the entire Russian capital.

But he picked up not a trace, not the faintest whiff of a clue as to Basil Anickin's movements. The man must have turned into a ghost to escape the net of Dmitri's vigilance, in addition to the handful of gendarmes whose help—no thanks to the chief—he had privately enlisted. He let it be known in dirty taverns and sleazy faro rooms that he was looking for the lawyer who was associated with the defense of revolutionaries, and that if Anickin had any backbone he'd face Dmitri like a man rather than assaulting helpless women.

He made himself a visible and available target. But to no avail. Either Anickin had long since fled the city, or he was too set in his wicked plan to kill Katrina before setting his sights on her husband.

Dmitri hunched over a glass of vodka. He had never been in this tavern before. It had always been his custom to do his drinking in other parts of town than this, but he couldn't be choosy these days, not if he hoped to locate his quarry. He had thought of swearing off liquor until he caught Anickin, but had not been successful at such a resolve. No man should be expected to face this kind of stress, this kind of challenge, without something to steady him.

He drank slowly, as if this would be his last glass of the foul stuff that was as responsible as anything for bringing his brief marriage nearly to ruins. For the hundredth time, or so it seemed, he mentally retraced his steps of the last three days. What could he have left out? Where had he not gone? He had thoroughly combed the island. This tavern now hosting his weary bones was the last and certainly the most vile. But most of his investigation had to be done without the aid of those locals he encountered. They made no attempt to hide their suspicions. A few he had been able to buy off, but their information was as suspect as their greedy countenances.

Dmitri could not believe Anickin would have departed the city so quickly. He had been by the estate two or three times, and from the guards posted and general activity about the place, it appeared Anna's Cossack friend had everything well in hand for his wife's protection. If he did not find the murdering doctor tonight, tomorrow he would bathe and shave and put on some fresh clothes and make another appearance, perhaps even take Katrina home and dismiss Grigorov and take up the duties of protection himself. But he would make one more attempt to flush the lawyer out of hiding.

Dmitri lifted his glass, grimaced when he found it empty, and absently ordered another.

He tried to remember everything Katrina told him about the attack—everything Anickin said. There had to be a clue somewhere.

Suddenly he remembered the blood! It had been on his sabre. He had seen a splotch or two on the carpet without realizing it. Of course . . . in Anna's attack, she had wounded Basil!

He wondered how serious it had been. To have drawn the kind of blood that would have splattered to the floor, the wound must have been somewhat severe. Anickin no doubt had required medical attention of some kind. No wonder he had not been seen or heard from! He was wounded . . . perhaps lying in bed someplace!

Dmitri tossed back the remaining vodka in the glass and jumped up from his seat. He threw a few coins onto the counter and hurried away.

There must be scores of doctors in the city. Dmitri's first thought was Basil's own father. But knowing Basil as he did, he realized his father would be the *last* person to whom he'd go for help. It would be too obvious. Besides, Dr. Anickin had openly disavowed his son when he had been arrested. Most other respectable physicians could be ruled out as well; for to assist a known escaped criminal, especially under the new tsar, could land them immediately in jail . . . or worse. He would have to begin his new search from the lower end of the physicians' scale.

70

The remainder of the day and well into the night Dmitri spent ferreting out every scurrilous medical practitioner—legal or otherwise—that he could get a lead on, beginning where he was on Vassily Island.

His quest finally took him to Grafsky Lane.

It was late. Thank heaven for the white nights that provided a small protection against the evil happenings that flourish best in darkness, and flourished on Grafsky Lane at *all* times, day or night. Dmitri moved warily, aware of the comforting pressure of the sidearm inside his jacket.

One of his interrogations, and fifty rubles, had put him on the track of a certain Dr. Bobov.

The fellow was, he had been told, a failed medical student who nevertheless called himself *Doctor*. He apparently used the few tidbits of knowledge he *had* gained at the university to prey upon the unfortunate wretches who could ill-afford even some of the more skilled charlatans Dmitri had encountered on Maly Prospect.

Dmitri located him easily enough. He plied his trade with seeming immunity from the law, which was more concerned with the revolutionary element than a harmless old quack who had failed his exams. The pounding of Dmitri's fist on the door must have startled the old man, for a crash of glass followed, and a string of curses sounded before the door was finally opened.

"What do you want?" shouted Bobov, hitching a suspender over his shoulder. His greasy gray hair was tangled and unkempt. His face showed a thick stubble of beard. His eyes peered out of the darkened room, bleary, red, and squinting as if the bright light of the long-set sun had suddenly shone in them. Behind him in the room, Dmitri noted a rumpled cot with a table beside it that held an overturned bottle of kvass. On the floor, the shards of a broken glass, apparently the cause of the noise and the curses, were scattered in the puddle formed by the spilled kvass.

"I would like to speak with you," said Dmitri, "in private."

The man squinted even more at the cryptic words, looking over Dmitri's shoulder as if expecting to see a squad from the Third Division at his back.

"What for?" Bobov gave a loud, noisy sniff.

Dmitri was in no mood for subtleties or delays. He shoved past the so-called doctor as if he indeed did have the Secret Police backing him up. Bobov stumbled backward as Dmitri spun around and slammed the door shut.

"I am looking for a patient of yours," he said with fire in his eyes as he turned back.

Bobov stared at him silently, his face revealing nothing.

"Don't act dumb. I won't stand for it," Dmitri went on quickly. "The man had a wound in his right arm, perhaps his hand or wrist. He would have sought treatment two or three days ago."

"Got a name?"

"His name is Anickin, though I doubt he would use it. Now tell me—what do you know about him?"

"Assuming I had seen a fellow such as you're describing, which I'm not admitting—"

"Look, Bobov," interrupted Dmitri, taking a menacing step closer, "I know well enough that you saw him! Now give me the information I want or it's *you* who will need a doctor, and a real one rather than the likes of you!"

"No need to get rough," whined the doctor with a whimper as he backed up a step or two.

But Dmitri misjudged the man's intentions. He quickly leaped forward, grabbed the man's soiled shirt with his fist, and slammed the pathetic body backward against the closed door.

"I told you, I'm in no mood to be stalled!" he yelled threateningly. "Did I mention I am armed?"

"I'm doing no such thing. You woke me up. Just let me have some spirits to clear the cobwebs out of my head."

"I've got no time for that . . . now talk!"

"Evie's friend, it was," began Bobov.

"Evie . . . who's Evie?"

"No-good woman—lives not far from here."

"What did the man look like?"

"He was a mess—blood everywhere. But once we got it cleaned up, it wasn't as bad as it looked."

"What did you do for him?"

"Took a few stitches, that's all."

"Where'd he go?"

"How would I know?"

But when Dmitri's raised fist whitened in front of the man's face, his memory suddenly improved.

"Evie's place," he said. "Least I got no reason to think otherwise. He'd lost some blood and was pale. So I told him he'd better lie low and—"

"Where is it?" Dmitri cut in impatiently.

"Round the corner—you'll know it. Sign on the door advertising spirits and the like, people coming and going."

"Where was he?"

"Upstairs, in Evie's private room."

The only reward the disreputable doctor received from the angry and intoxicated count was a final shove that sent him sprawling onto the floor next to the broken glass and spilled kvass.

71

As Bobov had said, Dmitri found the place easily enough.

The alleyway leading to the run-down, unsavory tavern was littered with garbage many days old. A tomcat screeched under his feet as Dmitri stepped into the dark passage, but he was so intent on his destination and the hopeful culmination of his hunt that he hardly paid it a second's notice. He stalked through the door into the vile place as if he were attacking a Turkish fort—with none of the qualms of conscience of his brother-in-law.

His soldier's instincts served him well, for he knew that the best position any man could hope for in battle was that of surprise. Hesitation now, even for a brief moment, could make him lose the advantage he possessed.

He stormed through the empty common room, took in the

scene in an instant, located the stairs, and bounded up them with no hesitation. As he took the stairs two at a time, he drew out his revolver and held it poised in readiness.

There was only one door on the landing above. It was closed.

Dmitri paused only momentarily, drew in a deep breath, then raised his leg and crashed his booted foot hard against it. The latch and fittings all snapped from the blow, and as the splintering wood was still raining down around him, Dmitri burst into the room.

Basil lay outstretched on a bed three meters from him, with such a look of astonishment and shock on his face that Dmitri might have found it humorous had his business been less deadly. A woman garbed in a flimsy dressing gown of faded reddish color lounged in a threadbare overstuffed chair next to the bed. She was some years older than Anickin, or at least looked it, even though a thick layer of rouge and powder tried to hide the fact.

Dmitri absorbed the scene in seconds, noting in particular the bandage around Basil's right wrist some five centimeters above the base of the hand. The brief interval filled with stunned silence ended as Basil regained his control.

"So," he sneered, "the swaggering count has found me at last." His glaring eyes seemed almost pleased at the turn of events.

"Yes, Anickin," rejoined Dmitri. "Now we will see how you fare when up against other than helpless women."

"Helpless, ha! ha!" Basil gave a croaking laugh, but his right eye twitched with anything but merriment.

"Get up!" Dmitri ordered.

"Why not kill me right here in my bed?" His tone challenged, his eyes dared.

"I, at least, have some regard for female sensitivities." Dmitri turned his head toward the woman. "But I *will* either kill you or see you behind bars today, one way or another! Now move!" He cocked the pistol.

Basil measured his adversary for one more moment before swinging his legs off the bed. Dmitri did not take his eyes off the lawyer, following his movements with the gun. He would put nothing past this lunatic! Yet despite his wariness, Basil's next move nevertheless caught Dmitri unawares.

As Anickin gained his feet, even before he had fully risen, he suddenly grabbed at the woman's arm and yanked her toward him with such force that he fairly lifted her bodily from the chair. She had not even time to let out a surprised scream before she was firmly grasped in his arms as an effective shield against Dmitri's weapon.

"How many lives will you take, Remizov?" he shouted.

"You are a vile animal!" cried Dmitri. He kept his weapon trained on Basil, cocked and prepared to fire at the first opportunity. There could be no thought of an honorable battle. The man was a wild beast, and must be approached and dealt with as such.

Keeping Evie in front of him, facing Dmitri, Basil slowly worked his way toward the door. Although the woman looked terrified, she made no attempt to escape, nor did she struggle in the least. Dmitri wondered if the whole hostage scenario was a charade and whether he ought to call Anickin's bluff.

But there was no time for moral debates. Basil was at the door, and suddenly threw the woman toward Dmitri and sprang for the latch.

The pistol fired out of control as the woman's body slammed against Dmitri, knocking the gun from his hand. She slumped to the floor.

Dmitri froze, aghast at what he had done. But his instincts allowed only a moment of horror before he sprang into action. Without pausing to retrieve his gun, he leaped over the woman's body and bolted down the stairs in pursuit.

Basil's weakened condition was no match for the strength and speed of righteous fury. Before the wounded lawyer had reached the outer door, he felt a vise-grip upon his shoulder. Dmitri yanked him around and slammed him up against the sooty wall of the empty common room in one quick, violent motion. Basil scarcely had time to catch what was left of his breath when he found himself the victim of an unrelenting barrage of blows to his face and midsection.

The superior strength he had exerted in their last encounter together had all but left him, and Basil was completely ill-equipped to fight back. Dmitri caught him by the throat, and, after several more vicious blows, began beating his head against the brick wall.

Suddenly the air exploded with the sharp report of gunfire.

With the force of the shot, Dmitri was thrown off balance. He felt a sharp, searing pain in his shoulder as he hit the ground.

"Good girl!" said Basil through swollen, bleeding lips.

The woman stood above them on the landing, bent and pale from her wound, holding Dmitri's revolver in both her trembling hands.

"I . . . I couldn't let him kill you, Basil," she rasped, then winced in pain as she slowly made her way down the stairs.

"Give me the gun," said Basil. "I'll finish him off."

She hobbled toward him. "You'll have to go now, won't you?" she said.

"There isn't time for all that now, Evie—give me the gun."

"Take me with you, Basil. They're sure to arrest me now, and . . . I don't know if I'll be strong enough to keep quiet. They'll ask about my wound. How can I . . . take me with you . . . please."

"Of course I'll take you. Now let me finish this rat off."

He grabbed the gun from her hand, and his lips twisted into a hideous grin as he pointed the gun back around at her and his finger squeezed the trigger.

She did not even scream as the bullet penetrated her heart. She was dead before hitting the floor. Yet even as she crumbled lifeless, her lips wore the same look of relief, even of affection, that had come over her momentarily when for a few brief seconds, she thought they would be together.

Even as the echo of the gunshot was reverberating through the room, Dmitri groggily came to himself. Hardly conscious of the burning pain in his arm, he lurched for the murderer's feet. Basil stumbled back, tripped over Evie's body, and reeled to the floor, the gun flying from his hand as he hit.

Dmitri rolled to his left, stretched out his hand, and in a single motion swept up the weapon.

Basil was back on his feet now. Dmitri fired.

He was dizzy and his aim went wide. Still he fired . . . again . . . then again. It was only as the gun clicked empty that some of his vision began to clear and he saw that he was firing into thin air.

Hurriedly he glanced around the empty room. Basil was nowhere to be seen. Dmitri struggled to pull himself to his feet. But his legs were sapped of all their strength. His head spun, and suddenly the wound in his shoulder came full force upon him. He staggered momentarily, then toppled over in a faint, collapsing in a heap over Evie's body.

When he awoke again, Dmitri had no idea how much time had passed. It could have been hours or only minutes.

He instantly recalled everything that had transpired. His first two sensations were of the horrific pain in his swelling shoulder, and the lump of cold humanity lying beneath him.

With revulsion, he crawled off Evie's body and attempted to stand. The stiffness of his joints and the dried blood splotches might have indicated to him the passage of more than just a few minutes, but his brain did not absorb that information clearly. His first thought was only to be after Basil.

He staggered to the door, grabbed the wall for support, then stumbled outside. The cool night air helped further to revive him, but the stench of garbage more than made up for it. The alley spun around and with effort he choked down his nausea. Inch by inch he gradually began making his way along the deserted close.

But it was no use. Basil Anickin had long since disappeared, swallowed up in the gathering fog.

Dimtri's consciousness had already begun to fail him again when slowly he sensed that he was not alone.

With blurry half-awareness he sensed that these people holding on to him were friends. Their uniforms indicated some royal regiment. They must have been sent to find him, to tell him all was well. They were now leading him home. And in a nice carriage, no less. It would feel good to get off his weary feet.

But his head and shoulder ached dreadfully, and he could not keep his eyes open much longer.

As Dmitri collapsed in unconsciousness, the two gendarmes on either side of him grabbed hold of his limp frame and stuffed him inside the paddy wagon. They climbed in beside him, yelling at the driver to make haste.

With a man of this importance in tow, it would not do to keep Chief Vlasenko waiting.

72

Anna crossed herself with one hand and prayed fervently, while with the other she clutched Katrina's squeezing fingers.

The princess cried out, the sound of her voice shuddering through the little house. Katrina had long since given up any illusions about trying to maintain the restraint and propriety expected of her class. This was the greatest thrill, the greatest pain, the greatest exertion of a woman's life. And for now, Katrina Viktorovna Fedorcenko was a woman, not a princess.

The contractions were coming in quick succession now. Sweat poured from her face faster than Anna could wipe it away. Sophia had correctly diagnosed the trouble during the night— the child was large, probably past due, and Katrina's womb was small. There had already been more bleeding than she liked. But the princess was holding on bravely. Anna had already washed three sets of linens and sent Misha to various of their neighbors in search of new dry ones. Notwithstanding these difficulties, the baby would probably have been born hours ago had it not been for the additional complication of its breech position. The final and most arduous stages of labor had already lasted from daybreak until now, and the loss of blood was gradually telling on Katrina's stamina. How much more she could take, the old peasant midwife could not tell. She tried to keep her anxieties to herself, and yet knew from the way Anna sought her eyes that her daughter was worried too.

Travail and Triumph

The day was well advanced. It had to be past the midday hour. Where could the doctor be?

Yevno had returned about dawn from Akulin, alone. He had been told the physician was nearby, attending to the broken leg of an old peasant man in a village south of Katyk. The mishap had happened when the man was nearly gored by his angry bull. Yevno rested only long enough for something to eat and a pot of fresh hot tea, then set out once more, this time taking Misha with him. If they had to search from farm to farm and door to door, two men were better than one.

That had been four or five hours ago, and still they had not returned. In her heart Sophia feared that even should all three men come through the door this very minute, it would probably be too late.

She glanced across the bed at her daughter, herself a grown woman now. Poor Anna was suffering as greatly as the husband or the princess's mother would if either were here. In their absence, Anna seemed to be carrying the full weight of her noble friend's life upon her own humble shoulders.

Suddenly Katrina's whole body tightened. She sucked in two quick gasps of air, then involuntarily held her breath in agonizing silence, holding herself off her back and clasping Anna's hand to the very bone. After ten or so seconds she relaxed, but not before a mournful wail escaped her lips.

"Anna . . . Anna," she whimpered, ". . . I can't—"

But her words were cut short by another scream.

Oh God, Anna prayed, *take care of the princess . . . bring her child out quickly and safely! Comfort her . . . please, Lord!*

As her daughter was silently praying, Sophia's heart skipped a beat from the dreadful outburst. She had watched over many births, but never one so difficult as this. She leaned forward to check closely.

"God be praised!" she exclaimed. "The baby has turned. I see the crown of its tiny head!"

"Does that mean it's safe now, Mama?" Anna asked.

"I don't know, child. We will hope for God's mercy."

"She is still screaming so hard, and looks like she has no strength left."

"It is the way of childbirth, Anna."

Before she could say more, another shriek came from the bed. A horrified look filled Anna's eyes. The sound pierced straight through to her heart as if she were feeling every one of her mistress's pains.

"She is close now," said Sophia. "Here, Princess," she said to Katrina, "bite down on this." She placed a rolled-up cloth next to Katrina's mouth. Katrina opened her lips and squeezed down on it with her teeth. "It will help her bear the pain," she added to Anna.

Katrina was breathing hard, her face pale and clammy and wet. Her eyes were closed and a look such as Anna had never even imagined filled her face. The pains were coming almost continuously now. Again she cried out, arching halfway up in the bed, grabbing on to the hands of both her peasant nurses with all the strength she still had as she pulled herself forward.

"Princess," said Sophia, "you must push now."

"I can't," moaned Katrina, totally spent.

Please, dear God, Anna prayed silently, *bring this baby safely into the world.*

"Princess, you must!" exhorted Sophia as Anna wiped a wet cloth across Katrina's brow with her free hand. "After this you will be able to rest for weeks," added Sophia.

Katrina moaned, then gritted her teeth together against the cloth, and bore down with all her remaining strength. Anna felt the bones in her hand grind together.

"Yes . . . praise God! That is good, Princess!" said Sophia, tears of joy beginning to slip down her round cheek.

The contraction lasted ten or fifteen seconds; then Katrina began to relax and lay back down, breathing deeply, her face relaxing, her jaw slackening. Slowly she opened her eyes a crack, sent a feeble smile glancing in Anna's direction, then closed her eyes again and lay still. It was the first smile she had given in a long time. She could sense that the birth was near.

Sophia left the bedside and went to the pot of water still standing over the fire. With a stick she lifted a fresh towel from the boiling pot and held it up to cool enough so she could wring it out, then brought it to the bed. As she pulled back the sheet and laid the towel over Katrina's lower abdomen, a look of concern crossed her face. Katrina was still bleeding, and the flow seemed to be increasing. But there was nothing Sophia could do to stop it, and the baby had to be birthed.

"Thank you . . . that feels good," Katrina murmured.

"Anna, go wring out some more cloths," said Sophia. "We must keep the entryway warm."

Anna did so. Just as she returned with two fresh towels, another contraction came.

Katrina winced, bit down, and held her breath. Then suddenly she cried out in a long exclamation of pain. She lurched forward, holding her breath again. By this time Anna had given her mother the hot cloths to apply above the birth passage, and was sitting down again. Katrina held on to her friend's hands for dear life until the pain began to subside a minute or so later.

On it went for some time. Between each contraction, Sophia changed the hot towels. In another twenty minutes the contractions were less than a minute apart, and the infant's head was partially exposed.

Two more brief pains came, then a pause. Then suddenly a fierce tightening struck Katrina's entire frame, too ferocious for her even to let out a howl from the pain. Her body lurched forward, and every last ounce of her ebbing strength pushed downward. This time there was no relief. There would be no more contractions. The climax had come and would last as long as it took to bring forth the baby.

Sophia grabbed the clean white blanket she had reserved for just this purpose and held it under Katrina's legs.

It did not take much longer . . . thirty seconds, perhaps forty. At length Katrina let out a long gasp of air as if the last bit of her life had been taken from her, and sank back prostrate in the bed, utterly exhausted and empty.

The infant lying upon the blanket in Sophia's hands was still and quiet. "Mama . . . ?" said Anna, not wanting to accept what this might mean.

But Sophia did not, or perhaps could not, hear. Her entire being was concentrated upon the task at hand. She bent over the flaccid infant, ran her finger through its little mouth, turned it over—rather roughly, Anna thought. Then she slapped its bluish bottom with a strong *whack*.

Anna gasped at the suddenness of her mother's unexpected

action. She had never seen Sophia strike a child so harshly.

But just as suddenly came a tiny high-pitched whimper, the next instant a loud gasping for air, and finally a full-bodied, lusty scream. The baby's cries were nearly drowned out by Sophia's, followed in a few moments by Anna's. Katrina's baby was alive!

Sophia cut and bound the infant's cord, wiped away what she quickly could of the blood and birth film and water, then wrapped the child in the blanket and handed it to Anna, who was standing at her side.

"Give the baby to your mistress, Anna," said Sophia. "I want you to be the one to tell her the good news."

In awe of what she had witnessed, and in deeper awe of the tiny life before her, Anna took the small bundle and cradled it in her arms. She could hardly take her eyes from the miniature face, its tiny lips pursed together like a flower bud, quiet now after having so firmly announced its claim to life. Her first thought was how much her nose looked like her mother's.

"Princess," said Anna, "you have a daughter."

73

Anna handed the bundle to Katrina and watched joyously as the princess reached up with feeble arms to take it. Her pale, weary face was radiant with happiness.

"I am so weak," she said. "I am afraid I will drop her."

"No, you won't, Princess. I will stay here with you."

Anna lifted one of Katrina's arms to hold it around the baby; and in this manner, with them both supporting the newborn together, Katrina at last beheld her daughter.

"Oh, Anna," she exclaimed in a soft, strained voice, "she *is* beautiful!"

"Of course, Princess. She is yours. How could she be anything else?"

"That's not what I mean, Anna," smiled Katrina. "Oh ... can you believe it, Anna—I have a daughter ... a little baby daughter!"

"A new little princess who will grow up to be just as fine and beautiful a woman as her mother," said Anna tenderly.

"I wish Dmitri could be here."

"He will be here soon, Princess."

"But, Anna, what if he never received Polya's message?"

Above all things, Anna did not want her mistress to be anxious just now. She needed rest, in both body and mind. She tried to divert the conversation back to the baby they held in their arms.

"Have you decided upon a name for her yet, Princess?" she asked.

"Yes, and it is none of the silly names we used to talk about."

"What is it?" asked Anna excitedly.

A faint smile flitted across Katrina's face. "I wish to name her Mariana."

"It is beautiful ... I love it already."

"It was a name my mother loved—my grandmother's name. Mariana Natalia Dmitrievna Remizov."

"It is a good Russian name, Princess."

"Even my father is sure to like it, but ..." She paused as her throat tightened momentarily. "Anna, I am so tired. Will you take Mariana?"

"Of course, Princess. You just rest, and my mother and I will take perfect care of you both."

"And when I wake up, Dmitri will be here."

"Yes, I am certain he will be."

Anna lifted the infant back into her arms, then pulled the blankets and covers up around Katrina. After making her as comfortable as possible, Anna went to join her mother in the kitchen area.

Sophia poured out two cups of tea, and the two women sat down at the table. Sophia shook her head, all her previous joy at the successful birth dimmed.

"Anna, it is not good."

"What do you mean, Mama? The baby seems fine, the princess is resting . . ." Her hopeful words trailed away, replaced by a deep frown of concern as she watched her mother continue to shake her head.

"The princess is bleeding," said Sophia.

"Is that not normal, Mama? There is always some blood and—"

"Not only from the tearing of skin, Anna. She is bleeding from *inside*. I have never seen such a hemorrhage."

"Surely there is something you can do."

"I have seen even the doctor unable to stop such a flow."

"But, Mama—"

"I think I must go after the priest."

"Mama!"

"Shhh, child!"

Sophia rose. "I will stop at Polya's to see the children. And the baby will need a wet nurse. I have a potion here, Anna. When the princess wakes, mix it in some tea and make sure she drinks it all."

Anna desperately grabbed her mother's hand.

"Mama!"

"I am sorry, child. I know how you love her. But all we can do for her now is pray."

74

As the door closed behind her mother, Anna gazed down at the baby still nestled in the crook of her arm. She crossed the baby, then herself.

God had spared this innocent life for its own sake, she thought, and for purposes only He knew. Such was the great mystery of life—only the Father of all knew its intricacies. But no matter what happened, this beautiful child would never be alone—not if Anna could help it.

What am I thinking? she chided herself. *Mama is surely wrong this time. The princess will sleep soundly, and all will be fine. The count will come soon to take his family home.*

The child stirred in Anna's arms, then let out a tiny sigh. She seemed so content just for these moments, now that her battle to enter the world was behind her. Tiny Mariana was unaware of all the turmoil of life's cares swirling around her. Several days earlier, Katrina had wondered aloud whether they would ever be happy again. Anna found herself wondering the same about this innocent infant she was holding.

"Anna," came a soft voice from across the room.

Anna laid the sleeping baby in a basket of dry laundry that she and her mother had prepared as a makeshift cradle.

Imagine, she thought to herself, *the noble child's first sleep among the poor rags of our laundry!*

She walked to her mistress's side.

"Anna, I am so warm . . . and wet," she said, her voice barely audible.

"You have just had a wonderful baby, Princess," Anna said. "A little bleeding afterward is to be expected."

"Are you sure, Anna? I feel so weak."

"Of course, Princess," said Anna cheerily, ignoring the lump in her throat. "I will change the bedclothes so you can go back to sleep." She stooped down, kissed the princess, then set about the task, not allowing Katrina to see the tears forming in her eyes, nor the red-soaked linens that were put outside the door after they had been replaced with fresh ones.

As Anna worked, she noticed that the princess was breathing rapidly and shallowly, so she assumed Katrina had gone back to sleep. Five or ten minutes of silence passed. Anna was almost startled when she heard her mistress's voice again, though it was so soft she had to go to her side and lean down to discern the words.

"Anna," she said feebly, "you won't leave me, will you?"

"Never, Princess."

"Anna, have I ever told you how much I love you . . . that

you are more like a sister to me than a servant."

"You have not needed to tell me, Princess. I have known."

"I always wanted to have a sister, Anna."

"I am honored that you would think such of me, Princess."

"Anna, would you call me by my name? You have never done so."

"Of course."

"I want to hear my name from your lips, as if we were friends."

"We are friends. The best of friends . . . *Katrina*."

Katrina smiled. It sounded even more precious to her ears than she had thought it would.

"Thank you, Anna," she murmured, closing her eyes again. "That is what you shall call me from now on."

Even before the words had died out, she was again asleep.

75

Anna dozed in the chair next to Katrina's bed. The baby still slept peacefully atop the laundry. The cottage was quiet.

Anna awoke with a start when she heard the door open.

Her mother had returned with the priest. A stab of dread smote her heart. Seeing the priest, attired in his best robes normally reserved for high feast days, brought a sudden immediacy to the reality she had not allowed herself to face. Her mother must have told him the esteemed identity of their suffering guest, accounting both for the robes and his haste in coming to the humble peasant cottage.

The priest walked to the bed. Anna rose and curtsied respectfully. "Anna Yevnovna," he said in greeting, with a grave nod of his head, his long gray beard brushing his chest.

"Father Corygov," returned Anna.

The priest looked at the figure lying on the bed. "Ah, so young," he said, then bowed his head, made the sign of the cross with his hand over her body, and began to chant a prayer. *Lord Christ, Son of God, have mercy upon us, sinners all. Gracious Lord, forgive our sins. Most merciful God, Thy will be done, which will have all men to walk before you in holiness of soul and knowledge of the truth. Bestow now upon this, Thy servant, your grace as she . . .*

Katrina half awoke, and without moving opened her eyes slightly to take in the scene, though she did not seem to apprehend its full solemn import.

"Anna . . ."

"I am here, Katrina." Anna stepped forward and took Katrina's hand. The priest continued his ministrations, almost as if no one else were present in the room with him. Anna understood none of his unctionary words, although the awful truth had begun to dawn on her. Tears silently spilled from her eyes and ran down her cheeks, yet she made no sound. At length Father Corygov dipped his fingers in the small jar of holy water he carried with him for the purpose, and quietly crossed Katrina's forehead.

"Do you wish to make a final confession, Princess Katrina Viktorovna?"

"Yes, Father," murmured Katrina, her voice scarcely audible.

"Leave us, Anna," said the priest.

"Anna . . ." said Katrina in a tone for the first time almost fearful. With the little remaining strength she possessed, she gripped Anna's hand in desperation.

"She will not go far," said Father Corygov, speaking in a tone that allowed no argument even from a princess.

Half an hour later, the priest bade them a grim farewell, stopping for a moment before he left to bless and pray for the new baby.

The afternoon wore on slowly. Sophia left again, returning with a woman from the village to suckle the baby. Anna changed Katrina's bedclothes again. Alas, they were as red as those she had washed an hour before, and her heart nearly failed her with grief.

When Anna returned inside, she went immediately to her mistress's bed. The princess was awake and seemed agitated and restless.

"Anna, I must speak to you," she said. Her voice was weak, but not so faint as before. A hint of her inborn spirit of determination showed through even at this hour, and Anna took hope just to hear it.

"Yes, Princess . . . I am right here beside you."

"You must make me a promise, Anna."

"You know I will, Princess."

"I have given this much thought, Anna," Katrina went on. "It is possible that . . . Dmitri may not come."

"Katrina," broke in Anna, "I know he will! He loves you too much—"

"Anna," interrupted Katrina, and though her voice was soft, it was yet firm in its resolve to speak directly to her purpose. "Anna . . . we do not know what might happen," she went on. "If it should be . . . if I should not see him again—"

She stopped, her voice choked with both emotion and weakness as of fading embers struggling to retain the last of their fire.

"Anna, promise me this," she continued, summoning a great breath as if to give her strength, "I want you to promise me . . . that you will raise Mariana. I want you to raise her here, in Katyk."

"I know the count will come!" said Anna, speaking in a tone of desperation, and weeping freely now.

"I do not want her exposed to the strife and duplicity of the city. And I do not want her raised by strangers. My father cannot even care for himself now, much less an infant granddaughter. Dmitri's mother—you cannot let me go thinking the baby might end up with that woman!"

"Oh, Princess . . . don't speak so!"

"You are the only one I would trust with my daughter, Anna . . . the only one I know who would love her with the kind of love . . . the love I will not be able to give her. I know I ask a great deal of you, dear Anna, but you are my best and closest friend, my dearest and most precious sister. . . ."

"Princess," said Anna, "I would die for you if I could. What you ask is no more than I would willingly and gladly do for you! But think of what you are asking. We are but poor peasants. Mariana is heiress to fortunes, to palaces—"

"And to grief, Anna—do not forget that."

"Grief comes to places like Katyk, too."

"Perhaps . . . but I will know that you will always be there to love her—as you have faithfully loved me. If you would give me peace, Anna, do not deny me this last request of my heart. I must know she is safe with you."

Anna could not refuse her mistress. Her heart was too full of love and heart-sickening anguish. But the words which came next from her mouth were not those of a servant but rather of a friend, a sister.

Anna knelt down at Katrina's bedside, weeping openly and without shame. "I promise, Katrina," she said. "I will do as you ask. I will love your daughter and serve her just as I have loved her mother."

"Thank you, Anna," came faintly from the bed.

The words were barely discernible. Katrina's strength was clearly spent. But a smile was on her lips.

She closed her eyes. Suddenly Anna's heart seized her, and she clutched her chest, fearful for a terrible moment that the end had come. But the next instant a thin breath exhaled through Katrina's nose, and then a steady—though faint and laboring—breathing from her lungs resumed.

76

A short time later the door opened. In walked Misha, looking nearly exhausted himself, followed a few paces behind by the doctor. Yevno arrived three minutes later, breathing heavily. By then the doctor was already at the bedside, and Yevno went straight to his own corner and collapsed on top of the family bed.

It was immediately clear to all three men the moment they stepped across the threshold that times of eternal import had descended upon the humble Burenin cottage, and none of them spoke. Misha's eyes caught Anna's and held them for several long seconds, feeling her anguish and trying to convey his sympathy and understanding.

It did not take long for the doctor to corroborate Sophia's bleak diagnosis. He examined the baby, pronounced her a healthy specimen, but said there was nothing he could do for the mother. Even had he been present at the birth, he doubted he could have saved her. Only God could stop a flow of blood like hers.

He did what he could to make her comfortable, then asked if he might have some sleep. He had been up most of the previous night, but rather than return home, he wanted to remain close by just in case some change merited his presence. Misha immediately took the doctor out to the bed in the barn.

Another hour slowly passed. Yevno slept, the doctor slept, Katrina slept. The wet nurse sat in the corner with the baby. Anna, Sophia, and Misha sat—waiting, praying, the latter two offering Anna what comfort and sustenance they were able.

Anna sat with Katrina's hand in her own. Her heart was heavy. Without her mind thinking about what might lie ahead, the soreness in her heart was yet molding and shaping new regions in her being, getting her ready for what she had to bear.

A slight movement told her that her mistress was coming to herself. She bent down and kissed the pale face. Katrina's eyes opened. She smiled.

"Have I told you I love you, Anna?" she asked wanly.

"Yes, Katrina . . . yes, you have. I love you too."

"How can you love me, Anna. I am so ugly and petty sometimes. You are so good and pure."

"Please, Princess, do not say such things," said Anna, her eyes filling afresh with tears.

"Do you remember the first day we met . . . in the garden?"

"Yes, of course. I could never forget it."

"We were as different as two people could be, weren't we,

Anna?" said Katrina, her voice strengthened after the sleep.

Anna nodded.

"We are not so different now, I think. I hope I have become a little like you, Anna."

"Oh, Princess, you have given me so much! I think I too have changed—for the better . . . in ways that have made me more like you."

"My friendship with you is the most special and precious thing I have ever had in my life, Anna. Do you know that? I want you to know it."

"Thank you, Katrina. You are the best friend I could have ever hoped for."

"You made life worth living for me, Anna." As she spoke, her face was serene. A perfect and deepening peace shone from her eyes, a peace as of a greater health and larger contentment than anything she had ever known in all the years of her life. Anna could not stop her tears, nor would she had she been able. She sensed the gentle winds of life and birth gradually carrying her mistress toward that faint border between this world and the next. Katrina herself had become like the newborn babe from her own womb. The birth of the one was ushering the other into that greater life, through the back side of the door called death. But on the other side of that door awaited the careful and loving hands of those who had gone before, that they might gently welcome their fellow pilgrim home. Katrina was going to see her own mother again, with a new kind of knowing. And if she had to leave her precious Mariana for a season, it would not be long before they would all—mother and daughter, granddaughter and maid—be sisters together.

Katrina looked deeply into Anna's eyes. And in the peace that radiated from her own, she who had been the learner now became childlike enough to be for a few moments the teacher.

"You mustn't cry for me, Anna," she said softly. "See, I do not weep. I think I have never been happier in my life than lying here with you."

"Forgive me, Princess. I cannot help being brokenhearted," said Anna. Indeed, how could she help it? She loved her mistress; they loved each other, and their very beings seemed to have fused into one. She had been her servant and friend, willing and loving and giving as any angel. But because she was not an angel, she could not keep her heart from breaking.

"You must not forget what you have been teaching me all this time—that the will of God is everything. You have taught me that, and so many other things about our heavenly Father, Anna, and I love you. I hope I love God too, but I could never separate the love I have for you from loving God. If it hadn't been for you, Anna, God would have remained as far away as ever. I am so glad He sent you to me!"

Anna continued to weep. She could not speak.

A long silence followed. Katrina closed her eyes again and relaxed. Anna thought her mistress slept. Suddenly her eyes opened wide and a flash, as though light from heaven, broke across her countenance.

"Anna!" she cried softly. "Anna . . . hold my hand."

"I have it right here, Princess, in my own."

"I . . . I can't feel it . . . I can't . . . Anna, where are you?"

"Beside you, Katrina—I am here."

"I can't see you . . . it is coming . . . the light is so bright . . . Anna, hold me, Anna . . ."

Anna rose from her chair, sat down on the side of the bed, and gently lifted the frail form. With the princess's head cradled in her lap, Anna softly stroked Katrina's hair and cheeks.

"Thank you . . . you have made me so happy . . . I love you, Anna . . . I—I . . . goodbye, Anna . . . I—"

"Princess . . . Katrina! I love you, Katrina!"

Anna felt the body give a little shudder as an expression of contentment came over Katrina's face. And thus, enfolded in the love of her maid and friend, anointed for her death by the passage of her own life into her infant daughter, baptized for the new life by the tears falling upon her face from the eyes of the one who held her, Katrina died in Anna's arms.

77

The gentle afternoon breeze carried on its wings the warm fragrances of summer—hints of full-blossomed flowers, suggestions of ripening fields of grain, and the moist sweetness of distant green pasture grasses.

In nearly twenty-four hours, Anna had scarcely been out of the house. But now she stepped outside. It was time to breathe deeply of the fresh country air and to try to restore her spirits.

In the distance she discerned the echoes of the noisy stream that meandered through the meadow. By its banks grew her favorite willow, where in the past she had often sought solitude. It was good to be reminded again of the world outside, and of the fact that life did indeed exist beyond the smothering sorrow that was engulfing her.

Anna found her papa gathering eggs in the chicken house. His thick, gnarled hands picked up each delicate egg with uncanny gentleness. Yevno had been given a physical body that contradicted his inner spirit. Big, husky, lumbering peasant man that he was, Yevno yet carried within his bosom the gentleness to mend a butterfly's wounded wing, or to soothe his daughter's breaking heart. He could not read, and in all his life had never traveled two hundred versts from his birthplace, yet he grasped more of the ways of the universe than many a learned scholar in the most renowned universities of the land.

They talked for an hour. Yevno gently comforted his daughter, and offered that greatest of all gifts of sympathy—a heart that understands. Anna cried a great deal, and upon the great chest of her father found solace, refuge, and the first tender, tentative shoots of a reviving hope.

She told him of her promise to Katrina and asked if she had done the right thing.

"Only your own heart can answer that question for you, little Annushka," he replied. "God speaks to your heart as well as to mine. If you listen close, you will know."

"How will I know, Papa?"

"I cannot tell you that, my child. You will have to speak to the baby's father. Your duty is now likewise to him as well as the child."

He smiled and kissed her cheek. "But if some harm has come to him, or until the present danger is past, our home is always big enough for another little one, eh? What joy that would bring to my old heart!"

Anna's eyes filled with tears.

"My poor Annushka!" Yevno set down his bucket of eggs and wrapped his great arms around her. "So many hard things have come to you. But they make you stronger, Anna. You do not need to be afraid. Your shoulders may seem little to you, but they are strong enough to bear this burden. And remember, you are never alone. Helpers abound—especially the Great Helper above."

Anna left the chicken house, lighter in spirit than when she had entered it. She walked to the stream, then sat down with her back to the trunk of the old willow.

How much time passed, she did not know. She heard the sound of a step behind her. She turned, then rose to her feet.

"Oh, Misha!" she said, falling into his arms. She clasped him tight as she wept afresh. "I loved her so much!"

Misha did not speak, only held her tenderly to him, stroking the top of her head gently, allowing her tears to flow without restraint.

They had not spoken a great deal all day. Misha had been busy with Yevno, making arrangements for the transporting of Princess Katrina's body back to St. Petersburg.

"Everything is ready," he said at length. "Your father and I must be off soon if we are to make Pskov before nightfall."

Anna nodded. "I do not like to leave you," Misha went on. "Not now..."

"I know," said Anna. "But you must."

Gently Misha released her, took her hand, and led her back toward the tree.

"Sit down, Anna," he said. "There are some matters we must talk about before I go."

She obeyed as if in a dull stupor and tried to focus her mind on the decisions that had to be made.

"The body will travel anonymously, so that Anickin, if he should ever attempt it, will not be able to trace Katrina's movements and get to the baby. When I arrive, I will make every effort to locate the count immediately. If I am able, I will commit everything to his discretion. If not, as you suggested last evening, I will go straight to Polya and Mrs. Remington. They will see to affairs at the two houses until I find Count Remizov or we otherwise decide what is to be done."

"What about poor Prince Fedorcenko?" said Anna.

"Yes, I've thought of him. The whole affair could look suspicious to everyone—to him, the count, Mrs. Remington. Here we are, a Cossack guard with no connection to the family, and a maid, saying that the princess *ordered* us to remove her from the city and to keep her child here in a peasant cottage rather than with her own family. Who are we that they should believe us?"

Anna sighed. "We must pray you find Count Remizov," she said. "He is the only one who fully knew of the danger. And he is probably the only one who knew Katrina well enough to know that what she did is exactly what she would have done under the circumstances."

She paused and sighed again. "I only wish—" Then she stopped herself. "No, I cannot think such thoughts. I cannot even say his name again. He is *not* here, and so we must pray for God to show us what is best to do."

Misha was silent. He knew her heart, and to whom she had given it.

"You know I will help you however I can," said Misha at length.

Anna looked up at him and smiled. "Yes, Misha, I know," she replied softly. "You have always been there whenever I needed you."

Silence fell between them. "Oh, Misha!" Anna exclaimed at length, "I can't help being fearful. I made a promise to Katrina that I would take care of her daughter if Count Dmitri does not return. But as you said, it all seems so . . . so complex and out of the ordinary. I don't know how I could do such a thing."

"You promised."

"Of course! I would do anything for Katrina. I would love her child as though she were my own. But what kind of life could I give her by myself? There are so many questions in my mind. Would I return to the city sometime, or always remain here? I cannot help being confused about what is best."

"I cannot answer your questions, Anna. Except that I do know you will give Princess Katrina's baby a happier life, one more full of love even in poverty than she would ever know without you, even in all the palaces in Russia."

No one spoke for several minutes. Misha seemed to be deep in thought. At length he pulled his gaze from the waving field of wheat in the distance and focused his eyes with probing earnestness directly on Anna's face.

"We have known each other several years, have we not, Anna Yevnovna?"

Anna nodded.

"Since that day I came upon you so frightened and nervous in the Winter Palace that you did not even have the presence of mind to bow before the tsar," he added, smiling.

Anna laughed lightly. It seemed such a pleasant memory now, and it felt good to think of happier times.

"You have indeed always been there to help me, Misha," she said.

"As I wish to be now."

"And as you *are*."

Misha pulled his gaze away again for a few moments, then turned back, deep furrows lining his brow.

"You are not the only one who has a promise to keep, Anna," he said. "I too made a promise to the House of Fedorcenko. But my promise was to do everything I could to take care of *you*."

Anna looked away.

"It seems that perhaps the time has come for me to fulfill that obligation, that promise—"

"I do not want you to feel duty bound to me," interjected Anna.

"Please, hear me out," Misha went on. "Perhaps obligation was not a good choice of word. I feel duty bound, as you say, only by the duty of love. As you fulfill your promise to the princess, I wish to fulfill mine to her brother . . . in a permanent way."

"Misha, what are you saying?"

"That I will tend the land and pay the rent, and do whatever I must to make for you and this child a good life. I wish to marry you, Anna—to care for you and share life with you, so that not the smallest taint could ever come to your reputation on account of the child."

"Oh, Misha . . . !" Anna could say no more for some time. Finally she spoke, her words soft. "I could never ask such a thing . . ."

"I do not say what I do because you ask, nor even because of my vow to the prince . . . but because I care for you. It would be a great honor for me to serve you, and to love you in this way, and to call you my wife."

Anna sighed deeply and her eyes filled with tears. Her first thoughts were of Katrina's brother. She had never so much as thought of loving or giving herself to another man. But perhaps their fairy tale romance had only been that—a fairy tale. Now suddenly so many realities of life had come pressing unexpectedly upon her. How *could* she raise a child alone? What would she do? Her parents could not care for them forever; they were advanced in years. And how could she prevent certain unwholesome stigmas from being attached to them, especially if she could not reveal the truth about the child's parentage? For herself she cared nothing, but Katrina's daughter deserved better.

"You would marry me," she said at length, "knowing that a piece of my heart would always belong to another man?"

"Do you not think I have weighed all these things in my mind?" answered Misha. "But life is not a storybook tale for young children. It is full of twists and hurts, full of the unexpected. I too have loved before, or thought I had until I met you. And if you have loved, and perhaps still love, I only pray there might be a piece of your heart that would grow to love me, too. Yes, Anna, I would, and I hope you will want to marry me."

"Have you spoken to my father?"

"Not yet. I wanted to ask you if there was reason for me to talk to him. With your leave, I will speak to him this very day and ask him for your hand."

"You may speak to him, Misha," said Anna at last. "But we must decide nothing. Time must pass. We must speak to Count Remizov. It will take time for me to absorb all that has suddenly happened."

"Of course, Anna. I understand. For now I must return to St. Petersburg with the princess. I must try to find the count. And I must see to my own affairs at the palace."

"What will you do, Misha?"

"If my life is to be here with you, I will resign my post. But for now I will try to explain to my commander the reasons for my absence as best I am able. I will call it a family crisis or some such. Then I will do my utmost to return to you as quickly as possible with news."

"Write me a letter as soon as you learn something."

"I would sooner trust information to my own lips, brought on the back of a horse. You know how Cossacks love to ride!"

"So I have heard," smiled Anna.

"But be assured I will notify you however I can and as quickly as I am able how things stand in the capital and at the two houses. You will be safe and provided for here, I am sure."

"My family will no doubt treat *me* as a princess!"

"And the child?"

"My mother and I will care for her as our own. Now, you and my father must go."

Misha rose and started back toward the cottage.

"You will hear from me before many days, Anna," he said. "I pray you will consider my offer."

"You may be certain I will ponder it deeply."

When Misha was gone Anna remained at the willow. She wept again, though whether for Katrina, Mariana, or herself, she did not know.

78

Yevno spent the night with Misha in Pskov and returned to Katyk the following morning.

Anna heard nothing for a week and a half. Then arrived, not a horseman, but a letter from the city. Hastily she opened it and read:

ANNA YEVNOVNA:

I had hoped to bring you news in person, but circumstances here prevent me, and there is still much to do. I have duties at the palace to attend to, but am allowed much liberty. Saving the life of the tsar's father continues to go before me.

I am happy to tell you that I have located and spoken with Count Remizov. I am sorry to report, however, that he is presently in jail. A woman was found dead on Vassily Island, killed by his gun, and with her blood all over the count's uniform. An investigation is underway, and though he will probably be released, it means that Anickin is still free and is desperate, for the count assures me he was the murderer of the woman. Remizov is despondent over the princess and I do not have great hope in his mental facilities at present. While he is in this state, I have not told him of his daughter. If I succeed in obtaining his release, I will then inform him how things stand, and will bring him to you.

As far as everyone else knows, the princess ordered you to take her out of the city, to escape Anickin. I did not hint at our destination, and have seen to it that the message left in Polya's care has been destroyed and Polya herself adjured to silence. I pray I am forgiven for lying: I said that the princess's baby was born in a country inn, that the child was dead, that the local doctor we found to attend the birth saw to the burial of the baby but was unable to save the princess, who had a sharp attack of hemorrhage following the birth. I said I then sent you home in mortal grief to your parents, and I accompanied the body of the princess back to the capital. For the present this has answered nearly all the questions that have arisen.

Mrs. Remington is naturally curious, though in her grieving state has no reason to doubt what I have told her. Prince Fedorcenko knows nothing, although he has been told everything. Mrs. Remington saw to the arrangements. The prince attended his daughter's funeral, but went away muttering something to the effect of getting it all straightened out when Natalia and Katrina return from the Crimea.

I myself am confident that accompanying the count to Katyk and putting his own daughter into his arms will bring him to himself. Then, I hope, he will be of a more rational mind to decide what is to be done.

There is great sadness here, as I am sure there still is in your heart. I share your grief.

I hope to bring the count, and to see you again soon. Whatever he should decide in the matter of his daughter, my offer to you still stands, and grows daily more full in my heart.

>I am,
>Your Servant,
>LT. MIKHAIL IGOROVICH GRIGOROV

Toward the end of the month of July, two horses rode into Katyk, bearing the Cossack and the count. They went straight to the cottage of Yevno Pavlovich. Misha was the first to dismount, and ran to the door. Dmitri wondered at seeing him embrace his sister's maid with such familiarity and obvious emotion, but he said nothing. Then Anna approached him.

"Count Remizov," she said, "I am so sorry about Princess Katrina."

Dmitri forced a smile. "Thank you, Anna Yevnovna. From what Lieutenant Grigorov tells me, I owe you a great deal on behalf of both my wife and my daughter. You have been faithful beyond most of your station. I am in your debt."

"Thank you, Count Remizov. Would you like to see your daughter?"

"Yes . . . yes, of course!"

Anna led the way into the cottage, introduced Dmitri to her mother and father, then stooped down to pick up the sleeping baby. Tenderly she placed her in her father's arms.

"Count Remizov, may I present Mariana Natalia Dmitrievna Remizov—so named by your dear wife just after the child was born."

Although somewhat awkwardly, Dmitri took her and gazed down into the tiny sleeping face as if trying to find himself in her countenance.

"She is beautiful, is she not?" said Anna after a few moments. Dmitri nodded. He was not a man accustomed to shows of emotion, and did not know how to cope with the rising tides now surging in his breast, his throat, and his eyes. He attempted to say something, but found he could not speak. He handed the child back to Anna, then turned quickly and walked back out the door, hoping to settle himself down in the fresh air.

Anna and Misha glanced at each other with a sigh. Misha then took a few minutes to fill Anna in on events since his letter, which chiefly were only that he had managed to obtain Dmitri's release, that he had, during the course of their journey together, explained everything to him, and that as yet no one else in St. Petersburg knew of Mariana's existence. Nothing had been heard of Basil Anickin since the attack.

After a few minutes, Anna left the cottage in search of the husband of her mistress. She saw him walking away along the pathway leading to the cottage. She hurried after him.

"Count Remizov," she said, falling in beside him, "what would you have me do?"

"What do you mean, Anna?" he said, still ambling slowly along.

"I was Princess Katrina's maid. I am yours now, if you want me, in whatever capacity I may serve you."

"Yes . . . yes . . . I see. Thank you, Anna," Dmitri replied, although his mind seemed distracted and disoriented. Suddenly he stopped, turned toward Anna, laid his hand on her arm, and spoke in a very different tone.

"But . . . how *can* you want to serve me?" he said. "Why do you treat me so kindly after what I have done?"

"My mistress loved you, Your Excellency. As I devoted myself to her, I can do no less to you, for you are my master as she was my mistress."

"But I left you, I deserted you both!"

"You could not have known Basil Anickin would break in."

"It's more than that, Anna—surely you realize that. I was an incompetent and foolish husband! I was so filled with apprehension the moment I learned she was going to have a baby that I returned to my old ways. You know how many nights I left Katrina alone, or arrived late or drunk. I have been a miserable excuse of a man, Anna—you of all people see it, you whom Katrina so admired as being innocent and pure and good. How can you now want to serve me?"

He turned away, but nothing could stem the tide that finally burst. Tears of despair and self-reproach coursed down his face.

"And then in her hour of greatest need," he went on, "I was not even man enough to remain at her side! Like a fool, I went away again, and when Anickin was trying to kill the two of you, where was I but playing faro and drinking vodka! I don't even deserve to be called a man. I am not worthy of the title!"

"You must not blame yourself—you could not have known," implored Anna.

"If I had a sensible head, I would have remained with you. But instead, I charged off to find him myself, and did nobody any good. I never deserved Katrina, and I don't deserve to be the father of her daughter! Anickin is loose, and we will always live in fear of his revenge. No peace will ever come to my house! Katrina knew me well, Anna. She knew she could not depend on me, so she had to leave the city, to try to protect you and herself and the child. And I never saw her again! I wasn't there when she needed me most! Where was I? In gaol, involved in a terrible murder caused by my own foolhardy recklessness!"

Anna had never seen him so broken, so consumed by his own guilt over the cruel turn of misfortune that had come upon him. His zest for life, all the old arrogance was gone, without even a lingering trace left in his eyes. He was a man who had come face-to-face with his greatest moment of trial and suddenly perceived his enormous failure.

"Dear God . . . do you realize what I have done?"

"To the very end, Katrina felt nothing but love for you," said Anna, a great new tenderness blossoming in her heart for this man she had always been afraid of. "You must believe me, she blamed you for nothing. She knew you were trying to protect her by going after Basil Anickin."

"But I didn't stop him! The monster is still loose, still hungering for my blood. If he learns of the birth of the child, I have no doubt he will make her a target, too. It will only be a matter of time. I couldn't stop him. I wasn't strong enough!"

"I'm sure you will find a way to guard against him, once we are back in your home in the city and—"

Anna stopped suddenly. "That is, Your Excellency," she went on, "if it is your desire to keep me with you, to help with the child or to serve you in some other way."

"Of course I want your help, Anna," said Dmitri disconsolately. "Katrina would want nothing more than for you to serve her daughter as you did her."

"I would be honored, Your Excellency."

"But don't you see, Anna . . . I can't take Mariana—or you either—back to the city! Neither of you would be safe. And I am scarcely capable of being a father or running a household."

"Mariana is your daughter, Count Remizov. She belongs with you."

"Perhaps . . . of course—certainly you are right, Anna. Eventually. But right now, I . . . I do not think—that is, I would much rather she be with you . . . here . . . away from harm."

"Your Excellency—"

"Please, Anna, I have made up my mind. It is best. Please . . . do this one last service for your mistress. I will provide for you both. When it is safe, and when I am in condition to be the father for her she needs, a father to make her mother proud of me, I will send for you. But until then, she will be far better off with you."

Anna was silent. Was this the sign of confirmation that she should trust Katrina's dying request as the best way? Misha had assured her that he had said nothing of it to the count, or of Anna's promise.

Yet Anna knew she had to do everything possible to unite Katrina's precious child with her father, whether he thought himself capable or not.

"Dmitri—" she said, hardly noticing that she had omitted his title and used his given name, "none of this changes the fact that you have a daughter now, who needs your care."

"*My* care! Haven't you been listening, Anna? I am worse than worthless to her, as I always was to Katrina—even before this attack by Anickin. You yourself must know it—even though you would never admit such a thing."

"But your responsibility—"

Dmitri turned away with an exclamation of disgust and shame, then walked several paces from her, his hand held to his head and a groaning coming from his lips. The word had stung him to the core. Anna trembled for what she might have done, and stood silently watching his back and heaving shoulders.

At length he stopped, then slowly turned to face her. A look of guilt and personal torment filled his face, and Anna's heart was stabbed with sorrow. He looked like a child who had lost his way and didn't know where to turn. For a few moments, Anna feared for his sanity. But when he at length spoke, his voice was measured and self-controlled, as if the words were being forced out to prevent him from breaking altogether into unreason and madness.

"Responsibility," he repeated slowly and softly, seemingly pondering its very meaning. "Responsibility was never my strong suit," he added, then went on, gathering resolve as he spoke. "Katrina knew me better than to depend upon me, and now you must follow her example, Anna. As I told you, my decision is made."

Anna hesitated to voice any further indecision.

"Little Mariana will be happy and content with you," Dmitri went on. "Love her as you loved Katrina. I will return to the city. I will make whatever arrangements are required. I will bring word back that confirms Misha's earlier story that the infant died in the country. I will have a smaller headstone engraved that will stand in St. Petersburg beside Katrina's, and in time, Basil Anickin and everyone else will forget that there ever was a baby. I will send for you and the child . . . two months, six months . . . perhaps a year. Please, Anna, do this for me . . . and for your mistress."

Anna sighed and looked deeply into Dmitri's pleading eyes.

At length she nodded. "Of course," she said, "I will serve you and your daughter in whatever way you think best, Your Excellency."

"Thank you, Anna. You are a faithful young woman."

"But I will serve Mariana for her *own* sake, Your Excellency," added Anna, "and for yours. I loved my mistress, and I am certain I will grow to care for those she loved just as deeply."

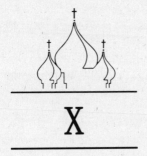

X

TRIUMPH AND NEW LIFE
(Fall 1881—Spring 1882)

79

Yevno shuffled down the road, leading old Lukiv behind him. The aging peasant's step was more labored these days, and his breathing heavier, yet he would not have dreamed of *riding* the faithful beast.

"Sitting on the back of a horse is for rich *moujiks* and the *promieshik*," he murmured in what was apparently an ongoing conversation with his four-legged companion. "You and I, Lukiv, are equals, eh? You walk, I walk, and we both grow weary together."

He chuckled into his tangled gray beard. The horse gave a whinnying snort of acknowledgment.

Yevno paused a moment for breath and, shielding his eyes against the midday sun, gazed across the surrounding valley. A light, cool breeze rustled the leaves of the birch and elms; the leaves were yellower than they had been only a week before.

Time indeed marched on, if not with the cadence of a military parade, then most certainly with the tenacity of an old man leading his workhorse and friend.

As the short warm summer drifts into the chills of autumn, so are our lives drifting into new paths, thought Yevno, the particular mood of the day casting his mind into a philosophical bent. For all his worldly ignorance, deep inside he was a man whose heart felt the changing and subtle tunes of the universe. And indeed, as sure as the air was turning crisp and the leaves yellow and brown with the new season, so too could Yevno sense the passing of the season of grief that had descended upon his home three months earlier.

Russians might revel in gloom and disaster, with their sonorous ballads in minor keys. But as with everything about the Motherland, on the other side lay the lusty, wild, vibrant grasping for *life* with all its riotous joy. Drudgery and joy, both went to make up Russia.

Old Yevno could feel the beginnings of change. As he trudged over the old wooden bridge, his sweeping gaze shifted toward the little crook in the stream beside the giant willow, where his eldest daughter sat in a most familiar pose. But instead of a book, a bundle of squirming blankets lay in her lap.

Once, in Pskov, Yevno had struck up a conversation with an ironmonger, as he had watched the burly artisan at his trade. Bent before the fiery cauldrons in which the metals were forged, the man told him that in melting together distinctive metals, he was able to produce a stronger tool in the end than was possible with only one element.

So it was with his own precious Anna.

She had passed through the fires of grief and loss and confusion—or at least was steadily passing through them. Into her grieving soul were being poured persons and situations, quandaries and decisions, that would never have come to her had she remained forever under his roof. The fires of suffering were melting into her very being, not breaking, not destroying, not consuming her, but rather strengthening her—adding depths of character that could come by no other means.

He knew well that it was not always so. Count Remizov displayed the sad example of a man who had let his troubles defeat him—at least for the present. Instead of forging a life for himself and his daughter, he had chosen to face life alone, turning his back rather than confronting the realities before him. They had heard no word from him since his brief visit in July with Lieutenant Grigorov. And as attached as they had all become to the count's daughter, they grieved that her own father would not desire to pour his life into her.

But his Anna was allowing the fires of affliction to purify her, even as the blacksmith's forge strengthened the poorer metals poured into it. Every day she grew with an inward stature toward a loveliness a father could be proud of.

80

Anna studied the child in her lap.

She could not help herself. Every time there was a quiet moment she found her eyes drawn to the contents of the little bundle. She thought by now she would have known every tiny nuance of that cherished face. Yet every time she gazed into it, some new facet of personality and individuality struck her.

Every day Mariana grew and was transformed into a being a little different than before, and new wonders presented themselves to behold. At this moment Anna found herself noting with particular marvel the vivid hue of the child's large eyes. They reminded her of Sergei's, a pale gray that was almost translucent. Mariana's innocent infant gaze made Anna feel as if indeed the child's own mother and uncle were looking into her spirit through the eyes of the child.

As these thoughts passed through her mind unbidden, Anna realized that for the first time she was able to think of Sergei without heartbreaking pain. To see him in tiny Mariana's eyes gave her a new and quiet joy, almost as if, in some unexplainable way, the child was in part their own.

There was enough of Katrina in the baby, however, to dispel any doubts as to her parentage. The silky locks of black hair grew thicker and richer every day. The full, expressive mouth, the little chin that, even at three months, jutted out ever so slightly with an expression of determination—both reminded Anna of her mistress. And already it seemed that Katrina's assertiveness was inbred and was beginning to show itself. Mariana's lusty cry in the middle of the night often woke the entire household, and the wet nurse testified to the child's hearty appetite.

Oddly though, despite the strong familial characteristics Anna observed in Katrina's daughter, many in the village claimed she looked just like Anna. Their comments could not help but make her swell with inner pleasure. But they were disconcerting at the same time. The thought reminded her that she had not yet answered Misha's proposal. He was a man of great patience, but the day would come when she would have to resolve the matter someplace deep inside her. It was no easy decision.

"Little Mariana," she said softly to the baby, "there is such wisdom in those gray eyes of yours. It is too bad you cannot speak to me."

She brushed her hand across the soft head and kissed the child on the forehead.

"Ah, little one," she went on in gentle tones, "what must the villagers think about your sudden arrival? They have been kind to me, and I suppose they are each drawing their own conclusions. Perhaps it is best not to disturb what they may think. Your papa—"

Anna's tone took a more somber edge momentarily, but then she quickly resumed.

"I will continue to pray that with the passing of time his wounds will heal, and he will have a change of heart. How much of all this you need to know, little one, I am not certain. Perhaps that same passage of time will enlighten me as well. As my own papa says, that is a bridge to cross when I reach the stream, but not before.

"I would like to teach you about your family one day, for they are noble people. Not in the social way, nor in the way the revolutionaries think of the nobility. You come from a good family, little Mariana. If only you could know your grandfather—as he was, at least. A man of high principles, and wise. Proud, however, perhaps too much for his own good. In the end that proved part of his own undoing. Maybe someday you may meet him, but not until your father comes for you.

"Ah, Mariana, we all will heal in time! And God will give His wisdom so we will know what to do. Listen to what I just read." Anna picked up the book lying at her side and thumbed quickly to the page in Psalms from which she had been reading: *"For thou, O God, hast proved us: thou hast tried us, as silver is tried. Thou broughtest us into the net; thou laidest affliction upon our loins. Thou hast caused men to ride over our heads; we went through fire and through water: but thou broughtest us out into a wealthy place.*

"Yes, sweet little one, the rich, green valleys lie ahead of us! And when more trials come, as surely they will, we can be certain of the joyous paths to follow."

Anna paused and gently rubbed the soft cheek with the back of her finger.

"But no matter what comes our way, you will always be loved. I will never replace your mother, but I will love you no less. I love you already, as much as if you were my own daughter!"

Anna grasped the child close to her breast, then kissed her gently. As her eyes probed the infant's face again, Mariana cooed contentedly, and the little pink lips twitched into a smile. Anna smiled in return. She didn't care what any of the old wives in the village might say. She knew this smile was real and was somehow meant just for her.

Mariana had chosen this moment to grace the world with this first sign of her most lovely expression, for somehow the God who had formed her knew it would be the best sign of all to confirm His eternal hope.

81

Anna looked up to see her father approaching her. His presence brought to her mind the perplexity of her present vacillation. Misha had been to Katyk again a week earlier, and though as patient and gracious and loving as ever, it was abundantly clear to Anna as well as to her father that her friend hoped a decision would not be many more weeks in coming.

Yevno tied Lukiv to one of the tree's low branches, then sat down beside her. Their eyes met.

"Oh, Papa," she said, "what *am* I going to do!"

"Do you mean about your baby or your Cossack?"

"Don't joke, Papa—I mean about everything! What should I do? Should I marry Misha? If you would only tell me, I would happily do as you say."

Yevno nodded seriously. "I know you would, daughter. You are as obedient as the sun which rises every day without fail. And because I know you would do whatever I say, for that very reason I will not say. You are twenty-one, and your heart must tell you, not your papa."

"Then tell me what you *think*, Papa."

"I think your Cossack is as fine a man as was your prince. That my little Anna should be loved by two men of such eminence makes an old peasant man such as Yevno Pavlovich very proud. Alas, you can marry but one of them, and only one of them appears left you."

"You are saying I should marry Misha?"

"No, daughter, only that Misha is here and your prince, if he yet lives at all, you may never see again. If you love the lieutenant, then you should marry him."

"It would be best for little Mariana for me to have a husband," said Anna, looking down again at the child in her arms.

"Ah, but you cannot say when Count Remizov will return for her," rejoined Yevno. "And perhaps for you both. You must not marry for the sake of the child, but for your own. The likelihood is that you will care for the child but for a season, but that in time the count will get over his troubles, perhaps himself marry again, and in due course take his daughter again into his own home. No, Anna, this is one case when you must follow your own heart rather than your love and loyalty to your former mistress."

"I could not wish for a better husband than Misha," Anna said. "And as he himself once told me, life is no storybook tale."

"He speaks the truth," agreed Yevno.

"And as long as I *do* have Mariana to care for, I shudder at Princess Katrina's daughter being thought of as . . . you know,

Papa—as a child born to an unmarried peasant girl."

"Are you anxious about what people think of *you*, Anna?" asked Yevno seriously.

"No, Papa. I am only anxious for what they think of *you* and Mama. I do not want your friends and our neighbors thinking ill of you because they harbor unclean suspicions about your wayward daughter."

"Anna, you are a daughter your mother and I are proud of and love with all our hearts. And we care nothing for what others may wrongly think."

"I know, Papa. I only care what they think of *you*."

"I care as little for that as I would to live in a palace."

"But I still must consider what people think of the princess's daughter. And for all these reasons, it seems my marrying would be best."

"Perhaps . . . perhaps, daughter. But you must follow your heart above all else."

"Yes, Papa."

Anna set Mariana down on the grass for a moment, then leaned forward to hug Yevno. He stretched his thick arms around her and held her close to him. The familiar smell of his body and shirt and beard all blended together, bringing tears of melancholy and nostalgia to her eyes. She lay on his chest for several moments, the little girl inside her wishing she could remain here forever, that she did not have to grow up and face a world too full of cares and decisions.

At length she drew back, wiped her eyes with the sleeve of her dress, and looked into his eyes. "I love you, Papa," she said.

A long contented silence followed. At last Yevno spoke. "So, daughter, what does your heart tell you?" he said.

"That he is a good and gentle man, and that I should probably marry him. But . . . after more time is passed."

"You speak wisely. It is never good to rush such things. Our God is never in a hurry."

82

Springtime had arrived, yet the chill of old winter still prowled about the northern regions of the Russian countryside.

Lt. Mikhail Igorovich Grigorov had been to Katyk as many times throughout the winter as the weather and his duties at the Winter Palace would permit. And now as the sun had begun to thaw the land, hope of a bright future began to stir in the earth. This sojourn to the poor village south of the capital would be unlike any previous trip for the Cossack. He came no more as a stranger, but as a friend, a brother—to join himself with one peasant family as a husband and son.

Anna awoke early. As nervous as her mother had been with the preparations they had been making for weeks, even she was still asleep. From where she slept in the corner the princess had occupied, Anna heard her father still snoring as well.

She smiled. How she loved them all! How good it was to be home again. Yet she had known from the very beginning that it would be temporary. Ten-month-old Mariana, sleeping peacefully next to her, insured that her life would never return to the childhood simplicity of the years growing up in her beloved Katyk. And the changes that would come to her on *this* day would be even greater. What would it be like to be a wife, perhaps a mother—not of the princess's child, but possibly one day of her *own*? She had scarcely allowed herself to think of such things, even through the long winter of her betrothal to Misha. There had remained almost a dreamy unreality to it all—a sense within her that she was following her ordained path, that events were simply coming to her and she had only to fall in step with their course. Even as her mother and Aunt Polya had fussed for two weeks over the final adjustments to her dress, she had felt like a spectator.

Until this night. She had gone to sleep thinking how good it would be once again to see Mrs. Remington and Polya—yes, and even Olga Stephanovna!—all of whom Misha had arranged to transport to Katyk for the wedding. How to explain Mariana's presence to the Fedorcenko servants had been a matter of great concern to Anna. None of them, including their master, the prince himself, knew of Katrina's daughter. But everything was being arranged by friends of her mother's, friends whose natural curiosity about the child had not caused them to draw erroneous conclusions concerning Anna's character.

Everything had been perfectly attended to in order to make this the most memorable wedding ever seen in the small village of Katyk—the perfect blend between the religious customs of peasant simplicity and the royal pomp of St. Petersburg itself. Everything—her dress, food, music, guests from the city and country—all had been seen to, except for one thing.

Anna awoke in the middle of the night with the sudden realization of what that one thing was. It was herself.

All this time, since she had informed Misha of her decision, she had considered the matter of her future resolved. But suddenly all the months had evaporated in a moment, and she felt as if she were back in the confusion of the previous autumn. She tried to dismiss it from her mind as she turned onto her side and attempted to go back to sleep. But it would not go away. The questions grew, and deep within her own soul gnawed a doubt as to whether she had indeed done the right thing in finally consenting to marry Misha.

Carefully Anna stole from the bed so as not to disturb Mariana, quietly dressed, and went outside. The sun would warm the ground later, but for now it was frozen from the night. Instead of her willow, on this occasion she sought the comfort of her father's barn.

She walked inside, glad that Misha and the other guests were staying in the inn at Akulin rather than here. She needed to be alone—with her thoughts, with God . . . and with her own deepest soul. How desperately she longed for her father's wisdom! How comforting it would be to ask him what she should do! But he had told her many months ago that in the matter of her marriage, she had to follow her own heart. This was one valley she could not share with any other. She had to walk through it alone.

She supposed there were always last-minute, lingering doubts. If no marriage proceeded where the bride or groom was seized by uncertainties and apprehensions the night before the wedding, then scarcely would a man and woman ever be joined! Jitters and doubts were surely normal.

But something deeper than that was stirring within her. The decision she had made to marry Misha bore all the marks of rational and logical certitude. It all made perfect sense. She had her father and mother's blessing and approval. Misha was a fine man. There was nothing whatever in *him* to cause her the least concern. She had been over all the pros and cons dozens of times, and everything her *mind* conjured up told her she had made the proper and prudent decision.

But what of her *heart*?

Even there, at first glance, there was nothing to cause her concern. She could easily envision spending her life with him, bearing his children, tending his home. He would be good to her, she knew that.

But the deepest question of all was one she had never forced herself to consider. Before it reached the very core of her being, her thoughts had always drifted toward Misha's integrity, and how honored she should feel that he would want to make her his wife. But at last the moment had come—within hours of being too late—when she knew she could look the other way no longer. She *had* to probe that innermost core of her heart. She had to look straight into her own self and ask the question she had not allowed herself to confront before now.

In the cold, silent predawn hours of her wedding day, alone in her father's barn, Anna Yevnovna, peasant maid and servant to the aristocracy, asked herself if she really loved the man she was about to marry.

She cared for him. He was the best of faithful friends. A more devoted and chivalrous squire no young woman could wish for—a man of integrity, stature, and honor. But . . . did she *love* him?

The disquieting sense that had awakened her and driven her from bed only grew stronger. Anna may have been an innocent, uncomplicated girl, but she was not naive. She knew that marriage must be founded upon the foundational bedrock of mutual care and commitment and sacrifice rather than fleeting schoolgirl passions. Yet inside she could not deny that her doubts were deeper than that. If the thing were right, she *would* love Misha. And whatever that love lacked on their wedding day, she would add to as the years went on.

But the question of whether she loved him only opened her to the larger question: was it the right thing to do? Was her marriage to Misha right in God's eyes?

And what of her love for Sergei? In the long year of his absence it had not altered one iota. Yes, Misha was aware of this, but did either of them truly know how this division of heart might weaken the bonds that must be present for a good marriage? And even if a marriage of convience and one-sided love was acceptable to Misha, was it really acceptable to *her*? Could she be happy with it? Her papa had indeed spoken wisely when he said she must not marry for the sake of others. In the end it would benefit *none*.

Moreover, could she give up so quickly on her prayers for Sergei's return? Perhaps it was in God's design that she and Sergei be forever separated. Perhaps he was even now dead. Yet was she ready to embark on a new life *now*, while doubt remained, and hope still stirred within her heart?

Marriage was too weighty a matter, too permanent, with too much at stake, to enter into its solemnity double-mindedly. *All* doubts might not be removed, but there should be none at the core of truthfulness.

Tears filled Anna's eyes. She knew what lay before her. She either had to keep these final-hour doubts to herself, silencing the reservations now shouting themselves at her, and go ahead with the day as planned, smiling as though all were well and right within her heart, or she must summon the courage to do what was right.

It would take more courage than she dreamed possible! The humiliation . . . the mortification! What would everyone say . . . her mother and father . . . Misha himself? After all the preparation and arrangements . . . how could she?

And yet would the embarrassment be worse than facing Misha on the night *after* their wedding, having to *pretend* to him on their first night together that all was well, having to hide from him the inner conflicts of doubt that swirled within her? And perhaps having to hide them from him all their days and years together?

Nothing, Anna concluded, would be worse than that.

She could not do that to Misha. She could not do that to herself. She *did* care far too much for him to enter into a marriage of duplicity.

If she was to marry him, it would be with her *whole* self. Whether it took months, or even years, before the doubts were removed, she must be in no more a hurry than God was. All the questions, especially those about Sergei, must be put to rest before she could take such an important step.

She had no choice if she wanted to be true to her convictions and to herself. She would have to endure the mortification and shame.

Anna knew what she must do.

83

The day after the canceled wedding dawned bright, crisp, and clear. A warming had set in during the night that would not send the frost away permanently, but which, for several days, would give welcome impetus to the approaching arrival of summer.

Anna lay awake long after slumber had overtaken the rest

of the household, reliving in her mind the events of the day. The dread with which she had anticipated it had not even been as bad as having to carry out her resolve. There had been such to-do about everything, such fuss, such talk, so many questions.

The only two persons whom she knew *really* understood were her father and Misha. Both had looked deeply into her eyes, then had smiled and conveyed a depth of respect for her courage to do what she had done. Whatever kind of love it was she bore for Misha—whether that of a brother and friend, or someday a husband—his handling of the untoward affair only made that love deeper and richer. He took a great share of the responsibility upon his own shoulders, spent the entire day soothing and explaining and making new arrangements, all so that the brunt of the awkwardness would not have to be borne by Anna alone. Everything about the day confirmed in everyone's mind what manner of fiber the Cossack was made of. It made Anna's decision both easier *and* harder to carry out.

And yet as she had gone to sleep that night, she sensed a lightening of the tension of uncertainty. She had been carrying it for months, but had only the night before become conscious of it. She slept soundly, and awoke more fresh and optimistic than she had felt in a long while. What the future held, she did not know. But as she walked outside on the new morning and breathed deeply of the unseasonably warm air, her spirit felt like smiling.

It *had* been difficult yesterday. Awfully so! She never wanted to face something like that again as long as she lived!

But now she felt right inside again . . . right with herself, right with God, even right with Misha. They had been such friends before, like brother and sister. Their engagement had subtly changed everything, although neither had spoken of it. Now, Anna hoped, they would be free to be the friends they had been before.

She also felt *right* about the future. Now God could do whatever He had planned for her. She would be in no hurry.

Anna walked outside. It was yet early, though daylight was fully abroad over the land. She walked toward the willow, breathing in deep draughts of the fragrant air—the aromas of wet earth and growing things and life's renewal . . . the odors of hope and new birth.

God, oh God, she prayed silently, *what do you have for me? What is it you want to teach me, what do you want me to learn from this? Show me, Father, what you would have me do. Make straight the paths of my life, my future. If I am to raise Mariana alone, if I am to return one day to St. Petersburg to serve her father, if I am to marry . . . guide my steps, Lord. Let me not stray the tiniest distance from your hand as you walk beside me. Make clear to the eyes of my heart and my understanding what is your will for me. Do not let me do what my own mind tells me would be best, but let me only seek what YOU would have for me.*

Anna stopped, then sighed deeply. There was another besides Misha in her heart, one whose memory she could never erase. And she knew *he* was at root the cause of her lingering doubts. She had been so sure of *his* rightness! She could not take hold of one hand before letting go of the other.

And, Lord, she went on, *give me some sign in the matter of Princess Katrina's brother. Let me not live forever in doubt. If he is dead . . .*

She could not complete the sentence, even in her silent prayers. A tear formed in her eye and she sent her hand unconsciously after it.

She walked on and sat down with her back to the tree. For more than an hour she sat, alone with melancholy, nostalgic, dreamy, prayerful thoughts of the man whose eyes she saw reflected in the innocent gaze of a tiny child.

84

As the day wore on, a thick sultriness seemed to descend upon Katyk. The sky was yet clear, but it felt like a storm. In his home, Reb Plotnick stirred uneasily. There was not a trace of wind. Yet *something* was at hand.

Misha arrived midway through the morning. He had put Polya, Olga, and Mrs. Remington on the train back to St. Petersburg, he said, and would himself return tomorrow, once he was assured all was well with Anna and her family. He commented on the peculiar feel in the air as well.

The stillness of the spring day seemed too full. Misha came upon Yevno early in the afternoon, standing beside the door of the barn, glancing with an almost bewildered expression this way and that, as if expecting something. Misha shielded his eyes with his hand and followed Yevno's gaze into the distance. But there was nothing to be seen.

An empty unsettledness gradually gave way to a vague sense of anticipation, which led to expectation. Before the day was out, Yevno finally declared, storm clouds would appear in the north and a fierce wind would kick up. There could be no other explanation.

Anna was not so sure the atmosphere was carrying a spring storm toward them, although she had felt the air heavy with premonitions since her time of thought and prayer at the willow tree. As the day had progressed, she had unconsciously begun walking with lighter step. Without even being aware of it, her heart had started to beat faster, and her lips began quietly humming long-forgotten melodies.

Even the children seemed restless. By the late afternoon all of Katyk had begun to share it. Anna became more and more agitated. Misha was preparing to leave. She did not know when she would see him again. Perhaps that was the cause for her disquiet.

She walked outside. There was her father, standing with his hand shading his eyes, gazing toward the southeast. She walked toward him.

A sound of plodding footsteps running toward them turned both of their faces toward the village. There was young Paplanovich hastening toward them, a boy of twelve who lived next to the tavern. He ran straight to Yevno, shouting something Anna could not make out at first.

"They told me to get you, Yevno Pavlovich. They said he has come back!"

"Who told you?" said Yevno.

"The men at the tavern. They said for you to come!"

"Who has come back?"

"The man . . . the man from St. Petersburg! You must come!"

Yevno began to follow as Anna approached.

"It seems your baby's father has returned at last," said Yevno to her. "Paplanovich says he is in the village."

"The count?" said Anna, glancing toward the buildings in the distance.

Whatever her father or young Paplanovich said in answer, Anna heard nothing of it. Suddenly she was running toward the village, strides ahead of either the boy or the old man behind her. The figure on horseback in the distance was small. But she knew Dmitri well enough to recognize in an instant that the regal bearing could not be his any more than it could be any promieshik for many versts around Katyk!

Her heart beat wildly within her. Tears streamed down her face.

How could it be? But with every step she knew it could be no other! The horse was plainly visible now, galloping toward her, clumps of dirt flying into the air behind it. On its back the princely rider wielded the reins as he had once swung a great scythe across the very field through which he now flew.

Even as Anna ran hysterically, joyously, laughing, and sobbing straight toward them, he reined the huge animal in amid a whinnying commotion of dust and hooves and rearing and snorting.

He was off the beast even before the four wild, skittish legs were stilled, taking three giant strides before scooping her into his arms. At the touch of the face he had dreamed of night and day against his own cheek, suddenly the floodwaters of tears were released and he wept with joy.

"Sergei . . . Sergei!" Anna cried, tears flowing without restraint. He held her to him, his chest heaving with great sobs of healing, deliverance, and love.

"Oh, Anna," he whispered into her ear at length, "how I love you!"

Time seemed to stand still for the two reunited lovers as

they stood blissfully in each other's arms. All the hundreds of questions would come later. For these few precious moments, there was nothing else in the universe than to drink in the glorious mere *presence* of the other. What were words alongside the yearned-for, dreamed-of embrace?

Thus they stood, eyes closed, still breathing heavily from the exertion, weeping freely, unconscious even of Yevno as his lumbering gait caught up with his daughter, unconscious of the cottage now emptying of its inhabitants, all now shouting and running toward them, unaware of Yevno's boisterous welcome to the nobleman he had once considered his friend and to whom he had agreed to give his daughter's hand.

Gradually sounds began to filter into Anna's and Sergei's ears. The rest of the world beckoned. They could not ignore it forever.

Slowly, reluctantly they fell apart, pausing just long enough to hold each other's eyes for a moment—a gaze which, like the embrace, said everything.

Then came the voices, the running feet, Yevno's handshake and slap on the back, Sophia's tears, Anna's laughter and more crying, and Sergei's attempted answers to the fast-flowing questions from the children.

Last of all, behind the others, walked Misha. He approached Sergei. Their eyes met, then the handshake, an embrace. Misha stepped back. There were tears in his eyes—not tears of loss, but rather of love.

"Welcome home, my friend," he said in a soft and somewhat husky voice. "Your Anna, as you see, is well. I pray I have been faithful to you in my care for her."

"I'm sure you have been," replied Sergei.

"She will tell you all," rejoined Misha.

He turned toward Anna, embraced her warmly, then took her hand and placed it in Sergei's. "Anna," he said, "you are as fine a woman as it has been my privilege to know. And now . . . I give you your prince."

85

Misha returned to Pskov the same day, and to St. Petersburg the next. If he bore any regrets, it was that his love for Anna had come too late. But for she and her prince, he had only the deepest approbation, knowing true love when he saw it, and glad that dear Anna had found hers. He was honored that her sisterly affection for him was as strong as ever, and he was content to be as her brother and to remain her dearest friend. As for Sergei, Misha counted him as friend and brother also, and would do so all their lives.

Sergei took up immediate lodgings in his former quarters in the barn. Straw had never felt so soft or the smell of hay and cow flesh so sweet. He was thin, and on the whole fit, though his complete health had not yet quite returned. More than a year of constant travel to Siberia and back had clearly taxed him heavily. He did little for a week other than eat and sleep and drink tea by the gallon. Sophia tended him like a mother caring for her own, and he obeyed her every whim like a compliant son, casting Anna or Yevno a wink every now and then to say he was only going along with the fuss for Sophia's sake. Anna's only frustration was that she wanted to have him all to herself for a hundred or two hundred hours so that she could tell him *everything* she had thought and felt in the nearly two years since she had seen him!

It all had to come out in pieces, however. Gradually his strength returned, the flesh between his skin and bone thickened, and the fiber of his muscles again became taut. He took to helping Yevno where he could, and walks with Anna became longer and more frequent.

Sergei grieved for his sister and blew up at his best friend's irresponsibility, but in the end wept for them both.

He doted on his infant niece, a look of wistful longing in his eyes when he gazed at her. Anna was gentle in telling him of his mother's accident and the effect it had on his father. Sergei was quiet, and the sadness he felt seemed genuine and healthy. A remarkable change seemed to have taken place in him; Anna had noticed it almost from the first moment. He was a full-grown man now. His face and eyes carried a settled look. All the old acrimony was gone. When speaking of his father, his tone was deeply filled with compassion rather than bitterness, and he seemed anxious to reconcile with him. He was quieter, and appeared at peace with himself.

There was more of a change about Sergei than mere maturity could account for. A faraway look would come over him, and it was clear he was reliving some portion of his recent sojourn. Anna knew he would tell her in his own time. Until then, she waited. It was enough just to have him again.

Anna had changed, too. She was no more a child, but a lovely woman, delicate yet firm and resolved, graceful yet strong. Curiously, she reminded Sergei of Katrina, a fact which was all the more evident whenever she held his little niece in the crook of her arm. More than once, when the mood turned light and gay, they reminded each other of their first day together on the shores of the frozen Neva. But as much as their shared love brought a bounce to their steps, these were days filled with as much melancholy as joy. There was much to be decided. And considering his father's condition, Sergei wrestled with the new dilemma of his duty to step forward and assume the mantle of leadership in his family.

Unfortunately, to do so would be no simple matter. It could endanger them all as much as Basil Anickin's vendetta against them. But whatever he did about his father, Sergei knew he had to speak as soon as possible with Dmitri. They were now related by marriage if not by blood, and his responsibility extended as much to little Mariana and the House of Remizov as it did to the House of Fedorcenko.

How to live out that responsibility was a question that contained enormous practical difficulties. The predicament of his situation was such that, Sergei now had to admit to himself, might even change everything with Anna.

"Nothing can alter how I feel about you, Sergei Viktorovich," said Anna one evening as they walked along through the fields.

"But don't you understand, Anna," he replied. "It is now even worse than when I left before. Now I am a fugitive, an escaped criminal." He touched the puckered scar on his forehead where his prisoner's tattoo had been removed. "If I am found, in all likelihood I will be shot."

"Sergei, please, don't speak of such things!"

"But how can you marry me, knowing that for the rest of my life this cloud will hang over us?"

"I would marry you if only for a day to be considered your wife," said Anna. "We will pray that our God will show us what to do. Perhaps someday you will be pardoned. If now you told me you wanted to leave the country, I would not oppose you as I did before, but only hope you wanted me to go with you."

"*Hope*, Anna? Of course I would want you to go with me! But there is also Mariana's future to consider, and the promise you made my sister . . . and my father."

"God will show us what is to be done. I am only so happy that you are here to decide things. It was so awkward suddenly finding myself in the position of making decisions for two noble houses, and caring for a newborn princess, when I was but a lowly peasant maid."

"You were never *merely* a peasant maid, Anna Yevnovna," said Sergei, smiling. "I saw more in your bearing from the first moment I laid eyes on you. And you will soon be the wife of a prince."

"Oh, Sergei, I can hardly believe you are really here! Are we finally going to be married, and never have to part again?"

"Yes, Anna. I promise it this time. You will be the wife of Sergei Viktorovich Fedorcenko, even if I have to change my name and live in hiding. Even if no one ever knows, you *will* be the wife of a prince!"

"You make me so happy!"

"I want to spend the rest of my life making you happy, Anna, love of my heart. And speaking of promises, that is another reason I must return to St. Petersburg soon—besides speaking to Father and Mrs. Remington and setting the house in order and finding Dmitri and knocking some sense into that skull of his."

"What other reason?"

"A promise I made you before I left."

The look of confusion on Anna's face made Sergei laugh.

"Don't you remember—the lapis cross. I promised you I would place it back into your hand when I returned. But as you see, I do not have it."

"Where is it?" asked Anna.

"After my trial, when I was convicted, I gave a small package to my father to take home for safekeeping. I knew it would be stolen before I was halfway to Siberia if I tried to take it with me. If what you say of his condition is true, he may remember nothing of it, but I am certain it will be somewhere in the house. And I fully intend to carry out my promise!"

"You will be careful when you go?" said Anna.

"I will take every precaution," insisted Sergei. "I will wear a disguise so that no one will know me—Basil Anickin, Cyril Vlasenko, not even my father himself. But I doubt the house is being watched. I'm certain word of my escape was followed by word of my death. No one returns from Siberia through winter. But to be safe, I will go to Dmitri's first."

"How *did* you stay alive and make it all this way, Sergei? You still have not told me of your journey. There is a difference in you, and I want to know of it."

Again the faraway gaze came into Sergei's eyes.

"I will tell you everything, Anna," he said. "But I want to wait until I am able to give you the whole story without interruption. Perhaps after we are married we can go away someplace together."

"I will eagerly anticipate it!"

"Where shall we go, Anna—England, the Crimea, Switzerland, Italy?"

"As long as we are together, I don't care *where* it is!"

"Then I must make haste to get things in the city set straight. I will return there at once so that I can come back to you."

"Another farewell between us," said Anna.
"But this will be the last," replied Sergei.

86

Sergei made good on his last two promises to Anna. He returned to Katyk in a week's time, bringing with him the lapis cross, and as he had vowed two years before, placed it back into her hand. She kept it only long enough to give it back to him on their wedding day, and henceforth it was *his*.

The other promise he had made her, that there would be no more farewells to endure, he also made good on. At least there were none of significant import for many years.

He had accomplished all that lay in his power to do concerning setting the houses of his two families in order. There would continue to be a considerable awkwardness, he said, owing to the incognito nature with which he would have to conduct affairs in the future. But Mrs. Remington was a shrewd one, he said with a smile, and he had every confidence she would be able to manage. His meeting with his father was disappointing at best. Viktor seemed only to vaguely recognize Sergei—not because of any disguise but because Viktor did not have the will to step outside the protective walls of his mental seclusion. Sergei told no one of the child, for her continued safety, nor that he had been to Katyk. There would also be no word of his marriage. For *everyone's* safety—including Anna's family—most of their future would have to be lived in secrecy from the eyes and ears of St. Petersburg society, even though it meant those closest to them knew nothing as well. He would remain in touch with his father's house by various circuitous means. Otherwise, he and Anna would live as commoners without anyone knowing that he was a prince or what had been his background.

Sergei and Anna were married in Katyk the first week of June 1882.

The prince was dressed in the clothes of a peasant, and never were his title or true name spoken. There was much speculation in the community. No one quite knew what to make of this sudden wedding in light of the previous canceled one. Those who had actually met Misha were few, and in the imaginations of the country peasantry, the prince who had visited and worked in Yevno's fields three years earlier had become almost a mystical figure of past legend. The faces of the Cossack and the prince, therefore, were neither known nor distinguishable. Most people assumed the two men were one, and that the earlier wedding had only been delayed two months. Nothing from the Burenin home was said to discourage such talk. The wider the confusion, the less likely it was that the full truth would be discovered and Sergei's whereabouts become known throughout St. Petersburg.

Of Sergei's and Anna's acquaintances from the city, only Misha was on hand for the wedding. He did not appear in his uniform, but dressed like Sergei in the simple attire of a commoner. Who he was, nobody ever quite knew, but there was talk of a distant cousin having arrived a short time earlier. Where that word had originated was unclear, though whenever it came within sound of Sophia's ears, the edges of her lip curled up slightly in an imperceptible smile.

With the love of true friendship, Misha wished the bride and groom both well, and saw them off for two weeks in the south, then returned to his own duties in the city.

87

"Are you ready to hear of it all?" asked Sergei midway through their first week together.

"If you are ready to tell me," replied Anna.

"I am a different man than when I left for Siberia."

"I knew that the first moment I was in your arms."

"Siberia changes everyone," said Sergei. "Mostly it embitters them. For me, however, it was the *return* from Siberia that made the difference. And in my case, the long sojourn healed me of my bitterness rather than added to it."

"I knew that too. You have compassion and love for your father now, I can tell."

"I only pray the opportunity comes for me to completely reconcile myself to him. I tried to talk to him when I was there. But it will take some time. Hopefully in such a reconciliation his mind will return."

"Most of all, Sergei," said Anna tenderly, "you are at peace with yourself."

"And with God," added Sergei. "It all goes together. The bitterness I felt, the guilt, even the hatred—none of it could have been healed without God's touch. I was bitter toward Him too. I had a great deal to learn . . . about myself, about being a man."

"How did you learn it?"

Sergei sighed, and led her along the path they had been following, thinking for a moment before going on. "Being alone with no company but yourself forces you to look at things more deeply than you might otherwise. But even then, if you don't have the perspective to see things truly, your own self can still be your own worst enemy. No, sometimes, Anna, you need someone else's eyes to help you to see yourself as you truly are."

"You found such a person?"

"I did. I found a man whose search was almost identical to my own—the search to find the meaning of manhood, I mean."

"The fellow Kaplan you told me about whom you escaped with?"

Sergei laughed. "No, not Kaplan, although there are plenty of stories about him I *could* tell!"

"Who then?"

Sergei smiled thoughtfully. "How I ever crossed paths with this man I can't imagine. Only God's providence could have arranged it. It's a long story."

"I'm not leaving your side until I've heard every word," said Anna. Sergei was silent for several moments. Then he drew in a deep breath.

"We almost didn't make it out of Kara at all. The river was fierce, and by the time I caught up with Kaplan, I was nearly drowned. My chains had taken me straight to the bottom, but the current was swift enough that the water tumbled me along, though I was submerged. The constant motion enabled me to push my way off the bottom with enough force that I could get my head above water for a breath or two before being dragged down again. In this way, bouncing from bottom to surface and back down, I managed to get enough air to stay alive, and gradually I worked my way toward the shore and the shallower current. Kaplan and I found each other. He traipsed off into the forest and found a thick chunk off a fallen tree. Wrapping my chains onto it, I was able to float and stay above water. He found a log for himself, and thus we swam and floated and were carried downriver a good distance out of range of discovery by the patrols from any of the prisons.

"By daybreak we were many versts away. We left the river, walked overland mostly through forests, avoiding villages, though in that region there are not many."

"Why did you avoid the villages?"

"Near the mines, the people fear escapees and are not inclined to help."

"What did you eat?"

"The forests are plentiful—berries, honey, insects, even

some grasses. And we stole, I am sorry to say," added Sergei. "If we came upon a cottage or a small village, we waited until night, then would creep into a barn or shed and try to find grain or cheeses."

"What about your chains? How did you walk?"

"Very slowly, I'm afraid, it was many days of difficult travel until we reached a moderate-sized village. We waited until the middle of the night, then crept into it. Not only did we manage to find enough food for two or three days, we located an ironmonger's. It was not difficult to get inside, though far too black to see well. But all we needed was a hammer and his anvil and a sharp pinching tool. Several good whacks of the hammer and I was free of my shackles."

"Didn't you make a racket?"

"Yes, which is why we fled from the place immediately, leaving the chains on the dirt floor where they had fallen. Even as we gained the cover of the trees nearby, we heard voices and shouts behind us!"

"I'm glad they didn't catch you!"

"Not half so glad as I was. Kaplan and I kept moving all the rest of the night to put as much distance between ourselves and that place as possible. And now that I was free, I could set a much better pace. Kaplan had led the way until then, but after I was free of my shackles he had difficulty keeping up with me!

"Kaplan's plan had always been to go over the mountains southward into Mongolia so as to get into warmer regions before winter froze all of Siberia. But as soon as we started up into the Khingahs, we realized we were not nearly strong enough for such a trek. Even if we had been capable of the climbs required, we would surely have died of starvation, for it is a desolate land. So we turned back, made our way down again into the river valley of the Shilka, and followed the valley to the river Amur, whose valley was lush and green and fertile and where, at that time of the year, it was easy to find growing things to eat. I think we ate better at that stage of our journey than we had at Kara. But starvation was never far from us, and the cold tried to kill us daily. I know we survived only by God's grace.

"The mountains rose above the valley on our right the whole way. Once we saw them giving way to the valley of the

Sungari, we turned south again. I was in favor of making for Vladivostok, but Kaplan convinced me otherwise. As long as we were in Russia, he said, we would not be safe. The great Russian seaport on the Sea of Japan was where all escapees tried to find some warm water passage home. Instead, it was where they were all recaptured, or so he said. In the end I went along with his plan to make for the Yellow Sea and the seaports of northern China. The thought of the Chinese intimidated me, but he assured me we would not find them so fearsome as I thought. We would even be able to converse, in the northern provinces, after a fashion, especially in the seaports and towns where we would readily find some European vessel where we could work our way to North Africa or Portugal or the Netherlands or England. If we could get our bodies back to strength, they would not mind where we came from. Good ship hands were hard to come by in China, and captains readying for the return voyage often had scant crews owing to desertion, sickness, and death. I don't know how Kaplan knew all this, but his words proved true in everything.

"We made Newchwang well into winter and, true to what Kaplan had said, found passage to Tsingtao in exchange for our labors. The port there was full of Germans and German ships. We had no difficulty in hiring on for a steamer bound around Africa to Lisbon. But I was a nobleman who had never done a day's work in my life, and Kaplan had been in Kara for fifteen years, but somehow we survived the rigors of ship life.

"My back and shoulders were never so sore in all my life, and we were both still weak from the imprisonment and our journey overland to the sea. Yet as the days went on, we gradually became more accustomed to the new life of sailing.

"A great storm hit us our first week out. We ran aground and took on a great deal of water, and the captain limped into Shanghai, where he proposed to lay over until the ship was fixed and seaworthy again. Kaplan and I found a man who removed our convict tattoos." He ran a hand over his forehead, wincing at the memory. "And it was in Shanghai that I met the man I spoke of."

"Was he Chinese?" asked Anna.

"No, hardly that," laughed Sergei.

"Tell me about him. I'm eager to know who he was."

"Before his influence upon me has meaning," replied Sergei, "you have to understand the state of my heart and mind at the time."

He paused, breathed in deeply, then began again, this time in a pensive tone.

"I had been sinking into a hole of great despondency for years. Surely you could not help being aware of it—the troubles with my father, my struggle with my position in the army, all the frustrations vented in my writing, the book, my trial, the sentence to Siberia. Anna, I tell you, after I left you, I became as lost a soul as ever crawled the face of the earth. I tried to take my own life once, halfway to Kara. I was a vegetable. I thought I would lose my mind—consumed by guilt, bitterness, anger, despair, frustration. And certainly there was no place in my soul for God. I had failed in everything—with my family, with my father, with the only woman I ever loved. I failed my country, my career . . . everything!

"I considered myself a man without a scrap of manhood left within me. I was less than nothing. I might as well have been dead. I *wasn't* a man. Whatever *manhood* means, I had lost it, although I don't know if I ever knew what it was in the first place. My own father wasn't exactly the ideal man in my sight. Strong, authoritative, stoic . . . but almost without a heart, without a place in him to feel and hurt and open himself to those around him. Your own father came as close as anyone, I suppose, to showing me the other side of what being a man might mean. And yet, Anna, as shamed as I am to admit it, the fact that your father was a peasant made me wonder if it was somehow 'different' for him than for me."

"There *are* differences when we are brought up the way we were, Sergei," said Anna.

"But not differences in what constitutes essential manhood. At least so it seems to me now. But then, I have been thinking on it a great deal since landing in Shanghai."

"What happened there?"

"As I said, I met a man. It was to take two or three weeks for the ship to be fixed. We left the ship and were walking through the city when we came upon what looked to be a street brawl. A big, good-looking fellow was in the middle of it. He towered over the rest, and it was instantly clear that he was European, not Chinese. Kaplan and I rushed in to see what we could do, and then we realized it wasn't a brawl at all. The fellow, who was speaking in Chinese but wasn't apparently making himself too well understood, was mixed up in an accident that had just happened and was trying to get them to help him lift an overturned cart of some peasant farmer.

"Before I knew what was happening, there we were side by side with the big brute of a man, and the three of us quickly had the thing set right. He turned to us and shook hands, and began thanking us."

"In Chinese?"

"No," laughed Sergei. "But I understood him no better than if it had been."

"What was he speaking then?"

"English. I can read it well enough, but I don't speak it sufficiently to be understood. Before too long we stumbled into French, and after that got on tolerably well together. I always knew my French studies would come in handy someday!"

"Was the man French?"

"No, he was a Scotsman. And his French wasn't much better than his Chinese. But I could understand him, and we got on."

"What was he doing there?"

"He was a sailor too. Or he *had* been. He'd come about a year, maybe a year and a half before. He found himself shipwrecked off the coast of China, and was rescued by some English missionaries who brought him back to life."

"It sounds exciting."

"The whole thing is one of the most captivating stories I have ever heard. Why, Robbie's adventures on the high seas and then in China make mine in Asia and Siberia seem tame by comparison."

"Robbie . . . that's his name?"

"Yes. Robbie Taggart."

"You sound as if you were quite taken with him."

Sergei did not answer immediately. He breathed deeply, gazed into the distance, and reflected on Anna's words.

At length he nodded slowly. "Taken with him . . ." he mused, repeating what she had said. "Anna, there is no other way to say it than that my whole life was changed as a result of him. The man altered my entire outlook . . . on everything! He became a friend, but so much more than a friend. He is just a remarkable man. There is no way I can describe or ever repay the debt I owe him. Without him, Anna, you would have no husband, at least not the one you *do* have now. I want you to meet him. I don't know how, I don't know when, but *someday* you *will* meet him. Because I *must* see him again, if only to look into his eyes and tell him what he did for me."

"He doesn't know?"

"Most of our time together I spent listening to him, listening to his father-in-law, a missionary by the name of Wallace, and especially *watching* Robbie. We talked, of course, but mostly I observed and absorbed. It was not until my return voyage, out there on the seas all these past months, that I had a chance to let it all sink into the depths of my being. I suppose you could say the *change* came mostly after Robbie and I parted."

"How long were you with him?"

"After our first meeting, Kaplan and I went back to his mission with him. He'd come to Shanghai for some supplies. It turned out we missed the sailing of our ship, and I remained at the mission two months before Robbie helped me arrange passage west on another vessel."

"What about your friend?"

"Kaplan? He decided to stay at the mission!" laughed Sergei.

"He must have been taken with it, too."

"He didn't say much, but I have the feeling he was asking himself a lot of questions about his own life."

"You still haven't told me what it was about Robbie that had such an influence on you," said Anna.

"It was just *him*—the man he was," answered Sergei. "There were so many similarities between us. We were close to the same age. He had left Scotland probably about the same time I left St. Petersburg for my reassignment on the Caspian. We both left behind us women we loved, and neither of us had an inkling of who we really were or what lay ahead. Our paths led us eastward—his around the Cape and eventually to China, mine to the Kara mines of Siberia. Maybe that is why he had such an impact upon me, because I could see so much of myself in him."

Sergei paused briefly. "But my pathway led me to despair and bitterness and guilt; he found something else at the end of his pilgrimage."

"What . . . what did he find?" asked Anna with wide-eyed interest.

"Himself . . . *that's* what he found," answered Sergei. "And that was *everything*! It was clear to see, from one look into his eyes, that however similar we may have been when we embarked from our homelands two years before, we were now worlds apart. Robbie possessed something. And I knew instantly, as I said, the moment I gazed into the peacefulness of his eyes that I wanted it . . . that I *needed* what he had discovered. How he had got it, where it had come from, even what it was . . . I had no idea. I could just see that here was a man at peace within his own soul—at peace with himself, at peace with his surroundings, at peace with what it meant to be a man. I had to find out what it was. I had to know. I had to have it! And that is why, from the very beginning, I plied him with questions, I listened eagerly for everything he had to tell me, and I watched his every move, his every expression, his every glance. I got to know him probably far better than he even realized. I *had* to know what it was in his heart that made him different from any man I had ever known!"

"Did you find out?"

"I think so. No . . . I *know* so! What made Robbie different was that he had discovered the secret of what it means to truly be a *man*. Dmitri always measured his worth by his manly exploits. My father was stoic and rugged to the end. It was how men were, how they were supposed to be. But then I found myself face-to-face with Robbie Taggart—a man as brawny and rugged and fighting tough as any man in the tsar's army—who spoke quiet words of *gentleness*, who told me of a change God had made inside him, and who told me he had discovered a deeper and more enduring manliness than he'd ever known on the high seas. I tell you, Anna, listening to him tell his story—the sailing adventures, the drama of fighting pirates and cutthroats, the love he left behind and the love he found, and what he discovered inside himself as a result of it all—was enough to change anyone. Had it not been for Robbie Taggart, you might never have seen me again. I'd have either died somewhere, or I'd have been nothing but a wreck of a man. As it is, for the first time in my life I feel whole and complete."

"Then I do want to meet your Mr. Taggart. I must thank him personally for sending my husband back to me," said Anna.

"I was sailing northward up the west coast of Africa," Sergei went on, "after several months at sea. Suddenly everything Robbie had told me, and all my own past, became vividly real to me. For the first time I *saw* with such clarity who I really was—that I was *not* yet truly a man after the fashion of Robbie Taggart and the *Man* he had told me so much about. And in that moment I realized how desperately I *wanted* to be.

"I was alone on the deck. It was late. The sea was relatively smooth, and we were moving fairly well under a full sail. The moon was up, but the sky was half cloudy, and so its reflection was obscured over the surface of the water. All at once the years of bitterness toward my father, my own guilt over my failure, all my frustrations and anger—and, I suppose, a deep resentment toward God, too—it all crashed over me like a giant wave.

"Suddenly without realizing what I was doing, I found myself on my knees on that lonely deck, crying out to God as I never had before. *God*, I said, *I don't want to live like this anymore! Please take away the anger and bitterness and unforgiveness in my heart. I have not been the man I should have been—not to my family, my country . . . not even to myself. But I want to be, God. I want to be a MAN! I want to be whole, I want to be gentle and kind like Robbie Taggart. Give me a heart full of love, God, not the gall and rancor that has been inside me for so long. Forgive me, and put forgiveness inside me, too. I need . . . your help . . . I need you, God! Make me the man YOU want me to be!"*

Sergei stopped. Anna had taken his hand as he spoke, and now gazed earnestly into his face, her eyes full of tears.

"I don't even know how to put into words all that happened, all that I felt, all that I prayed," Sergei went on. "I must have knelt there for twenty minutes, so much going through my heart and mind. I found myself releasing heavy weights I had carried for so long, just like cutting the chains off my ankles. But these were weights that had been tied to my heart. I found myself forgiving my father, forgiving Rustaveli, forgiving the guards who had beat me, and asking God to forgive me for my attitudes and words and actions against them. Mostly I had to accept God's forgiveness for myself. Robbie had told me about it, but until that night on the ship it didn't make sense to me. That night I realized it was the biggest weight of all, the heaviest chain around my heart.

"When I finally found that my mind was still, for the first time I realized I'd been weeping. My face was wet. I stood up slowly, and I felt almost as if I could see the chains falling off and splashing into the black ocean below the railing where I stood.

"I don't know how to say it any other way, Anna, other than that I knew there had been a change. I felt more like a true *man* than ever before in my life, because I'd finally let go of all the prideful trappings that men all over the world—including myself—mistake for manhood. And I suppose for the first time, I felt ready to come home . . . and ready to face you, and look into your eyes . . . and tell you that finally I understand a little of what love really means."

Anna squeezed her husband's hand.

"I do love you, Anna," he said. "I loved you before, but now it means so much more than it could have then."

"Oh, Sergei," she replied, "you cannot know how happy it makes my heart for you to be at peace. I knew the moment I saw you that much of your past ache had dropped away. I could see that you were lighter and more free. I love you so much!"

She slipped her arm through his and they walked on in silence. Now that Sergei's story was complete, they could truly begin the rest of their life together.

Gently she laid her head against his shoulder as they made their way along the path. Their waiting for this day had been long, and not without its sorrow. But now that it had come at last, the years vanished; and all of life became a glorious eternal moment of quiet, contented joy.

They had each other. Their hearts were joined as one. And for this blissful present, all was well.

Epilogue

Sergei had not been able to locate Dmitri during his time in St. Petersburg, nor in the months following his return with Anna to Katyk did he gain any trace of him. Keeping himself in the background, with Misha's help he had discovered from his regimental commander that Dmitri had requested, and received, a leave of absence from his duties and, it was presumed, had been away from the city for some time.

For the present, therefore, it appeared that the young princess of the House of Remizov would continue in the care of her mother's brother and maid.

Anna and Sergei prayed daily for her brother Paul in Siberia, but it would be many years before they heard even a tiny shred of information about him.

The bond and love between Anna and Princess Katrina Viktorovich Fedorcenko Remizov lived on, as Anna poured her heart's devotion into the growing young girl. Mariana possessed the strengths and personality characteristics of both young women who had cared for each other with such an uncommon love. Sergei often paused when watching the young face, then chuckling to himself and making comments about seeing both Anna and Katrina so visibly alive in his little niece. In the growing child the personalities of Anna, peasant maid, and Katrina, noble princess, fused and balanced into one.

As the little girl passed her first year and began to walk and talk and scamper about, there persisted in the community a sense of wonder concerning her origins. Speculations were subdued, though plentiful. No one doubted Anna's character, and Yevno and Sophia were held in sufficient regard that no one believed the unthinkable, that the baby had really been Anna's.

People talked—about the child, about Anna and her new husband, and the grandfather, who was suspected of knowing more than he told. Yevno had always been thought of as a somewhat odd and unusual man in things spiritual, and it was not unlikely that this tendency would carry into his eldest born. There were mysterious roots in the whole thing, that much was certain.

The rumors, as they reached their final stages, usually involved Anna's marrying a man of great importance, but whose cloudy past had toppled him from high rank. Some said he was a Cossack from the south who had fought in the tsar's wars and had even saved the grand duke's life. Others continued to insist that, whatever the mystery, the man was a peasant just like themselves, who had migrated north from the Ukraine. As to the child, well, the wild nature of Cossacks was well documented.

But most of the rumors were eventually dismissed, and Anna's new husband was said to have been a peasant and farmer all along. His regal bearing indicated otherwise, but the way he worked the fields alongside old Yevno said to any observer that he had been doing it all his life. And the rumors were quieted once and for all when he purchased a small plot and peasant cottage five versts southwest of Katyk on which to raise his small family. For a nobleman to do such a thing was unheard of, even in legend.

The child remained an enigma. Some of the old wives claimed that the Cossack—a good and compassionate man—had come across her abandoned somewhere in his travels and had brought her home to his betrothed.

The rumor that she was actually a princess was one of the more persistent and lingering threads of speculation. And, though most said there was not a word of truth to it, country peasants in Russia were always fond of turning whatever they could into a fairy tale.